MW00532268

DREAMWIELDER

THE
DREAMWIELDER
CHRONICLES
—

BOOK ONE

GARRETT CALCATERRA

DIVERSIONBOOKS

Diversion Books
A Division of Diversion Publishing Corp.
443 Park Avenue South, Suite 1008
New York, New York 10016
www.DiversionBooks.com

For more information, email info@diversionbooks.com

First Diversion Books edition March 2013.
Print ISBN: 978-1-62681-254-3
eBook ISBN: 978-1-938120-93-0-

For my mother, Shirley, who literally dreamt up Makarria, and long before that, ingrained into me a profound respect and love for the inner-strength of women.

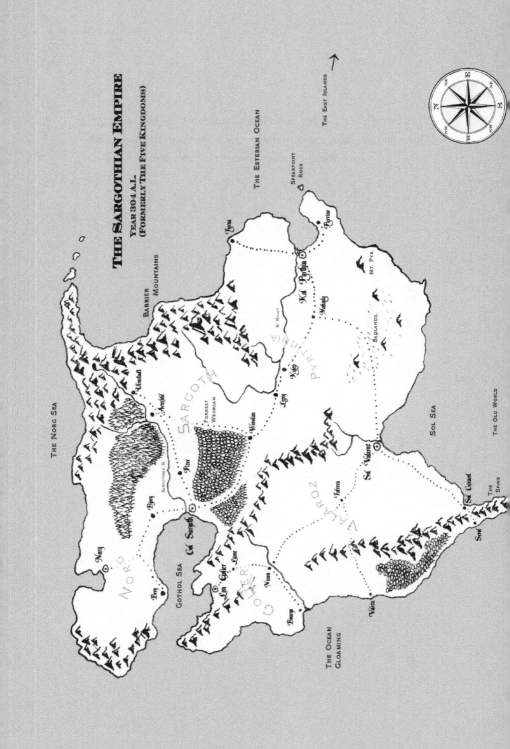

THE SARGOTHIAN EMPIRE

YEAR 304 A.L.
(FORMERLY THE FIVE KINGDOMS)

1
A Scent in the Air

Far from the soot-blackened walls and towers of Col Sargoth and the Sea of Gathol, south of the Forrest Weorcan and east of the sea-dwelling city of Kal Pyrthin, on a peninsula jutting out into the turbulent Esterian Ocean, sat a lone farmstead. It was a humble farmstead, with only a single A-frame barn and a tiny house, both built of rough-hewn timber and with thatched roofs of bound palm leaves. But on this night, beneath the stars and tendrils of purple clouds threaded across the sky, the farmstead suddenly shimmered and became a castle. Gone were the timber walls of house and barn, and in their place massive granite walls and turreted towers. Gone was the daub and stone chimney dribbling peat smoke into the night air, and in its place a rooftop pennon snapping in the wind. Gone were the sleeping plough horses and dairy goats, and in their place warhorses and hunting hounds mulling about the courtyard.

Inside the keep, Makarria—a princess—slept on a canopied bed piled high with cushions and sleeping furs. A simple violet gown hung on a brass rack beside the nightstand. Makarria sighed contentedly, but the sound of sudden pounding at her chamber door agitated her sleep and she rolled over to bury her head deeper in the cushions. The pounding persisted, however, and the doors groaned and finally burst open. Galen, Makarria's father, doubled over in the doorway to catch his breath from the exertion of kicking the door in, and Makarria's mother, Prisca, rushed past him, her gold embroidered sleeping gown billowing behind her.

"Makarria," Prisca gasped, shaking the sleeping girl by her

5

shoulders. "Makarria, wake up!" Makarria groaned and tried to push her mother away in her sleep. "Makarria, wake up this instant," Prisca yelled, feeling herself become dizzy and disoriented. "Makarria!" she barked again and this time she slapped her daughter across the face.

Makarria woke with a gasp and in a blink of an eye it was all gone: the sleeping cushions, the canopied bed, the ornate clothing, the castle, all of it except the violet gown, which fell to lie crumpled on the uneven wood-slat floor. Makarria put one hand to her burning cheek but gave it little thought. In her mind, the image of a glorious castle still lingered. She looked up at Prisca with her big green eyes. "Mother?"

Prisca took a deep breath and collapsed onto the sleeping mat beside Makarria. "It's alright now. You were just having a nightmare."

"A nightmare?" Makarria sat up, her stinging cheek already forgotten. "It wasn't a nightmare. I was a princess, and I was in a castle preparing for a grand ball. I had a dress, and I was to meet—"

"You're not a princess, Makarria," her mother interrupted. "Just a farm girl, and you were keeping us all awake talking in your sleep."

"I'm sorry, Mother," Makarria said, realizing her father was there too, standing at the curtain that separated her sleeping area from the rest of the one-room house. "Sorry, Father. Did I wake Grampy too?"

Her mother sat up and frowned. "No, your grandfather can sleep through anything it seems. Now go back to sleep. Remember, if you have any nightmares or dreams—no matter how fun they seem—push them away, forget them. You're not a little girl anymore."

"I'll try, Mother," Makarria agreed.

Prisca brushed back Makarria's tangle of dark brown hair and tied it up in a bun with a leather tie, then nudged her to lie back down. *"Close your eyes, fall fast asleep,"* she sang softly, *"Rest your head, without a dream. When you wake, you will see, a bright new day for you and me."*

Makarria smiled at the familiar song. "How am I supposed to be a big girl when you sing me nursery rhymes?"

"Never you mind," Prisca said, giving her a kiss. "Just close your eyes and sleep fast. The goats need milking at first light."

Makarria did as she was told and closed her eyes, and though she was still excited about her dream and cared not to go back to sleep, she was more weary than when she had first gone to bed that night. *Why am I so tired*, she wondered, grasping for the details of her dream, but already the images had flitted away like mist on a breeze, and she was fast asleep before even her mother bent over to pick up the gown from the floor.

"Some tunic for a farm girl," Prisca whispered as she stepped from the sleeping area and Galen closed the curtains behind her.

"Looks to be silk," Galen said. "Not likely to last long in the mud and salty air."

"I best wake my father and see what he thinks."

Galen nodded in agreement. "I'll check on the animals," he said and slipped outside.

Prisca stepped quietly to her father's sleeping area. When she opened the curtain, she found him already awake.

"Another dream?" he asked, pushing aside the strings of gray hair from his face and rubbing the sleep from his eyes.

"Did you not see the castle? Did you not see yourself? You were probably dressed in an ermine robe with a crown on your head."

"I saw none of it," he replied. "I just now awoke when I heard voices. Did everything go back to normal?"

"Everything but this," Prisca said, handing him the gown. "Her tunic. Or used to be, at least."

He ran the folds of the gown between his fingers. "Silk. Violet and real as could be." He looked up at his daughter with concern. "You and Galen are both alright?"

"Galen is fine. It made me dizzy and nauseous when I tried to wake her, but I'm fine now."

"And the animals?"

"Galen's checking on them."

"Have him check the flowers in the garden outside too. The color of this gown is no coincidence, I think. With any luck the sweet violets were the only things to be harmed. Better them than us or the animals." He handed her the gown. "You best put this in the fireplace and burn it."

Prisca took the gown and sat down beside his withered frame. Though the nausea was gone, she felt weary and weak, nearly on the verge of crying. "When will this stop, Father? What if a traveler passes nearby and sees something? What if one of us does get hurt? What if one of *his* agents finds out?"

"There's nothing more we can do, Prisca. Wake her when she dreams, keep people away, destroy anything she creates. Keep her occupied with milking goats and tending the garden, and she'll grow out of it soon enough."

"When? She's nearly thirteen already."

"When she has her first moonblood. No later than that."

"You're sure."

"Yes," he told her, though he was not so certain of it himself. He wanted it to be true, for everyone's sake—his own, Prisca's, Galen's, and most of all, Makarria's—but deep inside he suspected it was nothing more than wishful thinking.

The sorcerer Wulfram stooped through the doorway into a small round chamber at the top of the tallest tower in Col Sargoth. A cloak of shadow covered his body from crown to toe, a mottled mantle of black feathers and fur. His body, though shrouded beneath the cloak, was visibly misshapen: his legs were splayed forward and bent at a grotesque angle, his shoulders stooped forward, yet arched above his head, and his head—even hidden beneath his hood of feathers—was too long and too narrow to be completely human.

"What is it?" he growled at the man awaiting him. "Why have you summoned me from my sleep?"

The man wet his lips and swallowed before speaking. He was the most privileged servant in the Sargothian Empire—High Houndkeeper—and he'd been Wulfram's servant for nearly forty years, and yet he still was terrified by the sorcerer's presence. "The hound," he said, pointing to the large contraption in the center of the chamber, "she's smelled something, Master."

Wulfram turned his gaze upon the contraption, a copper compass five feet in diameter resting on four gilded legs, each fashioned in the shape of a woman's calf and foot. The outer ring of the compass was graduated like any normal compass, with 360 equidistant marks, but there the similarity ended. In the center, sprawled out on her back, was a scent-hound: a woman with the snout of a dog. She lay naked upon a copper wheel that rotated on an axle protruding up through her navel, and her outstretched, emaciated limbs were melded into the tarnished green metal, so that it was impossible to tell where flesh ended and wheel began.

Her snout twitched and sniffed at the air, but the wheel remained motionless. Wulfram followed the mark on the wheel extending from the tip of her nose to the outer ring of the compass. "One hundred and forty arc degrees off north. That's where she was pointing?"

"Thereabouts," the houndkeeper said. "The scent was weak and it only lasted a few moments. She couldn't sniff out the exact coordinate."

"If the scent was so weak, why did you bother waking me?"

"I, I'm sorry, Master. I didn't think you would be asleep. I—"

Wulfram glared at him, and the High Houndkeeper clamped his mouth shut. "I don't want an apology, I want an answer. Why did you summon me if the scent was so weak?"

The houndkeeper licked his lips. "Because, Master, the hound, she was whining when she smelled it, and she only whines when she smells one kind of sorcerer: a dreamwielder."

2
Visions of Fire

Prince Caile Delios of Pyrthinia reigned in his horse and called for his men to halt.

"What is it?" asked Lorentz, the captain of Caile's honor guard, which numbered only five including Lorentz.

Caile shielded his eyes against the sun and stared down the long ribbon of road stretching before them between vast fields of wild grasses. "Someone is coming."

Lorentz followed his gaze, but saw nothing. "Your eyes are better than mine then. Shall we take cover, Your Highness?"

Caile smiled. Lorentz had been his protector for as long as he could remember, and the two of them had long ago dispensed with addressing each other formally except when in the presence of royalty and dignitaries. "We're not in Valaróz anymore," Caile chided him. "These are Pyrthin fields around us."

"And those were Pyrthin badlands ten days ago when we were attacked," Lorentz reminded him. "It's been five years. Things change, even Pyrthinia."

Caile frowned at being reminded of the skirmish in the badlands. It had not ended well for the highwaymen who attacked them. The bandits were poorly armed and weak with hunger, and though Caile had taken pity on them, he could not in good conscience leave highwaymen behind to harry travelers on the high road.

"We're wardens of the realm," Caile said, as much to himself as to Lorentz. "We have a code of honor to uphold. I'd sooner wear a dress than take cover in our own lands."

Lorentz smiled. "If memory serves me, I seem to recall your sister putting you in a dress not so many years ago. I believe she was teaching you ballroom etiquette."

Caile turned to glare at his captain, but the corners of his mouth twitched upward into a partial smile, betraying his feigned anger. "That is vile hearsay, Captain," he said, drawing his sword melodramatically. "Now if you're quite finished with your japes…"

Caile commanded his mount forward with a yell, and his men spurred their horses behind him. It soon became apparent to all of them that Caile was correct; a group of mounted warriors was approaching, a score of them at least—too many to defeat if it came down to a fight. Caile did not hesitate, however, even though he knew Lorentz would lecture him later about charging an unidentified force.

The group of horsemen in the distance halted upon seeing Caile approach and raised a banner displaying the red and gold stripes of Pyrthinia. Still, Caile charged onward, sword in hand, ready for trouble. He could be reckless at times, he knew, but he was wary and paid more heed to Lorentz's advice than he let on. The Pyrthinian banner meant nothing; the armed horsemen could just as easily be highwaymen under guise as they could be official Pyrthinian troops. Only when Caile saw a face he recognized did he slow his mount and return his sword to its scabbard—and the face he saw brought a smile to his own.

"Well, little brother," his sister, Taera, remarked when he and his men finally came to a halt, "are you in such a hurry to be home that you meant to charge through a whole score of Pyrthinia's finest soldiers and your own sister to get there?"

Caile dismounted and said nothing as he walked over to her and pulled her from her saddle in a bear hug. Taera squealed, thinking the both of them would topple over, but her brother was no longer the skinny boy she remembered last seeing. He lowered her to the ground with ease, and the two of them held each other in a warm embrace.

"You shrunk," Caile said.

"Or you've grown. Five years and I hardly recognize you. Is that the beginnings of a beard I see? Have you started shaving, Caile?"

Lorentz cleared his throat. "Once a month, whether he needs it or not, Your Highness."

Caile shot Lorentz a dark expression, but Taera laughed and spoke before Caile could come up with a retort. "Captain Lorentz, it's a pleasure to see you again," she said.

"The pleasure is all mine, Your Highness. You've grown more beautiful by the day, I can well see."

Taera brushed her blond hair away from her face and smiled. "And you've grown more charming."

Caile groaned. "More disagreeable is closer to the truth. Let's be off. We can talk as we ride. I'd like to reach Kal Pyrthin while it's still light. It's been so long, I barely remember what my own home looks like."

"Indeed," Lorentz agreed, and the entire procession, now nearly thirty strong, made off to the east along the high road toward the greenbelt of trees skirting the River Kylep in the distance.

Lorentz joined the captain of Taera's honor guard at the forefront of the troops, and Caile and Taera settled in midway between the two groups of soldiers. "It's good to see you, Caile," Taera said. "I can't tell you how happy I am to finally have you back."

"You say happy, and yet sadness is plainly written on your face. What's going on, Taera? I was supposed to stay in Valaróz for two years still. Why has Father summoned me back?"

Taera dropped her eyes away from him to stare blankly at her saddle horn. She had insisted that she be the one to accompany the honor guard from Kal Pyrthin to greet Caile, but now that she was here, her courage seemed to abandon her.

"What's happened?" Caile asked again.

"It's Cargan. He's dead."

Caile took the news silently though his mind raced with a myriad of conflicting thoughts and emotions. He did not feel a pang of loss or grief, for his brother was older even than Taera, and Caile had hardly known him as a child. Rather, it was a dread that pervaded him as all the ramifications of his brother's death surfaced in his mind.

"What happened?" Caile asked after a long moment of silence.

"We don't know entirely. A messenger raven came from Col Sargoth. All the message said was that he'd been drunk and gotten in a fight and died."

Caile snorted, and Taera nodded silently in agreement; their brother had a well-known reputation for shunning drink, among other things, and he was not one to get into a brawl with drunkards—certainly not one to lose in a fight against drunkards.

"Did the message say anything else?" Caile asked.

"You know as well as I do what else it said. Emperor Guderian demands Father send a new ward to Col Sargoth."

Caile pounded a fist into his saddle, though his horse walked on unperturbed. "Ward? Hostage is more like it. How stupid does he think we are?"

Several of Caile's men took notice of his outburst, but Caile paid them little heed.

"I don't believe he cares how stupid or intelligent we are," Taera said, looking past her brother toward the first traces of Kal Pyrthin peaking over the horizon. "As long as we're scared and do as he says, that's all that's important—that we're frightened into obedience."

The tone of Taera's voice cut through Caile's anger and he realized he had completely neglected to consider how scared she must be. "Blast it all, Taera! Father can't seriously be contemplating sending you to Col Sargoth?"

"What choice does he have?"

"But after all the"—Caile caught himself near shouting and lowered his voice and leaned in closer to his sister so no one would overhear—"after all the visions? Have you had any more? Since Cargan died?"

Taera squeezed her eyes shut and flinched.

Caile instinctively reached out to grab her but realized what he had done and let her be. She clearly still did not like to talk or think about the strange images that came to her. When she had been younger, before Caile was sent to Valaróz, she had been told by their father to ignore the visions, to pretend they didn't happen so that they would go away. In a sense, it worked—as long as Taera chose to actively ignore and push away the images, they did not come to her—but Caile had a knack for reminding her, and on more than one occasion as children, he had triggered her visions and gotten them both berated.

"I'm sorry," Caile muttered, but Taera was lost in the images flashing through her mind.

"Fire," she whispered. "Everywhere. Pyrthinian soldiers dead. The red and yellow Pyrthin banner turned black… Ash. A woman…"

"Let it go," Caile said, grabbing her shoulder. "It won't happen. I won't let Father send you to Col Sargoth."

Taera opened her eyes and turned to him, more alarmed than frightened. "No, not in Col Sargoth. Here. Now."

"What?"

"Someone is coming, Caile! A firewielder."

"Lorentz!" Caile shouted, drawing his sword and surveying their surroundings. They had drawn nearer the River Kylep, and a new-growth forest bordered the road to their left, not tall or particularly foreboding, but thick with green foliage and undergrowth—perfect for an ambush.

"What is it?" Lorentz asked, at Caile's side almost immediately.

"Someone is in the forest."

Lorentz nodded. "We'll have the honor guard take Taera off the road, into the safety of the fields, and then take care of it."

Caile eyed the amber grasses to their right. "No, we'll all have to stay to the road."

Lorentz raised one eyebrow quizzically.

"We're dealing with fire, Lorentz. Those fields could go up in flames."

"Fire," Lorentz repeated flatly, considering Caile's words for a brief moment, and then he was issuing orders for the soldiers to take up their shields and don their helmets. Within seconds, the troops were gathered in tight formation around Taera, and Lorentz met Caile and the captain of Taera's honor guard at the front of the procession to start plodding warily forward. Unlike Caile and the rest of the soldiers, Lorentz had not taken up his shield and helmet. He held only a handful of arrows and a stout, short bow, which he strained and grunted to string.

"You know the drill," Lorentz said. "I'll hide in the grass, then sneak along behind you."

"I don't want to kill anyone," Caile replied. "Let me try to reason with them and await my signal."

"I'll await your signal or the moment you start getting showered in flames, whichever comes first."

"Just await my signal," Caile repeated. "I've spent the last five years in Valaróz—I can take the heat."

Lorentz snorted in reply then slid from his saddle and rolled to lay hidden in the tall grass alongside the road while the procession continued forward without him.

As much as Caile wanted to turn and glare at him, he kept his head forward and his eyes on the forest through the eye slits in his helmet. Lorentz still treated him like a child at times, and though Caile knew Lorentz was merely trying to keep him safe, it still aggravated Caile to no end. He was a prince of Pyrthinia, after all—the crown prince now that Cargan was dead, assuming they were to follow Sargothian law. Caile swallowed back the lump that rose in his throat at the thought. *I'm not a child any longer,* he repeated to himself.

They plodded onward, and the minutes dragged by with no sign of anything in the forest to their left. Caile began to wonder if his sister had perhaps misinterpreted her vision. She was distraught after all, with their brother dying and the prospect of being sent to Col Sargoth. Caile shook the idea aside. Taera didn't lack courage, that he was certain of, and he steeled himself to the task at hand— to focusing all his attention on whomever stepped foot from that forest.

Even prepared for it, they were all shocked by the sudden gout of flames that bellowed out from the trees. It swept over them in a flash, curling around shields, singeing horsehair, and setting the field behind them aflame. One soldier lost control of his panicked horse and was carried toward the forest just as a woman careened from the shadows like a feral animal. She flailed her hands above her head and brought them crashing down with an unintelligible shout, and horse and rider were enveloped in flames.

"Stay your position!" Caile yelled at the soldiers, as he struggled to calm his own horse well enough to dismount. He managed to jump clear of his horse just as the firewielder sent another gout of flames at them. He tucked himself behind his shield and could feel the intense heat curl around him. When the flames passed, he raised his free hand in sign of peace, palm up, showing he held no weapon.

"Stay your hand, firewielder," Caile hollered in the calmest, most authoritative tone he could muster. "We mean you no harm. We are your friends."

"Firewielders have no friends," the woman yelled. "Kill me or be killed."

"No, I beg you," Caile said, holding his shield away from his body and removing his helmet so she could see his face. "I am Prince Caile Delios. I promise you safe harbor. Please, just listen to me. I put myself at your mercy."

Caile dropped his shield and helmet to the ground and held both hands up. The woman glared at him and glanced warily at the soldiers behind him, but she stayed her hand. She was not as old as Caile had surmised at first glance—no more than twenty, at most—but she was filthy, covered in feculent rags, her hair clumped in muddy knots, and her face was lined with worry, her eyes wild with the burden of living a life of constant terror alone in the forest.

"I'm your friend," Caile said again, keeping his eyes squarely on her face and trying not to think about the burned soldier and horse smoldering nearby. "Come with me," Caile continued. "My father, the King, can protect you. You will have to stay under lock and key, but you will be well fed and treated kindly, that I can promise you." He reached his hand out toward her. "Please."

She smiled, and for a moment Caile thought he had reached her, but then the wildness repossessed her eyes. "Your father can't help me. No one can. It's too late. We're all doomed."

"No wait," Caile tried to plead with her, but she flung her hands above her head, drawing her power around her. Caile stood paralyzed, staring into her wild eyes, realizing he was about to die. Sparks danced at her fingertips, and her lips parted as she began to scream the command that would unleash his fiery death. His body tensed in anticipation, but then the young woman gasped in surprise and collapsed to her knees, the tip of an arrow protruding from one of her eyes. She crumpled face first to the ground, and Lorentz emerged from the forest behind her, another arrow notched and ready. He and Caile exchanged a look, not a look of victory but rather of sorrow and understanding. Lorentz returned to the troops, and Caile stood gazing upon the slain firewielder until Taera came and pulled him away by the hand.

"You tried, Caile," she said. "I'm sorry."

3
The Shadow Grows

Caile let out a weary sigh as he plopped down into a chair in his father's study, high in the upper reaches of Castle Pyrthin. King Casstian Delios, too, breathed heavily as he sat and stared into the flames of the fireplace before them. It had already been late by the time Caile, Taera, and their procession reached Kal Pyrthin, and then there was the formal reception with the well-rehearsed greetings and the state dinner in the dining hall where nothing but pleasantries could be uttered for fear of being overheard. That was all thankfully over now, and it was well past midnight. The two of them—king and son—sat silently for a long time, staring into the fire.

"Taera told me of Cargan," Caile said eventually. "I'm sorry."

"As are we all," his father replied, not looking up from the fire. "He was a fine man. He would have made a fine king."

"Have you learned any more of what happened? You can't believe this nonsense about him dying in a drunken brawl?"

"So was the word from Col Sargoth, so it was."

"Father," Caile said, leaning forward in his chair, "you know as well as I do that Cargan was a better man than that."

"A better man than you, for sure, but what can I do? Shall I call the Emperor a liar and bring his wrath down upon Pyrthinia? Is that what you want?"

"Of course not," Caile snapped, immediately regretting losing his temper and reminding himself to stay calm. "I'm not the foolish boy I was when I left, Father."

"Then what of this business on the road with the firewielder?

18

Are you mad? Trying to speak reason to such a person. You would have been killed if it weren't for Lorentz."

"She was a girl, no older than me, not some vile creature. When I left, you had an arrangement, offering amnesty for any sorcerers who turned themselves in and agreed to live here under your watch."

"That was five years ago. Times have changed. Emperor Guderian…"

"Emperor!" Caile spat. "This is no empire. This is the Five Kingdoms, and *you* are the King of Pyrthinia. Guderian is the King of Sargoth, nothing more."

"I'm afraid the Five Kingdoms are no more, son. With each passing day he wrests more power away from us. Nothing can be done."

Caile thrust himself back into the cushions of his chair, and neither of them said anything for a long while. Caile stared with a mixture of sadness and disgust at his father, a man who had seemingly shrunk since he'd last seen him. Five years before, the King of Pyrthinia had been a robust man, exuding energy and confidence. Now, Casstian Delios was old beyond his years. His arms and chest were still thick but lacked the hardened, muscular definition he was once known for. His face, too, was thin and ashen, and his once glorious mane of golden hair now hung limply above his shoulders, thin and mottled with gray.

"Do you mean to send Taera to Col Sargoth?" Caile finally asked.

"What choice do I have?"

"Send me. That's why you had me return from Valaróz, isn't it?"

King Casstian snorted. "The imperial mandate states I must send my eldest child as a ward to Col Sargoth."

"There are exceptions. Tell Guderian that Taera is too ill to travel, that I'm coming to Col Sargoth in her stead. All he cares is that he has his hostage."

"But she's not ill. Would you have me forge false documents? I don't take lying as lightly as you, especially when it means treason."

Caile could feel his face flush with anger. His father clearly was not one to let the past go. "If you ask me, it's better to lie to an evil man than to sign your daughter's death sentence."

"What's that supposed to mean?" Casstian demanded, sitting up in his seat, his face taking on some color and life.

"Don't pretend like you don't know, Father. She's a sorceress."

Casstian slumped back as if the wind had been knocked out of him.

"She's a seer," Caile continued. "She's the one who warned us to the presence of the firewielder today. She saw it in her visions. You can't send her into Guderian's grasp. That monster of his will sniff her out in an instant and they'll kill her just like they've killed every other sorcerer. I've met him, Father—I've met Wulfram. In Sol Valaróz. He's not human. He can see inside of you. He'll know. Sending Taera to him would be sending her to certain death."

Casstian was silent for a long moment. "And you think you will somehow fare better than Cargan or Taera?"

Caile sat up straight. "I have no magical ability to put me in danger. I've lived these last five years as ward to that usurper Don Bricio, and I stayed alive, bit my tongue while vile lies poured from his mouth. I met Wulfram and avoided his scrutiny. I know how to stay alive in a den of lions."

Casstian laughed without humor. "King Bricio and his court in Valaróz are a pack of kittens compared to what you'll find in Col Sargoth, boy."

Caile shrugged. "So be it. I'm not afraid."

"You should be."

"It makes no difference. I want to go and you can't send Taera. You love her more than me, I know. We're the same in that regard. She means more to me than you ever will."

King Casstian Delios looked into the flames of the fireplace and said nothing.

"Well?" Caile asked.

"Go then. Tell my porter to send for the physician, and I will compose the letter to Guderian."

"Thank you," Caile said, standing.

Casstian nodded and watched his son leave. It pained him that

Caile could see through him so easily. He bore Caile no ill will, but it was true he loved Taera and Cargan more. He simply couldn't help it. Casstian's wife, Hedia, had died shortly after birthing Caile, and as much as the King tried to tell himself he could not blame his son, the resentment had faded little over time, especially with Caile being so stubborn and overly-confident as a boy. *That boy is the heir to my throne now by Sargothian law*, Casstian mused, but that only reminded him of Cargan and fresh tears came to his eyes. He pushed the thoughts aside and wiped his face clean. He was King of Pyrthinia and could not be seen crying, not by the physician, not by anyone.

Taera was sitting on her bed with the lamp at her nightstand still burning brightly when Caile knocked at her chamber door.

"Still awake at this hour, Brother?" she asked as she ushered him in.

"I was worried you'd be the one asleep."

"So I could go back to my visions?"

"I'm sorry, I didn't mean to…"

She smiled for him. "It's not your fault. The visions are my concern."

Caile snapped out of his reverie and grabbed her in a nervous embrace. "No, it's all of our concern. That's why I've come to say goodbye."

She hugged him, then pushed him away, not unkindly, and straightened the leather jerkin he wore. "Goodbye? Is Father sending me off so soon then?"

"No, you're staying. I'm going to Col Sargoth in your stead."

"But how—"

"Please don't argue with me," he interrupted her. "I've convinced Father that it is best this way. I'm leaving now before he changes his mind."

"But you've not yet slept and you've been on the road already for weeks, and today, the firewielder…"

"Don't worry, I've learned to sleep in the saddle," he said with a grin. "Besides, I'll be safe in Col Sargoth—I'm no danger to the Emperor. Your job is the more difficult one."

"Oh?"

"You have to pretend to be deathly ill. And you need to get Father back. Remind him that he's the king."

Taera closed her eyes. "Be easy on him, Caile. He's weary. He must choose his battles with the Emperor. It's not easy."

"A king hasn't time for weariness. That's what he always used to tell us."

"I know."

"Remind him. Make Pyrthinia ready. I mean to find out what happened to Cargan. I don't know what will come of it, but it may be trouble."

Taera could only nod in agreement. As scared as she was for her brother, she knew it was pointless to try and stop him, for she had already foreseen him in Col Sargoth in her dream visions. Her own path lay in another direction. *A ship. A cavern of ice. A beautiful girl.* Whatever end fate awaited each of them, she could not say, but their paths were clearly set out for them in her mind. She kissed Caile on the forehead.

"Be careful, Brother."

"Careful is the way of old men. I'll stay alive. You do the same, and be wary of having too many visions—the houndkeeper here can sense magic as well as the ones in Col Sargoth and Sol Valaróz."

4
A New Moon Rises

From the rooftop, Makarria could see far beyond where Spearpoint Rock jutted out from the turbulent waters and off into the horizon where the Esterian Ocean and gray sky melded into an imperceptible border. Somewhere beyond the horizon, farther to the south, were the East Islands, and beyond that Makarria could only imagine. Maybe another land where the sun shone every day and a girl could run in the grass and wear a proper dress without having to worry about it being ruined by never-ending ocean squalls. Makarria smiled at the thought of actually being free of the salty air for once. She did love the ocean, especially when sailing with her grandfather, but she would love it a lot more, she decided, if she didn't have to live right next to it.

"Makarria!" her father hollered from where he lay sprawled out a few feet away from her. "Thatch!"

"Sorry," Makarria said, handing him one of the long palm fronds she'd set down on the roof beside her feet. Galen took it from her and threaded it into a gap in the roof where a frond had blown free the night before.

"You're not much help to me up here just staring off into the distance," he said when he was done. "Why don't you go see if your grandfather needs help?"

"Really? You're sure?"

"Yes, go."

"Thanks," she said, turning to tiptoe her way down the pitched roof along one of the main support beams.

Galen watched her leave with a wry expression, wishing he could navigate the roof with such ease. He had to crawl around on all fours in order to spread his weight out along two beams, otherwise, he'd crash right through the roof and into the house below. He'd hoped to teach Makarria to mend the roof on her own, but the girl seemed incapable of keeping her mind on any task for more than a few minutes. It was all well and good for her to daydream while tending to the garden or milking the goats, but it was too dangerous to be absentminded up on the roof. Galen sighed and grabbed the bundle of palm fronds, resigned to doing the job himself.

Back on the ground, Makarria raced from the house and down the grassy slope to the seashore where her Grandpa Parmo was pushing a skiff into the water.

"Wait, Grampy, wait!" she yelled after him, and he halted, knee-deep in the waves, until she got there.

"In you go," he said, giving her a boost into the boat. "You going to help me pull in the traps?"

"Yep."

"Hold on, then," he told her and pushed them off with the outgoing surf, timing it so as to pass between two breaking waves. He pulled himself aboard with a grunt and paddled them out past the breakers, then gave her the signal to hoist the small sail as he put aside the oars and grabbed hold of the rudder. Within a few moments, he had angled the skiff to catch the wind and they were racing toward Spearpoint Rock and their traps. "That's better," Parmo said, breathing heavily. "I'm getting too old to be launching skiffs from the beach."

"You're not too old, Grampy," Makarria assured him, smiling as the wind whipped her walnut hair across her face.

"If you say so," he replied, unconvinced. "How are you feeling? Is your tummy ache better from yesterday?"

"Yeah, mostly better, but Mother thinks I was pretending so I wouldn't have to do my chores."

"Nonsense," Parmo said with a wave of his free hand. "You may be absentminded at times, but you're no liar—that I'm certain of. Your mother is just worried. She's had a lot on her mind."

"Like what?"

"Nothing that need concern you for the time being. You just mind your parents and try to pay better attention to your chores. No more daydreaming."

"I know," Makarria said. "It's just that chores are so boring. Except for helping you pull in the traps, of course."

"Of course," Parmo agreed with a smile. "Ready the pole-hook and prepare to drop sail, First Mate."

They were nearing the first of their buoys, some thirty fathoms out from the leeward side of Spearpoint Rock. The red-painted coconut bobbed up and down on the rolling waves, functioning both as the marker for their traps and the hooking point for dragging the traps up from the water. Parmo steered them toward it and signaled for Makarria to drop the sail. As they slowed and drifted alongside the buoy, he threw the rudder to the side and they came to a near stop no more than a fathom out from the buoy.

"Pull her up," Parmo said. "Let's see what we've caught."

Makarria reached out with the pole-hook and looped it around the line receding beneath the buoy. When she tugged, though, the skiff moved more than the buoy line. "It's snagged on something," Makarria said, leaning out over the portside of the skiff to get a better hook on it.

"Careful now," Parmo warned.

"I've got it," Makarria said, but as she reached farther out she got the sudden sensation she was wetting herself, and in a panic she lost her balance. She dropped the pole-hook with a scream and toppled face first overboard. The water was shockingly cold, knocking all the air from her lungs and sending her into a panic to reach the surface. She had not sunk far, though, and she surfaced almost immediately, embarrassing herself by how loudly she gasped for air.

"Quit flopping around like a fish and grab my hand," her grandpa yelled. She took his hand, and he yanked her up over the side rail to plop on the deck. "Are you alright?" he asked, calm but breathing more heavily than she was.

"I think so," Makarria replied, but she wasn't certain. She was wet and cold, for sure, but it was something else. She felt like she was uncontrollably peeing in her britches but not exactly.

"What have you done, cut yourself?" Parmo asked.

Makarria followed his glance downward and saw that bloody water was indeed running down her legs where her short breeches ended above the knees. She ran her hands over her thighs; she didn't feel any cuts or pain, but when she looked at her hands they were covered in diluted blood.

"I, I don't think so," Makarria said, confused. "I don't feel any cuts. I…"

"Oh," Parmo said, with sudden understanding.

"What?"

"It's your first moonblood, Makarria."

"What!" Makarria jumped to her feet, covered herself, then spun around, only to find she had nowhere to go.

"Relax, it's fine," her grandpa said. "Just sit down. I'll take you home."

"I'm sorry, Grampy," Makarria said, too embarrassed to look at him.

"There's nothing to be sorry about. It's perfectly normal."

"But what about the traps?" she asked, now worried she'd ruined his chores.

"They'll still be here when I come back," he assured her. "But I'll never hear the end of it from your mother if I don't get you home and into her care straight away."

"I'm fine, really," Makarria insisted. "I don't need to go to bed yet."

Her mother was having none of it, and she tucked the sleeping furs tighter around Makarria. "It's not your moonblood that concerns me, it's that spill you took into the water. It's too late in the year to be swimming."

"I didn't do it on purpose, Mother."

"That's not what I'm saying," Prisca said, "and that's hardly the point, now is it?"

"No."

"Quit fussing like a little girl then. You're a woman now."

Makarria rolled her eyes. "What sort of woman gets tucked into bed by her mother when she's not even tired?"

"That's enough. I'll send in your grandfather. He wants to talk to you before you go to sleep."

"No!" Makarria said, louder than she intended to.

"Quit being silly," her mother chided. "He's a grown man, and he was *married* to a woman once, you know? I wasn't hatched from an egg. I did have a mother. And your grandfather was there when I had my first moonblood. It's nothing to be embarrassed about. It's part of being a woman. Besides, that's not what he wants to talk to you about, I'm sure."

Makarria only nodded, not trusting herself to speak.

Her mother kissed her on the forehead and left. A few moments later, Parmo stepped through the curtains and sat at the foot of her sleeping pad.

"How do you feel?"

"Fine."

Parmo nodded. "It's early still, and I thought you might like some company. Maybe a story or two? Unless you're too tired. Or too old for stories now."

Makarria couldn't help but grin. "I would like a story very much, but I want a real story this time, Grampy. No more of your nursery tales about mermen and talking whales."

"But those are real stories," he complained.

"I want to hear a story about something that really happened."

"Such as?"

"I don't know. Tell me about the Kingdom of Valaróz. Mother said you used to live there."

Parmo closed his eyes for a moment and nodded. "Indeed, many, many years ago."

"What was it like?"

"Well," Parmo began, "I'm sure it's much different now, but in my time Sol Valaróz was the greatest city in the Five Kingdoms. Some might disagree, but to me it was the finest place a boy could grow up. Castle Valaróz was nearly a city unto itself, made entirely of white marble mined in the high mountains to the north. When the sun rose over the Sol Sea, the entire city glimmered like a jewel. And the food, let me tell you. The waters are warmer there than they are here, and the fishermen would bring in all sorts of delicacies. Flying fish, swordfish, and clams, and squid, and octopus, and shrimp. The street vendors would chop them up, skewer them, and cook them seasoned with ground peppers and scallions grown in the terraced fields to the west.

"The fields were as much a marvel of human ingenuity as the castle and older, too. Legend holds that the terraces were already there when Sargoth Lightbringer crossed the Spine into the new world. Mile after mile of stone retaining walls, and the irrigation canals, so complex yet simple at the same time, relying only on gravity to feed themselves from the River Valaróz ten leagues upstream. Sol Valaróz was the first city Sargoth Lightbringer conquered, with the help of the mighty stormbringer Vala, of course. Valaróz became the first of the Five Kingdoms, Vala the first queen. From there, Sargoth Lightbringer and the other sorcerers moved east toward what is now Pyrthinia, but Vala stayed, and of all the Old World sorcerers, she had the most respect for the people and culture she came to rule. It's evident in the architecture of the buildings, in the food, the festival days, and even the clothes people wear. Apart from some of the tribal villages in Norg to the far north, none of the other Five Kingdoms retained so much of the culture from the indigenous peoples as Valaróz...."

Parmo glanced down and saw that Makarria's eyes were already wavering closed. "It seems you were more tired than you thought," he said softly. "Or perhaps my history lesson was too boring."

Makarria muttered something unintelligible, too far gone to fight off her slumber. Parmo sat there for a moment longer, letting himself remember the blue waters of the Sol Sea where he'd learned to sail as a boy. It had been a long time since he'd allowed himself to think of it. With a sigh, he stood to leave, but the air caught in his throat, and he felt a wave of dizziness wash over him. A breeze inexplicably ruffled his hair and tunic and the curtains around him. *Has someone opened the front door?* He sat back down, thinking for a moment he must be ill, but then Makarria muttered something in her sleep again, and Parmo yanked her sleeping furs away to see that her sleeping gown was shimmering, halfway transformed into a blue dress.

"Makarria," he wheezed, shaking her by the shoulders.

Makarria's eyes batted open and the dress disappeared, once again a sleeping gown.

"Grampy?" Makarria asked, confused.

"No more dresses tonight," Parmo whispered. "No more dreams. Push them away."

"No more dreams," Makarria repeated, already half-asleep again. "No more dreams."

Parmo—still short of breath and lightheaded—watched her drift back to sleep, then pulled the sleeping furs back over her and straightened his hair. He'd have to tell Prisca and Galen. They wouldn't be happy, but there was nothing for it. He cursed himself for a fool. There was no more pretending anymore. Not for any of them. Makarria's power was here to stay, moonblood or not.

5
A Final Breath

When Makarria came in for lunch after finishing her morning chores, Parmo was still asleep. Makarria joined her parents at the small dining table beside the iron cooking stove in the center of their home and eyed his empty stool.

"Why's Grampy so tired today?"

Her parents exchanged a glance but said nothing. Prisca filled Makarria's wooden bowl with crab and leek soup from the pot boiling on the stove and handed it to her wordlessly. Galen kept his eyes focused on his own soup. They had been acting like this all morning, as if Makarria had done something wrong, and they were angry with her. As far as Makarria knew, though, she hadn't done anything wrong. Although tired and lethargic, she had gotten up in time to milk the goats before sunup, she'd pulled weeds in the garden and harvested the leeks for their soup, she'd fed the chickens and checked for eggs, and she'd done it all without a complaint or daydreaming.

"I think I'll go wake Grampy," Makarria suggested, wanting nothing more than his warm presence there with her right now.

"Let him be," Prisca said. "He was up late last night. We all were but you."

"But his soup will get cold."

"Makarria, I said let him be."

Galen frowned. "It is nearly noon. The old man should be up by now, having stayed up all night or not."

Makarria had no idea why her grandfather or the rest of them should have been up all night, but her eyes lit up at the prospect of waking him nonetheless. "Can I, Mother?"

"Fine," Prisca relented. "You can ask him but don't badger him into getting up if he's still tired."

Makarria dashed up from the table and threw aside the curtains separating Parmo's sleeping area from the rest of the room. "Grampy," she said, shaking his shoulders. But he did not stir, and his face was covered with sweat. His breaths came in rapid, shallow rasps. "Grampy?" she said again, and this time a thin moan escaped his lips. "Mother," Makarria started to say, but Prisca had heard the worry in Makarria's voice from across the room and was already at her side.

"Father," Prisca said sharply. She flung the sleeping furs off of him and saw that his nightclothes were soaked with sweat. "Go draw up a hot draught with worm root and anise like I taught you," she told Makarria. "Quickly, go! Galen, fetch water and a washrag."

Galen had been coming to see what the fuss was about but now turned and rushed outside to fetch the water and rag while Makarria ran to the stove to pile on more wood and stoke the flames. Galen returned a moment later with a pail of water and filled the kettle atop the stove before hurrying into Parmo's sleeping area with the remaining water and the washrag.

Once the flames were going strong in the stove and the water in the kettle heating, Makarria hopped onto one of the dining stools to reach the drying rack hanging from the roof. There were dozens of the little muslin sacks on the rack with a wide assortment of herbs, roots, dried berries, and fruits within them. All of them were similar-looking, but Makarria knew how to identify each one by smell; in a quick few moments she was back on the ground, crumbling with her fingers one pinch each of worm root and anise root into her grandfather's large bronze stein. The water in the kettle was not yet boiling though, and Makarria saw that her father had nearly filled it to the top. She dumped half of it out into the pot of crab and leek soup so that the water in the kettle would heat faster; the soup would be thin and tasteless now, but that was the least of her concerns. She could see that her parents had stripped Parmo of his nightshirt and were wiping him down with the damp washcloth. Galen lifted Parmo's head and torso so that Prisca could wipe his back, but it sent the old man into a fit of coughing.

"The draught, Makarria!" her mother yelled.

"Coming," Makarria said, checking the kettle. The water level was so low now she couldn't see if it was boiling or not. Without thinking, she stuck her finger inside to test the water and withdrew it with a sudden yelp, nearly knocking the kettle from the stove in the process. *"Merda!"* she silently swore, echoing her grandfather's favorite curse and sticking the pulsating finger into her mouth. *Think before you act, you daft girl.* She grabbed up the kettle handle with her other hand and filled the stein with steaming hot water. The pungent smell of anise filled her nostrils. She grabbed a dried honey-bead from one of the muslin sacks and tossed it in the stein where it instantly melted.

"Makarria!" Prisca yelled again.

"Here," Makarria said, rushing to her parents' side and handing off the stein to her mother.

Galen still held Parmo up in a sitting position from behind and now grabbed the old man's jaw with one hand to lean his head back and hold it steady. Prisca moved the stein to Parmo's lips and tilted it, forcing him to drink. Parmo sputtered at first on the hot liquid but then began swallowing as Prisca continued to pour it into his gullet. Most of the draught spilled down his chin and onto his bare chest but enough went down, and when Prisca pulled the empty stein away and wiped Parmo clean with the washcloth, his breathing seemed to slow and become more regular.

"Is he going to be alright?" Makarria asked, wedging herself forward between her parents to see if Parmo was opening his eyes.

"Get back!" Prisca yelled.

"I want to help."

"You've done enough, Makarria. He's sick because of you."

Makarria was dumbstruck and she staggered back. Her fault? What had she done?

"Just go," her mother said, regretting what she had said but still terse. "Outside and let us tend to him."

"It's alright. Go on, Makarria," her father said, and Makarria turned and fled outside.

The sun had burned through the cloud cover low in the sky to the west, and the blustering winds of midday had subsided into a gentle breeze. Makarria was laying on one of the large rocks that comprised the little jetty she and her grandfather had built to shelter their skiff from the relentless ocean surf. She was just lying there and letting the waves wash over her outstretched hand to soothe her burned finger. From the corner of her eye she saw her father walk down from the house, but she ignored him, even when he sat on a rock beside her.

"Makarria," he said, but he didn't know where to start. He had convinced Prisca the night before to not yet tell Makarria about her ability. There was still a chance she might grow out of it, and he was certain Parmo had overstated the danger of the Emperor. They were hundreds of miles away from Col Sargoth and Makarria was just a girl after all. What danger did she pose to the mightiest man in the Five Kingdoms, even if she could turn tunics to gowns? Isolated as they were here on the peninsula, she wasn't a danger to anyone but her own family. Galen couldn't bring himself to tell her that though. She was still his little girl, and he wanted her to enjoy the innocence of her childhood while she could.

"Your mother didn't mean to yell at you," he finally said. "It's not your fault that Grampy is sick."

"Is he alright?" Makarria asked.

"I don't know, Makarria. He hasn't woken up yet. Your grandfather is getting very old, you know? There's a chance, he…"

"No, he's not going to die," Makarria insisted. "He's not too old."

"I hope you're right. I really do. Do you want to come

and see him?"

Makarria nodded wordlessly and got up to follow her father up to the house. Inside, they found Prisca at Parmo's bedside. Parmo lay bundled beneath his sleeping furs, his breaths shallow but smooth and steady at least. The sleeping area smelled of dried sweat and anise.

"Prisca," Galen said. "Why don't we go get some rest now."

"No, I'm fine," Prisca said, but Makarria could see that her mother was weary. Galen was too. Between tending to Grampy and whatever had kept them up all night, they were visibly exhausted.

"It's alright," Makarria assured them. "I'll stay with him. I'll get you if he wakes up, or starts coughing, or…"

"Come," Galen said, grabbing Prisca's arm to help her to her feet. Prisca seemed about to protest, but she finally stood, kissed her fingertips and touched them to Makarria's forehead, then let Galen lead her to bed.

Makarria returned her attention to her grandfather. Though his face was relaxed, it seemed to be creased with more wrinkles than she had noticed before. And his skin sagged loosely from his cheeks and chin. Maybe her father was right. *No*, she insisted. *Grampy's not going to die.* She refused to believe it and instead focused her thoughts on the wonderful things the two of them would do together when he was better. The sails on the skiff needed patching, for one thing, but they would need to get more sailcloth first. Maybe Parmo could sail her to Pyrvino to buy it. He had always promised he would take her there, and her father said he would allow it once she was old enough. She'd had her first moonblood now—how much older could her father expect her to be? *Yes*, she decided, *Grampy and I will sail to Pyrvino. We'll get new sailcloth. We'll stay at an inn. I've never even seen an inn. And when we get back, we'll mend the sail and make new traps. I'll finally let Grampy show me how to tack the skiff, or beat the windward, or whatever he called it. Maybe we can explore Spearpoint Rock.* And the ideas came, one after another—all the wonderful things she and Grampy would do.

It became dark as she sat there at her grandfather's side and the time passed when they would normally eat dinner, but her parents did not stir from their slumber, and Makarria did not want to disturb them even if she was hungry. She could go one night without supper, and she meant to stay at her grandfather's side all night or until he woke. As if her thinking the idea somehow prodded him, Parmo stirred beside her and let out a low groan.

"Grampy?" Makarria whispered, grabbing his hand. "Are you alright?"

"Makarria?" His voice was a thin rasp, barely audible. He tried to sit up but grimaced in pain and fell back into his pillow.

"I'll go wake Mother," Makarria said, but Parmo reached out and grabbed her by the wrist.

"No. Don't bother her. Help me up, Makarria. I need to go outside."

There was urgency in his voice, and Makarria obeyed without question. She reached beneath his shoulders and helped him up and onto his feet. He leaned heavily into her as she guided him through the dark living area and to the door. He had to brace himself against the wall while she pulled open the door. When they were outside, the fresh ocean air seemed to invigorate him, and he stood on his own power, only taking her hand for support.

"To the beach," he said. "I want to be near the ocean."

They walked together down the hill, along the path through the grass to the pebbled beach, and there Parmo's strength left him. His legs went limp and it was all Makarria could do to break his fall as she toppled down next to him with a thump. Parmo's breaths again came in ragged spurts, and he could only open his eyes with great effort.

"Grampy?" Makarria asked. She wanted to run. To get her mother. To make another draught. To do something.

"Stay with me," Parmo said, holding onto her hand with what little strength he had left. "It's alright. Don't be scared."

"But, Grampy—"

"I know, I know." He closed his eyes and forced himself to calm his breathing before reopening them. "My time has come,

GARRETT CALCATERRA

Makarria. I was born of Tel Mathir, and now She wants me back.
It's part of the great cycle. You needn't be sad."
    Makarria shook her head. "I don't want you to die, Grampy.
You can't. I won't let you."
    "That's enough, Makarria," he said, though it was getting harder
for him to breathe. "Listen to me. Your parents love you. But they
don't understand the danger. You're special, Makarria. People will
fear you. The—" A wracking cough tore through him and his entire
body shuddered.
    Makarria grabbed onto him and held tight, not knowing what
else to do. "Grampy?"
    "Go," was all Parmo could wheeze, too weak to push her away.
"Go," he tried telling her again, but it only came out in an inaudible
whisper, and he lost consciousness.
    Makarria held onto him, saying his name over and over again as
his rasping breaths slowed. She looked at his face and through her
tear-filled eyes saw not his withered features but what she imagined
his visage to be when he was still young and full of life, when he
lived in Sol Valaróz and sailed the Sol Sea in a mighty carrack. His
body went limp and his breath become nothing more than a sigh,
but still Makarria grasped onto him and held that image in her mind.

6
A Sacrifice From the Sea

The scent-hound bayed, waking the High Houndkeeper in Col Sargoth with a start.

The second howl was so loud the houndkeeper jumped to his feet and stood paralyzed for a moment before remembering what he was supposed to do. When his wits returned, he released the lever that held the inner ring of the giant compass in place, and the scent-hound swung about on the axle protruding through her navel—steel bearings screeching with protest—only to lurch to a sudden halt pointing southeast. The hound bayed again and began whining as her nose centered in on what she smelled. When the compass quit moving altogether, the houndkeeper checked the coordinates, then went to the sprawling map of the Sargothian Empire hanging on one wall. The coordinates were the same as last time: 140 arc degrees off north. The scent-hound was still whining though, whereas last time she'd only fussed for a moment. Whatever this dreamwielder was doing, it was big.

The houndkeeper snatched up one of the steel balls from a rack below the map and rushed to a U-shaped flue pipe in the corner of the chamber that looped up through the flagstone floor and back down again. He opened the door hatch on the flue and placed the ball inside as steam billowed from the opening. He then closed the hatch and turned the valve lever, and a burst of steam shot through the pipe, hurling the steel ball down the flue toward the bottom of the tower where the alarm would be sounded.

The scent-hound bayed again. *Yes, whatever this dreamwielder is doing, it's big,* the houndkeeper thought. *And this time she's given herself away. Wulfram is going to be pleased. Very pleased.*

Parmo lay on the beach with his eyes open for a long time before he realized he was alive. There were no stars, only lightless clouds above him, but in the distance a thin swath of the black veil was illuminated gray with the promise of an imminent sunrise. He had not expected to ever open his eyes again, and he didn't trust his senses at first. He could hear the surf at his feet though, and he could smell the salty air and feel Makarria curled up at his side, sleeping in the crook of his left arm. He was surprised to find that he could move his free hand with ease and brush her hair from her face. His breaths came to him in a painless, natural manner. The more he thought about it, the more he realized nothing was causing him pain except for the tingling sensation of his arm falling asleep beneath Makarria's head.

"Makarria?"

He shook her gently, but she woke with a start and gasp.

"Grampy?"

"I'm here."

Makarria sat up with the sick feeling that she'd done something horrible, that something bad had happened. When she looked at her grandfather though, she saw that he was alive and well—more than alive and well. Even in the predawn darkness, she could see that he was no longer old and sick, but rather the young man she had seen in her mind. She remembered having fallen asleep with that image burning through her.

"You're not old anymore," she said simply.

"What?" Parmo asked, incredulous but realizing even as she said it that it was true. He ran his fingers over his face. The wrinkles were gone. He felt his arms, stout with the sinews of a seafaring man. He breathed in deeply the sea air, and his lungs did not protest. *How is this possible? I was dying.*

"Grampy?" Makarria said, suddenly noticing the hundreds of

small dark shapes on the beach around them. "What's happened?"

Parmo stood and followed her gaze. All around them—covering the beach for a mile in either direction—were sea creatures. Dead sea creatures. Fish, crabs, squid, gulls, swallows, turtles, jellyfish, starfish, oysters, snails, all of them dead.

"*Merda*," Parmo swore in disbelief. The enormity of what Makarria had done slowly hit him. *The Emperor must have sensed this.*

"What's happened to them?" Makarria asked, the sick feeling rushing through her body again. "Is it my fault?"

Parmo grabbed her by the shoulders. "No, look at me, Makarria. You saved my life. You made me young again."

"But how? The fish, they—"

"I'll explain it all to you later, Makarria. We haven't time right now. We need to leave. It's not safe here for you anymore." He prodded her toward the jetty. "Go, untie the skiff and make ready to set sail. Make as much room as you can. Get rid of all the traps, the pole-hook, and anything else we don't need to sail. I'll get supplies from the barn."

"What about Mother and Father?"

Parmo turned back to face her. "We can't take them with us, Makarria. There's not enough room, and they'll try to stop us besides. They'll be safer if they don't know where you are. I'll leave a message for them so they know you're safe with me. That's the best for everyone right now. Alright?"

Makarria didn't understand, but she nodded in agreement.

"Go then," he urged and spun away to sprint up the hill to the barn. He was amazed at how effortlessly his legs propelled him up the incline. *I'm not an old man anymore*, he marveled.

Inside the barn he found what he was after: two wooden chests he had not opened in ages buried in the back corner behind a stack of old harnesses and disused tack for the plough horses. The rusted hinges squeaked as he opened the chests, but the contents inside looked to be unharmed. He threw down two wool blankets from the first chest and piled everything he thought they would need in the middle, including a parcel of salted goat meat from the storage shelves and two skins he filled with fresh water. Lastly he pulled a long object wrapped in burlap from one of the chests. He set it down beside the wool blanket and unwrapped one end of the burlap to reveal the tarnished hilt of a sword. Tied to the hilt with a piece of twine was a ring, almost as blackened with tarnish as the sword hilt. He untied the twine and went to the barn doors. There he tied the ring to the door handle. Prisca would know what it meant. They had discussed scenarios in the past of what to do if Makarria were in danger. Prisca would be livid with him, but she would at least know that Makarria was safely gone with him and know to burn all of Makarria's belongings—all evidence that Makarria ever existed. Parmo didn't dare tell Prisca more. It pained him to abandon his daughter this way, but there was nothing for it. There was no time to argue.

His decision made, Parmo ran back to the blanket, grabbed up the four corners to pick up the supplies in a big bundle, then grabbed the still-wrapped sword with his free hand and hurried out of the barn toward the beach. Makarria stood ankle-deep in the surf waiting for him, holding the stern of the skiff nervously. A flood of conflicting emotions ran roughshod through her: excitement; shame at leaving her parents without saying goodbye; dread at the thought of all the dead fish on the beach and floating in the shallow waters around her; but mostly excitement about the adventure of sailing away in the dark. When Parmo got there, he heaved the bundle of supplies into the skiff then helped Makarria in.

"Off we go," he said, pushing them forward, and they vaulted over the first wave, then the second, and Parmo pulled himself in and took up the oars. "Prepare the sails."

"Where are we going, Grampy?"

"To the East Islands, Makarria. We'll be safe there."

Makarria's eyes bulged. "The East Islands? I thought you had to have a ship to get there. I mean, a real ship."

"For any ordinary sailor, yes," Parmo said with a grin. "But your grandfather isn't any ordinary sailor."

• • •

Natarios Rhodas, youngest of the three houndkeepers, stared out of his tower window in Kal Pyrthin sick with anticipation. Castle Pyrthin loomed in the distance to the west, and below and between sprawled Kal Pyrthin, a city bustling with people tending to last minute business and errands before nightfall. But Natarios's concern was not with the city or with King Casstian in the keep. Rather, his eyes were drawn to the northwest, where some thousand miles away stood Col Sargoth. It had been almost twenty hours since Natarios's scent-hound had gone nearly mad with its howling and crying. The poor beast had worked herself up into such a frenzy Natarios thought she was going to die. Whatever sort of sorcerer she had sensed was powerful. That's why Natarios was looking to the west, watching and waiting.

When he first saw the fleck on the horizon, he thought his eyes might be playing tricks on him, but the black form approached rapidly, and within minutes he could make out the shape of a raven. He shuddered as the raven loomed larger. *I'm a pitiful houndkeeper,* he lamented and threw open the shuttered balcony doors. The raven, larger than any bird had a right to be, slowed to a near hover above the tower and glided toward the balcony. Natarios stood clear as the bird swooped inside and skidded to a halt with an ear-piercing squawk. It stood nearly as tall as Natarios and regarded him with its obsidian eyes for a long moment before shaking itself spasmodically. Its feathers began to mottle and bubble, and Natarios could hear tendons and bones rearranging themselves beneath feather and skin. He had to lower his eyes away, lest he vomit. When he looked up, Wulfram stood before him, his fur and feathers now shrouding his human frame like a cloak.

"Master," Natarios greeted him with a stiff bow.

"Which direction?" Wulfram demanded.

"The southeast. But the hound couldn't pinpoint it exactly, master. I'm sorry. The scent was strong—it nearly killed the hound."

"You're sure it came from the southeast?"

"Yes, Master."

With a savage hiss, Wulfram grabbed the scent-hound's nearest foot and sent her spinning wildly on her axle. The hound screamed, a scream more human sounding than canine. Natarios wished there were a way to close his ears as well as his eyes.

"That's the same reading the hound in Col Sargoth came up with," Wulfram snarled. "This dreamwielder could be anywhere between here and the East Islands. We need the reading from Sol Valaróz to triangulate her position."

"It's a dreamwielder then?" Natarios said, a lump suddenly in his throat.

"What else, you fool?"

"She… she must be close, Master—the scent was strong. Probably right here in Kal Pyrthin, certainly no farther than Pyrvino."

Wulfram swept his cloak free of his hunched shoulders and moved toward the balcony. "I think not here; it's too bold. Still, send your agents into the city to find word of any strange happenings. If they find nothing, take your men toward Pyrvino and search every farmstead and hovel along the way. I'll meet up with you after I go to Sol Valaróz and get the last set of coordinates."

"Of course, Master," Natarios said, but Wulfram had already leapt from the balcony.

7
The Dark City

It had been a wearying three-week journey from Kal Pyrthin, first along the River Kylep, then across the border from Pyrthinia into Sargoth and into the highlands past Lepig, and lastly through Forrest Weorcan, which loomed dark and foreboding even though the massive trees had been cleared for a half mile to either side of the high road. Caile's journey was near complete though, and exhausted as he was, he bristled with nervous energy as Col Sargoth came into view. He had heard stories about the city, of course, but nothing could have prepared him for what he now rode toward. The hair at the nape of his neck stood on end, and his left hand involuntarily gripped tighter at his horse's reins.

"It's a dreary looking cesspit, isn't it?" Lorentz remarked.

Caile could only nod. The city stretched outward before them for miles to the south and east of where the Sargothian River emptied into the Gothol Sea. It looked like some great malignant, black sore spreading over the land, Caile thought. Even the seawaters around the city had turned black, and the white sails of the ships entering and leaving the harbor stood out in stark contrast to the inky backdrop.

They had been watching two plumes of black smoke loom larger on the horizon for hours as they approached, but now they could see the actual source of the black smoke. Two sprawling smelting factories at the north and south edges of the city belched out sulfurous black fumes from chimneystacks that rose into the air nearly as high as the five towers of Lightbringer's Keep. The keep itself glimmered like obsidian, and from this distance it looked like a black claw reaching its taloned fingers skyward from the center of the city.

Caile realized that the horses had all stopped of their own accord, and he urged his mount forward toward the south gate of the city. "We best raise our banner and make this official," he said, and Lorentz ordered the red and gold banner of Pyrthinia be raised.

By the time Caile and his honor guard reached the south gate, their banner had been noticed and a retinue of twelve Sargothian cavalry soldiers was waiting to receive them. The soldiers wore mail coifs over their heads and hauberks with articulated shoulder plates beneath black surcoats emblazoned with the symbol of Sargoth: a white sun radiating five shafts of light. Their riding pants were black leather with steel thigh plates sewn in and shynbalds to protect their lower legs. In addition, each soldier had a round shield and a flail strapped to his saddle. The flails were evil looking, crude weapons—huge spiked heads attached with chains to the long ash-wood handles. *Hardly ceremonial weapons,* Caile thought.

The captain of the guard, who wore an open-faced helm adorned with ram horns to signify his rank, rode forward to greet them, but the confusion on his face was obvious when he saw only Pyrthinian men before him.

"Where is the Princess Taera?" the captain asked, dispensing with any pleasantries.

"She is ill," Caile said. "I have been sent in her place."

"And you are?"

"Prince Caile Delios of Pyrthinia."

The captain sniffed and turned away with a curt waving motion for them to follow. Caile shot Lorentz a glance and Lorentz merely shrugged in return. Caile urged his mount forward, and they followed the retinue through the south gate, which was only a gate in the loosest of terms. There were two columns of granite on either side of the road and an archway spanning the distance between them, but unlike most cities in the Five Kingdoms, Col Sargoth had no outer wall. Rather, the city boundary was wherever the ramshackle hovels and tents on the outskirts of the city stopped. The south gate merely marked where the high road joined the main thoroughfare leading north toward the center of the city.

Once past the outer buildings, the streets were lined on either side with lampposts that smoked and sputtered, their filaments burning a dull orange even though it was still hours before nightfall. The road itself was not paved with flagstones but rather with tar and gravel. Caile watched as it came up in black clumps beneath the horses' hooves only to fall again and get trampled back into the road. The buildings were all tall rectangular affairs—two or three stories high, constructed of soot-stained cedar timber or granite blocks—and they seemed to trap in the choking stench of smoke and naphtha. What really stood out to Caile, however, was the fact that there were very few animals in the streets. In Kal Pyrthin and Sol Valaróz, the streets leading toward the city center were filled with horsemen, horse-drawn wagons, mule-drawn carts, and farmers leading pigs, sheep, goats, chickens, and any number of other animals to market. Here though, there were only the Sargothian cavalrymen on their horses and Caile and his men on their own mounts. There were plenty of city folk hustling about, but all were on foot. The carts were drawn by hand, and the few wagons they passed were self-powered vehicles that were propelled by steam engines, wheezing like bellows and spewing black soot from their smokestacks. Caile had heard of such things but thought them a myth before now.

As they moved deeper into the city, the buildings gradually grew larger, but they remained drab and uniformly rectangular. The people themselves cleared a wide path before the cavalrymen, and no one said a word to Caile or his men. They hardly even said a word to each other, Caile realized. That was partly what unnerved him so much—there wasn't the cacophony of voices he had grown accustomed to in a city. The near silence was eerie.

They reached the outer wall of Lightbringer's Keep and the Sargothian captain quickly ushered them past the guards. Inside the outer walls, it was nearly a city in and of itself, but they soon reached the inner wall, which connected the five towers together.

"We will dismount here," the captain said. "Your horses and belongings will be tended to. Please follow me."

Caile and his men did as they were told and followed the captain on foot. Six of the cavalrymen proceeded in front of them and six followed behind. All of them carried their flails, Caile noted. They proceeded through the inner courtyard toward the central keep, which was connected to the five towers via long narrow wings like spokes on a giant wheel. At the entryway to the central keep courtiers bowed deeply to greet them, but Caile barely had time to pay them notice, for the captain led them on at a brisk pace into the entry hall and down a long central corridor. Caile glanced upward and saw the ceiling in the corridor was vaulted some fifty feet or more. To either side, the walls were decorated with expansive tapestries depicting Sargoth Lightbringer in various scenes from ancient lore.

The hall ended at a set of wide double-doors, and the captain halted to speak with a courtier. The courtier slipped inside, and a moment later the double-doors opened. Caile realized with a jolt that they were entering the throne room; he was being ushered in to see the Emperor himself. Decorum usually called for visiting dignitaries the chance to bathe and change into proper attire before meeting, but clearly the Emperor cared not for decorum. Caile hastily combed his hair back out of his face with one hand and unbuttoned the top of his cloak to reveal his Pyrthinian surcoat before stepping inside with his honor guard flanked to either side behind him.

Like the central corridor, the ceiling of the throne room was vaulted, and there was a high balcony lining the rear and side walls, but apart from that it was similar in size and layout to the throne room in Castle Pyrthin. The stark difference was the man sitting on the throne. Few people outside Lightbringer's Keep had ever seen Emperor Thedric Guderian. Wulfram was the one who traveled to the other four kingdoms when necessary, and popular sentiment throughout the Five Kingdoms was that Wulfram was the true power behind Guderian. Caile had always imagined the Emperor to be an old, frail weakling of a man. He couldn't have been further from the truth. Even sitting upon his throne, Guderian towered above Caile. He was tall, broad-shouldered, thickly muscled, and appeared to be in the physical prime of his life, though Caile knew he was more than fifty years old. His jet-black hair was close-cropped to his scalp and a well-trimmed line of a beard ran along his jawline to where it connected with the mustache that outlined his mouth. His disdain for decorum extended to his wardrobe. He didn't wear a robe or crown even, but rather a black leather jack with plate armor at the forearms and leather trousers stitched with thigh plates and shynbalds much like the ones the cavalrymen wore. Next to the throne stood the Emperor's man-at-arms with Guderian's claymore: a massive two-handed sword nearly five feet long. Caile found himself gawking back and forth between Emperor and weapon.

"Your Excellency, I present to you Prince Caile Delios of Pyrthinia," said the courtier who had ushered them in.

The introduction snapped Caile to attention and he knelt down to bow before the Emperor. His men followed suit behind him.

"I was expecting a princess," Guderian said in a low quiet voice that nonetheless filled the entire throne room.

Caile raised his head to address him but remained kneeling. "Your Excellency, my father King Casstian Delios regretfully informs you that Princess Taera suffers a malady which makes her unfit for travel. He has sent me in her stead."

"A malady?"

"We bring a letter from the royal physician describing her illness," Caile replied, motioning for Lorentz to retrieve the letter from his satchel.

Lorentz withdrew the letter, and a scribe whom Caile hadn't even noticed before stepped from the shadows behind the throne and snatched up the letter. The scribe cracked the wax seal, read it, and nodded wordlessly to the Emperor.

"Very well then," Guderian said. "Tell me a bit about yourself, young Caile. You were ward to King Bricio, is that correct? How go matters in Valaróz?"

"Yes, Your Excellency, I was ward to King Bricio for five years and in charge of maritime relations with Pyrthinia and to a lesser extent the Old World. As of the time I left, two months ago, all was well. Pirates from the Old World raid some of the smaller villas near the Spine on occasion, but otherwise, everything is orderly." Caile didn't deem it necessary to elaborate upon how Bricio kept the realm orderly; Bricio had been hand-picked by Guderian, and the secret agents, the rewards for turning in dissenters, the ever increasing standing army—all the deceptive and tyrannical methods Caile had observed in his five years in Valaróz—were quite clearly methods passed down by the Emperor himself.

Emperor Guderian was nodding. "It seems Valaróz is more orderly than Pyrthinia then. I received word of the sorceress."

Caile's breath caught in his throat, and he felt himself on the verge of panic. *How could he possibly know about Taera?*

"You did well in killing the firewielder," Guderian continued.

"The firewielder, yes, thank you," Caile said, realizing the Emperor wasn't talking about his sister at all. Caile was relieved yet still disconcerted. He'd ordered his men and the other Pyrthinian soldiers to remain silent about the firewielder, and he himself had only told his father. There were the scent-hounds of course, but still, the Emperor shouldn't have known any specifics. "I had hoped to apprehend her," Caile admitted, "but she was mad with rage, she burned one man alive, nearly burned me, and my man Lorentz here was forced to kill her."

"You'd do well to take better heed of your man Lorentz then. I sense that more trouble is afoot in Pyrthinia. Your fool father treads a thin line in resisting the mandates I send him, and your brother was the bigger fool."

Anger welled up inside Caile, but he forced himself to respond in an even tone. "It was my understanding Cargan was killed by drunkards."

"Indeed, drunkards and traitors. Your brother made the mistake of trying to befriend them."

"I don't understand."

The Emperor smiled and stood, though there was no humor

in his smile. "Walk with me, Caile," he said, then strode away to one side of the throne room, and Caile had to jump to his feet and nearly run to catch up. Guderian led him up the balcony staircase and stopped to gaze out of a lead glass window. Two of the massive towers obscured their view to the left and the right, but their vantage point was still high enough to see over the inner and outer walls of Lightbringer's Keep to the city beyond. "Tell me what you see," the Emperor said.

Caile hesitated, unsure what the Emperor wanted of him. "I see Col Sargoth, Your Excellency."

"You lack vision then, boy. When I look out this window I see the pinnacle of technology. I see man's triumph over nature and evil. I see a city where smelters are making the strongest steel mankind has ever known. I see a city where beasts of burden will soon be obsolete, where steam powers our carriages, where machines power our mills, tan hides, and pump ether to the lanterns that burn night and day. I see a city where the roofs and roads are sealed with tar—a city that is impervious to storm and rain. Most importantly, I see a city free of sorcery. Sorcery is a malady that breeds evil in the minds of men, Caile. It was the sorcerers who nearly brought the Five Kingdoms to ruin and started the Dreamwielder War. It was the sorcerers who tried to allow the armies of the Old World to cross the Spine like they did nearly 300 years ago. Fortunately, like my ancestor Sargoth Lightbringer then, I am here now to stay the hand of evil."

Caile couldn't help but respond. "Sargoth Lightbringer himself was a sorcerer, though."

"Indeed, as were Vala, Golier, Pyrthin, and Norg. But times have changed, young prince. Mankind has evolved. Civilization has evolved. The New World was a wild land then, populated by shiftless savages, and our forefathers were hardly more than savages themselves. They needed sorcery to conquer the New World and set us upon our path, but sorcery has outlived its usefulness. We needn't the help of stormbringers now that we've mastered irrigation. There's no use for beastcharmers when beasts themselves aren't needed. Those who support the old ways—men like your father and brother—stand in the way of progress. During your stay here, Caile, I hope you'll come to see things correctly. Men who share my vision stand to inherit much. The day of the Five Kingdoms is over. We've evolved. This is the Sargothian Empire now, an empire where all may live without fear of sorcery."

"And what of your servant Wulfram?" Caile asked.

The Emperor turned from the window to face Caile. "He knows as well as I that when his job is done, I must kill him. Believe me, he longs for the day I will finally put him to rest."

Storm clouds surround a lone farmstead, and a woman looks up from her garden where she pulls weeds. Soldiers approach, led by a dark, shrouded figure. The woman yells for her husband, but by time he steps out of the barn, the soldiers are there.

Where is she, the shrouded figure asks. Where is the dreamwielder?

The woman shakes her head, and her husband tries to step forward protectively, but one of the soldiers clubs him to the ground. The soldiers crowd around, kick him savagely.

Stop, please, I don't know what you're talking about, the woman cries.

Liar! She was here. Where has she gone?

I don't know. Please, leave him be.

Kill them both, the dark figure says. They're of no use.

One soldier steps toward the woman, knife in hand. The others beat the husband with their clubs. His head cracks open and everything turns red...

Taera woke with a gasp and scrambled to her feet expecting to find herself surrounded by soldiers. She was in her own room though, standing on her bed, wearing her own nightclothes, soaked in sweat. It took her several seconds to realize it had all been a dream, but even with the realization, her heart did not calm in her chest because she knew it was more than a dream. It was a vision, and somewhere soon, if not already, there would be soldiers approaching a lone farmstead.

8
A Storm on the Horizon

Makarria stared into the distance from the bow of the skiff. The view had been the same for five straight days—endless ocean as far as the eye could see and an occasional puffy cloud in the sky—but now dark clouds loomed on the horizon. She'd pointed them out to her grandfather when she first noticed them several hours before, but he'd merely told her not to worry about it. He'd been saying that a lot since they set voyage, but Makarria couldn't help but worry. Parmo had told her what she was when the sun had risen on that first day: a dreamwielder. He hadn't meant to tell her much, but she was relentless with her questions.

In the days before Emperor Guderian, dreamwielders were the most revered and powerful of all sorcerers, Parmo had told her, but she didn't entirely believe him. She'd heard him mention the Dreamwielder War often enough in the stories he used to tell her. She knew how the dreamwielders had created horrible monsters by melding humans and beasts together. Parmo assured Makarria that she wasn't capable of doing anything of the sort, that what she'd done to save him was entirely noble, but still, here they were running away. People would be scared of her if they knew what she was. Particularly the Emperor. No wonder her mother had continually told her to not have any dreams. A pang of guilt shot through her at the thought of her mother. *I didn't even say goodbye to her or Father.*

"Grampy," Makarria started to ask, but her grandfather interrupted and corrected her. "Parmo," he said. "You need to call me Parmo from now on."

"Right," she complied, sitting up and turning to face him where he sat manning the rudder at the stern. "Parmo, won't people in the East Islands be scared of me too when they find out what I can do?"

"Perhaps scared, yes, but they won't try to harm you like back home. Besides, we're going to work on learning to control your dreams, right?"

Makarria nodded. She didn't have the foggiest notion how, nor did Parmo for that matter, but it seemed a reasonable notion. When Parmo had told her about her ability, she was not surprised. It was as if she'd somehow known all along she was a dreamwielder and that her grandfather had just put into words something she never knew how to say before. She could think of a half-dozen times when her dreams had seemed so real that she had awoken and thought them to be true, and in a way she had made them true because she really wanted them to be that way. The castle, the dresses, the ponies, the flowers. But what about the dreams she didn't want to be true? What about nightmares? Did she have the ability to make them come to life?

"Makarria!"

"What?" Makarria asked, realizing Parmo had called out her name several times.

"You best secure the yard arm to the bow and tie yourself in," he said, and she could see he had a look of concern on his face.

The wind was whipping her hair about, and she turned toward the bow to see that the storm was rapidly approaching. The sky was nearly black before them, and the first of the huge ocean swells swept the skiff up onto its crest, then back down into a trough so deep the clouds were blocked from sight for several seconds. Parmo lowered the sail, and as he furled it away, Makarria lashed the diagonally-angled yard arm to the bow of the skiff, so it wouldn't swing about wildly on the mast and knock one of them overboard. Once Makarria had the yard arm secured, she turned her attention to the rope belt she wore and tied the loose ends at either hip to the extra oarlocks at the front of the skiff so that she was securely tied-down in her seat, facing her grandfather at the stern of the skiff.

Parmo had made herself tie-in every night while sleeping, but this was the first time she had to tie-in on account of bad weather.

"Alright," Parmo said, grabbing up the oars, "You're tied in now and you have the bucket. When water starts coming over the sides, you bail out water. If it gets really bad, you'll have to wait until we're in the troughs between waves. Don't look behind you. I'll steer us with the oars and make sure we crest the waves safely. You just bail water and keep your eyes on my back. Understood?"

Makarria nodded.

Seeing that she had the bucket in hand and seemed unperturbed, Parmo sat himself down facing the stern and tied himself in. He secured the oars in the oarlocks and made sure everything was in place. The rudder was fastened secure—he'd steer using the oars now—and he'd mounted his convex navigating mirror at the starboard corner of the stern so that he could see where they were going. It wasn't a pretty sight in the mirror. The waves were big and the sky dark.

They rode up the steep incline of one of the first big waves, and from Makarria's position in the bow it seemed the mainmast and Parmo were directly below her. Parmo leaned heavily into the oars to propel them over the crest of the wave, and suddenly the bottom dropped out beneath Makarria and Parmo was above her as they plummeted down the backside of the wave. Sea spray splashed up and around them, and rain started coming down, slowly at first but increasingly heavy as they started climbing the next wave.

"Have you ever sailed through a storm like this before, Grandpa Parmo?" Makarria yelled over the howling wind.

"Of course, don't worry about it!" Parmo yelled back over his shoulder, but he neglected to mention that the last time he'd navigated a storm like this it had been in a much larger ship and the ship had nearly been torn to pieces in the process.

• • •

Natarios Rhodas shivered and tightened his black cloak around his shoulders as he strode through the streets of Kal Pyrthin toward the castle. A storm was fast approaching and he desperately hoped his business with King Casstian would be brief so he could return to his tower before the rains started. He knew such would not be the case though. King Casstian Delios always argued about the decrees the Emperor and Wulfram sent to him, and if the previous days' events were any indication of how things would turn out, the business with the King would be unpleasant. Natarios grimaced inwardly at that memory of what had transpired at the small farmstead on the coast. Wulfram had sensed that the dreamwielder was there at one point, but the farmer and his wife hadn't been cooperative. With Wulfram it was always best to be cooperative, and the farmers had learned that lesson the hard way. Not that it had helped Wulfram in the least bit; all they learned was that a skiff was missing from the farm. The dreamwielder was still out there somewhere, and she could have sailed anywhere along the coast: south toward the warmer waters of the Sol Sea, west toward Pyrvino, or to Kal Pyrthin. Natarios had left some of his men in Pyrvino to keep a look out for her, and Wulfram had flown south to skirt the coast all the way to Sol Valaróz in hope of tracking her down. That left only Kal Pyrthin to tend to, hence the unsavory task Natarios now had before him.

The people in the streets scurried out of his way, recognizing him as a houndkeeper, and he reached Castle Pyrthin without a single person hailing him or barring his way. He was immediately granted entry and audience with the King. Once inside King Casstian's study, Natarios unbuttoned his cloak to let the warmth from the fire seep into his bones.

"To what do I owe this displeasure?" King Casstian asked, taking a seat in the larger of the two chairs beside the fireplace.

Natarios smiled thinly and sat down in the smaller chair across from him. "There's a sorceress about it seems. The hound detected her a few days past, and Wulfram thinks she may be heading here, to Kal Pyrthin. The Emperor has decreed that a reward of one hundred crowns be offered to the person who turns her in."

King Casstian sighed. "How many times do I have to tell you, these methods don't work. The only thing you get when you offer a bounty is a bunch of paranoid people and fearmongering. If I offer a reward of a hundred crowns, common folk will be turning in their neighbors because they heard a strange noise in the night. Ruffians will be bringing me the heads of every spinster and crone this side of the highlands, demanding reward for killing some innocent old woman. It's madness."

"It's the decree of the Emperor," Natarios remarked. In actuality, the decree came from Wulfram, but it amounted to the same thing.

"It's madness," Casstian said again.

"I'll do you a kindness and not mention to Wulfram you said that. You know as well as I do that the Emperor wants what's best for all. We can't have a sorceress running loose in the city."

"I don't need any favors from you, houndkeeper. You're a blight on my kingdom. What do I care if a sorceress is running about as long as she keeps her business to herself? This reward you want me to offer will do nothing but cause panic. My soldiers will be running around on wild goose chases for weeks, chasing nothing when they should be standing ready to protect Pyrthinia from pirates or an attack from the Old World. You want to put my vassals in harm's way. I'll not allow it."

Natarios wrinkled his nose and scratched at the mat of hair beneath his hood. Even when he was trying to be cordial, Casstian showed him nothing but disdain. "I didn't come here to ask your permission," Natarios said, continuing on quickly before the King protested, "and you needn't worry about distracting your troops— my men will handle all investigations. Anyone with information about the sorceress is to come to my tower."

King Casstian narrowed his eyes. "That's beyond your realm of jurisdiction, houndkeeper. The Emperor and I clearly came to an agreement that you had no authority to carry out investigations, try criminals, or punish them. I have it in the Emperor's own writing that—"

"The scenario has changed," Natarios interrupted. He stood up, hoping to give the impression he was unconcerned and aloof of the King's protest. "I'm not asking your permission," Natarios continued, "I'm merely here to inform you of what I'll be doing. As a courtesy. If you take issue with the Emperor's decree, you can discuss it with Wulfram when he returns from Valaróz within the week."

With that, Natarios turned and hurried out of the study. Casstian wordlessly watched him leave, then turned to glare into the fireplace. For over thirty years he had been fending off the Emperor to maintain control of Pyrthinia, but he was slowly losing, he knew. Every day it was something—some new decree that left Casstian powerless to protect his people. He sighed deeply. It was a helpless feeling, and each day more so. There had been a time when he contemplated standing up to the Emperor, but he'd foolishly thought he could persuade the Emperor to see his way with reason, or if nothing else, he could keep Pyrthinia isolated and out of harm's way if he stayed quiet and didn't draw attention to Pyrthinia. It was clear now he had been wrong. Casstian had known for a long time but was reticent to admit it to himself. He had been whittled down to nearly nothing—a figurehead. That's all he was, and the little resistance he had posed over the years had been in vain. It had already cost him the life of one of his sons, his other son was in the lions' den, and now, he feared, the Emperor was after his daughter.

9
A Voice in the Dark

Caile downed his third ale and called for a round of spiced grain spirits from the tavern keeper. At his side, Meinrad tried to follow suit but spilled most of the ale down his chin. Meinrad was Caile's officially appointed liaison to Col Sargoth, but Caile hadn't been fooled for a moment by the title. Meinrad was the Emperor's agent. Whenever Caile wasn't attending court sessions pertaining to Pyrthinian trade matters, it was Meinrad's task to watch over Caile; Caile literally could not go anywhere beyond his private chambers in the keep without him. More importantly to Caile's mind, Meinrad had also been Cargan's liaison and witnessed Cargan's death at a tavern several blocks east of where the two of them now sat drinking. Caile had been in Col Sargoth for nearly a week now and had learned little more than that from Meinrad. The man was taciturn and rigid, but Caile had been showering him with praise and mock adoration for days, pretending to be a spoiled prince looking for nothing more than debauchery and easy thrills. The ruse seemed to be working, and each day Meinrad let his guard down a little more. It had taken a good amount of pleading and prodding to get Meinrad to escort him out of Lightbringer's Keep and to a tavern, but Caile had won out in the end, and here they were, mingling in the noisy tavern like any other city folk. While the mood on the streets of Col Sargoth by day was somber, the people inside the dim, low-roofed tavern seemed to be having no shortage of merriment and mirth.

The tavern keeper slammed down two pewter glasses filled with pungent grain spirit onto the table in front of Caile and his liaison. Caile clinked his glass against Meinrad's and lifted it to his lips, silently thanking Don Bricio for the only useful skill the usurper ever taught him: how to hold his liquor. Bricio had migrated from the Old World and brought with him the technique for distilling fire nectar when he was given the throne in Sol Valaróz. The fire nectar was potent and lived up to its name. *Learn to drink and enjoy it now when you're young and impervious to hangovers, and as you grow older your body will have learnt how to handle it,* Caile remembered Bricio saying during one of the many occasions they sat drinking from crystal goblets on the royal veranda overlooking the Sol Sea. Those were the times Caile would pick up on Bricio's dirty little secrets about how the people of Valaróz were kept in line, during the hour or so when the sun set, before Bricio would stagger away to bed one of the women in his harem.

Meinrad couldn't hold his liquor nearly as well as Bricio. He was big, even for a Sargothian, and several years older than Caile, but drinking spirits clearly wasn't in his repertoire. He slammed the pewter glass back into his mouth and tilted his head back, sloshing most of the grain spirit up his nose. He sputtered and coughed, and Caile slapped him heartily on the back.

"Easy now. No need to show off by drinking it through your nose."

"I'm alright," Meinrad wheezed.

"I take it you and my big brother didn't drink much over the years?"

"He never drank. Said it rotted the mind."

Caile shrugged, projecting an air of indifference. "He always was a bit stuffy from what I remember. But he still dragged you into the city, yes? What was it for if not ale and spirits? Women?"

"I wish," Meinrad replied, slumping forward onto the bench.

Caile grinned. "A bit of a bird dog yourself, eh, Meinrad?"

"No, it's not that. It's just that I wish Cargan was after women instead of... instead of..." Meinrad slurred to a stop realizing he was saying too much.

Caile leaned in closer. "You can tell me, friend. I'll not speak a word of it. I like it here in Col Sargoth. As far as I'm concerned, my brother dying was the best thing to ever happen to me."

Meinrad tried to look Caile in the eyes, but his own pupils wandered involuntarily, making it impossible for him to focus. "Let's just say—let's just say he was seeking out people who dislike the Emperor. I wasn't sure why at first… hoped it was 'cause he wanted to turn them in, but no…"

"Treachery, then," Caile remarked. He desperately wanted to know how Cargan had died—he suspected it was Meinrad or one of the Emperor's other agents who had killed him, not drunkards— but he dared not pry further, and instead waved the tavern keeper back over.

"No, no more," Meinrad protested when the tavern keeper refilled their pewter glasses.

"One more," Caile insisted, shoving one glass into Meinrad's meaty fist and raising up the other. "For my brother, the traitor, and to his well-deserved death."

Caile watched Meinrad's reaction to his words as he drained his glass. The Sargothian seemed dispassionate one way or the other and merely lifted his glass to his lips. He drank about half of it before choking and lurching to his feet.

"I'm going to be sick."

Caile jumped up and took his liaison's arm. "Easy now. I'll help you outside." He guided Meinrad clear of their bench and tossed a few coins onto the table to pay for their drinks, then led the way out the back door. Outside, a cool ocean breeze blew through the alleyway. The rear of the tavern was comprised of a decrepit stable— little more than a lean-to with a water trough, some moldering straw, and a few posts for patrons to tie up their horses. There wasn't a single horse there. From what Caile had seen, no one used horses in this city except for travelers and the Emperor's cavalrymen. The city folk seemed content to get by on foot or to take the steam-propelled rickshaws and wagons that clogged the nighttime streets.

Meinrad grasped one of the stable tie-posts and retched violently.

"That's right, get it out," Caile encouraged him, and when

Meinrad was done he led him to the horse trough. "Some water will make you feel better. Drink up."

Meinrad leaned forward to do as he was told but slipped on the vomit-soaked ground and toppled head first into the trough. Caile grabbed the Sargothian by the waist to keep him from tumbling fully in, and the scent of stagnant water and filth washed over Caile, almost making him gag. It occurred to him that he could easily let Meinrad drown in the acrid water, but he brushed the thought aside and merely let Meinrad thrash about and make bubbles for a few more seconds before pulling him back out. Meinrad gasped, choked, then retched again. Caile led him farther into the stable away from the trough and guided him to lie down in a patch of straw. The big man didn't protest, and the moment his head touched the ground, he passed out.

"That was easy," Caile muttered, surprised by the opportunity now afforded to him. He had only intended to loosen Meinrad's tongue, but Meinrad was likely to be out cold for several hours or more, and that meant Caile could do as he pleased with no one the wiser. Without a second thought, he hurried out of the stable.

Once clear of the alleyway and on a main street, the sea breeze was much stronger. The air smelled of salt and the fisheries near the wharves, but it was more pleasant than the smell of tar and smoke that choked the streets by day. *No wonder there are more people on the streets at night,* Caile mused. The streets were indeed filled with more people than anytime he'd seen before. The scene was far from cheerful, however. Apart from those who'd been enjoying the taverns, most of the city folk scurried about silently and swiftly beneath the yellow-hued light emanating from the street lamps.

"Turnips?" a peddler woman asked, holding up a basket full of her produce for him to peruse.

"Thank you, no," Caile replied. "If you had kabobs or something better suited to ale and spirits…"

The woman waved her hand at him dismissively and shoved her basket toward another passerby. Caile shrugged and walked farther down the street to hail the driver of a steam-powered rickshaw. "To

The Thirsty Whale," he said, handing the driver a coin and sitting down on the small bench at the front of the contraption. The driver pulled a lever, and the entire rickshaw shuddered and jerked forward. It crept down the street, wheezing like a bellows and slowly building momentum. Caile could feel the heat at his back from the boiler, and more than once he twisted his head backward to examine the steel contraption and watch the piston-driven crank thrust up and down spasmodically to rotate the massive flywheel. When they finally came to a stop in front of The Thirsty Whale, Caile decided it was an altogether disappointing experience. He'd expected something more, something faster, something powerful, something to make all the noise and smoke worthwhile.

The rickshaw was the least of his concerns right now though, he reminded himself. This was where his brother had been killed.

He stepped inside the tavern and glanced about. It was largely the same as the tavern he'd just left. It was comprised of a low-ceilinged, rectangular room furnished with square tables and squat benches. The tavern keeper's alcove was partitioned off at the back wall, and along the wall to Caile's far left was a huge fireplace, though there was no fire burning this early into autumn. Most of the tables were occupied with small groups of patrons, but there were several empty tables. Caile sat at one and caught the tavern keeper's attention and hollered for an ale. When the tavern keeper came with his ale, Caile opened his mouth to speak but thought better of it and merely paid for the drink. He knew an opportunity such as this was not likely to come his way again—to be here without Meinrad—but he didn't want to be overzealous and get himself killed. The truth of the matter was he really had no idea how Cargan died. He suspected Meinrad, but it could just as easily have been a random drunkard, or it could have been another agent of the Emperor's lurking about in the tavern. *I wish Lorentz were here,* Caile thought. *He'd know what to do.* But Lorentz and the rest of Caile's men were on lockdown in their barracks every night, and most of the days for that matter, by the Emperor's decree. Caile pushed the thought aside. *Lorentz would probably just tell me to forget about the whole business, anyway.*

Caile gulped down the head and first several inches off the top of his ale, contemplating. The tavern keeper would have likely witnessed Cargan's death, but he was also sober and probably a suspicious man. In Caile's experience, tavern keepers were an unreliable lot; they were too worried about keeping their doors open and making money and would rat out their own family at the first sign of trouble. Caile needed to find a regular patron, he decided, one who was good and drunk and wouldn't remember him or suspect anything when Caile started asking questions.

His decision made, Caile glanced up from his ale intent on scoping out a good candidate only to see that someone had sat across from him at his table.

"Tsk, tsk, Prince Caile," the man said. "It's not nice to get your liaison sickly drunk and then abandon him in a back alley."

Caile curbed his surprise and regarded the man silently. The man looked completely ordinary. He wore gray breeches and a dark tunic like nearly everyone else in Col Sargoth, and like most men in the city, he had short hair and a close-cropped beard. He didn't appear to be armed. There was little point in denying being Prince Caile Delios, Caile decided. Clearly the man had been following him. Caile had done nothing to reveal his identity, and he was wearing clothing nearly as nondescript as what the man across from him wore. The question was whether this man was one the Emperor's agents.

"You're more resourceful than your brother was," the man said when it was clear Caile did not plan on replying. "Cargan was a bit too direct in his attempts to contact us."

"And you are who exactly?"

The man ignored him and hailed the tavern keeper: "Two spirits and two more ales."

The man paid for the drinks when the tavern keeper came, then held up his glass of spiced grain spirit. "May the Emperor drown in his own privy," he said loud enough for only Caile to hear. Caile said nothing but raised his glass, and the two of them drank. The man sucked his cheeks in afterward then took a sip from his ale.

"Call me Stephen."

"What do you want from me, Stephen?" Caile asked.

"That depends on what you want from me and my comrades."

"Did you kill my brother?"

If Caile's bluntness caught the man off guard, he didn't show it. "In a sense, yes, but it was by necessity."

"Necessity?"

"Stay calm," Stephen said, and Caile realized he'd nearly shouted his question.

"What do you mean it was necessity?"

"Your brother came to us, but his liaison and the Emperor had grown suspicious. There were men following him the night he died. He was too sure of himself and was on the verge of giving away our identity—our whole organization. We killed him, pretending to be drunkards, but it was only to save the organization. The Emperor would have surely killed him if we hadn't, and the rest of us would've died with him. What we did was for the greater good of the organization."

"What organization?"

Stephen regarded him silently for a moment before responding. "Why do you want to know, Prince? Is it for vengeance or something more? Answer me truthfully."

Caile was silent. He'd assumed an outward air of calmness, but his insides were churning with nervous tension. He knew what Lorentz would be telling him if he we there: *get up and leave right now*. Caile was too close to just up and walk away though. "I'm looking for something more," he finally said.

Stephen nodded. "Very well then. Finish your ale, then go to the privy at the back of the tavern. When you're done, head out the back door into the alley. Two buildings down on the right, you'll see stairs heading into a basement. Knock five times on the door and we'll talk." The man drained his ale and stood up. "Take your time. We shouldn't be seen leaving together."

Caile lifted his mug to his face and watched silently as Stephen left through the front door. He was nervous now, suspicious of everyone in the tavern. Any one of them could be watching for all he knew. Any one of them could be an agent of the Emperor. He turned toward the front door and caught a brief glimpse of a woman stepping out. *Was that the turnip lady? Did she follow me?* His pulse was thrumming in his ears, and he forced himself to calm his breathing and relax. *You're being paranoid,* he chided himself. *Just relax. Don't draw attention to yourself. There's no reason for anyone here to suspect you're up to no good.*

He finished his ale slowly, keeping an eye on the front door, but saw no sign of the turnip lady or anyone else who looked suspicious. When he was done with the ale and went to the privy, he found he earnestly needed to relieve himself. After urinating, he stepped out the back door and meandered down the alleyway toward his right. There was another man in the alleyway vomiting, but otherwise no one was in sight. Caile hurried past the drunkard and found the stairway Stephen had described. He rapped on the door five times; it opened immediately and Caile stepped down into darkness.

"Are you armed?" a voice asked. It was not Stephen's.

"A boot knife, nothing more," Caile responded. Light suddenly shone in his face and he shielded his eyes enough to see someone had lifted the damper on a lantern. "Where's Stephen?"

"I'm here," Stephen said behind the darkness. "We must know we can trust you before we reveal ourselves. Please listen and answer all the questions asked of you. If you move, you will be killed. If you do not answer a question, you will be killed. Do you understand?"

"Yes."

"Good," the other voice said. "Who do you swear fealty to— the Emperor or your father, King Casstian?"

"I swear fealty to no one—I swear fealty to Pyrthinia," Caile said without hesitation.

Taera opened her eyes and gazed at the canopy over her bed. She was breathing normally and was not covered in sweat, which surprised her. She'd seen a ship and a cavern of ice in her sleep again. And the beautiful girl. Those visions had become common enough, but the new visions—her father in chains, and Caile lying in a dank cellar with his throat slit—would have frightened her into hysterics in the past. Yet for whatever reason, ever since the incident with Caile and the firewielder, she'd taken the visions in stride. Whereas before she would force the visions away and do everything in her power to ignore them, it was as if she'd subconsciously decided to accept the visions now. This realization made her feel better. She was frightened, but she didn't feel so powerless anymore. She glanced toward her window and saw that it was still several hours before dawn. In the morning, she would warn her father about the danger to him and Caile both, she decided. She'd warned Caile last time, and it had saved their lives.

10
Tђe Uŋcariŋg Oceaŋ

The Esterian Ocean was flat as far as the eye could see in every direction. Overhead the sun glared at its apex in a windless, cloudless sky.

"Can I jump in the water again, Parmo?" Makarria asked, standing up at the bow of the skiff to stretch and wipe the sweat from her face.

"Not now," her grandfather said, not bothering to look back from where he sat at the oars. "I saw the dorsal fin of a shark a few minutes ago, so you best stay out."

Makarria's eyes widened at the mention of sharks, but she said nothing and sat back down at her bench. It had only been two days since the storm passed, but it had been the most difficult two days of her life. They had lost most of their sail in the heavy winds when one of Makarria's knots came loose where it was battened down to the yard arm; all that was left was a tattered strip less than a yard wide. Their food stores had been ruined too, when the skiff had been washed over by wave after wave and the briny water soaked through the wool blankets and oilskin covering the salted goat meat. That left them with nothing to eat but fish, which there were plenty of, but they had no way of cooking their catch, and Makarria could only eat so much raw fish before gagging on the spongy texture.

The two of them had been taking turns at the oars, but to Makarria it seemed as if they were standing still. With no land mass or even clouds as a point of reference, it was impossible to tell they were moving at all. Makarria was hot and tired and hungry, and she wanted nothing more than to curl up on her sleeping mat back home. Parmo had insisted she wrap the remnant of the sail around her like a shawl to keep from getting sunburned, but the canvas was coarse and itchy—nothing like her soft sleeping furs. Makarria realized quite suddenly that she missed her mother, and the memory of Prisca tucking her into bed every night nearly brought her to tears. She sniffled them back though. She'd not yet cried in front of her grandfather on this voyage and she didn't mean to start now.

Facing away from Makarria at the stern, Parmo paddled on, his muscles sore and the novelty of having a young body forgotten for the time being. He knew Makarria was miserable too, but there was nothing for it. He'd gotten them into this mess with his rash decision to cross the ocean, and he now needed to focus his whole attention on getting them out of it. *Prisca would flay me alive if she knew what I've done,* he chastised himself. *Just because I'm living on borrowed time now, it doesn't give me the right to drag Makarria into more danger than she was already in.*

He had set their initial course from Spearpoint Rock due east, intent on sailing through the northwesterly trade current then veering southeast to the East Islands. Now that they were without a sail though, he had reversed course. He knew they wouldn't make it to the East Islands paddling, so instead he meant to catch the trade current and head north beyond the Kal Pyrthin Bay along the coast to Tyrna. Makarria would be happier with land in sight, and once they reached Tyrna they could find work on one of the fishing trawlers that worked the northern waters. There were only another two months of fishing before icebergs began forming in the waters off the Barrier Mountains, and then all the trawler captains would take their ships and crews south to fish the warmer waters near the East Islands or Valaróz. It would be hard, dangerous work, but the Emperor would never think to look for Makarria on a fishing boat, and in three months time they would be safe and warm on the East Islands. Makarria would have to cut her hair short in the meantime and pretend to be a boy, but Parmo decided he'd break that news to her when the time came. *Let's keep it to one piece of bad news at a time,* he told himself.

• • •

The news Taera had told him weighed heavily on King Casstian. There was nothing he could do to help his son Caile, but he would not sit idly by and let his daughter be taken away from him by Wulfram and that damned houndkeeper Natarios, he decided. Casstian's men had spied Natarios taking the scent-hound out of his tower and loading her onto a covered wagon. Clearly Natarios was narrowing down his search and Casstian didn't dare keep Taera around a day longer and risk her having another vision. She'd seen a ship in her visions two nights before, so he meant to send her away on one.

At the mouth of the River Kylep in Kal Pyrthin Bay sat *Pyrthin's Flame*, the new flagship for Pyrthinia's navy. In truth, she was still under construction—the bunks in the main hold had yet to be installed, and the captain's quarters and guest cabins were only partly furnished—but the master shipbuilder assured Casstian *Pyrthin's Flame* was seaworthy, and so Casstian had moved the launching ceremony forward by two weeks time.

Taera observed the ceremony at her father's side. He had yet to tell her she was leaving, but she knew what was happening as soon as she saw the ship. She paid little heed to the crew members introduced to her and to the blessing her father gave the ship in the name of Tel Mathir. It was as if she had lived the entire experience before in a dream, and she followed her father around wordlessly. It wasn't until the captain took them on a tour of the ship and Taera found herself standing face to face with a half-naked young woman in the royal guest cabin that it all became real.

"I'm sending you away, Taera," Casstian said. "It's not safe here for you anymore."

"I know."

"Kiss me then and dress this girl in your gown. She will stay here in Kal Pyrthin and pretend to be you for a while at least so no one knows you've left."

Taera kissed her father on his thin cheeks and hugged him, then he spun away and left the room along with the captain. Taera turned to regard the young woman waiting before her. She was younger than Taera by a few years, but she had the same blond hair and a similar build. She stood nervously, wearing only her undergarments.

"What's your name?" Taera asked.

The girl blushed and lowered her eyes. "Nessa, Your Highness."

"And you live here in Kal Pyrthin?"

"Yes. I am a lady at The Olive House."

Taera sighed inwardly. The Olive House was a brothel. *How is it that fate made me a princess and yet made this girl—who could be my sister by her looks—a whore?*

"Well from now on you're a princess, Nessa," Taera said, smiling for the girl. "Unlace my gown and I'll help you into it."

The girl did as Taera said, and half an hour later Nessa was adorned as the Princess of Pyrthinia.

"Once you get onto the deck of the ship, put up your parasol to keep your face in the shade and hidden as much as possible," Taera told her. "Keep it up until you get into the royal coach, and try not to speak to anyone. I've been in a dour mood all day, so no one will think anything of you ignoring them."

The girl nodded wordlessly, and Taera ushered her out the door with a reassuring smile. Alone and now half-naked herself, Taera went to the wardrobe mounted to the wall beside the bed. Inside she found several simple dresses. She chose one, dressed, then sat on the narrow bed. Within the hour, the captain began yelling orders up on deck, and the moorings holding *Pyrthin's Flame* were released.

So the voyage begins, Taera mused, knowing she would soon meet the girl from her visions but wishing she knew so much more.

11
Beneath the Dark City

Caile sat watching Lorentz run his men through combat drills in the training yard of Lightbringer's Keep. Across the yard, outside the armory, a small audience had also gathered, comprised of soldiers from the Imperial Guard and Cavalry. It was commonplace enough for soldiers to observe and weigh one another's worth on the practice field, but Caile knew this was more than casual observance: there was animosity between the troops. Caile's men were confined to private barracks—little more than a dungeon, really—located in the basement beneath one of the palace wings. It was all Caile could do to convince the Emperor's chamberlain to allow his men an hour a day to practice in the yard, and even that seemed to be an affront to the Emperor's troops. There was nothing for it though. As much as Caile put on a facade of being a loyal servant, the truth of the matter was he wasn't, and with the potential for trouble, he wanted to keep his men as sharp as possible.

When Lorentz finally called a halt to the drills, the lot of them joined Caile to sit in the shade for the last few minutes they had before returning to their barracks.

"Where's your shadow?" Lorentz asked, looking for Meinrad amongst the onlookers near the armory.

"I've been reassigned a new liaison," Caile informed him. "Apparently the Emperor didn't take kindly to Meinrad getting fall-down drunk last night. My new liaison is the giant lout there with the bushy black beard and the battle-axe. His name is Lindy."

Lorentz narrowed his eyes and glared at Caile. "What sort of tomfoolery have you been up to?"

"As far as anyone else knows, just that: tomfoolery. A few ales, a few drams of spiced spirits. That's all."

"I know you better than that, Caile. Your foolishness doesn't stop with a few drinks."

"Foolishness?" Caile said with mock indignation. "I'd hardly say finding my brother's killers is foolishness."

"You're serious?"

Caile nodded and leaned back onto his elbows so as to get closer to Lorentz but still look casual to the onlookers. "There's an underground society, Lorentz," he whispered, so even his own men couldn't hear. "They want to overthrow the Emperor and kill Wulfram. They claim to have a sorceress in league with them."

"But they killed Cargan?"

"By necessity. He was unwittingly bringing the Emperor's men right to them."

"And yet they let you just walk away?"

Caile shrugged. "I was alone, and I offered my help."

"Pyrthin's arse, Caile," Lorentz hissed. "You're going to wind up dead just like your brother. What were you thinking? You didn't tell them anything else did you?"

"I didn't have much choice in the matter," Caile said, remembering what he had glimpsed in the dim light of that basement. "They had cross-bows trained on me, and they wanted to know whether they could trust me or not."

"What did you tell them?"

"Mostly what secrets I knew about Bricio, but they seemed to know about all that already. They were more interested in Kal Pyrthin. They said the houndkeepers are after someone—a sorceress. I told them about the firewielder, and then…"

"You didn't tell them about Taera?"

Caile looked up at his friend and protector. "You know about Taera?"

"I'd have to be a lackwit not to, Caile. I was watching over you when you were a child, and the two of you would play. I was there when the firewielder attacked. I certainly know it wasn't you who read the future. How could you tell them about her, Caile? Your own sister."

"They said Wulfram is after her, Lorentz, but that they would help protect her. My father can't protect her. He has no power anymore."

Lorentz was quiet for a long moment as he took it all in. "Just because we have a common enemy," he finally said, "it doesn't mean these people are our allies or friends. We have no idea what their motives are."

Caile was grateful Lorentz acknowledged being on his side at least, an enemy of Emperor Guderian, but he knew his friend was right. Caile had never intended to say anything about Taera to anyone the previous night, but after getting Meinrad drunk, then drinking with the man who called himself Stephen, he had found himself more than a little drunk and nervous being surrounded in that dark basement by unknown faces.

"They want to meet with me again tonight," Caile said. "They want me to meet with their sorceress. What should I do?"

"Did you promise them anything?"

"I said I would come. I think they want as much information I can give them about Taera and Castle Pyrthin. I think they mean to steal her away."

"You'll stay put then. Lie low for a while so we can both think this through. Keep that big brute of yours nearby. With any luck, these people have some spies here in the keep. They'll hear that your old liaison was replaced and think you're being forced to stay inside for a bit. They can't fault you for that, and I'm more worried about the Emperor anyway. If he finds out you've been consorting with these type of people, it'll be certain death for all of us."

"But we have to do something," Caile said. "They know about Taera. We have to find out if they're allies or not."

"In due time, Caile. Your father is not as weak as you think him; he'll keep Taera safe. We can find out more when things quiet down and the Emperor is not expecting anything. Patience is the key, my boy."

Caile could only nod in agreement.

Later that night, long after his meal in the mess hall alongside his hulking liaison, Lindy, Caile laid on his bed staring at the dark ceiling. He'd jokingly asked Lindy over dinner if he wanted to visit some taverns, and the man had shrugged indifferently. Caile still had free reign to leave Lightbringer's Keep it seemed, but he was uncertain whether that was a good sign or not. The Emperor either suspected nothing or wanted Caile to think he suspected nothing. Whatever the case was, Caile heeded Lorentz's advice and told Lindy he intended to stay in for the night. The big man locked Caile in his room, the same as Meinrad had done on previous nights, and now Caile was there to stay until morning whether he liked it or not.

Several hours passed beyond the hour when Caile had agreed to meet the sorceress in the city, and he couldn't help but wonder what might have happened. Likely trouble, as Lorentz suspected, but perhaps not. *What if they're friends? We need all the help we can get if we want to oust the Emperor.*

A scraping noise in the corner of the room interrupted Caile's reverie and he sat up, expecting to see a rat or roach scurrying about. There was nothing though, only the floor and the noise again. The hair at the nape of Caile's neck stood up on end, and he quickly grabbed his boot knife, the only piece of weaponry he'd been allowed to keep. He slowly rose from the bed and approached the noise. It was definitely the sound of something scraping on stone, and as he got closer he saw that one of the floor-stones was slowly lifting upward. Caile pressed himself against one of the walls and knelt low to be within striking distance of whoever or whatever came up out of the hole.

A set of fingers poked through the crack beneath the stone and began pushing the stone aside. Caile waited until the opening was wide enough, then thrust his free hand into the hole and grabbed a handful of hair. There was a startled yelp as Caile yanked the intruder up and held his knife to the intruder's throat.

"Your Highness, it's me," the intruder whispered. "It's

me Stephen."

"What are you doing here?" Caile hissed, letting go of Stephen's hair.

Stephen rubbed his neck where Caile had drawn a bead of blood with his knife. "You missed our appointment."

"I'm locked in my room."

"We suspected as much. That's why Roanna sent me to fetch you."

"Roanna?"

"The sorceress. She needs to see you now, before she leaves the city."

Caile swore beneath his breath. Lorentz would be furious, but there was no way Caile could get around it now. "Where is she?"

"Follow me. I'll take you to her."

Stephen's head disappeared beneath the floor again, and Caile followed after him with another curse. The passage beneath the floor was cramped and dusty and four feet high at most. Stephen thrust a lantern into Caile's hands and replaced the floor-stone in Caile's room. Caile held the lamp up to get a good look at the stone so he could recognize it if he needed to find it on his own.

"This way," Stephen said, snatching the lamp from Caile's grip and hurrying away.

Caile followed as quickly as he could without smacking his head on the ceiling. They passed several connecting passageways, and at first Caile tried to make a mental note at each intersection of which passage led to his own room. There were dozens of turns and intersections though, and when he glanced down at the floor he saw that their footprints in the dust had left a clear trail to follow regardless, so he gladly gave up trying to memorize their route. The passage sloped continually downward and eventually opened into a wide corridor where they could walk upright.

"How is it the Emperor doesn't know about these passages?" Caile asked, feeling more at ease.

"Lightbringer's Keep is over 300 years old, and Guderian has been here for little more than thirty of them—there's much about the keep and this city he doesn't know about."

"How long have you been around?"

Stephen shot a glance back at Caile over his shoulder. "Me personally? Or the guild?"

"The guild," Caile replied quickly, not even knowing what guild Stephen was referring to.

"Since nearly the beginning, in the year 27 A.L., when the armies of the Old World first invaded the Five Kingdoms."

Caile was dumbstruck. *Who are these people?*

The passage veered sharply to their right, and suddenly they found themselves in a sewer tunnel. Stephen led the way along a narrow ledge above the brackish water, but the stench nearly gagged Caile.

"It's just a little farther," Stephen spoke through his shirtsleeve he held over his mouth.

Caile followed suit and less than a hundred feet down the tunnel was a wooden ladder which Stephen motioned him toward. Caile climbed up without question and at the top found a wooden trap door.

"Knock five times," Stephen instructed him.

Caile did as he was told and moments later the hatch opened and two sets of hands reached down to pull him up into an old wine cellar. Stephen followed directly behind him, and the two men who had assisted them then pulled up the wooden ladder and closed the hatch. Like Stephen, both of the other men wore nondescript clothing and appeared nonthreatening.

"Hello, Prince Caile Delios," a voice said behind Caile.

"Roanna?" Caile asked, turning about to regard the woman who had hailed him. She was late in her middle ages and completely unremarkable in appearance. Her gray hair was bound back and tucked into a caul, and she wore a simple gray dress with a sagging black bodice that did little to hide her rotund shape. She was hardly what he expected of a sorceress. The firewielder Caile had confronted outside of Kal Pyrthin had exuded a mad aura of power around her, but this woman exuded nothing.

"I am Roanna," the woman confirmed.

"I apologize for missing our earlier engagement," Caile said, bowing slightly and trying not to reveal his disappointment in the tone of his voice. "After last night, I was assigned a new liaison and was unable to leave the Keep safely."

"It's of no consequence. You're here now."

She motioned for him to sit at one of several wooden crates that had been arranged in a circle and took a seat herself at one of them. Caile nodded politely and sat across from her. Stephen and the other men took seats to either side of Roanna.

"Stephen and the others told me of your sister," Roanna began. "I'd like to know more about her."

"Of course," Caile said, outwardly calm but frantically thinking of what to say. "What is it you'd like to know?"

"Tell me about her power."

Caile nodded. "What assurance can you give me that you won't just go off and kill her? I need to know you mean her no harm before I tell you anything."

"Of course," Roanna said with a smile. "Perhaps it would be best if we started at the beginning?"

"Yes," Caile agreed though he had no idea what beginning she spoke of.

"You've lived in Sol Valaróz—you know that Guderian killed King Pallma and gave the kingdom of Valaróz to Don Bricio, I presume?"

Caile nodded.

"Well, the murder of Pallma scared the remaining three monarchs into subservience, including your father, who was newly anointed, if I'm not mistaken."

"He was only fourteen," Caile replied.

"I remember it well enough, but that's about as far as most people know. The lesser-known story is how Guderian exterminated the sorcerer's guilds. The guilds were a shadow of their former selves after the Dreamwielder War, it is true, but there was still much power in them. Do you know how it was that Guderian destroyed them, my young princeling?"

"Wulfram?"

"Wulfram is a mighty sorcerer, perhaps the mightiest sorcerer the world has ever known after the dreamwielders transformed him, but even he could not have defeated the guilds on his own."

"How then?" Caile asked, getting caught up in her story despite himself.

"Guderian. He has no magical ability in any traditional sense. He can't wield fire or storms or dreams, he can't manipulate animals or see the future, but he is nonetheless of Sargoth Lightbringer's bloodline. There is power in him—the power to stint sorcery. For hundreds and thousands of years, dating back to the Old World and the holy wars over Khail Sanctu, war has always been fought steel against steel, sorcery against sorcery. Armies would face each other on the field while the sorcerers fought behind the lines, trying to gain an advantage, always escalating the stakes, but usually counteracting one another. Guderian changed all that. With his immunity to any sort of sorcery, he himself faced the sorcerer's guilds and cut them down with his steel blade, while Wulfram annihilated any troops or warriors who defied them. The two of them were unstoppable. I bore witness when Guderian clove the head from my father's shoulders on the streets of this very city. I was twelve years old."

Caile nodded. "I do not doubt your animosity toward the Emperor, but what do you want from my sister?"

Roanna smiled. "If your sister is who I think she is, she is Guderian's one weakness. It has been foretold that a daughter of one of the five monarchs would be born who would be a sorceress, and that she would destroy Guderian. Such was the vision of the mightiest seer in all of the Old World on Guderian's tenth birthday, many years ago when he was still in exile."

"How do you know all this?"

"As you can well see, my dear boy, the guilds are not as dead as Guderian thinks them to be, and our connections go beyond the borders of his so called empire."

Caile was silent for a moment as he let everything sink in. "So you want my sister then, so you can throw her at the Emperor and defeat him?"

"If she is indeed the one foretold by prophecy, I don't intend to throw her at anyone. My plan is to take her away someplace safe, to train her and cultivate her abilities until she is ready to face Guderian and destroy him. I would not throw a defenseless girl in harm's way, Prince."

"What is it you need to know?"

"I need to know if she's the one. What sort of ability has she shown?"

"She's a seer," Caile said. "Ever since we were children she's been able to see events before they happen. She saw the firewielder that attacked us outside Kal Pyrthin in a vision and warned us."

"Has she done anything else? Started fires or brought on storms? Spoken with animals? Transformed anything?"

"Not that I know of," Caile said, shaking his head.

"How old is she?"

"Eighteen."

Roanna rubbed her chin, lost in thought. "It's possible she will develop more powers. I myself saw visions long before I developed my greater abilities as a mature woman. If she's seeing clear enough visions to warn you of danger, her ability is stronger than most." Roanna stood and smiled. "Thank you for your help, Caile. It's unfortunate you had to learn so much about us, but I suppose there was no other way. You seem like a nice boy."

Stephen and the other two men stood and each pulled a dagger from their belt.

"Wait," Caile said, jumping from his crate and grabbing his boot knife. "I gave you what you want. I hate the Emperor too. I can help."

"In other circumstances, perhaps," Roanna said, "but you're a ward of Guderian now and you know too much. You'll slip up eventually, and he knows how to get information out of people, willing or not. We can't risk him finding out about us."

The three men had backed Caile up against the old wine racks lining one wall. Caile scooted to his left to position himself in the corner of the room and crouched into a defensive position. None of his assailants were fighting men, and if he had his sword, Caile was certain he could kill them all handily, but with only his boot knife he knew he stood little chance if they all attacked at once.

"All at once," Stephen said. "On the count of three."

Caile swore and gripped his knife tighter.

"One...two..."

Caile didn't wait for three to come. He lunged forward at the man who stood to his far left and slashed at the tendons on his outside knee. The man went down with a cry and Caile sprung up just in time to block Stephen's knife thrust. Caile let his momentum carry him into Stephen and wrapped his arms around him in a bear hug that kept Stephen's knife hand pinned to his side. The third man feinted toward them, but Caile spun Stephen around as a shield and the man backed away.

Roanna was yelling. "Kill him, Stephen. Kill him!"

Caile couldn't help but grin at the madness of it all. He freed his right hand and held his knife to the side of Stephen's throat. "Let's all just calm down now. There's a door behind you, Roanna. Take your other two friends out with you, and Stephen and I will just head on down the ladder. We'll all go our separate ways, and no one else gets hurt or killed."

Roanna glared at him. "I'm sorry, Stephen."

It took a moment for it to register in Caile's mind that she said Stephen—not Caile—but by then it was too late. Roanna made a terse gesture, and suddenly Stephen screamed as his chest burst into flames. Caile pushed him away with a curse and scurried toward the trap door in the floor, but Roanna yelled out some guttural phrase and the door burst into flames too. The injured man on the floor grabbed at Caile's ankle, toppling him to the ground, and then the other man was on top of Caile, trying to force his dagger into his chest.

"Quickly," Roanna yelled. "Kill him!"

Caile could feel the strength in his arms waning as the man on top of him used all of his weight to force the dagger downward. The injured man had a firm grip on Caile's legs, keeping him from twisting free. Caile let loose an animal-like scream as he tried to push the man on top of him away with all his might, but to no end. Caile's surge of energy quickly left him, and the dagger continued its inexorable and agonizingly slow path toward his chest. Caile couldn't help but wonder if this was how his brother had died. *Lorentz warned me,* Caile chastised himself, thinking it would be his last thought, but suddenly there was a massive explosion and the man atop of him was blown sideways into the wall. Caile choked on the dust and rose to his knees just in time to see Roanna run past him and plummet down the trap door into the sewer below.

Disoriented, Caile looked about the room, trying to discern what had happened. The main door leading from the cellar had been blown off its hinges, along with half the doorway and the surrounding wall. In the ragged opening stood a woman. She was dressed similarly to Roanna but looked younger and had darker hair, though it was hard to make out her features clearly in the choking dust. Still, she looked familiar to him.

The turnip lady! he realized as he rubbed the dust and tears from his eyes. She regarded Caile for a moment, then motioned for him to follow her as she lowered herself down the trap door into the sewer. Caile glanced toward the blown-out doorway leading upstairs but heard shouting and yelling from that direction and decided it best to follow the turnip lady.

She stood waiting for him in the sewer. "Roanna has fled," she said. "No doubt, she'll leave the city and not return now."

Her demeanor and voice was nearly unrecognizable from how she'd acted the night before when they'd met in the street. She had been hunched over and spoke with a distracted voice when trying to sell her turnips to him, but now she carried herself and spoke with authority.

Us meeting was no accident, Caile realized. *She was following me.*

"Can you find your way back to the keep?" she asked him.

"I think so."

"Go then. Hurry back before you're found missing. The scent-hound will have certainly detected what Roanna and I have done, and soldiers will be searching the city soon."

The woman turned to go off in the other direction.

"Wait!" Caile said. "Who are you?"

"A true ally and more than a turnip farmer. That's all you need to know for now."

12
The Meeting

Makarria and Parmo saw *Pyrthin's Flame* long before anyone on *Pyrthin's Flame* spied their tiny skiff. It was mid-morning and Makarria at first thought the white sails on the horizon were nothing more than clouds. When she realized that it was actually a ship, she was overjoyed, hoping they would be rescued, but Parmo shook his head in worry and told her to lie down out of sight as he yanked in the oars and crouched down beneath the rail to join her.

"That's no fishing boat, Makarria. It's a naval brig if I've ever seen one. Two masts, fore and aft sails…" Parmo glanced around frantically for his sword. *I haven't even had time to take off the rust and put an edge on the blade,* he lamented.

"You think it's after us?" Makarria asked, peeking up over the rail.

"I hope not. It's best not to find out, so stay down and out of sight."

Makarria saw that her grandfather was worried, but she didn't find herself the least bit scared for some reason. "It's flying a red and yellow flag. Aren't those the colors of Pyrthinia, Grampy—I mean, Parmo?"

Parmo found his sword still wrapped up in the burlap but paused to glance over the rail at the ship to see if Makarria was correct. *Pyrthin's Flame* had gotten closer but had not altered its westerly course, which was merely tangential to the northwesterly path they were on.

"It looks like the gold and red stripes of Pyrthinia," Parmo agreed. "That means nothing, though. The Emperor could have sent word to King Casstian."

Makarria didn't believe it. "I think they'll help us. We should wave at them with the sail."

"No, we'll stay put," Parmo said, his tone making it clear the matter was not up for debate.

Makarria sighed and rested her chin sullenly on the rail of the skiff and Parmo turned his attention back to his sword.

On board *Pyrthin's Fire*, the sailor assigned to the crow's nest glimpsed Parmo's skiff, but even through his telescope, it was so small and distant, he could discern little more than that it was a single-mast skiff—drifting aimlessly in the current without a sail, it seemed.

"Fishing boat, starboard side, looks to be abandoned or stranded," the sailor yelled down to the first mate on the main deck.

The first mate turned to the starboard and saw the skiff as an intermittent speck bobbing up and down on the swells in the distance. They were already a full day out from Kal Pyrthin Bay, which was farther from the coast than most fishing boats would dare venture, and normally the first mate would change course to check on a boat in distress, but the captain had made it clear this was no normal voyage. Their orders had been strict: stop for no one and make for the East Islands with all due haste. The first mate sighed inwardly at having to leave fellow mariners stranded at sea, but orders were orders. He turned from the starboard rail, intent on heading to the quarter-deck, and nearly ran smack into Taera.

"Your Highness," the first mate stammered in apology, "I didn't hear you approach."

Taera hardly heard the man speak. She had been in her cabin and seen a small boat in her mind. "There is a girl on that boat. We must rescue her."

"Your Highness, we are on strict orders to not delay for any reason."

"It's not a request—it's a command, sailor."

The first mate hesitated for only a moment, then dashed to the quarter deck to relay the orders to the helmsman.

Taera made her way to the forecastle as *Pyrthin's Flame* came about to the starboard side. The captain found her there a few short minutes later watching the skiff slowly loom larger in the distance.

"Your Highness, we haven't time for delay," the captain began to protest. "Your father has entrusted me with your life."

"My life may depend on the girl in that boat," Taera responded. "All of our lives. If you're in such a hurry, then get her on board quickly, and we can be on our way again."

"Of course," the captain agreed, and he hurried off to join the first mate at the quarterdeck.

When it became apparent to Parmo and Makarria that *Pyrthin's Flame* had spotted them and was approaching, Parmo knew there was no sense in trying to hide anymore.

"Grab up that sail and start waving it," he told Makarria. "When they get here, try to let me do the talking, but if anyone asks you, we're from a little village south of the badlands. I'm your Uncle Parmo, and we were sailing to visit relatives in another village to the north before we got caught up in a storm three weeks ago. Our sail was ruined and we've been drifting in the trade currents ever since. Don't mention anything about your parents or the farm or Spearpoint Rock, and certainly don't mention anything about dreams or me being your grampy. What's my name again?"

"Uncle Parmo."

"Good," he said and turned his attention to their belongings. There were an awful lot of things in the little boat, but he would claim they were family heirlooms for their relatives if anyone asked. He re-wrapped his sword in the burlap, then bundled the sword and everything else worth saving in the wool blankets. He didn't like the idea of being unarmed, but he knew a sword would do him little good against an entire ship crew. *We can only hope they're not looking for us, and if they are, then let's just hope they don't realize it's us they're looking for.*

The captain of *Pyrthin's Flame* ordered his crew to drop sail thirty fathoms out, and the frigate drifted to a near-stop six fathoms from the skiff. Makarria happily waved to the crew of the much larger ship, now plainly visible on deck, and Parmo took up the oars of the skiff to paddle them to the brig's portside. When they got close enough, the crew of *Pyrthin's Flame* threw out a guideline, and Makarria grabbed it up out of the water and quickly tied it to the cleat at the bow of the skiff. The crew began towing them in, and moments later they clunked into the hull of the *Pyrthin's Flame*, which towered above them. The crew lowered a rope ladder and Parmo helped Makarria get started before grabbing his bundle of belongings and following after her.

On deck, sailors helped Makarria and Parmo over the main rail. Makarria was so happy she couldn't stop saying thank you. Parmo quickly spotted the captain and thanked him for his generosity, then began the quick rendition of the story he had concocted explaining their predicament.

A short distance away Taera stood staring at Makarria. She had seen Makarria's face so often in her visions of late she felt as if she already knew her. "Hello," she said, touching Makarria on her shoulder. "I am Taera. I've been waiting to meet you."

Makarria hadn't even noticed Taera at first, but she looked at her now and smiled. She had never seen a woman so beautiful before. Apart from her mother and the farmer's wives at the few nearby farmsteads, she had not seen any other women at all.

"You're a princess," Makarria said in awe, her eyes soaking in Taera's golden hair and her simple, yet elegant dress.

"Yes. I am Princess Taera Delios of Pyrthinia. What is your name, if I may ask?"

"Makarria."

Taera bent forward and grabbed Makarria in an embrace. Makarria had no idea why a stranger would want to hug her, but she returned the embrace, and after a moment she realized she was crying and did not want to let go.

"It's very good to meet you, Makarria," Taera said, holding her tighter. "You're safe now. Everything is going to be alright."

• • •

The full moon rode high in the night sky, but beneath the canopy of cypress trees skirting the River Kylep it was utterly dark. Natarios swore and held up the hem of his black cloak to keep it from dragging in the puddles between the gnarled cypress roots and tripping him up. A chorus of bullfrog croaks reverberated through the stale air, punctuated by the occasional shrill cry of a nocturnal bird. It was enough to make the hair at Natarios's neck stand on end, but he was thankful it was only frogs and birds he heard and not some predator.

At the bank of the river, the moonlight glimmered off the glass surface of the water, and at the far bank, a hundred yards distant, was another black wall of cypress trees. What caught Natarios's eye though, was the ship sitting at anchor in the middle of the river. It was strangely umbrageous—somehow not catching a glint of the moonlight—and it appeared to be inverted to Natarios's eye. The top half was long and cylindrical like the hull of a warship, but the bottom half was no larger than the cabin on a small fishing trawler. Natarios couldn't begin to imagine how the thing stayed afloat in the water. *Best not to worry about it,* Natarios decided. *It's certainly no more bizarre than seeing a man turn into a raven.*

Natarios opened the shutter on the small lantern he carried—twice in quick succession to signal the ship. Shadowy figures moved along the bottom half of the ship in immediate response, and a few short moments later Natarios could make out a rowboat with two people on board heading his way. When the boat reached the shore, Natarios helped the female passenger onto solid ground, but the giant of a man who held the oars made no effort to disembark.

"Mistress Roanna, it is a pleasure to finally meet you," Natarios greeted the woman.

"Well met, Houndkeeper Natarios. I hope you were not followed? The Flying Wolf knows nothing?"

Natarios felt a sharp pain between his legs and looked down to see that Roanna was pressing the tip of a dagger into his groin. "No, no one knows," he stammered.

"Good," Roanna said, pulling the dagger back into one sleeve of her heavy cloak. "Tell me what you know of the Princess. Have you sensed anything from her?"

DREAMWIELDER

"Yes. Since Wulfram was last here, the scent-hound has been smelling much activity. I've been moving the hound around the city to pinpoint the exact location, and there's no doubt: it's coming from Castle Pyrthin."

"Excellent. The renewed activity coincides with the return of her brother, it seems."

"Perhaps. There was the firewielder the Prince killed, but there has been much other strange activity of late, even before that. We found something on the peninsula east of Pyrvino, and Wulfram has been off chasing that lead ever since. He seemed unreceptive when I suggested there might be a sorceress in Kal Pyrthin…"

Roanna spat. "Wulfram is a fool, more animal than man. It's the Princess we're after, I'm certain. Between what the dead brother told us, and the young one, and now your own hound, it has to be her. We'll steal her away tonight before the Flying Wolf returns. We'll need your help."

"I'm afraid that's not possible," Natarios said.

"You needn't worry about any harm coming to you. I'm not asking you to get us past the gates—we'll be entering from above. I just need information: what tower she resides in, how many sentinels are on watch, what their routine is…"

"No you don't understand. She's gone."

"Gone?"

Natarios nodded and grinned, still rather smug with himself for having figured it all out. "Two days ago come morning the hound quit sensing anything. That very afternoon the Princess allegedly took ill and only the physician and the King have been allowed to see her since. Other members of the household staff have seen her from a distance, but none of them have gotten close enough to see that it's not really her, that it's a decoy. You see, there's a classy brothel a few streets in from the harbor, and they have a young girl there who's known for being as beautiful as the Princess herself. Courtiers and courtesans that find themselves lovestruck over the princess pay good money to—"

"What are you getting at, imbecile?" Roanna snapped. "Where has the Princess gone?"

"She's sailed off on a ship, heading to the East Islands," Natarios grumbled, bristling at her dismissal of his story. "They used the girl as a decoy."

"What ship is it?"

"*Pyrthin's Fire*. It's brand new, a two-master, probably the biggest ship you'll find outside of the Sol Sea. I doubt you'll be able to catch her in that ship of yours, and even if you did, it's manned with every sailor in the Pyrthin navy worth his salt."

"You needn't worry yourself about it anymore," Roanna said, turning to get back into the rowboat. "Return to your normal duties for the Emperor. This conversation never happened."

"And my money?"

The big man in the boat flung a coin purse, smacking Natarios square in the sternum and knocking him backward over a root into a mud puddle.

"You'll get the rest when we have the Princess and the Emperor is dead," Roanna said as the big man pushed the boat off and began rowing toward their ship.

Good luck getting past Wulfram first, Natarios quipped silently as he opened the drawstring on the purse and counted his money. It was less than he had hoped for but more than enough to be worthwhile. He had no love for Wulfram and the Emperor, and as much as he'd like to see the both of them dead and get paid the rest of his money, he'd seen well enough what Wulfram was capable of. He was skeptical any sorceress could pose harm to him. In all likelihood Wulfram would return soon, and Natarios would have to tell him that the Princess had fled. Wulfram would go after *Pyrthin's Fire*, and if Roanna got in the way, he'd kill her. *Serve her right for not letting me talk.*

Natarios pushed himself to his feet, intent on getting away from the river and trees and back to his tower as quickly as possible, but Roanna's ship caught his eye, and he turned just in time to see it pull up anchor. He stood there staring in disbelief, because rather than drifting downstream, it drifted up into the air.

"An air-ship," he marveled. "Even the Emperor doesn't have one of those."

13
The Bond

With the sun at his back, Parmo could see for miles on the eastern horizon: nothing but blue sea and a few puffy white clouds. They were heading east again, toward the East Islands, as luck would have it. Parmo could still hardly believe it. The captain of *Pyrthin's Flame* had told Parmo that they would return to Kal Pyrthin afterward, and Parmo readily agreed to work on the ship in exchange for passage. He didn't tell the captain that he meant to stay on the East Islands with Makarria. The man seemed nice enough, but Parmo didn't trust anyone. It would be an easy enough task, and safer for everyone, for Parmo to slip away with Makarria once they were in port in the East Islands.

"Hey there," one of the sailors barked, interrupting Parmo's reverie, "those whippings aren't going to finish themselves."

"Aye, right you are," Parmo said pleasantly enough, but inwardly he cursed the man. *I know more about sailing than you and the rest of this fool crew combined.* Still, Parmo took pride in his work, and he turned his attention back to the whippings he'd been at all day. There were nearly one hundred and forty lines on *Pyrthin's Flame,* and the ship still being new, none of the ends had been finished. The captain had tasked Parmo with finishing them all, which involved binding the ends of the three-stranded ropes with an intricate combination of sewing and knotting to keep the ends from unraveling. Parmo was not yet even a quarter of the way done. He picked up his sail-needle with a sigh and tightened the leather palm he wore over his right hand. It was tedious work, but at least it passed the time he figured.

He would have preferred to spend his time with Makarria, but the Princess on board had more or less adopted her. Parmo still could not fathom why the Princess was on board in the first place, but he knew better than to ask questions and arouse any suspicion. *Just stay quiet and Makarria will tell me all about it when we get safely off ship in the East Islands,* he reminded himself.

Makarria, for her part, was having a perfectly wonderful time with Taera. The Princess had helped her bathe the day before when they'd been rescued, then insisted that Makarria stay with her in her cabin. The cabin did not have a particularly comfortable bed by Taera's standards, but to Makarria it was the most luxurious thing she had ever experienced, especially after sleeping in a skiff for the last week or more. Makarria still couldn't believe that she had met a princess. Taera, with her long blond hair and clear blue eyes, was more beautiful than Makarria ever imagined a woman could be. By comparison, Makarria with her brown hair and dark-tanned skin felt like a wretched-looking whelp.

"You don't speak much, do you?" Taera asked her.

Makarria looked up to see Taera staring at her from across the bed where she sat combing her hair. "I don't?"

"No, you're very quiet, and sometimes you're not even listening when I speak. Your eyes see me, but you're somewhere else."

Makarria glanced away, embarrassed. "My mother says that too. She says whenever there's work to do I go off into my own little world."

Taera smiled and rubbed Makarria's shoulder. "Don't worry, I was the same when I was your age."

"Really? Did your mother yell at you too?"

"No. I didn't have my mother around much growing up. She died when I was very young."

Makarria covered her mouth in shock.

"It's alright, sweetie," Taera assured her. "As I said, I was very young and I barely remember her. I was well taken care of. I imagine it's quite different being a farmer than it is being a princess. No one has ever depended on me to milk goats or tend to a garden."

Makarria shrugged. "It's not so bad. If I work hard, I'm usually done with all my chores before dark, and then I can hike around by myself or go out on the skiff to help my grampy get the crab traps."

"Your grandfather or your uncle?" Taera asked.

"My grandfather. Parmo is my…" Makarria caught herself and remembered the story she was supposed to tell. "Parmo is my uncle, not my grandfather. A different skiff. They each have their own."

Taera stood up and placed her hairbrush in a drawer of the tiny dresser secured to the far wall of the tiny cabin. "I want you to know that you can trust me, Makarria," Taera said. "You don't have to keep secrets."

"I'm not keeping secrets. It's just, I'm nervous, you being a princess and all."

"I don't think that's it. You're scared but not because I'm a princess."

Makarria averted her eyes and adjusted her tunic.

"Can I tell you a secret?" Taera asked. "You can't tell anyone, otherwise my life will be in grave danger, but I trust you."

"Alright," Makarria agreed.

Taera sat back down on the bed and leaned in close to Makarria. "I can see things before they happen," she whispered. "I'm a seer, Makarria. My father is sending me away so that the Emperor can't kill me. I'm to hide away on the East Islands and hope Guderian and Wulfram never find me."

Makarria's eyes went wide. "The Emperor is real, then? And Wulfram? They'd really want to kill you because you see things?"

"Yes, very much so. And I think you are running from them too, Makarria. I've seen you in my visions. Our fates are tied together somehow. It's not clear to me yet, but you are a very important young woman, and I swear to you, I mean to do whatever I can to keep you safe."

Makarria nodded. She knew that Parmo would be mad at her for talking, but she couldn't help it—she trusted Taera. "I can make things when I sleep," she blurted out. "Grampy says I'm a dreamwielder."

Now it was Taera's turn to go wide-eyed. "A dreamwielder? You're sure?"

"Yes. Grampy was taking me to go hide at the East Islands, just like you, but a storm came and ruined our boat."

"Parmo is your grandfather?"

"Yes."

"But he's far too young to—" Taera stopped mid-sentence as a vision of Parmo's face transforming from old to young flashed through her mind. "You changed him," she said, hardly believing it.

"Yes," Makarria admitted. "It was an accident, and I killed a lot of fish. It's alright though. Grampy says when we get to the East Islands he's going to help me try to learn to control my dreams. And if you're there too... we'll be safe, right?"

Taera closed her eyes and inhaled deeply. "Yes, we probably would be safe there, but I have a bad feeling we're not going to the East Islands, Makarria. I've not seen the islands in my mind. Our fate lies elsewhere I'm afraid."

King Casstian Delios rubbed his eyes to get the bleariness out of them. The stack of documents on his desk was a cluttered mess, and Casstian hardly knew what to make of it all. He had been King of Pyrthinia since the age of fourteen when his father was killed, and in all that time Pyrthinia had never been at war. There'd been a few naval skirmishes with pirates from the Old World and the squelching of a small uprising in Tyrna when two stormbringers riled up the townspeople against the Emperor, but Pyrthinia had not fully mobilized for war since the Dreamwielder War, a year before Casstian was even born. *I've spent my whole life trying to forge peace between Pyrthinia and Sargoth,* Casstian mused, *and now here I am—an old man— considering rebellion.*

Casstian had been meeting with his most trusted advisors and looking at numbers and reports all day. As it stood, Pyrthinia did not have anywhere near a large enough standing army to march on Col

Sargoth. There was also Valaróz to consider. Don Bricio would be the first to come to the Emperor's aid, and the Pyrthin navy simply could not compete with the Valarion navy. The best Casstian could hope for would be for the Pyrthin navy to blockade Kal Pyrthin Bay and keep the Valarion ships out, while ground troops marched on Sol Valaróz. That would mean fighting on two fronts though. Even if Casstian marshaled every able-bodied Pyrthinian into service, they would still be undermanned. At best, Casstian could hope to surprise Sol Valaróz by attacking there first, but the casualties would be massive, leaving them with too few troops to march on Col Sargoth. Plus, attacking Valaróz first would give the Emperor too much time to prepare, and give Lorimer, King of Golier, time to send reinforcements. And then there was Wulfram to contend with, whom Casstian had no answer for. The odds seemed insurmountable. Casstian knew he had to do something though. The Emperor would find out sooner or later that Casstian had sent Taera away, if he didn't know already, and that would be reason enough for the Emperor to come after him. *It's either strike first or give up and surrender myself,* Casstian decided. *Is my life worth the lives of thousands of Pyrthinians?*

An odd clank at the window roused Casstian from his thoughts, and he got up from his desk to peer out the window. He saw nothing at first except for the night sky and the dimly lit windows of the city below him. Directly below his study tower, however, a small regiment of troops was marching toward the main gates of the keep, and they weren't Pyrthinian troops. Casstian spun around to go find his chamberlain but stopped dead in his tracks.

"Greetings, King Casstian," Wulfram spoke, his voice more a growl than human speech.

Cold fear surged through Casstian's gut. "How did you get in here?"

"That's not important, King. What is important is what *you've* been doing. Why have your captains been marshaling troops? And where is your sick daughter?"

"I've sent her away to keep her out of your hands, you filthy animal," Casstian said, drawing himself up to his full height and pushing aside the fear in his belly. A deep wheezing groan emanated from beneath Wulfram's robes, and Casstian realized Wulfram was laughing.

"I admire your honesty," Wulfram said. "But you've needlessly sacrificed yourself. I'll find your daughter eventually, and she will still die."

"You first," Casstian said, lunging forward as he drew a dagger from his belt. Wulfram merely stood there, and for a fleeting moment Casstian thought he had been quick enough, but then Wulfram struck with such speed that Casstian was on the ground with his arm slashed open before he even realized what had happened.

"Fool old man," Wulfram growled, his clawed right hand still protruding from the sleeve of his black cloak, his talons dripping with Casstian's blood. Casstian watched in horror as he lifted his hand to his shrouded face and licked the blood away with his elongated tongue.

There was a ruckus in the corridor outside the study and Casstian's chamberlain barged in through the door.

"Your Majesty—" the chamberlain started to say, but he stopped in stunned silence when he saw Wulfram standing over Casstian. His mouth kept moving for a few seconds more before he could get words out again. "…I, I'm sorry, Your Majesty, I tried to keep them out."

Heavy footsteps approached from the corridor and in barged Natarios, followed by a dozen of the houndkeeper's henchmen in dark uniforms emblazoned with the symbol of Sargoth.

"Excellent work, houndkeeper," Wulfram said. "Shackle the King and take him to the dungeon."

"Not man enough to kill me?" Casstian spat, clutching at his rent open forearm to stop the bleeding.

"I'll leave that honor to your son when he returns with the Emperor."

"What? Caile? He wouldn't."

"He will if he wants your throne," Wulfram stated simply, and with that he turned and strode out the door.

14
Night Flight

Taera woke with a start. She had seen the cavern beneath the ice in her dreams again and a new face: a woman who was smiling, beckoning from above. When Taera had first seen the cavern in her dreams, weeks before, it carried a foreboding sense of danger with it, but now it was different. The thought of the cave warmed her somehow. And the woman, too. Taera sat up and checked on Makarria, who lay sound asleep beside her. Taera hated to wake her, but she felt compelled to go up onto deck. *The woman is waiting for us,* Taera realized.

"Wake up, sweetie," Taera whispered, shaking Makarria's shoulders.

"What's wrong?" Makarria asked, sitting bolt upright. "Was I dreaming?"

"No, everything is fine. I just need you to come with me."

"Where to?"

"I'm not exactly sure," Taera replied as she got up and shed her sleeping gown. "Just come along. Get into your britches and tunic. It won't do for us to travel in our nightclothes."

Makarria was confused, but she did as she was told. When the two of them were dressed, Taera grabbed Makarria by the hand and led her out of the cabin and up onto the main deck. It was well after midnight, and not even the moon was up anymore. Only the stars lit the waters around *Pyrthin's Flame*. The damp, salty air around them was completely still, and the only sound was the water sloshing against the hull of the ship.

GARRETT CALCATERRA

"Where's the crew?" Makarria asked.

"Sleeping," Taera replied, leading Makarria toward the stern castle.

"But shouldn't there be a helmsmen or a watch at least?"

"Don't worry about it, sweetie," Taera said in a flat, dreamlike tone.

Something wasn't right, Makarria could tell. The flaccid sails were raised, but no one was on deck. It was like a ghost ship. "Taera?" Makarria asked, but Taera was already climbing the ladder up to the stern castle. Makarria hurried up after her. "Taera?" she asked again as she reached the top.

Taera paid her no heed though. Her attention was instead focused on the woman standing at the stern of the ship, the woman from her vision: Roanna.

"Greetings, Princess Taera," Roanna said with a slight bow of her head.

"Who are you?" Makarria asked.

"I am Roanna. And you?"

"She's my attendant," Taera said. "She'll be coming with us."

"You know that I'm taking you away then?" Roanna asked.

"Yes. I've seen it in my visions. And I've also seen that Makarria will travel with us. She must come along. It is not negotiable. If she stays, I stay."

"No need to make threats, Princess. There's plenty of room for two." Roanna turned and grabbed a rope ladder that swayed in the air behind her. Makarria gasped as she followed the ladder upward with her eyes to see the dark airship floating above them. "Quietly now," Roanna said. "Up you go. Both of you."

Makarria opened her mouth to protest and say she couldn't go anywhere without Parmo, but Taera hushed her and pushed her toward the ladder. "Please, just trust me," Taera said. Makarria nodded and grabbed the ladder from Roanna. She climbed easily, despite the sway of the rope ladder, and thirty feet up she reached the deck of the airship. Two massive hands reached over the starboard side rail to help pull Makarria on board, and with little effort on her

96

own part Makarria found herself on deck, face to face with a huge, dark-bearded man clad in furs.

"Who are you?" Makarria asked.

"Siegbjorn, captain of this ship. Now move aside so I am able to help the others."

Makarria shuffled as far back as she could on the small deck and quickly looked over the vessel while Siegbjorn pulled Taera on board. There was a small cabin behind them and a series of control levers at the bow, but apart from that there was little to the gondola portion of the airship. The vast majority of the ship was the giant cylindrical air-filled hull above them. Makarria had never seen anything like it before. She had never even heard of such a thing before.

Roanna climbed up onto deck behind Taera and began pulling up the rope ladder. "Get us away from *Pyrthin's Flame*," she commanded Siegbjorn.

Siegbjorn turned away wordlessly and grabbed the control lines that released a short burst of flames up into the hollow center of the hull above them. With the added heat in the hull, the airship slowly rose up and away from *Pyrthin's Flame*.

"You're to take us to the cavern in the ice, is that correct?" Taera asked.

Roanna silently regarded her for a long moment. "Yes, that is correct but not until we take care of some unpleasantness first."

Roanna turned away from them and looked over the rail of the airship down toward *Pyrthin's Flame*. Sparks flashed at the tips of Roanna's fingertips, and Makarria suddenly felt every hair on her body prickle. Before Makarria or Taera realized what was happening though, Roanna grunted from deep within her core and thrust her hands downward, sending a stream of flames tumbling over *Pyrthin's Flame*.

"No!" Makarria screamed. "Grampy!"

"What are you doing?" Taera gasped, rushing toward Roanna, but Siegbjorn grabbed her up in one arm and wrenched her from her feet. Below them, *Pyrthin's Flame* went up in flames and lit the night sky.

"Let this be your first lesson, Princess," Roanna said. "Did you know I was going to burn your ship? Did you see it in your visions?"

"No," Taera whispered.

"That's because I am able to block my intentions from you. Around me, you will only see what I choose for you see. I mean you no harm, Princess, but if you are to learn from me and come to harness your powers as is your destiny, you must first fear and respect me. Is that clear?"

Taera could only nod.

"Good," Roanna said. "Now take her inside, Siegbjorn, and let's be away."

Roanna swept past Makarria into the cabin of the airship, seemingly oblivious to Makarria, who had backed herself against the portside rail. Makarria looked over her shoulder at the burning ship below them. Even with the sails aflame, still no one stirred on deck. *I have to get down there to warn Grampy.*

Siegbjorn glanced at Makarria, but he was holding onto Taera and pushing her toward the cabin. Makarria knew this was her one and only chance. She climbed the railing and shot a glance below. It was a long way down, maybe fifty feet to the surface of the water. She stopped, paralyzed with fear for a moment, but the thought of Parmo being burnt in his sleep sparked her into action. She let go of the rails with her hands and sprang forward. Her brief hesitation had been all that Siegbjorn needed though. He snatched Makarria by the back of her tunic before her feet even left the railing and heaved her to the deck of the airship.

"No, let me go!" Makarria yelled, scrambling toward the other rail. "Grampy! The ship's on fire!" Siegbjorn reached down to grab her, but Makarria slapped his hand away. "Grampy! Gram—"

This time Siegbjorn was not so gentle. He thumped Makarria along the side of the head with the open palm of his hand, and she fell to the ground, stunned, barely conscious. Siegbjorn picked her up by the scruff and dragged her inside the cabin along with Taera.

Roanna regarded the three of them. "You should have let the

little one jump and saved us the trouble."

"No jumpers on my ship," Siegbjorn grumbled, and he dropped Makarria to the ground where she landed in an unconscious heap.

Parmo woke to the sound of timber creaking and the thick stench of smoke. He tumbled out of his hammock, grabbed up his sword, and sprinted toward the ladder leading out of the hold beneath the forecastle. Up on the main deck, a wave of pure heat swept over him from the flames enveloping the rear of the ship.

"No," Parmo said, stunned. "Makarria!"

He bolted across the main deck, pushing through the intense heat to the stern castle, and leapt through the doorway to the main cabins where he was nearly blinded by the thick smoke filling the corridor. The wooden floor beneath him burned his bare feet, but he forged on, using his left hand to guide himself along the wall and feel for the door to Taera's cabin. An explosion blew the door off a cabin farther down the corridor and Parmo had to shield himself against the flames and debris just as he found Taera's cabin. He thrust the door open and stumbled into the room only to find it deserted.

"Makarria?" he yelled, looking beneath the bed, but she was nowhere to be found nor was Taera. Smoke from the corridor flooded into the room, and he knew he had to get out of there quickly before he was trapped. *"Merda!"* he swore as he covered his mouth with one arm and stumbled back into the corridor. Another cabin behind him flashed over and flames licked at his back as he ran for the exit.

Back out on the main the deck, there was only slightly less smoke than in the corridor. The entire stern castle was up in flames, and the mainsail burned so brightly Parmo had to shield his eyes. He spun around, trying to orient himself and choking on the acrid smoke all around him. *Where's the damned crew?* he asked himself, perplexed. There should have been men bustling everywhere, trying to put out the flames or helping people evacuate. Someone should have cried out a warning when the fire started. There wasn't a single person on deck besides Parmo though.

Parmo ran to the hatch leading to the main hold and felt a sense of dread fill him. The hatch covering the passageway had been battened down and barricaded shut with a barrel. Someone had purposely trapped the crew in the hold, he realized. He pushed the barrel aside with a mighty heave, then hacked away the ropes holding the hatch closed with his sword. The hatch burst open with a torrent of smoke and heat that knocked Parmo to the ground. He choked back the stinging tears in his eyes and peered down the hatch. The flames inside the hold lit up the smoke with an eerie, mottled, orange hue, but even through the veil of smoke he could see bodies at the bottom of the stairs. Without a second thought, he tossed aside his sword, took in a deep breath, and darted down the stairs. He grabbed the first man he came to and dragged him up the stairs, then went down and grabbed another man. He turned back to go again, but the flames had reached the stairs, and with the newly fresh air the fire billowed up out of the hatch like a furnace. Parmo had no choice but to back away.

One of the sailors Parmo had pulled out of the hold coughed and came to. Parmo knelt down over him. "Are you alright? Can you get up?"

The sailor blinked his eyes and shook his head to clear his mind. "Aye, I think I can stand."

"Then get up, man, and help me grab your crew mate here," Parmo ordered him as he grabbed up his sword. The man pushed himself up to do as he was told, and the two of them grabbed the unconscious sailor from beneath the shoulders and dragged him to the portside of the forecastle. Parmo looked over the rail to see his skiff hanging there where the sailors had hoisted it up out of the water two days prior. "Down into the skiff," Parmo told the sailor beside him. "I'll lower him down to you."

"Aye," the sailor said, climbing over the rail and dropping down to the skiff.

Parmo yanked the unconscious man up and lowered him as gently as he could to the other sailor. Still, the unconscious man hit the deck with a heavy thud.

"Lower the skiff down to the water," Parmo yelled down. "I'll be there in a moment."

The sailor nodded and began loosening the ropes to lower the skiff, and Parmo turned his attention back to *Pyrthin's Flame*. The stern half of the ship was a wall of fire. The main mast was a giant burning tower, and the square sails on the foremast had caught fire too. Parmo hacked a line to drop the triangular trysail from the foremast and bundled the sail up as quickly as he could. "Here," he yelled as he dropped the sail over the rail into the skiff. The sailor below caught the sail with a grunt and a curse, but Parmo paid him no heed. He instead cut loose a water barrel lashed to the railing and rolled it down the main deck to where the side rails ended.

The heat was intense, and Parmo could feel the skin on his face dry and crackle. He pushed ahead though. He knew without fresh water, all of his efforts would be in vain, and they would survive the fire only to die of dehydration in a few days. When he reached the section where the rail finally stopped, he rolled the barrel off the deck into the water below, then turned to see if there was anything else he could salvage from the ship. The deck rumbled beneath his feet. There was a massive splintering noise, and Parmo realized that the main mast was uprooting itself from the deck. It was falling like a great burning tree right toward him!

Parmo jumped and pummeled into the water below, gripping the hilt of his sword tightly, determined not to lose it. The main mast split in half as it hit the side of the ship above him, and the top half battered down into the water beside Parmo with a hissing torrent of steam. He kicked his legs to propel himself away from the smoldering timber and found the water barrel bobbing up and down several yards away. He grabbed at the barrel gratefully to keep himself afloat and took a deep breath. It was no easy thing to tread water with a sword in one hand, even if he was without boots.

"Where are you?" a voice came out to him, and Parmo looked

up to see the sailor paddling the skiff toward him.

"Here," Parmo hollered, and within a few moments Parmo was on board and the two of them hoisted the water barrel up into the skiff. "We best get away from her," Parmo said, looking up at *Pyrthin's Flame*.

"Aye," the sailor agreed and they both took up paddles and rowed themselves clear of the burning ship.

Pyrthin's Flame groaned, and the stern slowly began sinking into the water, sending the bow high up into the air. Parmo looked on in wonder. Just the day before he had been grumbling to himself about being relegated to sleep in the forecastle where he was constantly being jarred around as the bow rose and fell over each ocean swell. And yet, if he'd not been in the forecastle hold, he would have been trapped with all the other sailors in the main hold.

Pyrthin's Flame continued to burn, and soon the bow and the burning foremast were the only parts of the ship protruding from the dark waters.

"Pyrthin's arse," the sailor whispered. "What happened?"

"Treachery," Parmo answered, and even as he said it he saw a shadow move across the stars in the eastern sky. He saw the silhouette of the airship in the distance, heading back toward the Five Kingdoms, and he gritted his teeth with anger and determination. *Stay strong, Makarria. I'll find you.*

15
The Throne of Fire

In a private chamber in the upper reaches of Lightbringer's Keep, Caile bowed deeply and rose to face Emperor Guderian. At Caile's side, Lorentz stayed prostrate for a moment longer before rising. Behind them, Caile's liaison, Lindy, stood barring the exit from the chamber, and in the corridor outside, four more guards stood at the ready. The Emperor, himself, sat in a modest throne atop a raised dais, and to either side of him were racks full of weapons: swords with barbed blades, maces, flails, short handled battle-axes, and bladed weapons Caile had never seen the likes of before. The rest of the room was unadorned and black. There were no windows, only a half dozen wall torches, and the room reeked of iron or blood—Caile couldn't tell which.

Apart from the court sessions and public hearings in the throne room, it was the first time Caile had been summoned by the Emperor since arriving, and he knew whatever was going on wasn't good. *This chamber is meant to intimidate people,* he told himself. *Just remain calm, think before speaking, and everything will be fine.*

"Leave us and close the door," the Emperor told Lindy.

The giant man did as he was told, and the Emperor regarded Caile and Lorentz silently for a long moment before speaking again.

"Your father is a traitor, Prince," he finally said. "He sent you instead of your sister, not because she was ill, but because she is a sorceress. You knew and yet said nothing."

"I cannot speak for my father, Your Excellency," Caile responded, "but I can assure you I knew nothing of the sort. I barely know my sister. I've been gone these last five years in Valaróz, and before that I was but a child."

"But you do not deny that she is a sorceress?"

"Who am I to question you, Your Excellency? I've seen no signs to suggest she is, but you would know better than I, and as I said, I've been gone. All I know is I was summoned back to Pyrthinia two years early and immediately sent here without so much as a night's rest. I was informed that my brother had died and that my sister was too ill to travel, that is all."

"You can vouch for his words?" the Emperor asked Lorentz.

"Yes, Your Excellency. It is as the Prince says. We were summoned to Kal Pyrthin and stayed not even a day before being sent here. King Casstian himself told me that the Princess was unfit for travel and asked me to watch over young Caile."

Caile bristled inwardly at being called young but let it go. "The Royal Physician himself penned the letter I brought you, Your Excellency."

"Yes, that is why he has been stripped of his office and put in chains along with your father," the Emperor stated flatly.

Caile heard the menace in Guderian's voice and picked his words carefully. "If I may ask, Your Excellency, how is that you are so certain my sister is a sorceress and my father a traitor?"

"The houndkeeper in Kal Pyrthin identified sorcery in your father's keep, so I sent Wulfram to investigate."

A sense of dread filled Caile at hearing Wulfram's name.

"But your father knew he was caught," the Emperor continued. "Before Wulfram arrived, he sent your sister away on a ship and began marshaling forces to wage war against the Empire."

Caile found some small triumph in the fact that Taera had escaped, but he showed no outward sign of his emotions. "I must say, I'm stunned," he said. "I did not think my father was capable of revolt. He has been a loyal servant to you ever since he took his throne."

"Outwardly loyal, perhaps, but he has been a constant impediment to my vision of progress. He has clung to the old ways and harbored sorcerers, endlessly petitioning me for amnesty. It all makes much more sense now, knowing one of his own children is a sorceress. Parents will go to no ends to protect their children, even treason it seems. And yet, he had no qualms about sending you here to me." The Emperor grabbed up one of the axes beside him and spun the handle in his hand. "Why? Is it because he has little regard for you, or is it because he knows you're clever and thinks you can talk your way out of danger?"

"If I may venture a guess, I would say it is the former," Caile said. "I have done my best to be a loyal son and servant of both Pyrthinia and the Sargothian Empire, but I admit to having little love for my father, and he has never shown any respect or love for me. Don Bricio has shown more regard for my welfare and growth than my own father."

The Emperor stood and stepped down from the dais, axe still in hand. "Be that as it may, you are in a dire predicament, young prince," he said, circling Caile and Lorentz. "You were sent here as collateral to ensure your father's loyalty, but Casstian Delios is King of Pyrthinia no longer. That means you are of little value to me anymore."

Caile eyed the weapon racks on the dais as the Emperor swept past him. If he was quick, Caile might be able to leap away when the Emperor's back was turned and arm himself, but he knew that would mean Lorentz's death, and alone, Caile would have little chance fighting his way past the Emperor, Lindy, and the other guards in the hallway. The best he could hope for would be to strike a mortal blow to the Emperor before the guards rushed in. *Keep your cool,* he reminded himself and took a deep breath.

"If you have declared my father and sister traitors under the powers vested to you by the wartime privileges of Sargoth Lightbringer, then by the same laws decreed by the founders of the Five Kingdoms, I am rightfully the successor to the throne of Pyrthinia," Caile said. "I understand how easily you could end the Delios line of succession," Caile went on, nodding in the direction of the axe in the Emperor's hand, "but I think we might find a mutually beneficial solution."

The Emperor stopped in front of Caile and stared down at him with a thin smile. "So you have some cleverness in you after all, my princeling. Don Bricio has taught you well. You see how we both may gain by helping one another. It is true I could hand pick my own ruler for Pyrthinia, but I've seen the problems it has caused in Valaróz. The Pyrthinians will be more content if Caile Delios sits on the throne rather than some stranger. And Pyrthinia will thrive with a ruler who shares my vision. So I leave the choice to you. Pledge your allegiance and loyalty to me and the Sargothian Empire, and the throne is yours."

Caile opened his mouth to respond, but the Emperor held up a finger to silence him. "But before you answer, you may want to hear the terms of your pledge. If you are to be King of Pyrthinia, your first task as my servant is to carry out the execution of your father. When his head lies on the courtyard of Castle Pyrthin, you shall take the throne."

Panic flooded through Caile. He had not lied before when he said he felt little love for his father, but there was more love there than he was willing to admit. He knew he could never kill his own father.

"What would the people think, having a kinslayer as a king?" Caile asked, his voice less firm than before. "It would undermine my power in their eyes."

"No, quite the opposite," the Emperor said, leaning in close to Caile. "It would show the people that King Caile and Emperor Guderian are unified in thought and purpose, that the old ways of sorcery are death, and that the future lies within grasp of the human mind and technology." The Emperor stepped back and sat back down in his throne. "You have provided wise council to your prince in the past, Captain," he said to Lorentz, "Perhaps you have some advice to him now?"

Lorentz nodded. "A wise and just king will never find it easy to execute someone, but he must find the strength in him to do what is right, to lead by example. When despair reigns supreme, when defeat seems near…"

Caile recognized the words Lorentz spoke. It was an old saying from the time of the Dreamwielder War that Lorentz left unfinished. Caile knew it well; it was meant to inspire troops going into a hopeless battle. *When despair reigns supreme, when defeat seems near, stand by your brothers, follow orders, and even in death we will be victorious.* But that wasn't the way Lorentz ever recited it to Caile in private. *Don't ever throw your life away needlessly,* Lorentz always told him. *When despair reigns supreme, when defeat seems near, do what you must to live and fight another day…*

The Emperor nodded in approval, oblivious to Lorentz's hidden message. "Sage advice, Captain. Follow orders. Is that something you are capable of, Caile, or are you still too young and headstrong to realize what's good for you? If you can trust in me and do as I say, you will live a life of privilege and see the Sargothian Empire become the greatest civilization the world has ever known. You will come to see the truth in my vision of the future. However, spurn me and pain and death will be all you know. I extinguished the royal line of the Pallma family in Valaróz, and I have no qualms about doing the same with the Delios line in Pyrthinia."

"The choice is simple, Your Excellency," Caile said. "I will gladly trust in you and do as you say. Upon your word, I will strike my father's head from his shoulders."

"Good. Sharpen your sword then. We leave for Pyrthinia tomorrow."

Natarios Rhodas leaned back into the deep cushions of King Casstian's throne with a contented sigh. *I could get used to this,* he thought. *The rats and ravens can have that smelly tower and the scent-hound too.*

"Excuse me, sir," the chamberlain interrupted. "By tradition, a regent of the realm shall not sit in the monarch's throne but rather sit off to the side so as not send the wrong message to vassals."

"When I want your official take on tradition, I'll be sure to ask you," Natarios remarked.

"But sir," the chamberlain persisted, "Wulfram said you were to abide by all standing laws until such time as he or the Emperor arrives."

"Yes, laws, not traditions. Show me an official writ that states regents can't sit on the throne and I'll move. Until then, kindly quit your yammering. You're giving me a headache."

The chamberlain pursed his lips and stormed out of the throne room.

"Have the kitchen send me a tankard of ale!" Natarios yelled after him, but he knew the chamberlain would ignore him. *No doubt he'll be off to the scroll room to find some antiquated law making it illegal for regents to place their buttocks on the royal cushions.* Natarios sighed again. Ruling a kingdom was wearisome work, especially with half of King Casstian's most trusted advisors locked up in the dungeon with Casstian himself. Natarios had ordered all the makeshift militias Casstian had mustered disbanded. He had found little resistance to that decree, but every other decision he made had caused him endless grief. If the chamberlain wasn't objecting, it was the craftsmen guilds or the harbormaster or some rich merchant. Natarios had half a mind to march down into the dungeon and negotiate the release of King Casstian. If Casstian was willing to part with some of the gold in the royal treasury, Natarios would be happy to leave it all behind. *Along with the gold I got from Roanna, I could take a ship to the Old World and buy myself my own little villa. I could buy a nice, comfy, cushioned throne of my own to sit in and not have to make all these tedious decisions.*

Natarios knew that Casstian was not the type of the man to bargain with though. *He's too damned stubborn with his "principles,"* Natarios scoffed. If he released Casstian, Natarios would likely find himself in shackles, locked up in the dungeon. And then there was always Wulfram to worry about. Taking a bribe here and there was nothing worthy of Wulfram's attention, but letting Casstian loose would be grand treason, and the Emperor might take exception. The thought of Wulfram coming after him did not particularly appeal to Natarios.

No, no, Natarios mused, *I'll just stay here in my luxuriant chair and avoid everyone's wrath. Who knows, if something bad happens to that foolhardy prince, the Emperor might even give me the throne, and then I can choose my own advisors to make all the tough decisions...*

16
Mistakes in the Dark

Caile paced his room frantically trying to figure out what to do. He knew what Lorentz would say—*just be patient and wait for the right opportunity to escape*—but waiting wasn't an option. The Emperor intended on going himself to Pyrthinia to oversee King Casstian's execution, and in all likelihood Wulfram would be there too. Even if Caile managed to slip away with his men on the road to Kal Pyrthin, the Emperor would track them down and kill them. *No, if I want to get my men out of here and have any chance of saving my father, the only option is to escape tonight,* Caile decided. *But how?*

He could use the secret passage beneath his room and save himself, of course, but he couldn't bear the thought of leaving his men behind to certain death. As far as he knew, there was only one entrance into the guarded barracks where his men were staying, and that meant getting out of his room past Lindy. There weren't any other options.

Past Lindy it is, then.

Once his decision was made, Caile moved with purpose, deliberately avoiding the gravity of what he was about to do. He pulled out his boot knife, pried up the floor-stone covering the secret passageway and tossed the stone onto his bed. He then laid down on the floor as if he had been knocked down, and began yelling.

"Help! Lindy! Help!"

The door flew open and Lindy barged into the room, battle-axe in hand.

"A man came up through the floor," Caile said breathlessly,

pointing toward the hole. "He tried to kill me."

Lindy rushed forward to hunch over the dark passage, and Caile pushed himself up to stand beside him. "He jumped back into the hole when I started yelling," Caile said, pausing with uncertainty for only a moment before thrusting his boot knife into the base of Lindy's skull directly above the spine, just as Don Bricio had taught him years before. The knife stuck in Lindy's massive vertebra, though, and rather than killing him instantly, it merely stunned him. He staggered to his feet with a groan and his arms flailed about to find Caile. Caile grabbed up the first thing he could find, the floor-stone, and brought it crashing down over Lindy's head. The stone split in two over the back of Lindy's thick skull, and the giant of a man toppled face first into the hole in the floor, only to get wedged halfway in.

Caile fought back the wave of nausea and faintness that washed over him. *What's done is done,* he told himself. He grabbed one of Lindy's limp legs and tried to pull him up, but the man was too massive to lift. Seeing no other options, Caile instead stomped on Lindy's rump and forced him inch by inch down into the passageway. On the last kick, Lindy's body fell and landed below with the sickening noise of bones snapping. Caile lowered himself into the passageway to find Lindy's head twisted backward at a grotesque angle.

"I'm truly sorry," Caile said, yanking Lindy's cloak free and pilfering the battle-axe and a belt knife from Lindy's dead body. Lastly, he yanked free his own boot knife from Lindy's neck and wiped the blood from the blade.

With the weapons and cloak in hand, Caile pulled himself back up into the room and covered the passageway entrance with the broken pieces of the floor-stone. He donned Lindy's faded black cloak and hacked the bottom foot and half off so that it wouldn't drag on the ground. With the cloak on, he was able to tuck the battle-axe up against his chest and keep it hidden. The boot knife he stowed in one boot, and the other knife he put into his belt.

Not wasting another moment, he strode out of the room, leaving the door wide open and walked calmly down the corridor.

Boldness had served well in the past, and that was his only semblance
of a plan now. Back in Sol Valaróz, Caile had snuck into all sorts of
places he wasn't supposed to go simply because he had learned to
walk as if he knew where he was going. People rarely questioned
someone who walked with confidence and a sense of authority.

Caile knew a sentinel passed by his room every quarter hour,
but with any luck the guard would think nothing of Lindy being
gone since the door was wide open, and Caile was also gone. In all
likelihood, the sentinel would assume Lindy had escorted Caile to
the privy or to get a late meal in the kitchen. That left Caile free to
barge right through the entire keep to his men, or so he hoped.

He strode down the corridor, trying not to think about what he
had just done. He had killed several men before, but all of them had
been in battle—either pirates from the Old World or highwaymen.
This was the first time he had ever killed someone in cold blood. *You
did it to save your men, so it's not murder,* he told himself and tried to
focus on the task at hand. The entire keep seemed to be asleep, and
he met no one in the main corridor or in the side corridor leading
to the training yard. Outside the air was crisp and pungent, reeking
of smoke and soot. The moon had already set, and Caile surmised
it was only a few hours before dawn. He heard distant voices from
the armory to his left, and the faint orange glow of the forges cast
long shadows across the training yard, but otherwise there was no
sign of life.

Caile grabbed a wooden bucket beside one of the drinking
troughs, filled it with water, and walked across the training yard to
the stairwell leading down to his men's barracks. The single flight
of stairs led to a dank, narrow corridor, lit only periodically by wall
torches. Some fifty paces down the corridor, a half-asleep sentinel
stood guarding the door to the barracks. He didn't notice Caile
approaching until Caile was almost upon him.

"What's this?" the guard asked, groggily lowering his short pike
toward Caile's chest.

"Water for the Prince's men."

"Water?"

"That's right," Caile said, and he flung the bucket into the guard's face.

The man flailed back from the sudden onslaught of water and fumbled for his pike. Before he could get a good grip on it again, Caile hefted his axe from his cloak and swung it in a tight arc right into the crook of the guard's neck. The man collapsed with a gurgling noise and did not move again. Caile knelt down over him and yanked the keys from his belt. There were only three keys to choose from, and the second one he tried opened the door the barracks.

"It's me," Caile said, knowing his men would have been awoken by the commotion.

"Caile?" Lorentz hissed from inside. "What are you doing?"

"I'm saving you. Let's go."

Lorentz stepped from the pitch-black barracks into the dim light of the corridor and eyed the slain guard. "Did you get the other one too?"

"What other one?"

"Damnit, Caile, we're not alone down here. There are more prisoners and another guard."

"No," Caile muttered, peering deeper down the corridor just as a dark figure came into view.

"What's going on down there?" the second guard asked.

"Uh, nothing," Caile stammered. "I'm relieving you of duty."

The man took another step forward and squinted his eyes to get a good look at Caile and the collapsed guard at his feet.

"Halt there a moment," Caile started to say, but before he could finish, the man swore and ran off in the other direction.

Caile sprinted after him, oblivious to Lorentz's shouts behind him to stop. The guard was portly and didn't move fast. Within a dozen steps, Caile had closed the distance to ten yards, but then the guard inexplicably stopped and reached up to grab something: a rope pulley. Before Caile could reach him, the thrum of a bell rung out overhead sounding the alarm.

"No!" Caile screamed, and he took off the guard's head with one swipe of his axe. Caile stood there over the decapitated man, stunned—as if in a dream—and for a moment all was silent, but then other bells sounded overhead, relaying the alarm.

"Caile," Lorentz yelled from the mouth of the corridor. "Get over here!"

Caile grabbed up the slain guard's pike and rushed back to join his men. Lorentz had taken up the other guard's pike, but the rest of Caile's men were unarmed. Caile handed off the pike he held and the knife from his belt, but held onto the axe for himself and pushed his way forward to Lorentz's side at the top of the stairs. A few scattered guards were running their way from the barracks, but otherwise, none of the Emperor's troops had yet taken up the warning call.

"Damnit, Caile, you should have just run away on your own," Lorentz said. "Now you've endangered your life."

"You can lecture me later. Right now we need to get out of here and to the gates. To the armory, go."

Caile sprinted forward before Lorentz could protest, and his men had no choice but to follow him. The three of them with weapons rushed to the forefront, and the brief skirmish in the center of the training yard left the guards from the armory dead. Caile's two unarmed men took up weapons from the slain guards, and they pushed forward again. Before they reached the armory though, a full regiment of the Emperor's Imperial Guard marched into the training yard to bar their escape. The Imperial Guardsmen were fully armed with long swords and bucklers, and they outnumbered Caile's men, four to one.

"Go, get out of here," Lorentz said, holding Caile back.

"I'm not leaving you," Caile said, despair washing over him.

"You have to. Our only chance is for you to live and fight another day. We'll buy you time."

"But where?"

"To your room, fool," Lorentz hissed.

Across the yard, the captain of the Imperial Guardsmen shouted a command, and the regiment surged forward.

"Use the passageway," Lorentz yelled, pushing Caile away. "Get back to Kal Pyrthin and free your father. Go!"

Caile handed over his axe. "Here, this will serve you better. There's a passage behind the forges that leads to the gates if you can break through."

"Yes, go," Lorentz said, shoving Caile away. "Go!"

Caile spun and sprinted back into the corridor from which he had come just as the Imperial Guardsmen reached his men. Shouts and the concussion of swords on shields receded away behind him, and after a moment, Caile realized he was weeping. He wiped away the tears so he could see where he was going and rounded the corner to the main corridor only to run smack into one of the sentinels. The man stumbled backward, and without thinking, Caile kicked him in the face, sending him reeling back to slam into the ground. Caile stomped on his face one more time, then snatched up his mace and raced down the corridor to his room.

He found his bedroom door still wide open and rushed inside to close it behind him. He didn't even bother gathering up the few belongings in his room. Time was of the essence, he knew. He grabbed the bulky table lamp from his nightstand, yanked up the broken floor-stone and lowered himself down into the passageway where he stood on Lindy's corpse while he slid the stone halves back into place overhead.

The table lamp was cumbersome, and Caile had to hold it steady so as not to spill oil on his hands and set himself aflame, but it lit up the passageway well enough. He could clearly make out the footprints in the dust from when Stephen had fetched him a few weeks prior, and he had no trouble navigating the intersecting passages. Before long, he was in the sewers looking for a way out. He didn't dare risk going up into the same cellar where he had met Roanna, but he was certain there were other ways out of the sewer. In fact, there proved to be dozens of exits, depending on what sort of drek he was willing to climb through to get out. None of the choices were appeasing: excrement, fouled water from the bathhouses, slop from butcher shops and millers, oil from the streets, and an assortment of other unidentifiable liquids flowed into the main sewer channel from a multitude of side-passages and shoots. Caile just had to pick one.

Seeing no better options, he picked a broad side-passageway that angled upward and started climbing. The stench was unbearable, and he had to toss aside the lamp so as to have at least one hand free to help climb the steep incline. In the other hand, he used the mace as a walking stick to keep from sliding back into the main passage.

It was a ten-foot climb and at the top Caile yanked himself up into a back alley gutter between a host of shops. He flopped onto the ground and rolled onto his back to breathe in the cool air, not caring that he was soaked in filth. The alley was filled with rancid trash and refuse, but after being in the sewer, the air seemed the sweetest he had ever breathed. When he finally caught his breath, he dragged himself to his feet and cast aside Lindy's sodden cloak.

It was still dark, perhaps an hour before sunrise. *Not much time to get out of the city.* He jogged to the edge of the alley and stopped unsure which way he should go. South was the most direct route to Pyrthinia, but the Emperor would know that, and if the guards hadn't already figured out Caile was gone, they would soon. Without a horse, Caile could probably make it out of the city before daybreak, but then he'd be out in the open on the road and easy to spot. He'd be safer heading east and skirting Forrest Weorcan, but that would take him a week out of the way and by then his father might already be dead. His only other option was to head for the harbor and try to sneak onto a ship making for Valaróz, but that would take even longer than heading west. His father would certainly be executed well before he could make it to Sevol as a stowaway, then travel by foot across the entirety of Valaróz and Pyrthinia to Kal Pyrthin. *East it is then,* he decided.

He moved swiftly, staying close alongside the buildings. There were lights in the windows of a few buildings—bread makers mostly and a few early-rising craftsmen—but the city was still largely asleep, and all was quiet except the occasional tolling of a bell from Lightbringer's Keep behind Caile. Those bells were not a good sign, Caile knew, and sure enough, before he had made it more than a few hundred paces eastward, the sound of horsemen approaching echoed through the streets. Caile tucked back into another alleyway, and a few moments later a half dozen of the Emperor's cavalrymen sped by. Caile swore. They would be heading for the east gate, no doubt, to keep an eye out for him trying to escape. *How am I going to get out?* He stood there for a long moment, again weighing the option of heading for the harbor. *Perhaps it would be safer to head back into the sewer for a few days and wait,* he pondered.

A new noise interrupted his contemplation. It was one of the noisy steam engines approaching. Caile tucked himself back into the shadows. The cacophonous cart lumbered his way, and he fully expected it to speed on by, but instead it stopped right as it reached the entrance to the alleyway. The engine slowed to a drumming drone of two intermittent steam pistons. Caile knelt down and peered into the street, the mace in his right hand loose and ready. The steam contraption was much larger than the rickshaw he had ridden in a few weeks before. It appeared to be a wagon drawn by a steam engine, although it was hard to tell in the dark. A lone figure sat at the helm of the controls. Caile shot a glance backward to make sure no one was sneaking up on him from behind. He couldn't be certain, but he felt like the person on the wagon was staring right at him.

"If you're heading east, I could perhaps give you a ride," the person said over the noise of the engine.

Caile recognized the voice instantly. It was the turnip lady, the sorceress who had saved him from Roanna. "You," he whispered.

"Yes," she said. "Come quickly. I'd like to be on the road before the sun rises."

"How do you keep finding me?"

"There's no time for that now. Come. You must trust me."

More bells sounded from Lightbringer's Keep, and Caile knew more troops would be coming soon to search for him. He didn't like this woman's damned secrecy, but he didn't see that he had any better options. *She's saved me once—why not again?* He darted out of the alley and pulled himself up into the wagon.

"Bury yourself under the turnips and stay quiet," the woman

said, and before he could reply she was at the controls, throttling the engine up to speed.

Caile laid down and wormed his way beneath the turnips as the wagon lurched forward. The hard vegetables were far from comfortable, but they were big enough to keep him from feeling suffocated when he burrowed his head down beneath them. The noise of the engine was near deafening, and it took several seconds for Caile to notice when the wagon suddenly slowed and came to a stop.

Voices carried to him over the alternating pistons.

"...got caught up in the market late yesterday and didn't want to risk the roads at night," he could hear the woman say. "Cows need milking, so I'd like to get home by first light."

"Have you seen anyone suspicious on your way through the city?" a man's voice asked.

"Just me and my turnips," the woman answered.

"Alright, away with you," the man said, and then the engine wound up again and they were rolling forward.

Caile let out a deep breath. With it, the last of his strength dissipated. He relaxed his right hand and felt the blood rush back into his fingers that were clenched around the mace handle. Everything had happened so fast it didn't seem real. He'd killed Lindy. And the guards in the corridor. He'd left Lorentz and his men trapped in the training yard. They were probably dead now, he realized, and the mere thought of them dead brought tears to his eyes. Before he could stop himself he was sobbing uncontrollably. *Stupid, stupid,* he told himself. *You're too old to be crying.* But he couldn't stop himself, and the noise of the steam engine drowned out the noise anyway.

17
Amongst the Clouds

Makarria sat huddled in the corner of the cramped cabin of the airship watching Taera. The princess lay silent and unmoving in the lower bunk bed along the back wall, as she had all night. She had not said a word or even made eye contact with Makarria. Makarria could not begin to understand what the princess was so upset about. *She's not the one who had to leave her grandfather behind on a burning ship.*

Apart from the two bunks, the only other pieces of furnishing in the cabin were a small round table and two stools that were secured to the floor. Makarria had been relegated to the corner where Siegbjorn had tossed her aside, but the uncomfortable quarters were all the better as far as she was concerned. There was no escaping now, and if Roanna was powerful enough to know about and even influence Taera's visions, then she would surely notice if Makarria began dreaming and accidentally used her power in her sleep. *Better not to sleep at all,* Makarria had surmised the night before when she regained consciousness and, indeed, she had done little more than doze off and on throughout the night, mindlessly twirling her hair and repeating over and over again in her mind the song her mother used to sing to her. *Close your eyes, fall fast asleep. Rest your head, without a dream. When you wake, you will see, A bright new day for you and me.* Whenever Makarria did doze off, the image of *Pyrthin's Flame* bathed in fire forced itself to the forefront of her mind, and she would wake again with the stinging memory that she had left her grandfather caught in those horrid flames. She refused to believe that he was dead though. *He heard me yell, I just know it,* she kept telling herself. *He's fine.*

It was morning now, and Roanna had left the cabin to check on Siegbjorn at the helm. Makarria considered getting up to talk to Taera, but she was afraid of speaking lest Roanna overheard them. Plus, Makarria didn't know that she had anything nice to say to Taera right now. Makarria knew it wasn't the princess's fault, but still Makarria had tried warning her back on the ship.

The door opened, letting a gust of cold air into the cabin and Roanna bustled back in, quickly closing the door behind her and rubbing her arms to ward off the chill.

"Are you awake and done pouting now, Princess?" Roanna asked.

Taera said nothing.

Roanna snorted and turned to Makarria. "How about you, whelp?"

"I'm awake."

"Well, keep quiet then and out of my way," Roanna said, sitting down at one of the stools. "And you, Princess, get up. It's time for the first of your lessons. We'll arrive at the caves tomorrow, and you must be prepared."

Taera pushed herself up slowly from her bunk. "Why did you have to burn the ship?" she asked.

"Because it was full of worthless peons," Roanna remarked, "and yet all it takes is one peon to see our airship and our guise is up. When the world finds out who you are, Princess, and what you are capable of, many people will be after you. Already the Emperor's agents sniffed out your presence. That is why your father tried to send you away. No, I think it's best that we keep your whereabouts hidden, and if that means killing a boat full of peons, so be it."

"One of those peons was my grandfather," Makarria said, unable to bite her tongue.

"And peons spawn more peons, so keep your mouth shut or I'll seal it shut for you," Roanna snapped.

"Leave her alone," Taera said. "She's just a girl. Why don't you go outside, Makarria. Get some fresh air."

"By all means," Roanna agreed. "Do us all a favor while you're out there and hurl yourself overboard properly this time."

Makarria said nothing but got up and went outside as she was told. The air outside was shockingly cold, and the strong headwind whipped her hair back over her shoulders. Goosebumps covered her arms, but she ignored the chill and peered over the portside rail. *Pyrthin's Flame* and Parmo were long gone behind them. All she could see was the ocean glimmering in the morning light hundreds of feet below them, and far off in the west she could see the first hints of landfall. Makarria felt like she should be afraid so high up in the air, but strangely she was not. It reminded her of a recurring dream she used to have where she was a bird gliding on the ocean squalls, just like the seagulls she saw every day and knew so well. It wasn't like her dreams where she changed things, just a fun dream she used to have when she was a little girl.

"If you mean to stand near the edge, I would ask of you to keep ahold of the rail," Siegbjorn said from the helm, no more than a few yards away.

Makarria had nearly forgotten about him, lost as she was in her own thoughts. She grabbed hold of the rail as Siegbjorn said and looked over the ship, now fully visible in the daylight as opposed to the night before when she'd climbed aboard. The entire front deck, from prow to cabin, was no longer than fifteen feet, and Makarria guessed the entire gondola was no more than thirty feet long.

"If a sudden crosswind were to come up," Siegbjorn said, "and trust me, I have been captain of the airship long enough and seen it many a time—the crosswind will send you flying right over the edge."

With the blustering wind, Siegbjorn's words blew past her in staccato, wavering bursts. He spoke, too, with a strange accent that made his words hard to understand.

"I know how to take care of myself on a ship," Makarria said after a moment.

Siegbjorn snorted. "If that is the truth, then I would ask you to make yourself useful and take up the slack in that line you see flapping around."

Makarria glanced at the loose line he indicated and saw it was merely an extra rope wound between two cleats on the deck. "It's just an extra line," she remarked.

"Extra line or no, it should not be loose," Siegbjorn said. "If you were to show me you could tie it off properly, I would be persuaded to let you help with the ballast lines and not throw you overboard. By 'accident,' of course, as Roanna has said it."

Makarria regarded him silently for a moment. She didn't know what to make of him—whether he was joking or serious about throwing her overboard. And she hadn't forgotten the fact that he'd hit her in the head and knocked her senseless. In either case, she knew he was testing her. *He thinks I can't do it because I'm a girl.* With a derisive snort, she tied the rope off and stepped back for him to look it over.

Siegbjorn nodded with approval and, to Makarria's disappointment, seemed unsurprised by her ability. "Grab then the first ballast line," he said, "the one you see connected to the furnace vent, and pull on it with your strength."

She did as he said, and a burst of flames shot upward into the hull above them. "We're going up," she observed.

"We are getting closer to land, and it is nearing day. We cannot risk being spied by those below, so up we go. Pull again."

Makarria gave the ballast line another yank and the ship lurched slowly upward again. "It's the heat, right? Heat always rises my grampy told me."

"Yes."

"But what's pushing us forward? I don't see any sails."

Siegbjorn locked the steering levers in place and took two long steps to come to a halt right in front of her. His dark hair was tied loosely in a knot at the back of his head, and his woolly beard concealed his mouth so she could not see his expression. Makarria bit her bottom lip, fearing she had angered the man with her questions, but after scrutinizing her for a few seconds with his bay-colored eyes, Siegbjorn merely unwrapped a strip of fur he wore around his neck and draped it over her shoulders. "I will show you, but first you must bundle up. You are of no use if you are frozen and shaking. Make sure to keep your arms free, and you will be safe for grabbing on to the rails."

Makarria gratefully wrapped the fur around her shoulders and chest, then followed after Siegbjorn who deftly guided his immense bulk along the narrow plank running down the starboard side of the ship. At the stern of the airship he pointed up to the tail end of the main hull above them where a propeller some ten feet long spun rapidly, driving the ship forward.

"It is powered by the same furnace that heats the air in the hull," he said over the whirring of the propeller.

"What does the furnace burn? I don't see any firewood."

Siegbjorn shook his head. "Wood is too heavy. This ship—it burns peat. Roanna and Kadar make it of metals and wood and magic, and I know not what else. It is light and yet burns long and very hot."

"And how do you steer?" Makarria asked, glancing over the stern of the ship below them. "I don't see a rudder."

"Rudders," Siegbjorn corrected. "There are four of them, but they are not below, they are above: two on either side to control our elevation and two on top to control our direction."

"But I thought the heat made us go up and down."

"It does, yes. Certainly when we are not moving forward, but for the most, the heat only makes us buoyant, like a log in water is made to float. The rudders guide us up and down as we cut through the air."

Makarria couldn't see the rudders from where they stood, but she pictured them in her mind and the concept made sense. Always being on a boat in water, she had only thought of rudders controlling their lateral direction—starboard or portside—but it made perfect sense that in the air a rudder could steer them up or down too. She was a bit peeved she hadn't thought of it herself, in fact.

A gust of wind rocked the ship and snapped Makarria from her reverie.

"We would be best to return to the helm," Siegbjorn said and turned to lead the way.

Back on the main deck, Siegbjorn put Makarria to work. The cold wind froze the watery snot running from her nose, but Siegbjorn gave her a swipe of bear fat from a jar to keep her lips from chapping and cracking. During their idle moments—which there were many of—Makarria did as Siegbjorn did and tucked her hands beneath her furs to keep them warm. She bombarded him with questions, and if he was annoyed by them he showed no outward sign. The only questions he refrained from answering were those regarding Roanna and where they were going. Makarria was content to learn about the airship though, and was plenty curious to fill the time with questions of sailing the skies.

The two of them snacked on dried elk meat periodically and sipped on a sweet honey wine from Siegbjorn's scuttlebutt. The meat was hard to chew and salty, but the wine washed it down and warded off the chill, and Makarria found both to be an exotic departure from the typical fare of fish she had been relegated to eating over the last few weeks. By mid-afternoon they had reached land, and they changed course slightly to skirt the coastline far below them. Makarria could make out little apart from the irregularly partitioned fields; the farmers she knew had to be down there tending to the fields were much too small to make out. Siegbjorn steered the airship in a northwesterly direction and as evening fell, the Barrier Mountains loomed large in their path like a jagged, impenetrable wall. The temperature dropped drastically with the setting of the sun, and Siegbjorn sent Makarria back into the cabin for the night.

"You have been a good first mate," he told her. "Get some rest and tomorrow you can help me land."

"But don't you sleep?" she asked, realizing she was exhausted and that he must be more weary than her considering he had not slept the night before.

"I will sleep when we arrive. I am like a bear: I hibernate when I can, work when I must."

Makarria smiled and turned to go back in but stopped and turned back to him. "Did Roanna really tell you to throw me overboard?"

Siegbjorn shrugged. "She suggested that she would not be angry if you were to fall overboard, but I say no men overboard on my ship."

"I'm glad to hear that," Makarria said. She liked Siegbjorn, she decided. He treated her just like her grandfather did when they were on the skiff fetching their traps. "Goodnight, Siegbjorn," Makarria said, then went inside where she found it to be significantly warmer.

Roanna looked none too pleased to see her. "You're still here?"

Makarria said nothing in reply and instead went and sat on the bunk beside Taera, who was slouched back against the wall, completely unaware Makarria was even there.

"Taera?"

"She's in a dream trance," Roanna said. "And failing miserably."

Makarria grabbed one of Taera's hands, and the princess blinked her eyes, slowly regaining awareness. She looked about for a moment, confused as to her whereabouts, then remembered where she was and realized Makarria was beside her.

"Your hands are freezing," Taera said, seemingly drunk. "You've been outside this whole time. You'll take ill. I completely forgot. I…I…"

"I'm fine," Makarria assured her. In fact, her hands and face were quite cold, but because of the honey wine she felt flushed and hot now that she was inside the comparatively warm cabin.

"No, you'll be sleeping with me in my bunk tonight. It's freezing in here, and we'll keep each other warm."

Makarria nodded. She was still a little angry with the princess, but the thought of sleeping on the bed instead of the floor was enticing. Besides, Taera looked to be more distraught than Makarria was. Her face was pale and drawn and she exhibited none of the confidence or excitement she displayed back on *Pyrthin's Flame*. Makarria felt a pang of guilt for blaming her for their predicament, but no harm had been done—she'd not voiced her anger.

"I suppose we're done with your training for the day, Princess," Roanna said.

Taera said nothing.

Makarria ached with curiosity to know what sort of training Roanna was giving Taera, but she didn't dare ask with Roanna there in the room. It would just have to wait along with everything else. *Don't think about Grampy, Mother, Taera, or anyone else,* Makarria told herself. *And whatever you do, don't dream.*

And so the three of them said little. They ate a meager dinner of dried bread and cheese, then laid down to sleep. Drunk as she was on honey wine and warm on the bunk alongside Taera, Makarria fell fast asleep, completely forgetting her worries that she might dream.

Makarria woke fresh with energy the next morning and went out onto the main deck to join Siegbjorn at first light. The sight before her nearly took her breath away. Towering above them to either side were jagged mountains, in some places covered with ice and snow, and in other places nothing but sheer faces of granite too steep for snow or ice to stick. Larger precipices loomed before them, and though the sky above the airship was clear, clouds hung on the highest of the mountain peaks. Siegbjorn had chosen a route through the lowest of the mountain passes from the Esterian Ocean, but even still, they were far higher up than they had been at any point prior. They were approaching the realm of Norgland, and this far north in the hemisphere the tree line was lower than it was in the southern reaches of the Barrier Mountains. Below them in the valley there was a deep forest of pines and firs, but the mountains themselves were barren and frozen: glimmering white ice and impenetrable gray rock.

"The air is thin and hard to breathe when this high in the mountains," Siegbjorn remarked, seeing that Makarria had joined him. "The winds can be dangerous, too. They come blowing from the mountaintops in many directions, but the weather is quiet and warm today. *Svell Módir* has smiled upon us."

Makarria shivered and wrapped her fur tighter around her neck and shoulders. "If this is warm for the mountains, I don't want to be here when it gets cold."

Siegbjorn smiled and his breath came out a white plume of steam. He gave Makarria a nip of his honey wine, then put her to work. They picked their route slowly between the mountains, sticking to the low valleys and passes between the peaks, sometimes dropping as low as the tree line, but more often than not high above it, and on occasion so high up over a saddle between two peeks that Makarria found herself becoming dizzy. Though the sun rode low in the sky to their port side, it reflected blindingly from the south faces of the mountains on their starboard side, and combined with the thin, cold air, it made Makarria's head ache. She stubbornly ignored the pain though, and stayed at Siegbjorn's side.

Noon passed and the sun raced away in front of them. "Winter is coming and the days have become short here in Norgland," Siegbjorn said. "It will be dark no more than six hours past noon."

"We won't be stuck in the mountains in the dark, will we?" Makarria asked, disconcerted. As stunning as the mountains were, she decided she liked the sea much better.

"No," Siegbjorn replied. "Indeed, we are almost there. Grab the fore-ballast line and give us more heat."

Makarria did as she was told, and Siegbjorn steered the ship up over one last saddle. At the apex of the ridge, a huge valley opened up before them, and sitting in the middle of the valley was a vast lake, glimmering like a sapphire jewel. Makarria breathed in sharply at its beauty. The mountains were not to her liking, but a lake in the mountains was another matter.

"Is that where we're going?"

"We travel not to the lake itself," Siegbjorn replied, "but to the caves you will find at the south end. Grab the aft ballast line and let us down slowly."

Again Makarria followed orders, and Siegbjorn steered the airship down in a wide spiraling path to a meadow nestled between the mountainside and the southern end of the lake. When they got low enough, Makarria saw there were men standing there in the meadow, dressed much like Siegbjorn. When they reached shouting distance, Siegbjorn gave out a cry in a language Makarria did not understand, and Siegbjorn's comrades greeted him in return.

"Drop our tether lines," Siegbjorn told Makarria.

Makarria tossed the lines to the men waiting below, and in a few brief minutes they were anchored safely on the ground. Siegbjorn poked his head into the cabin to tell Roanna they had arrived, then hopped overboard to greet his companions. They spoke in gruff tones in their foreign tongue but wore smiles on their faces.

The talking and smiling ceased the moment Roanna stepped foot out onto deck. She snapped for Siegbjorn to lower the gangplank, then led Taera off the airship and across the meadow without a word. Makarria shot Siegbjorn a glance, but he kept his eyes averted, and she was forced to scurry after Roanna and Taera on her own. They followed a well-worn path up an incline from the meadow some hundred yards to where an ice-filled crag cleaving the granite face of the mountain before them opened into a tunnel. The tunnel opening was smooth—clearly widened by human hands from the natural cleft—and large enough for five men to walk in abreast. In the opening stood a tall, slender man with dark skin and oily black hair slicked back over his head. He had a long, straight nose and pointed sideburns that made his face look bird-like, and draping back from his shoulders was a deep burgundy robe.

Roanna stopped and kicked Taera in the back of the legs to send her to her knees. Makarria quickly knelt down behind them as Roanna shot her a dark look.

"Bow down before Kadar," Roanna said. "He is your master now."

Kadar smiled, revealing a narrow mouth filled with jet-black teeth. "Many years I have been waiting for you, Princess. Welcome to your new home: the Caverns of Issborg. You have done well, Roanna, but who is the little one?"

"She is my servant," Taera said.

Roanna struck Taera across the face. "Silence! You will speak only when spoken to." Taera bit back tears, and Roanna turned apologetically to Kadar. "I am sorry, Master. I've had little time to prepare her. I will have the men kill the young one if you want. The Princess needn't have any distractions, so it is probably for the best."

Fear welled up inside Makarria, but Kadar paid her no attention. His attention was on Taera. "No," he finally said. "She is a princess— let her have a servant, her little friend. She will need it."

18
The Cavern of Ice

Sweat poured from Taera's forehead. She focused on the ball of energy she had envisioned in the core of her chest and tried to move it to her fingertips, but still nothing happened. No flames, no sparks, nothing.

"Stop," Roanna said, irritated. "You're trying too hard."

Taera relaxed her body with a sigh and opened her eyes wearily. She sat cross-legged on a wooden pallet facing Roanna in a small chamber deep inside the mountains. The chamber was small—no more than fifteen feet from one cold stone wall to the other—and dimly lit. Only a lantern in the corner behind Roanna provided any light; there were no windows, of course, only a metal-banded door of rough-hewn softwood planks. On a metal tray between Taera and Roanna was a small pile of pellets: the same peat pellets used to fuel the airship.

"All you need is the tiniest of sparks to start," Roanna explained again. "From there, you project it toward the peat and let that be the fuel for the flames. You are merely providing the trigger. If you keep trying to hurl your entire body energy through your fingertips, you're going to exhaust yourself, or worse, die."

Taera said nothing. She was already beyond exhausted and convinced she could do nothing Roanna asked of her. On the day they arrived at the caverns, Kadar had met with Taera privately—asking her questions, making her perform small tests of mind and body, and physically examining her in a way that made her skin crawl. When it had all been done, Kadar looked disappointed and sent her away without a word. For the three days since that meeting, Taera had been awoken early to work with Roanna on an assortment of exercises: everything from forced trances to trying to start flames at her fingertips, to predicting the future of an assortment of fur clad northmen Roanna paraded before her. Taera had failed at every task. Even her ability as a seer failed her. Still, Taera's biggest worry was keeping everyone's attention on her and away from Makarria. Taera had no idea what Roanna and Kadar were capable of, but she knew if they learned of Makarria's abilities—and what she were truly capable of—they would take her away and subject her to something worse than what Taera was going through.

"Watch me again," Roanna said. "And not just with your eyes. Open up the rest of your senses and feel what I'm doing."

Roanna held her arms out in front of her, palms up. "Sense how I force the heat of my body from my core to my fingers." Slowly, energy accumulated at her fingertips until light crackled from them like tiny sparks of static electricity. "And then the projection, the release." She lowered her hands slightly, and the pellets on the tray took flame. "It is quite simple."

Taera shook her head. "I'm sorry. I see the fire at your fingers and then the pellets burning, but I sense nothing else."

"We're done for the day then," Roanna said, lurching to her feet. "You may go back to your quarters." Roanna went to the door and held it open for Taera to leave.

Taera stood and moved sullenly from the chamber into the main cavern. The main cavern was vast, stretching for unknown miles at the base of the icy crag in the mountain they had seen from outside. Along one wall of the crag, a series of chambers were carved into the rock face, including the one Taera had just exited. Along the opposite wall of the crag was the very glacier which had cleft the mountain and created the crag. It was a curious glacier, a great slab of ice like a blade between the living rock, hanging down into the cavern with a series of dripping stalactites to feed an underground stream that flowed into the lake outside. Its most curious feature, however, was that the glacier stretched unimpeded from the cavern to the very surface of the mountainside, thereby providing a pathway for the daylight to illuminate the cavern. It was by no means bright, and the hue of the light was a dreary blue-gray, but it was still far better than a cavern illuminated only by sputtering torches, and it provided a gauge for the passing of time along with the rise and fall of the sun each day.

Taera had at first been awestruck by the cavern—it far surpassed the visions of it she had seen back in Kal Pyrthin—but now she gave it not a second glance. Rather, she shuffled her way deeper into the cavern to where one of the large northmen stood guard at the door to her private chamber. He opened it wordlessly for her, and she entered to see Makarria doing a handstand along the back wall of their sparsely furnished room.

"Keeping yourself entertained, I see," Taera remarked as she stepped inside, and the guard closed the door behind her.

"Taera! You're back. What happened? What did you do today?" Makarria rushed to Taera's side and hopped up and down like an excited child.

"Not now," Taera said, pushing her away and slumping down onto a wooden bunk. "I'm exhausted."

Makarria knelt in front of her and looked her over. "You are. You look horrible. Can I get you some water? Some food? Anything?"

Taera merely waved her away and said nothing. Already her eyes were closed, and she was drifting off to sleep. Makarria turned away with a huff. She knew she shouldn't be angry with Taera, but she couldn't help it. She had been cooped up in their chamber for three days straight with nothing to do but eat two meager meals a day and entertain herself. She had grown bored of doing handstands, cartwheels, and somersaults, but she'd found nothing better yet to pass the hours.

When a guard came a short time later bringing their supper, Makarria woke Taera and they ate in silence for as long as Makarria could bear.

"I know you're tired, but could you maybe tell me what it is they're teaching you?" Makarria asked.

"Nothing I can do," Taera said with a shake of her head.

"Is Roanna getting cross with you? Maybe I can help."

"No!" Taera snapped. "You are to do nothing of the sort."

Makarria felt tears welling up in her eyes and stood quickly to hide it from Taera.

"Makarria, no, I'm sorry," Taera said with another sigh. "It's just, I don't want you to get hurt. If they find out…" She left the rest of her thought unsaid out of fear that Roanna or Kadar might somehow be able to overhear what she said.

"But it's so horrible in here," Makarria said, unable to hold the tears back any longer. "At least you get to leave our room everyday. What am I supposed to do?"

Taera stood and hugged Makarria. "I don't know. I'm sorry. There's nothing for it. I know we are meant to be here, but I don't know what we're supposed to do. My visions have left me. I've seen nothing since we arrived here. We are just going to have to bide our time and see what happens. Roanna and Kadar are unkind, but I don't think they mean us harm. We just have to wait."

"Can't you take me with you in the morning, at least?" Makarria pleaded. "I promise just to watch."

"Roanna won't stand for it. I'm sorry, Makarria."

More tears came. Makarria felt foolish. *Quit being a baby,* she told herself. *You've had your moonblood—you're a grown woman now,* but the tears would not stop.

In the morning, Taera left again, and again Makarria was left to her own devices. She resolved to make use of her time by exercising to keep her agility and balance sharp. *I might be back on that airship any day now, or Grampy might come to rescue me.* She didn't really believe either scenario would happen, but it gave some purpose to her day. She walked the perimeter framework of her bunk with her eyes closed; she spun herself in circles until she was dizzy and then hopped on one foot and tried staying upright; she tried to climb the walls, but found the stonework too smooth to provide adequate hand holds. All in all, it kept her busy for a few hours, and then she plopped to the ground bored and dejected. She considered practicing her letters as her grandfather had taught her, but there was nothing to write with. There was literally nothing for her to do.

Just when she thought she could take it no more and would scream, the door to her chamber suddenly opened and in walked Siegbjorn. "Come with me," he said gruffly.

Makarria wanted to scream with joy, but his tone of voice silenced her. *Am I in trouble?* she wondered. She silently followed after him past the guard and into the main cavern. She had no idea where he was taking her, but she didn't care, she decided. Anything was better than being trapped in her room. Siegbjorn's heavy footfalls echoed in the cavern around them, and apart from the incessant dripping of water from the glacier, there was no other sound in the vast emptiness. He led her past the chamber where Taera was locked inside with Roanna, and past numerous other chambers— some with closed doors, some open—until they finally reached the opening to the meadow outside. They passed no one the entire way.

A thin blanketing of snow covered the ground outside, and the sky was gray, but still Makarria had to shield her eyes against the brightness after being in the dim cavern for so long. She glanced back toward the cavern opening to make sure they were alone before she finally spoke.

"Siegbjorn, where are we going?"

"To check on the airship, of course. I cannot be expected to do an inspection without my first mate."

Makarria let out a squeal of excitement and jumped forward to embrace him around the waist. The big man stopped awkwardly, but smiled nonetheless, and patted her shoulder roughly.

"Where have you been the last three days?" she demanded of him as they continued on into the meadow toward the airship.

"Sleeping."

"For three days?"

"I told you, I am like a bear. I would not have slept so long if I knew you were to be locked up, but I was tired and it did not occur to my mind that Roanna would leave you under lock and key."

Makarria cringed at hearing Roanna's name. "Will she be angry that you've freed me? You won't be in trouble, will you?"

Siegbjorn snorted. "She has probably already forgotten you exist. And I do not mean to free you. I am merely putting you to work, and when night comes it is back to your chamber with you. Yes?"

"Aye, Captain," Makarria said smartly, and Siegbjorn grinned from beneath his big beard again.

They found the airship still tethered where they had landed. Siegbjorn put Makarria to work checking all the lines on the gondola for frays while he examined the furnace and the controls at the helm. When they were done with that, Siegbjorn then had her climb the thickly braided ropes that attached the gondola to the main hull floating in the air above them. The main hull had an internal skeleton, but the shell itself was made of a thick, black, canvas-like material that squished beneath Makarria's hands and feet. It supported her weight well enough but was not easy to traverse. She climbed to the very top to check the two vertical rudders, then to either side to check the horizontal rudders, while Siegbjorn exercised the rudder controls.

When Siegbjorn was satisfied that all was in working order, he had her hoist up a giant canvas tarpaulin. It was easily larger than even the mainsail of *Pyrthin's Flame*, and Makarria marveled at the time and effort that must have gone into making it. She had spent hours mending the sail of her grandfather's skiff back home, and she couldn't begin to imagine how long it must have taken to sew each section of the tarpaulin together. For that matter, the egg-shaped main hull must have been even more work, she realized. *It must be nearly airtight to hold in all that hot air,* she mused.

"Makarria!" Siegbjorn shouted up at her. "What is the delay?"

"Sorry," she yelled down at him and scurried back across the length of the hull, dragging the tarpaulin behind her. Once she had the tarpaulin draped over the entirety of the hull, she lowered herself to the ground, and the two of them staked down each of the two dozen ties to keep the tarp from blowing away.

"The tarpaulin will keep the snow and ice from stacking on the hull of the ship and freezing up our lines," Siegbjorn told her. "As it is, winter is coming and it will be hard enough to unbury her from the snow if we must needs fly anywhere."

"What next, then?" Makarria asked, cold, but excited to do more.

"Back into the caverns. I will show you where the peat is prepared for the furnace."

Siegbjorn led the way back inside, and they passed the same series of chambers, now on their left. The cavern narrowed beyond that and began rising in elevation as it followed the lower edge of the slab-like glacier. At points, the underground stream beneath the glacier came to the surface in a peacefully bubbling brook. The sound comforted Makarria but reminded her also how much she missed the sound of the surf and her home. She wondered what her parents were doing at that moment, but the thought pained her, so she quickly turned her mind to other thoughts, lest she start crying again.

"Did Roanna make this cave?" she asked.

Siegbjorn snorted. "This cavern has been here long before Roanna was ever born, long before men even walked the world, I think. The ice above us—it carved this cavern many ages ago. Indeed, it continues to carve it as the ages pass."

"But it didn't carve out all those rooms," Makarria pointed out.

"No, my people, the *Snjaer Firan* as we once called ourselves, discovered this cavern many hundreds of years ago. Before even Norg, Sargoth, and the other sorcerers came to conquer this land. My ancestors wintered in the cavern, then in the spring and summer would venture out for months at a time into the valley outside where they would fish, hunt, and gather all that they needed for the coming winter. When the Five Sorcerers came, the *Snjaer Firan* in name fell under dominion of Norgland, but even Norg himself never ventured so high into these mountains more than once or twice in his lifetime. We went on living much as we had in the years before, that is until Trumball came."

"I've heard that name before," Makarria said, trying to remember what she knew of him. "My grampy must have told me a story about him, but I can't remember much."

"He was the son of our chieftain and had strange powers, much like those of Roanna and Kadar I imagine, but to greater ability and better purpose. When he was still young, he left our cavern and explored far beyond the Five Kingdoms to the Old World, learning what he was able. He returned many years later a wise and powerful man and became the mightiest of our chieftains. In his travels he had learned well the workings of Tel Mathir, whom we call *Svell Módir*, and he taught our people much. They extended the cavern through the core of the mountain to make an entrance on the south face, so we were no longer cut off from the outside world, and they built the fair city you are about to witness. After that, the Dreamwielder War began, and of the Dark Queen and her son Guderian we do not speak. Let it be enough to say that when Trumball was murdered we destroyed the southern entrance of the cavern and again kept to our own ways. So things remained until Kadar came unbidden seven years ago."

"He's not one of you, is he?" Makarria asked. "I mean, he's not *Snjaer Firan*."

"He is certainly not. Nor is Roanna, though she is at least of the Five Kingdoms."

"Where is Kadar from then? And what's wrong with his teeth?"

"Of his teeth I cannot say, but he travels here from Khail Sanctu in the Old World."

"You don't like either of them, do you?" Makarria ventured.

"Whether I like them or not is unimportant and best left unspoken. You have asked enough questions for now. Be content to know that Roanna and Kadar prefer to stay in the chambers of old, near the valley entrance, and let us abide in our city so long as we provide for them and do their bidding."

They had been continually climbing upward, and Siegbjorn

stopped now at the crest of the incline where the cavern opened into a vast chamber that took Makarria's breath away: the glacier itself comprised the western wall to their right and stretched upward hundreds of feet to disappear again into the dark ceiling; running alongside the ice wall was a narrow lake, spanning the entire length of the chamber, nearly a half-mile long; and on the upward sloping rock bed above the lake was a city. Many of the buildings were freestanding, made of quarried granite blocks into rectangular one- and two-story structures, but the vast majority of the city was literally carved into the granite wall that comprised the eastern edge of the chamber, and hundreds of stairwells and windows in the rock face glowed cheerfully with lamplight.

"Welcome to Issborg," Siegbjorn said and led the speechless Makarria forward.

19
The Shrouded Path

Caile had slept fitfully throughout what remained of the night and well into the morning hours as the steam-powered turnip cart carried him along the eastern road away from Col Sargoth. The mysterious sorceress driving the cart did not slow or stop until the sun had nearly reached its apex, at which point she steered the cart off the main road down a muddy tract leading to an abandoned farm. There she parked the cart in a dilapidated barn, roused Caile, and ushered him into a single-axle wagon. Caile rubbed the weariness from his eyes as she hitched a sway-backed plow horse to the cart, and then they were off onto the main road heading east again. Caile started to speak on several occasions, but the cart clacked loudly on the rutted road, and if the woman heard his half mumbled questions, she ignored them.

When the sun set over the horizon at their backs, the woman steered the cart from the road into a copse of trees and finally called a halt. After so many hours of not speaking, Caile found himself nearly mute, unsure where to start or what to ask the woman who had rescued him. The fact that he had abandoned his men in Lightbringer's Keep weighed heavily on his heart, and he realized with consternation that he had forgotten his mace back in the turnip cart earlier that afternoon. Again, he was armed only with his boot knife. He knew the sorceress had rescued him twice now and seemingly had good intentions, but that didn't mean Caile should trust her. *Roanna and her men were pleasant enough, too, until they got the information they wanted from me.*

Caile helped the woman unbridle the horse and make camp, and neither of them said a word. Not until after she had a fire going and they were both nibbling on crumbly flat bread beside it did he finally speak.

"Why did we abandon your steam cart?" he asked between bites. "It's faster than your crippled horse, I imagine."

The woman answered without looking up from the fire. "Because the Emperor's men will be looking for a steam cart full of turnips when the guards tell him they let it pass freely through the eastern gate. Besides we were nearly out of fuel. The steam cart is fast, but it has a limited range."

"How far are we from Col Sargoth?"

"Nearly a hundred and fifty miles since last night."

Caile raised his eyebrows, impressed. "Not even the Emperor's fastest horsemen could catch us at that pace."

"No," the woman agreed, "but Wulfram could."

Caile digested her words silently. "Who are you?" he asked finally.

"My name is Talitha. I am a sorceress."

"But you're not part of the guild?"

"No. I am in league only with myself and hopefully with you now."

"You know who I am then, I take it?"

She nodded at him and narrowed her eyes. "I'm quite aware of who you are and the foolishness you've been up to, Prince Caile Delios."

Caile felt his face heat with embarrassment, but he bit back the rash words on his tongue. "How is it that you know so much? How were you able to find me?"

"I'm merely observant, Prince. There is much to see when you know what to look for."

"Well, I appreciate what you've done for me," Caile said, annoyed by her cryptic words, "but I must leave you and head south."

"You can make that decision when we reach Arnsfeld, unless you mean to forge your way through the thick of Forrest Weorcan."

"We are on the eastern high road, then?" he asked.

"Yes. Your path is decided for you for the time being, I'm afraid. Behind you is Col Sargoth, to the north is the Sargothian River, and to the south the Forrest Weorcan. The only way to go is forward."

Caile said nothing, and so their conversation ended for the evening. He was impatient to get back to Kal Pyrthin and help his father, but he knew Talitha was right. There was nothing to do but keep heading east for now. In the morning, they broke camp hastily and were on the road before the sun crested before them. Caile insisted on taking the reigns at intervals throughout the day to give Talitha a rest, but they said little and their actions were short and purposeful—they steered the cart ever eastward, stopped for water and food breaks only when the horse needed it, and made camp for the night when the sky darkened, nothing more. For four days straight they did this, and then on the evening of the fifth day out from Col Sargoth the road drew within sight of the Sargothian River and they reached the farms bordering Arnsfeld.

"There is an inn I know of on the far side of the city," Talitha said. "We will stop there for the night, and you can decide then which way you will go in the morning."

Caile nodded silently and they continued on. Arnsfeld was unremarkable after having been in Col Sargoth, and Caile paid little attention to the layout of the city and the people inhabiting it. It was not unlike the cities in Valaróz or Pyrthinia, except that even the largest buildings were predominantly made of wood rather than stone. The roads were laid out in the same grid-like pattern, and the people moved about with the same busyness as people in any city. There were no steam-powered carts, no smelting factories, no tar paved streets, and no gas lit street lamps. In fact the city was rather small, and they passed through it unimpeded and soon found themselves at the The Lonely Pine, the inn Talitha had spoken of.

The stablehands at The Lonely Pine promptly took their horse and cart, and after a few brief words with the innkeeper, Talitha acquired a private room and a warm supper to be brought up for the two of them. Before retiring to the room, however, she insisted that Caile visit the bathhouse at the back of the inn.

"You reek of turnips and feces," she remarked.

"Hardly surprising considering I've crawled through the sewers and been buried in turnips," Caile said with a shrug, but he did not protest. In fact, the thought of a bath sounded almost better than a meal and strong ale did to him at that moment.

The bathhouse was hardly elegant—the water in the wooden tub was lukewarm and far from clean—but Caile emerged feeling like a new man. The innkeeper's wife took his feculent clothes to wash, promising to deliver them to his room dry and clean in the morning, and in the meantime she gave him a spare set of baggy britches and a ridiculously large tunic to wear for the night. The tunic hung nearly to his knees and looked like a dress on him. "Some fat man forgot 'em behind several months back," the woman said. "Not pretty, but they'll keep you from having to run around bare skinned."

When Caile was finished in the bathhouse and finally retired to their room, he found Talitha waiting and their food already delivered. They ate the barley and lamb porridge ravenously, and when the two of them were done, Talitha for the first time looked Caile in the eye and regarded him from where they sat facing each other across the small end table between their two beds.

"Well, Prince Caile, you are not the pampered boy I expected you to be," she said. "You work hard and do not complain."

Caile shrugged and pulled the loose tunic tighter around his shoulders. "I don't see what I have to complain about. My men I left behind to die in Col Sargoth, and my father waits execution. They are the ones who have reason to complain."

Talitha smiled, though with little joy. "You mean to make for Kal Pyrthin then and save your father? Or try at least?"

"What else am I to do?"

"Did it ever occur to you that I might have rescued you for a reason?"

Caile shrugged. "I suppose. What reason?"

Talitha sighed and closed her eyes. "I know you think you've already made up your mind, that you have no choice but to head for Kal Pyrthin, but that is not the case. You sit at a fork in the road and you can choose one of many directions. In one direction, yes, you can make haste southward and try to save your father, but that is not the only path before you."

"You see a better path, I take it?" Caile asked.

"Yes, you could continue with me."

"And what is there for me along your path?"

Talitha leaned her head back in deep concentration. "Your sister, and perhaps much more."

"Taera? Where?" Caile edged forward on his bed, a brief glimmer of hope in his heart for the first time in days.

"I see the caverns of ice from my childhood, and my instincts tell me I must return and that I will need your help if I am to succeed."

Caile narrowed his eyes. "Who are you, really? And why do you insist on speaking in riddles?"

Talitha opened her eyes and smiled. "I am who I said I am, and I am sorry if I speak in riddles. I have great strength in many areas but seeing the future is not one of them. All I can see are images shrouded in fog and doubt. It is left to me to interpret their meaning. But this I am sure about, for I have seen it clearer than any other image in my life. Your sister is captive in the Caverns of Issborg, or will be soon, I am certain."

"And what does she mean to you?"

"Everything," Talitha said, "for her fate is tied to mine. Few things are clear to me, but your sister is—or protects—the key to defeating Guderian. That I am certain."

Caile nodded. "Roanna spoke of a prophecy. She said my sister was foretold to defeat the Emperor. Is it true?"

"Whether your sister is the one, I cannot say. But Roanna is there in the caverns with your sister, and the prophecy she spoke of is no lie. It was foretold by the mightiest seer in Khail Sanctu on Thedric Guderian's tenth birthday."

Caile leaned back onto the straw mattress of his bed and rubbed one hand over his face. He had been so certain of himself when he'd left his sister and father in Kal Pyrthin, but now he was certain of nothing. He had thought Stephen and Roanna allies at first, but they had tried to kill him. *How do I know I can trust her?* he asked himself of Talitha.

"I cannot give you any better token of trust than to beg you for your help," Talitha said.

"You read my thoughts," Caile accused, but Talitha shook her head.

"I do not need to read your thoughts, Prince Caile. Your concern is written plainly on your face, and it is not unfounded. There are few you can trust, but I will tell you in all sincerity that I am one who you can trust. I am an enemy of the Emperor. I am a worshiper of Tel Mathir, and I dream of a day when the Sargothian Empire is gone and once again the Five Kingdoms are intact. I dream of a day when those with the capacity to wield magic are not feared and hunted."

Caile was silent for a long moment as he weighed his thoughts. "I think you are being honest with me, so I will be honest with you. My heart tells me to follow you and help my sister, for I have little love for my father. But still, loyalty drives me to Kal Pyrthin. Casstian is my king and sire. What sort of prince would I be if I let the Emperor kill him without a fight?"

"What if I were to tell you that you could not help your father?" Talitha asked. "What if I told you help was already on the way?"

Parmo woke with a start. "What? What is it?"

Rufous was standing over him shaking his shoulders, and at the bow of the small skiff Gaetan, the other man Parmo had rescued, stood waiving his arms frantically.

"A ship has spotted us," Rufous said. "We're saved."

Parmo pushed himself up from where he lay curled up in the stern of the skiff and looked in the direction his two shipmates were pointing. There was indeed a ship heading right toward them, rising over the ten-foot swells with ease. It flew no colors at its mast and appeared to be a merchant ship. *Probably for the best,* Parmo surmised.

They had spotted land earlier that morning and while Parmo guessed it was the shores of Pyrthinia they saw, he could not be certain, and it was safer to be picked up by a merchant ship than one from the Valarion navy.

It had been six days since *Pyrthin's Flame* had burned and sunk into the Esterian Ocean. Parmo and the two sailors he saved had set a course due west, but they had with them only a makeshift sail and none of Parmo's navigation equipment, so they were relegated to navigating by the sun and stars, which was sufficient for the first two days, but then the winds came and the formless gray clouds blotted out the sky above. To make matters worse, they had been rammed on the third night by a whale or a shark—it had been too dark for them to be sure—and the tiller was ruined beyond all repair. That left them with nothing to do but steer with their oars, no easy task with the strong south-blowing wind filling their sail. It was wearying, imprecise work, and they took turns at using an oar as a rudder and slept when their shift was through. All they were certain of was that they were exhausted and bearing in a somewhat westerly direction, and so they had no idea from where this new ship was approaching them or where it was going.

The ship lowered her sails as she approached, and after a few exchanged shouts back and forth, Parmo informed them they were indeed stranded. The sailors on the larger ship threw down tethering lines, and after securing the skiff in tow Parmo, Rufous, and Gaetan climbed up to the main deck of the larger ship.

"Thank you," Parmo said to the sailor who helped him over the rail. "Where are you bound for?"

"Kal Pyrthin," the man replied, but before Parmo could pry further, the captain of the ship pushed his way forward.

"I'll be the one asking questions," the captain said. "Where are you from and where are *you* bound?"

Parmo looked the men over silently for a moment before responding. By their accents and the look of them, he was confident they were Pyrthinian, not Valarion. Valarions were of darker complexion and tended to roll their r's slightly.

"We are the only survivors of *Pyrthin's Flame*," Parmo said finally. "She went down six nights ago, sabotaged by pirates and put to flame."

The captain eyed Parmo, unconvinced. "*Pyrthin's Flame* is the King's flagship, and I'll be a porpoise's teat if you're a Pyrthin naval man. You're a Valarion if I've ever seen one."

"You're quite right," Parmo conceded. "I was but a passenger on the ship, but these men are Pyrthin naval men and can vouch to the truth of my statement."

"Aye," Gaetan said. "Able Seaman, Gaetan Sodonia at your service."

"Third Mate, Rufous Delphinos," Rufous followed. "It is as he says. Someone killed the night crew, barricaded the main hold, and set the ship aflame. It was Parmo here who saved the two us and cut loose the skiff before *Pyrthin's Flame* went down."

"I tried to save the captain first, but the captain's quarters were the first to go up in flames," Parmo explained, somewhat by apology.

"This is disturbing news," the captain said. "Did you see your attackers?"

"They were already fled by time we were awoken," Rufous said. "All we saw was the shadow of a... a ship of some sort."

"You seem uncertain," the captain probed.

"It was night, and we were all half-choked and blind with smoke," Parmo explained, not wanting to reveal too much. "We saw the silhouette of something retreating to the west. That is all we can say for certain."

"*Something*, eh? Perhaps it was the same flying ship people say passed over Kal Pyrthin almost a fortnight ago?" the captain probed.

Rufous shot Parmo a glance but said nothing.

"It was certainly strange, whatever it was," Parmo answered. "Captain, if I may, I suggest we set off for Kal Pyrthin with all due haste. The King needs to know what happened immediately. There was valuable cargo on that ship."

"I'm afraid we have more strange news for you, friends," the captain said. "We have been told that King Casstian has been dethroned. For high treason the Emperor's dogs are saying. Word has spread to Tyrna even, where we are bound from. The entire Kingdom is in disarray."

"This is dire news," Parmo replied. "What do we do now?"

20
The Face of Terror

Natarios Rhodas stood silently in the courtyard of Castle Pyrthin watching Wulfram inspect the crowd of women who had been brought up from the dungeons. Since putting out a bounty on sorceresses several weeks prior, mercenaries, cut purses, and all sorts of unsavory characters had been dragging in women in droves. Natarios had kept them locked up in his own scent-hound tower at first, but once King Casstian had been taken captive, he moved them to the dungeon beneath the castle in order to accommodate the sheer number of them. There were forty-seven of them according to his records. Most were harmless, he was sure: old spinsters who gossiped too much, homeless orphan girls, street trollops, and other such guttersnipe. They were a bedraggled and pathetic lot, but Natarios's orders had been clear; he was to pay the bounties on all of them and let Wulfram sort them out.

They all stood now huddled together in the center of the courtyard, wrists tied behind their backs. Wulfram stalked amongst them, giving most of them no more than a glance. A few he examined carefully, touching their temples with his taloned fingers or sniffing their heads. Some of the younger women were no more than children, and they balled in fear when Wulfram regarded them. Around the perimeter of the courtyard, twenty Pyrthinian archers stood at the ready should any of the women actually turn out to have power of any sort. Their captain stood rigidly at Natarios's side.

A minor commotion at the main gate distracted Natarios from Wulfram's inspection, and he turned to see one of his henchmen hurrying his way across the courtyard.

"A raven came from Col Sargoth," the man said between heavy breaths, thrusting a scroll into Natarios's hands.

Natarios started to break the wax seal but saw that the scroll was addressed to Wulfram and thought better of it. He instead dismissed the man back to his tower and tucked the message into his robes to await Wulfram. *I can't say that I miss that dank tower,* Natarios thought to himself as he watched his courier scurry off. He had assigned the three most trustworthy of his men to stay in the tower and attend to the scent-hound and for himself had appropriated King Casstian's private quarters. It certainly made it easier for him to attend to daily matters concerning the governing of the city and kingdom in Casstian's stead, and the comforts were the least he could ask for in reward as far as he was concerned. Wulfram, for his part, stayed in Casstian's study high up in the tower. *Probably so he can fly off in the night to prowl around,* Natarios mused.

After what seemed an interminably long time to Natarios, Wulfram finally walked from the throng of woman to join Natarios.

"Find who you are looking for?" Natarios asked.

"No. There are a few women of minor ability among them, but they are of little concern to us."

"Shall I order their release, My Lord?" the captain of the archers asked, keeping his eyes averted toward Wulfram's feet.

"No," Wulfram said without hesitation. "Have your men kill them all."

The captain's mouth opened in protest, but the words choked back in his throat.

An emanation of danger prickled across Natarios's skin. He was no fool. He knew the captain and his men held no loyalty to Wulfram or the Emperor. They obeyed out of fear alone. "Master," he said in a neutral tone, "there are children amongst the captives. Surely they pose no danger to us? Let us take them back to the dungeons, and then I'm sure the captain will have no reason to object to your commands. Isn't that right, Captain?"

"No," Wulfram growled before the captain could respond. "I

said kill them all."

Wulfram's voice carried throughout the courtyard, and the archers and the captive women both heard his words. A handful of sobs and cries for help sprung from the crowd of women, and the archers shuffled uncomfortably as their eyes darted from one another to their captain to the panicked women. Already sweat had formed on the captain's brow, and he began to shake his head.

"I can't, I can't."

"Have your men take aim and shoot," Wulfram commanded.

"No," the commander replied, stealing what courage he had left and standing straight.

"Have it your way then," Wulfram said and he turned to face the women. His hand gesture was subtle, and few at first noticed the flames, but within seconds the fire spread from the feet of the captive women to climb up their skirts. The women screamed, at first only startled, but their yells quickly turned to cries of pain as the flames enveloped them. A few of the women at the edge of the fray tried to bolt, but they managed to make it no more than a few steps before tripping to writhe, burning on the ground.

"No!" the captain yelled, unable to stand it any longer. He rushed forward to aid the women in whatever way he could, but before he could take two steps, Wulfram swiped at him with wolf-like quickness and he fell dead, his throat rent open with four mortal gashes.

The cacophony of screaming was near deafening now, and smoke billowed up from the burning women. Around the courtyard, the archers turned away in shock. Some of them vomited at the smell of smoke and cooking flesh.

"Let this be a lesson to all of you," Wulfram bellowed over the mayhem. "If you wish to show mercy to others then you will obey my orders without question."

Natarios kept his eyes steadily on the scene of fiery horror before him, but he turned his mind to other thoughts to distract himself. It was a skill he had taught himself long ago to cope with the unsettling acts he was forced to watch. And sometimes perpetrate.

The screams one by one ended, and the women quit struggling as they slowly succumbed to their painful deaths. One girl only, no more than twelve or thirteen years old, continued to struggle after all the others. She had thrown herself to the ground and tried rolling, but the flames were unrelenting, and eventually she too came to a stop as her long blond hair burned away to nothing, and all but her bones were consumed by the flames.

"You have a message for me, I believe," Wulfram said suddenly.

"What?" Natarios asked, realizing Wulfram was addressing him.

"The message from Col Sargoth."

"Of course," Natarios replied, scrambling to reach into his pockets and turn over the scroll. He had completely forgotten about it already.

Wulfram tore open the message and read it, then crumpled it and tossed it aside as it burst into flames. "I must return to Col Sargoth at once," he said, striding away toward the main keep. "The prince has escaped."

"But wait," Natarios said, rushing after him. "What am I to do with the King?"

"Keep him locked up," Wulfram said. "I will return before long."

High in one of the five towers of Lightbringer's Keep, Lorentz retched on his own blood. His neck muscles strained to tilt his head forward, but like the rest of his limbs, it was lashed to the crossbeams of the rack, and he was forced to remain upright and let the blood and bile run over his chin and down his neck.

"Where has he gone?" the Emperor whispered again, leaning in close to Lorentz's ear. "Tell me."

"I told you already. He means to rescue his father."

"And I've told you, he's not passed along the south road. You think I would not expect him to flee for Kal Pyrthin? He has not gone that way. He is in league with sorcerers, I know. Tell me. Where are they? In Norgland? Golier? Valaróz?"

"I don't know," Lorentz said.

The Emperor picked up his tongs again. "Don't make me pull out more teeth, my dear man. This will all be much easier on you when you tell me everything."

Lorentz groaned but said nothing, and the Emperor reached toward him again.

21
Lore From the Past

Taera sat bolt upright in her bed and screamed. Across the stone chamber, Makarria jumped up in her own bed, startled by the sudden outburst.

"What's wrong?" Makarria asked when she gathered her wits and remembered where she was. The wick on their lantern had burned low in the night and all Makarria could make out was Taera's wide eyes and pale face from across the room. The bed, covers, and walls all were lost in the shadows. Makarria feared that someone or something had snuck into their room. "What is it, Taera?"

"I saw Lorentz. He was in pain. And dozens of women and girls screaming. They were dying, Makarria. They could have been us."

Makarria let out a small sigh of relief, realizing the danger wasn't imminent. She threw her covers aside and toed her way across the cold floor to sit beside Taera. "It's alright, you just had one of your visions."

Taera could only nod. She hadn't experienced a vision in days, and these new visions were not the manner in which she had hoped to rediscover her power. "I'm scared, Makarria," she said, and she realized she was crying.

"I know," Makarria said, hugging her. "Don't worry, I'll help you."

• • •

The next morning in her training chamber, Taera said nothing of her visions to Roanna, but the sorceress too seemed perturbed. "You had a vision, yes?" she asked Taera.

"Yes."

Roanna pursed her lips grimly. "I do not have the clarity of vision you do as a seer, Taera, but images still come to me on occasion. Last night... their faces were not clear to me, but I saw many women—some of them girls still—in great pain. And I saw enough of their killer to know it was *him*."

"Him? Who?"

"Who else? Wulfram." Roanna drew in closer to Taera, and spoke in almost a whisper. "Always, women with power have been feared. Even Vala, I imagine, was feared and hated by Sargoth, Pyrthin, Norg, and Golier when they came across the Spine to create the Five Kingdoms. In their greed and lust for dominion, men have always gone to great lengths to subjugate women. But at no time in the history of the Five Kingdoms or the Old World have we sorceresses been so hated as we are now, Taera. Do you know why?"

"No."

"Because of the prophecy. When Thedric Guderian was still a boy, he was exiled in the Old World and a mighty seer came upon him. This seer foretold that a sorcerer with great power and the blood of one of the Five Monarchs would be the downfall of Guderian. Guderian and Wulfram have known this from the start, and for decades now they have toiled to root out all magic. People already feared sorcerers from the time of the Dreamwielder War, but Guderian and Wulfram declared a secret war on those with power, especially women. It was Wulfram himself who skulked into the villages and cities of the Five Kingdoms and performed the atrocities the Emperor then blamed on the sorcerer guilds. And when the last of the guilds were destroyed, and the great sorcerers killed—including Trumball, whose cave we now inhabit—Guderian and Wulfram continued to wage their war, particularly against women with power. And women of royal blood of course. King Larimore sacrificed his own daughter, who had some minor ability as a beastcharmer so as to appease the Emperor. She was only five.

"Certainly, plenty of male firewielders and beast charmers and stormwielders have been killed during the Emperor's reign, but always the focus has been on finding women with the power to wield magic. Why is this the case, I have always wondered. Is it merely because men fear women, or is it something more?"

Taera looked on at Roanna intently. "I don't know."

"Nor do I for certain," Roanna continued. "But I have my suspicions. Kadar does not share my belief, but could it be that there was more to the prophecy than we've heard? Possibly the mighty seer in Khail Sanctu foretold it would be a particular sort of sorcerer who would kill Guderian. Did you know, Taera, that it is dreamwielders who have always been the mightiest of sorcerers? Not firewielders or stormbringers. Dreamwielders. Of all the sorcerers, only dreamwielders use their power to create something rather than destroy it. And like with childbirth, only women are able to become dreamwielders. You did not know that, did you?"

Taera could only shake her head.

Roanna closed her eyes and breathed in deeply. "Now you know why you are so important," she said gravely. "Now you know why your work here is so important and why I must be stern with you. You are the one, Taera. We must delve into your powers and unleash your ability to wield dreams."

Caile and Talitha rode at a trot on the road heading northeast to Ulmstadt. Earlier that morning, Talitha had bartered her wagon and swaybacked horse in the Arnsfeld marketplace for the two horses which they now rode. They were shaggy horses typical of the northern realms and barely worthy of being pack animals in Caile's estimation, but they were nonetheless better suited to the impending cold weather and frozen terrain than Talitha's wagon would have been. Caile, too, had done some bartering in Arnsfeld, exchanging his boot knife for a dinged up arming sword, a careworn bow, and a half dozen arrows. His knife was easily worth five times as much as all the other weapons combined, but Caile could hardly explain to the merchant that the knife had been forged by Pyrthinia's royal armorer without arousing suspicion. As it was, he had no choice but to be content with the weapons and horses both. Talitha had been quick to remind him before leaving the inn that he was an outlaw now.

The Barrier Mountains rose ahead of them in the distance and to the left of the road, beyond the Sargothian River, was the great evergreen forest of Norgland. Talitha surmised they had five days of travel to reach Ulmstadt, and there the high road ended and they would seek the long abandoned forest tract leading into the mountains and the caverns of Issborg.

A few hours before noon, Talitha reigned her horse in and dismounted. "We've been pushing the horses hard enough for a while," she said. "We'll walk for a bit, then stop for a brief rest."

Caile dismounted and led his horse forward to walk beside her. "Do you think we're being followed?" he asked, stealing a glance behind them.

"It's not likely. The Emperor has no reason to suspect you would go this way, and he does not even know of my existence. Or so I hope."

"What about Wulfram?"

"He is probably the mightiest sorcerer to walk the earth, but he has no ability as a seer. The both of them will think you are making for Kal Pyrthin as you yourself had intended. And once we reach the caves we seek, we will be shielded against detection from the scent-hounds even should I be forced to use my power. No, I don't think they will find us. We have more pressing foes to worry about for the time being."

They walked in silence for a while as Caile silently weighed her words. "That sorceress you fought," he said after a time, "she told me there used to be guilds of sorcerers, but that the Emperor destroyed them. Is that true?"

"Yes."

"I don't understand, then. If we have a common enemy, why aren't we allies? This sorcerer—Roanna—she has a whole underground following in Col Sargoth. They could help us. Why don't you trust her? And for that matter, why didn't she trust me? Why did she try to kill me?"

"The answer lies in your last question, Caile," Talitha replied. "Why *did* she try to kill you?"

Caile threw his hands up in exasperation. "I don't know. That's why I'm asking you."

Talitha smiled despite herself. "It's because that is the way of the sorcerer's guilds. Their only goal is to preserve themselves and gain power and influence over those without the ability to wield magic. If they had their way, they would lord over everything and everyone, and the Five Kingdoms would be no better off than they are now with the Emperor in charge. The Old World was plagued with the warring of such guilds. The mightiest of the guilds would put themselves in power, only to be overthrown by the next, and on and on, and the whole time the common people were left to suffer. That is why Sargoth Lightbringer left the Old World. He had seen the beauty of Tel Mathir. He saw the true role of the sorcerer as that of a guide in the ways of how we interact with nature, the mother of all things living and dead. Together with Vala, Pyrthin, Norg, and Golier, he crossed the Spine to create a new civilization, one that could live and prosper peacefully, in harmony with Tel Mathir."

"They couldn't have all been that peaceful," Caile remarked. "I've heard stories from tribesmen in the hills of Sevol, north of the Spine. They tell how the great chieftains of their ancestors were forced to bend their knee to the Five or be killed."

"You are more right than you know," Talitha conceded. "It is a mistake great rulers have made since the dawn of time, believing they can use force and violence to enforce peace. I do believe the intent of the Five was well meant, but they nonetheless set the precedent for sorcerers to have domain over the Five Kingdoms. There *was* a long age of peace and prosperity, but with the passage of time, people became lazy and those with the power of sorcery abandoned the ways of Tel Mathir and formed into guilds to exert their power and control the Five Kingdoms. They grew greedy and contentious, and when Col Sargoth was laid siege by the treachery of Lon Golier at the start of the Dreamwielder War, the guilds broke the ancient pact the Five had made hundreds of years before: the pact to never use their powers in war unless attacked by a force from beyond the Five Kingdoms. The guilds openly fought with one another, sold their services to whichever monarch bid the highest, and gladly created the creatures of war you have no doubt heard of. Creatures like Wulfram, though he was created by Queen Guderian, not the guilds. The only sorcerer of strength who still held to the ways of Tel Mathir was Trumball, but alone he could not stem the tide."

Talitha stopped suddenly and turned away from Caile to gaze at the mountains before them. "I digress," she said after a moment. "I did not mean to give you a history lesson. My point was, the guilds were just as much to blame for the Dreamwielder War as the Dark Queen, and they are nearly as much to blame for Guderian's empire of terror as he is. This is why Roanna gave not a second thought to killing your brother. This is why she tried to kill you. She uses her powers for ill gains and does not know the ways of Tel Mathir. She cares only about herself and her guild, which is no more than a shadow of the guilds of old. This is not to say she can be taken lightly. She has much destructive power in her, and she is not alone I am afraid."

"You think there are more sorcerers?"

"Yes. Roanna couldn't have become as powerful as she is without a master. The sorcerers of old are all dead in the Five Kingdoms, except for Wulfram, and anyone born with power since the war has had to escape to the Old World to find someone willing to teach them. It is very likely Roanna has taken league with just such a sorcerer. The sorcerers from the Old World are always looking to escape the constraints of their own lands."

Caile felt his stomach knot at the thought of having to face multiple sorcerers. He had come along expecting that Talitha would deal with Roanna and that he was there merely to help with any of her ruffians like Stephen. "If it comes down to it, can I even kill a sorcerer?" Caile asked. "I mean, would I even have a chance armed only with a sword?"

Talitha shrugged. "We are still human. You can catch us unawares or surprise us as you could any else. It is very difficult though. A well-trained sorcerer uses more than her eyes and ears to sense out danger, and she can strike quickly, whether it be with fire, wind, animals, or something else. Your best bet is to do the unexpected."

Caile nodded, remembering how Lorentz had snuck up behind the firewielder back in Pyrthinia and killed her with a bow and arrow. "Well, I always manage to surprise Lorentz, so perhaps I can surprise a couple sorcerers," Caile put in, though he was not so sure himself. "Still, I'd prefer it if there were only one."

"As would I," Talitha agreed.

22
Allies Forged

Parmo casually came to a halt in the teeming central market of Kal Pyrthin and examined a basket of olives at one of the plethora of produce stands filling the massive marketplace. Or he pretended to at least. In his peripheral vision he watched the man who had been walking behind him for the last several minutes, a man wearing the colors and insignia of Sargoth. Parmo hoped he had not aroused enough suspicion to be followed, but still it was best to be cautious. Since arriving in Kal Pyrthin two days prior, he had busied his days chasing down rumors of the flying airship, and while he had tracked down dozens of witnesses who had seen the ship heading out to sea, no one had seen the airship return. The ship had either made landfall farther to the north or skirted south and gone to Valaróz. It was impossible to say which.

While Parmo had been discreet in his inquiries, he could not be certain that the Emperor's men weren't watching him. It was very possible they too were looking for the airship. Parmo had initially assumed the airship belonged to Emperor Guderian, but that was not necessarily the case. From the rumors Parmo had picked up on, the Emperor's men were questioning people and trying to track down the Princess Taera, too. And then there was the matter of Parmo's cohorts—the two men he had rescued. After learning that King Casstian had been imprisoned, Rufous and Gaetan had surreptitiously entered the city along with Parmo when they arrived in port. If it were widely known that they were survivors of *Pyrthin's Flame* there was no doubt that the three of them would be taken prisoner. The new regent—the houndkeeper—was ruling the city and ostensibly the kingdom now, and he had not been shy about throwing dissenters into the dungeon or simply executing them. That was why Parmo was so wary: Rufous and Gaetan were more than mere dissenters. The two seamen had been rounding up as many allies as they could find among the military and administrative ranks of King Casstian's government. Rebellion was in the works.

Parmo sniffed at the olives in his hand, then tossed them back into their basket as the man he had been watching walked obliviously on into the center of the market and was lost in the crowd of people. The Emperor's agent either wasn't following Parmo in the first place, or he was sloppy and had lost track of Parmo. In either case, Parmo turned in the opposite direction and headed for The Herdsman, the inn where he rented a room along with Gaetan and Rufous.

Outside the central market, the streets were decidedly less crowded at this late morning hour. The trouble brewing in the city seemed to have scared most people into staying home and out of sight unless they had business to attend to, especially since rumors had spread of Wulfram burning old women and girls alive in Castle Pyrthin. Parmo saw no more than a half dozen people on the side streets, and he arrived at the dilapidated harborside inn only a few short minutes later. He found Rufous drinking an ale all by himself inside the nearly empty common room.

"Parmo!" Rufous hailed from where he sat at a lopsided table.

Parmo joined him and waved for the bar maid to bring him a stein of ale.

"Any luck?" Rufous asked.

"More of the same. Plenty of people saw the airship head out after us, but no one saw her return. She could be anywhere now. How about yourself? How goes your... business venture?"

"The venture goes well," Rufous replied. "We've recruited several more partners, so to speak. The question now is not whether we have enough partners but what our plan is. Everyone has their own ideas, and all of them seem lacking."

"You're the one bringing everyone together."

Rufous rolled his eyes noncommittally. "I'll be honest with you, Parmo. I know how to sail a ship. I can command a crew of sailors when it comes to skirting a reef or storming an enemy vessel. But this business—it's a bit beyond my area of expertise."

The bar maid arrived with Parmo's ale, and both of them went silent until she left and went back to her business.

"The key is to delegate," Parmo said, pausing to quaff deeply from his stein. "You needn't know everything. All you have to do is get the right people involved and coordinate it so that everyone carries out their plan at the exact right time."

"Coordinating isn't my strong suit," Rufous admitted. "I was a supply sergeant once, for Pyrthinia's old flagship. It didn't last very long. I tried to feed a hundred sailors with four loaves of bread and five gallons of water. Numbers and schedules don't agree with me."

Parmo laughed. "I'm sure it wasn't that bad."

"Damned close," Rufous replied. He took a swig from his tankard and turned to Parmo, the humor gone from his features. "Perhaps you could meet with the men. You know, see what they have to say. You've got a good head on you. You don't seem to get riled up like the rest of us. Passion and fury are well and good in the heat of battle, but they're not worth a damn when it comes to strategy."

"I wish I could help, but I have to find my granddaughter."

"You said yourself you have no idea where she is," Rufous pointed out. "She's with the princess, and the best thing you can do right now is help us free the King. He loves that girl of his, and he'll go to all ends of the world to find her. Find the princess and you'll find your granddaughter."

Parmo pursed his lips. As much as he hated to admit it, Rufous was right. Parmo was at a dead end. He could pick a direction at random and try to track down the airship, but the chances of actually finding it on his own were slim. On the other hand, if he successfully helped free King Casstian, they would have infinitely more resources at their disposal. The thought of Makarria alone— captured by an unknown assailant—pained Parmo, but there was nothing he could do about it. Running around blindly wasn't going to help either of them. Here, in Kal Pyrthin, he could be of help. *Be strong, Makarria. Be strong.*

Makarria sifted through the crumbling rock in her hand as the men at the end of the tunnel continued digging with their picks. "It just looks like normal rock to me," she remarked to Siegbjorn.

"It looks to be normal rock to me also, but the miners know what they are doing. The veins of the magnesite are many here in the caverns, I am told. Our people find it, they dig it out, then Roanna mixes it with the other ingredients to make the peat. It burns much longer than any wood we can gather in the valley."

Makarria tossed the rubble in her hand back into the wheel cart and shrugged. The whole mining operation was much less intriguing than she had hoped. It amounted to little more than a bunch of big, hairy men digging long tunnels and carrying out cartfuls of boring looking rocks and sand. Still, it was better than sitting locked in her chamber. It had taken some doing on Makarria's part to convince Siegbjorn to take her to Issborg again. Siegbjorn had been commanded to keep the airship grounded, and when Siegbjorn had nothing to do Makarria was relegated to sitting in her chamber day in and day out. As uninteresting as the mines were, visiting them was better than her alternative.

"Come along," Siegbjorn said, sensing Makarria's restlessness and leading the way back down the narrow mining tunnel toward Issborg with his lamp held out in front of him.

"Are there any fish in that lake next to your city?" Makarria asked.

"There are a few pale creatures in those waters but nothing you would be able to catch. Certainly not any creatures you would want to eat."

"Maybe we can go to the lake outside then?"

"The day is nearly gone," he told her.

"Tomorrow then?"

Siegbjorn shook his head. "I am sorry. Tomorrow I will be gone. I am to leave on the airship tonight."

Makarria felt hope surge up inside her. "Where are you going? Can I go with you?"

"No," Siegbjorn said, again shaking his head forlornly.

"But I'm your first mate."

"Yes, I wish it was so. But Kadar himself has made it very clear to me: you are to stay with the princess. She is not having an easy time. She needs you. I risk much by taking you way for even a few hours as I do today."

Makarria nodded. It was true enough. Taera had been increasingly quiet of late, ever since the dream she'd had. Nothing Makarria said or did seemed to reach the princess. Taera would smile for Makarria and that was about it. She returned every night from her sessions with Roanna more exhausted than she had been the previous night. Makarria wanted to help, but Taera wouldn't let her. It was exasperating. Everything Makarria offered to do, Taera promptly forbid. She was worse than Makarria's mother.

The narrow tunnel suddenly opened up before Siegbjorn and Makarria, and they were standing in the enormous cavern housing the city of Issborg. It was significantly brighter than it had been in the mining tunnel, but the light emanating through the ice wall on the far side of the city was already waning.

"Night approaches," Siegbjorn noted. "I must return you to your home."

Makarria sighed and said nothing. She followed Siegbjorn away from the city to the north end of the caverns. When they reached Makarria's chamber, she waved silently goodbye to Siegbjorn and walked inside to find Taera already asleep. Makarria pulled the covers up over the princess, then went to her own bed where her dinner—a bowl of porridge, now cold and coagulated—sat at the foot of the mattress. Makarria set the bowl aside and laid down, much too bored to sleep. *I wonder where Grampy is right now? I wonder where Mother and Father are? I bet they're all worried about me.* Makarria remembered how worried they all were when she had gotten her

first moonblood and fallen into the water. And before that, they had
been worried about her dreams. Makarria had been good about not
dreaming ever since she'd turned her grandfather young. She'd not
dreamed since then, and the last dream she could remember before
that was the one where she was a princess. *Yes, the castle and the violet
dress. It was so pretty.*

Taera suddenly gasped and jumped up from her bed. "No!
Makarria, no."

Makarria jumped halfway out of her own bed she was so
startled. "What? I wasn't dreaming, I swear. I wasn't doing anything."

Taera squinted the sleep out of her eyes and shook her head.
"No, I'm sorry. It wasn't you who was dreaming. It was me. I've seen
the truth of it all."

"You've seen the truth of what?" Makarria asked.

Taera was silent for a long moment, still shaken by what she
had seen in her visions. She had told Makarria next to nothing of
what took place each day in Roanna's chamber, and she had certainly
not told her anything of what Roanna said about the prophecy.

"Please, you can tell me," Makarria said, sensing her reticence.

"I know why we are here," Taera said at last, and with those
words the last vestige of her will to keep things secret from Makarria
disappeared. *I can barely keep myself safe,* she realized. *What point is there
in pretending to protect Makarria by sheltering her from the truth?*

"There is a prophecy foretelling how the Emperor will die,"
Taera began, and she proceeded to tell Makarria everything Roanna
had said. The more she spoke, the easier her words came. She told
Makarria about the Emperor's ability to stint magic, about the
prophecy, about how only women could be dreamwielders, and how
Roanna thought Taera was the one spoken of in the prophecy.

Makarria listened intently as Taera recounted everything.
"Are you going to do it?" Makarria asked after a long moment of
contemplation. "Are you going to kill the Emperor?"

"No," Taera told her. "I couldn't even if I wanted to. I'm not
who Roanna thinks I am."

"You're not?"

"No, *you are*, Makarria."

"That's a silly thing to say," Makarria said, forcing a laugh. "How could I be you?"

"That's not what I'm saying. I'm saying that *you* are the dreamwielder who is foretold to kill the Emperor, not me."

"But you said the prophecy was about a princess."

Taera got up from her bed and walked across the chamber to sit beside Makarria. "Yes, that is exactly what I said. I had another vision tonight and never before has a vision come to me with so much clarity and certainty."

"What did you see?"

"You, Makarria. And you were not the farm girl you claim to be. You were not the tomboyish sea urchin skulking about on a ship that I first met. You were a princess, clad in a violet gown and with a great weight on your shoulders."

"That's impossible," Makarria said, but even as she said it the dreams she'd had back home flashed through her mind.

"I am no dreamwielder," Taera assured her. "Roanna has been trying to teach me, but the power isn't there. It's not in me, it's in you. I don't know how or why, but you have the blood of kings and queens in you, Makarria."

Makarria sat there, too stunned to speak. She didn't know how or why it could be true, but she believed Taera.

"I always suspected there was something more to you," Taera said, "but I wasn't sure and I didn't want to frighten you. I thought I could protect you, Makarria, but all I've done is drag you into further danger. Roanna and Kadar—they're sworn enemies of the Emperor, but I fear they are no better than he is. If they find out who you are, they'll throw you at him. They will try to train you like they do with me, but in the end they will use you to their own ends, they will use you like a weapon to kill the Emperor."

"I don't want to kill anyone," Makarria said, shaking her head at the very thought. She feared the Emperor, she knew her grandfather cursed his name, but that didn't mean she could bring herself kill him, evil or not.

"That's why we must keep this secret and get you out of here," Taera said. "You've made friends with the captain of that airship, yes?"

"Siegbjorn? Yes, but what—"

"He's told you that he has no love for Roanna. You must convince him to take you away, now, before winter fully arrives and you are trapped here."

"I'm not leaving without you," Makarria said.

"Roanna and Kadar won't let me escape, but they have no reason to seek after you. If you disappeared, they would hardly notice. I overheard Roanna say that Siegbjorn might be leaving, to gather news before the first winter storms come. You could steal away with him, then escape when the ship lands."

"It's too late," Makarria said. "He's leaving tonight."

"There's still time then," Taera insisted.

"We're locked in here until morning, Taera. Plus, Siegbjorn told me that Kadar himself said I'm supposed to stay with you. He'll notice if I'm gone."

Taera's hopes dimmed at hearing this, but she was not willing to concede. There had to be a way to protect Makarria, she was certain. "The city you told me about then. The people there will hide you perhaps. They can take you to the other side of the mountain and show you the way out."

"I told you, they collapsed the tunnel on that side," Makarria reminded her. "I could maybe stay in the city, but I wouldn't know who to ask. Siegbjorn only introduced me to a few people and most of them don't speak our language." Makarria realized that she truly didn't want to leave Taera. The Emperor and ancient prophesies were far away and meant little to her. As far as she was concerned, it was more important to stick together, especially now that Makarria knew what was going on. "I'm not going anywhere without you," she declared.

Taera held her head in her hands. She felt completely empty. Hopeless. She considered what her father would do in her position. Or Caile. As much as the two of them did not see eye to eye, they were not so different from each other. Neither one of them would ever give up. They would continue doing what they thought was right until their lives were ripped away from them. Cargan had been the same. Taera owed it to them, she decided, to do nothing less. The problem was, she didn't know what she could possibly do.

"We wait," she said after a long silence. "We'll keep your secret and wait out the winter. I'll do what I can to appease Roanna and keep her hope alive that I am the one. That is all we can do for now. I am sorry, Makarria."

No more than forty yards away from Makarria and Taera's chamber, Roanna sat down on a velvet cushion in Kadar's chamber. The room was furnished with a carven oak bed and desk; embroidered tapestries hung on the walls; a rug of crimson kork-wool covered the floor from doorway to bedside; and yet, even with the warm glow of many lanterns, it still seemed very much a cave.

Kadar sat on a cushion across from Roanna and stroked his dark eyebrows with his slender, long-nailed fingers. "It takes too long," he said.

"She's only been here a few weeks," Roanna replied, annoyed at his presumptuousness. "We knew it would take time. She's had no training whatsoever before now. We can't expect her to be a mighty sorcerer yet, and besides, we agreed to give her a year or more before even considering confronting Guderian."

"I speak not of confronting *him* yet. I am telling you it has taken too long to discover her abilities beyond clairvoyance. She is nineteen already. A fully matured woman and yet I detected nothing in her during my examination. And your teachings, they have been fruitless. If her other abilities do not blossom yet of their own accord, we are wasting time—your exercises are not going to awaken them. No, I think we must accelerate matters."

"No, I will not allow it," Roanna snapped. "You promised to let me work with her until she was ready."

"Do not tell me what you will or will not allow, woman!" Kadar snarled, and though his voice was quiet, it filled the chamber with menace. Roanna shrank back on her pillow. "You know as well as anyone how effective my methods are," Kadar went on. "This princess has lived a pampered life. Her mind is soft. We must shock her entire being if we are to reach her true potential. She must suffer pain, know agony. And if that works not, I will give her a child to change her chemistry and draw forth the power inside her."

"Please, just give me more time with her," Roanna begged of him. "I know I can awaken her ability without resorting to those measures."

Kadar regarded her silently for a long moment. "You have three days more, Roanna. That is all. If we see no sign of an awakening in her, then I will be taking over her training."

23
The Rebellion Begins

Parmo looked over the small group of men gathered around him in his upstairs bedroom of The Herdsman. Their plans had come together quickly after Parmo agreed to stay and help. Rufous and Gaetan had already recruited soldiers, sailors, and officials from every arm of the Pyrthinian government, and they already had all the workings of a plan. All Parmo had to do was bring an outside perspective and settle a few arguments, and now here they were on the cusp of staging a coup. Nearly a dozen men were packed into the room, standing around the sagging bed which had become a desk of sorts with a large map of the city spread out across it.

"What news do you bring?" Parmo asked of the newest member of their group, an archer whom Gaetan had recruited from Castle Pyrthin.

"I was witness to the butchering of those girls three days ago," the man said. "After Wulfram killed my captain and all those girls, the houndkeeper gave Wulfram a message. Wulfram said he was summoned back to Col Sargoth. I was standing close enough to hear it with my own ears. He said that the Prince had escaped, and I can only assume he meant Prince Caile."

"Those are good tidings," Parmo said, pushing aside the thought of the girls being butchered by Wulfram and turning his gaze upon Gaetan. "Have you confirmed the sightings of Wulfram leaving the city?"

"Aye," Gaetan replied. "We've confirmed over thirty sightings of him flying off. People around the castle, in the city, and even in the farms to the west saw him making toward Col Sargoth."

"We must act now then," Parmo said, taking a deep breath and making sure he had everything straight in his mind before continuing. "Who's in charge of the archers?" he asked the new recruit.

"Me. I'm the captain now."

"Perfect," Parmo said. "How many men can you steal away from the castle unnoticed tonight? Men you can trust?"

The captain of the archers eyed Parmo silently for a long moment before responding. "Six, including myself."

"Then you will go with me to the houndkeeper's tower. I'll go into the tower myself to deal with the houndkeeper's men, but if they keep their wits about them they will try to send a warning to Col Sargoth. We can't risk any ravens getting loose, Captain, otherwise Wulfram will be right back here to make a short end of our work. Make sure nothing gets out of that window alive."

"If I may?" the captain said, looking to his fellow Pyrthinian soldiers and sailors. "Why is it that we are taking orders from a Valarion? And one five years my junior by the look of him."

Parmo pursed his lips. He still couldn't keep his head around the idea that his body was young now. Before Makarria had remade him, his distinctly Valarion features had been hidden beneath wrinkles, sagging skin, and grayed hair. No one would have ever suspected him of being a Valarion. In addition, his aged appearance had lent him an air of wisdom and dignity. *No one instinctively trusts a young man though*, he reminded himself, *particularly if he's not your countryman. You've got to earn it.*

"I apologize if I sometimes presume to give orders," Parmo said. "I'm merely making suggestions, and I promise you, we share the same goals, Captain. I want to see King Casstian free and on the throne again. My niece has been abducted along with the princess. I want to get them both back. I want the Emperor and Wulfram dead. I want to again see the day where Pyrthinia and Valaróz are the closest of allies."

"Parmo's proven himself," Gaetan said. "He saved my life and Rufous's, both."

"That's right," Rufous affirmed. "And no one is giving orders to no one. We're all in this together. We all have our own areas of know-how and skills. It just so happens that Parmo's is with strategics."

The archer nodded. "If you vouch for him, it's good enough for me, I suppose."

"Will you go with me to the tower, then?" Parmo asked.

"Me and my five best men. It is done."

"Thank you," Parmo said with a nod. "The rest of us then, let's proceed as planned. Gaetan, you know where to find the houndkeeper's new harbor master: kill him."

"With pleasure."

"Jeremo, Arsino, Callum, you'll split up and take the three gate-keepers."

The three men nodded.

"Loukas and Eudecio, you must secure the treasury."

"Consider it secured."

"And the rest of you," Parmo said at last, "Castle Pyrthin is yours. Wulfram has left it sorely unguarded. At best, the houndkeeper has ten of his own men there. The rest of the inhabitants are loyal Pyrthinians; they obey the houndkeeper now out of fear, but they will join you if you have the courage to take charge. All of you, use your name and rank to command whatever troops you can to do your bidding. Rufous, don't forget, you're now the captain of the King's flagship and that makes you an admiral. You'll find few in the castle at night who outrank you. Are we all clear?"

Every man in the room nodded in assent.

"Very well then," Parmo said, "at midnight, we all act at once."

No one said a word, and in the silence Parmo couldn't help but wonder if he'd made the right choice in staying. His heart had told him to keep searching for Makarria, and yet here he was caught up in revolt. *You might have a young body now, but the world is moving faster than your mind,* he warned himself. *Keep your wits about you tonight.*

. . .

Natarios Rhodas woke with an unsettling feeling. He'd been dreaming that he was being pecked to pieces by ravens while simultaneously being burnt alive. He pushed the images out of his mind and tucked his fur blanket back around his shoulders. *I shouldn't have such nasty dreams when I'm sleeping in this big, lush bed,* he mused. *I don't know how Casstian found the willpower to get out of bed every morning.*

He rooted his head deeper into one of the down pillows and clamped his eyes shut, but sleep would not come to him. His stomach began grumbling after a while and he decided the only thing to do was to head down to the larder to grab some warm milk and a bite of cheese. His mind settled, he threw aside the covers, grabbed his night robe from the bedside, and stepped into his slippers. When he slipped out the door into the corridor, he found his guard asleep in his chair. "Worthless fool," Natarios muttered, but he shuffled past without waking the man and made his way down the stairs to the kitchens and the larder. A few solitary cooks were there kneading dough for the morning meal, but they paid him no heed. He helped himself to a jug of milk and broke off a sizable chunk from a wheel of cheese, then sat on a step stool to enjoy his snack. *This is the life,* he told himself. *You won't find milk and cheese in the middle of the night in your old tower. No warm, comfy bed with big cushy pillows. No warm robe and slippers. Just that smelly hound. Those squawking ravens. And always on the lookout for that wretched Wulfram.*

A shout suddenly rang out disrupting his thoughts, followed by heavy footsteps in the corridor outside the kitchen. Perplexed as to who could be shouting at this hour, Natarios set aside his jug of milk and peered out from the larder doorway. He saw Pyrthinian soldiers hurrying by and realized they were heading in the direction of the stairs toward his quarters.

"Sargoth's hairy arse," he swore beneath his breath and stepped back into the larder. He could hear the men running up the stairs now and beating on his door. Without a second thought, he crept to the back of the larder and let himself out the back door into the service yard where stores and wares were delivered each day. No one was about at this time of night, however, and Natarios simply unlocked the service gate and exited Castle Pyrthin's outer walls unimpeded. *You have quite the nose for danger,* he congratulated himself. *Quite the nose, indeed.*

Parmo withdrew his sword and held the blade before him in the wan moonlight alongside the houndkeeper's tower. The blade— now polished and honed to a fine edge—felt odd in his hands. It had been decades since he last wielded it. The last time he had killed a man with the sword he had been in Valaróz, and he had been wearing his ring, the ring that he left with his daughter. *Prisca, I'm so sorry,* he lamented. *I didn't mean to take her away from you. I'll make it right again, I promise.* He exhaled sharply and strode to the entrance of the tower where he banged on the door with the pommel of his sword.

"Who's there?" a voice shouted from inside.

"My name is Parmo. I bring news of the princess. I know where she is. I want my bounty."

The door opened a few inches and the guard inside peered through the crack. "What is it you know?"

"This," Parmo said, and he jabbed the tip of the sword into the man's exposed eye. It was not a clean thrust, though, and the man squealed out in pain as he fell back, merely maimed. Parmo kicked the door open and swore as he thrust the sword again, this time into the guard's heart. The man collapsed to the floor and Parmo leapt over his body to sprint up the spiraling staircase. There were two more of the houndkeepers's men upstairs, at least, and Parmo knew they must have heard the cry of pain. If they had any sense at all, they were hurriedly trying to write messages to send off with the ravens.

The stairs went on and on and Parmo found himself dizzy by the time he reached the first doorway some sixty feet up from the ground level. He paused a moment to gather himself and gripped his sword tightly before kicking the door in. With a shout, he lunged into the chamber only to find it empty but for the scent-hound on her giant compass wheel. Realizing he was in the wrong room, Parmo turned back into the stairwell and hurried up the last section of stairs. Inside the second chamber he found his quarry: two men bearing the seal of the Emperor. One of the men lunged at him while the other hurriedly reached into a cage to grab one of the ravens. Parmo parried the first man's knife thrust and kneed him in the groin. The man went down to his knees with a grunt and Parmo bashed his head with the pommel of his sword, splaying him out across the floor. The other man saw Parmo charging and screamed in panic as he hurled his raven toward the window. Parmo cut him down from behind, but too late. The raven opened its broad wings and took flight.

"Raven!" Parmo yelled, and even as he said it, three arrows whistled up from the darkness below to strike the hapless bird and send it flailing to the ground.

Parmo slumped to his knees over the window sill and sighed. "Well done, Captain," he said out the window after a long moment, then he turned to the two men lying in the chamber. The second was clearly dead, and after a quick examination, Parmo found the first one dead as well. He had been hoping to merely knock the man unconscious. *Not quite used to the strength of this youthful body,* he thought wryly. Still, it saved him the trouble of having to bind and drag the man downstairs. His part in carrying out the coup was complete. *Now it's up to the others.*

When he caught his breath, Parmo started back down the stairs, intent on joining up with the captain of the archers and going to the castle to see how their co-conspirators were faring, but as he passed the lower of the two chambers an odd noise caught his attention. He stopped and poked his head into the scent-hound's chamber. The hound's body quivered and Parmo heard the noise again. It was the hound itself. She was whining.

Parmo stepped into the chamber and eyed the creature warily. He had heard of the scent-hounds before, of course, but never seen one. Few people had. The sight of the miserable creature both disgusted him and stung his heart with pity. Its eyes were watching him, he realized, and it whined again.

"I can't help you," Parmo said. "I'm sorry."

The creature groaned—half-growl, half whimper—like an injured dog begging for help. "I can't help you," Parmo repeated, seeing the ghastly shaft through the creature's navel, and how its flesh was melded into the metal spokes of the giant compass. "There's no way to release you."

The creature kept at its whining and Parmo steeled himself. There was only one act of mercy he could perform, he knew. Taking a deep breath, he set his feet and raised his sword high over his head. He brought it down with all the force and precision he could muster and for a split second—right before the blade clove the dog-head from the woman's body—the creature went silent and Parmo swore he saw gratitude in its eyes. He hoped it was gratitude, at least, and told himself it was best this way. He then stepped out of the chamber and went slowly down the stairs.

King Casstian pushed himself up from the straw and muck covering the floor of his cell and looked through the small window slot in the iron door. The sound of heavy footsteps and a confusing array of shouted orders in the adjoining corridor had roused him from his muddled, half-asleep, half-awake state of consciousness. After the first few days in the dungeon, he had lost track of all sense of time. He had no idea how long he had been locked up and stood now only to interrupt the unceasing monotony his existence had become.

When a half-dozen soldiers congregated outside his cell then unlocked the door, he hardly realized what was happening.

"Your Majesty," one of the men said with a curt bow, "Castle Pyrthin has been retaken. We await your orders."

Casstian shielded his eyes against the glare of the torches they held. "I'm free?"

"Yes, Your Majesty."

"What of Wulfram, and that snake Natarios?"

"Wulfram left two days ago for Col Sargoth. The houndkeeper seems to have escaped, but we have killed or captured the rest of his men."

Casstian regarded his men silently for a moment. "You realize that by your actions, you have thrown Pyrthinia into war against the Emperor?"

"With all due respect, Your Majesty," one of the men replied, "war began the moment you were thrown into the dungeon."

Casstian smiled grimly. "Well said, man. Release the rest of my advisors from their cells and lead the way out of here. I need to wash the filth from me and eat a proper meal if I am to think straight again."

Parmo and the six archers found the main gates of Castle Pyrthin guarded when they arrived, but when the captain of the archers identified himself and mentioned Parmo's name, the guards quickly ushered them inside the courtyard.

"The King said to send you in straight away," one of the guards said to Parmo, leading the way into the main keep.

"He's safely freed, then?" Parmo queried.

"Alive and well," the guard said with a big grin on his face. "He's bathed already and in the mess hall eating like a man half-starved."

True to the guard's word, they found King Casstian in the mess hall. Rufous, Gaetan, and all but a few of the other conspirators were there with him already, though none of them shared his same interest in eating.

"And who is this?" Casstian asked, setting his fork and knife aside when he saw Parmo and the archers approaching.

Parmo gestured for the captain of the archers to speak first.

"I am Tharon Phaedros, new Captain of the Royal Archers, Your Majesty," the man said. "I regret to inform you that my predecessor, Ras Ambros, is dead, slain by the hand of Wulfram."

"So I have been told," Casstian replied. "You are to be commended, Captain, and are hereby promoted to the rank of First Constable for your deeds tonight. The men who accompanied you tonight are promoted two ranks and given all the wages and privileges afforded to such. Thank you, gentlemen."

The archers bowed thankfully and moved to the side, for already the King's attention was on Parmo. In fact, Casstian had recognized Parmo the moment he set foot into the mess hall. His face looked strangely familiar to him, yet he could not say who he was or how he knew him.

"You, sir," Casstian said. "You are the one called Parmo?"

"Yes, Your Majesty," Parmo answered with a polite bow of his head.

"My men tell me you are the one who organized them and strategized my release."

"I merely facilitated the meeting," Parmo replied. "Your men found one another and devised the individual components of our plan. I did little more than storm the houndkeeper's tower."

"Your modesty is unfounded. Taking the tower is no small feat itself, and I'm inclined to believe your role was larger than that. And yet you are clearly not Pyrthinian. Who are you, if I may ask, and of what concern to you was my release?"

Parmo hesitated. With all the work he had done to engineer Casstian's release, he had neglected to consider what he would say to the King now that he was free. "Rufous has told you what befell *Pyrthin's Flame*, I assume?" Parmo asked, sidestepping the King's question altogether.

"Yes. He says you swear that my daughter was abducted from the ship before it sank."

"That is my belief," Parmo confirmed. "The princess had befriended my granddaughter, and when I discovered the ship was burning, I went to rescue them first. Their cabin was empty, and there was no sign of violence or struggle. I am certain they were bore away on the strange flying ship we spotted afterward, as outlandish as that may sound. And hence my concern with your release, your

Majesty. We are joined in purpose to find our kin."

Casstian narrowed his eyes and leaned forward in his seat. "What I find outlandish is that you claim to have a granddaughter—you who are less than half my age and barely old enough to have children of any age."

Parmo swore inwardly at himself for forgetting his own story.

"Well?" Casstian asked. "Who are you, really? I will have the truth."

Parmo sighed and decided that nothing would serve but the truth at this point. Part of it at least. *We are at war with the Emperor now,* he conceded, *and Casstian needs to know who I am if I am to be of any help.*

"My name is Parmenios Pallma."

Casstian shook his head. "That's impossible. The Pallma bloodline was extinguished thirty-odd years ago."

"So the Emperor has said and so he believes, but I live." Parmo closed his eyes and recalled the scene that had nearly faded into his memory. "I was at sea when Wulfram and Guderian attacked Sol Valaróz and killed my family. I received warning barely in time when my ship reached the harbor. I was rash and meant to fight and avenge my family, but my crew would not allow it, and they threw me overboard as Guderian's men boarded my ship. The Sargothians fired arrows at me, but I was a strong swimmer in my youth. I went under and held my breath as long as I could then surfaced at the transom of the ship, concealed by the rudder. I stayed hidden there all day, then in the cover of night swam to a merchant ship at a pier across the harbor and climbed aboard as a stowaway for seven days in the harbor and two weeks more at sea before slipping away in Pyrvino. The Emperor's men never found my body, but they declared me dead nonetheless, figuring I must've been shot or drowned."

"Do you take me for a fool?" Casstian demanded. "Parmenios Pallma would be twice your age if he were alive."

"I am not as young as I look—I am sixty-four years old, Your Majesty. I myself find it hard to believe, but the passage of time has somehow been turned back in me by the hand of a sorceress. I have lived a life of modesty in hiding since my escape; I married, had children, a grandchild, and grew old. Then somehow, beyond my comprehension, I awoke young again. I cannot explain it, but it is the truth. Do you not recognize me, Casstian? We met once when you were still a boy."

Casstian shook his head, still not believing it.

"Look at my sword," Parmo said, handing his weapon over hilt first. "The blade bears the crest of Pallma on it."

"That makes you nothing more than a thief."

"Recall then the time I visited Kal Pyrthin," Parmo said. "You were no more than seven perhaps, but you joined your father and mine on a boar hunt. I rode at the rear of the procession with you, and one of the boars escaped the hunters' spears. You were unhorsed as our fathers made chase after it, and in your fright you began to cry. But you were too proud to let your father or anyone else see. I offered to help you up, but you stubbornly refused and made me swear your tears to secrecy."

"How could you possibly know that?" Casstian asked, the memory coming back to him quite clearly.

"I have kept that secret until this day, Casstian, and would have kept it secret still if there were any other way to prove my identity. I know it is hard to believe, but I am Prince Parmenios Pallma, the rightful King of Valaróz."

24
Secret Paths

Caile stopped at the top of the small ridgeline clearing and dismounted to wait for Talitha to catch up. The nearest peaks of the Barrier Mountains towered before him. They looked close enough to touch, but Caile knew firsthand how their tremendous size fooled the eye and warped one's sense of distance. For two days now they had been climbing through the wooded hills beyond Ulmstadt, and the mountains looked nearly the same now as they did then. Perhaps even more foreboding were the dark clouds coming in from the south to nestle along the base of the mountains. Caile turned away and looked back in the direction they had come. Ulmstadt was long gone from sight, but from his vantage point he was able to make out sections of the forest tract they had been following. The tract had long ago been abandoned and was little wider than a game trail now. At times, it disappeared altogether, buried beneath a landslide, blocked by a tree fall, or merely overgrown with time. Still, they had been successful thus far in always finding the trail again, and they had made good time—better at least than they would have fared setting out cross-country through the heavily wooded hills.

Talitha reached the top of the ridge and slid from her saddle to join Caile. "You set a grueling pace," she said.

"The horses are doing most of the work," he replied with a shrug. "They're sturdier than they look."

"Northern animals always are. It takes strength and fortitude to live out here."

Caile motioned toward the clouds in the distance. "Are we

going to make it before the snows come?"

"Those are not snow-bearing clouds. At least not yet. We have another two days before we reach the caverns. With any luck, the first storms will hold out until then."

"And then what?" Caile asked.

"Then we journey into the mountain. It is another four days from the entrance to Issborg."

Caile had refrained from voicing all his concerns for fear of sounding too worrisome and cynical, but he had heard of Trumball before and the caverns of Issborg. "I thought the caves were gone," he said. "Weren't they destroyed when Trumball was killed?"

"The southern entrance was collapsed, that is all."

"That's where we are going isn't it? The southern entrance?"

Talitha smiled. "Trust me. I know another way."

"You say that a lot," Caile remarked. "You'd be a lot more trustworthy if you were more forthcoming with information."

"And you'd be a much more pleasant traveling companion if you weren't so worrisome."

Caile waved one hand at her in exasperation and hopped back onto his horse. "Lead the way then. These caverns aren't going to find themselves."

Makarria was awake, but she did not stir when Roanna entered their chamber. Typically she was up and awake when Roanna arrived to fetch Taera each morning, but with Siegbjorn gone Makarria saw little reason to get out of bed and so stayed hunkered down beneath her covers.

Taera, on the other hand, threw aside her covers and started to get dressed out of rote habit as soon as she heard Roanna enter.

"Don't bother," Roanna said. "You're staying here today."

"What?" Taera asked, still groggy. "Why?"

Roanna sat Taera back down on her bed then sat beside her. "The time of reckoning is upon you, Taera. Kadar grows impatient with your lack of growth. I have been stern with you, I know, but you will find he is a much crueler master than I if you fail now."

"What is it he wants?" Taera asked, instantly wide awake, bristling with danger.

Roanna sighed. "He wants to tap the power inside of you. He feels that if it has not come out naturally, then he must pry it out of you."

Taera stared at her, confused.

"I've convinced him to give us one last chance," Roanna continued in a near whisper. She handed Taera two metal hoops that were linked together, about the size of manacles.

"What's this?" Taera asked.

"It is a test. In the Old World it was the first test that young dreamwielders had to complete before continuing their training. To pass the test you must separate the rings. Metals have always been the most pliable materials to the mechanizations of dreamwielders. I've taught you as best I can how to go into a dream state. Imagine the rings in your mind, then imagine them separate, and make it be. You have until tomorrow morning to complete the test."

"And if I fail?"

"Then Kadar will try his methods upon you," Roanna replied. She stared at Taera long and hard before continuing. "He will torture you at first. Pain and fear trigger a certain response inside our bodies. In normal people this response is to fight with more fierceness or to run from danger more swiftly, but with sorcerers it sometimes awakens new powers. Kadar has many tools at his disposal. He will cut you, he will burn you, he will press your eyeballs until you think they will burst, he will bend your hands and feet in ways that will make you want to die, he will use his powers to hurt parts of your body you didn't know existed. And if none of that works, Taera, he will bed you as many times as it takes to get you with child. Nothing changes a woman's body more than carrying a child—not the coming of your moonblood or the waning of it when you are old. Sorceresses of old were known to gain and lose great powers when they gave birth." Roanna's eyes glistened with tears, but her voice remained steady. "I do no wish this fate upon you, but Kadar will stop at no ends to see your power come to fruition."

"I can't do it," Taera whispered.

"You can!" Roanna barked, leaning in close. "You are the one, Taera. I don't have the power to show you or help you any more than I already have, but I know it is within you. Find your inner strength, delve into your darkest fears, do whatever it takes to accomplish this. You don't have a choice anymore." Roanna stood. "I return in the morning with Kadar. If you have not separated the rings then I will have no choice but to let him have his way with you. Be scared, Taera, because if you are not, I promise you, you will fail."

With that, Roanna turned and left, slamming the door behind her.

Makarria waited for a long time to make sure Roanna wasn't coming back before pulling the covers away from her face. "Taera?"

"Don't worry," Taera replied, crying softly. "I won't tell them. When they come in the morning, Kadar can take me away and do whatever he wishes, but I won't say a thing. I won't tell them about you, Makarria."

Makarria got up and walked across the room to take the rings from Taera. "No, I can do it for you. I've done things before. I've changed dresses. I made my grampy young again. I can do this."

"And then what?" Taera whispered. "They'll think I did it, and they will expect me to do more, to pass more tests. They'll find out it wasn't me at all and that it was you this whole time. Then what? Then Kadar can beat and rape you instead of me?"

The tone of Taera's voice was quiet, but intense—frightful—and Makarria stood silently for a long moment as she considered what she was proposing to do. She was scared, but at the same time, she was not willing to let her friend be harmed needlessly. "It'll give us more time at least," Makarria reasoned. "Siegbjorn will be back soon. He will help us if I ask him."

"I said no!" Taera said, snatching the rings from Makarria's grip with more force than she intended.

Makarria yelped and pressed her stinging fingers against her lips in surprise.

"No, I'm sorry," Taera sobbed, crying harder now. She tossed the rings aside and reached her hands out for Makarria. "I'm sorry, Makarria. I just wanted to keep you safe. I never meant for any of this happen. I never thought this would happen. I was so naïve. I thought… I thought… I don't know. I thought I was stronger."

Makarria put her arms around Taera, her fear suddenly gone. She felt oddly misplaced, consoling the friend who had mothered her and was five years her elder, but it felt right. Protecting her friend made her own fear disappear. "It's not your fault," Makarria said. "It's going to be alright. I promise."

Taera said nothing and only wept into Makarria's shoulder for a long time. After a while her crying subsided, and Taera slumped back into her bed. Makarria covered her up the best she could, then quietly treaded to the far end of the room to where the rings had landed. She picked them up, ran her fingers over the entirety of them, then went and sat down on her own bed. She had already made up her mind: she was going to separate the rings, no matter what Taera said. *You've been obeying others your whole life. Mother, Father, Grampy, and now Taera. They can't take care of you anymore. It's time to start making your own decisions.* She laid down with the rings in hand over her chest and closed her eyes. *You can do this, Makarria. You just need to dream it true.* She pictured the rings in her mind and tried to go to sleep, but found she was anything but tired. Her heart was thumping in her chest, and the anticipation of what she was attempting to do kept distracting her. After a while, she gave up trying to sleep and sat back up. She recalled walking in on Taera that first day on the airship and finding her sitting up in a trance. *A dream state, Roanna called it.* Makarria closed her eyes with her back against the wall and again pictured the rings in her mind, but the thought again distracted her and made her think of Roanna and Kadar and his black teeth. With an exasperated snort, she pushed all those thoughts aside and focused on her breathing. *Relax,* she told herself. *You didn't change Grampy when you were scared and sobbing, you changed him when you were half-asleep.*

Makarria focused on the sound of her heartbeat in her head and the air moving through her nose with each passing breath. Her body relaxed. Time passed—how much, she lost track of—and eventually she realized she had forgotten about the rings. Remembering them quickened her pulse again, so she pushed the thought of them aside. When she was relaxed again, she allowed herself to picture the rings in her mind but only for a moment before turning her attention back to her breathing. She repeated this multiple times, then forced herself to remember her goal. *Separate them,* she told herself. The next time she envisioned them in her mind, she pictured the rings melded together, the border between them blurry. Then again and again. Then she envisioned them separate. A chill swept over her body, but she shook it off and forced herself to stay focused on the image. *Two rings, separated.* She repeated the statement in her mind. She duplicated the image in her imagination over and over again. She duplicated it so many times it became instinct and soon she began to forget what she was doing. Her breathing slowed even more, and she lost track of what she was doing. Her mind wandered, fatigue swept over her. It was as if she was climbing a hill that got ever steeper.

Two rings, separated...

All thoughts were gone from Makarria's mind, and her body—completely exhausted—began to slump over. As she hit the mattress, the rings fell from her hands and clattered onto the stone floor and startled her awake. She pushed herself up and shook her head but could see nothing.

"Makarria?" Taera said from across the room. She too had been startled awake by the sound of the rings hitting the floor.

The room was nearly pitch black. The lone lamp in the corner near the door had almost been extinguished and burned now only with the faintest of lights. Taera got up slowly and felt her way toward the lamp. When she reached it, she adjusted the lamp to draw more of the wick up into the globe. It sputtered, then glowed brightly again, and Taera turned back toward the center of the room.

Makarria and Taera both stared at the two rings in the middle of the floor: two rings separated.

Makarria spoke first, nothing more than a whisper. "I did it."

"Yes," was all Taera could reply. After a while she got up from the floor beside the lamp and grabbed up the rings. "You will speak nothing of this," she told Makarria. "I will stretch out what little time you have bought us."

Makarria found that she could only nod. Taera tucked her beneath her covers, and she slept. Sometime later, the *Snjaer Firan* tribesman who guarded their door brought them their midmorning meal and escorted them to the privy. Makarria woke and dutifully followed him and Taera to the privy chamber and back but remembered hardly any of it or any of their dinner many hours later. She could barely walk or lift her arms to eat, and Taera silently assisted her, ashamed that in her moment of weakness she had let a girl bravely do what she could not. When they finished eating their evening meal, Makarria laid down and again fell into a deep slumber, while Taera returned to her own bed to sleep fitfully throughout the night.

When morning came, Roanna and Kadar entered without knocking. Taera wordlessly handed Kadar the rings. He examined them for a moment, then handed them over to Roanna. "Get working then," he told her. "I want constant progress now that you have opened her."

"Yes, Master," Roanna said with a stern nod, but when Kadar exited and left them alone, Roanna smiled. "I told you, Taera. You are the one."

25
War Plans

King Casstian's study bustled with people and a chorus of disconnected conversations. In one corner, Casstian's supply sergeant met with the Minister of Agriculture and the guild masters for the millers and butchers to begin procuring the food necessary to feed an army. In another corner, the Royal Armorer met with the guild masters of the smiths, fletchers, and ore miners to expedite the manufacturing of more weapons. Around the fire, Rufous and the other high ranking officers of the Pyrthin navy tallied the number of ships in port at their disposal—naval and merchant vessels, both— and discussed how they would structure the chain of command between the navy and the civilian captains. And around the desk, Casstian himself looked over a large map of the Five Kingdoms with his top advisors, including the archer Tharon, and Parmo.

"We will make Kylep our marshaling point and base for attack," Casstian said, pointing on the map to the city that sat at the northwestern juncture of the high road and the River Kylep. "Lepig would be better in some ways, perhaps, but folk there are of mixed loyalty, and the Emperor has a garrison with two-hundred cavalrymen. It would be a crippling blow if we could take the city from him, but we cannot hope to hold Lepig if the Emperor brings the entirety of his forces south from Col Sargoth. Kylep is better suited to that. It sits upon a high vantage point making it impossible to approach unnoticed, and it has outer walls which can be fortified. We can access it by both road and the river to begin sending supplies immediately."

"And what of Valaróz?" one of the advisors asked. "If they come by land through the badlands, they will cut off our supply lines between Kylep and Kal Pyrthin."

"We will send our advanced troops to Makady to begin fortifying the town against attack from Valaróz," Casstian said. "Prince Parmenios assures me that Valaróz will be disinclined to attack by that route, however, and I agree."

"Their strength lies in their navy," Parmo explained. "They will look to attack with their eastern fleet by sea and come at us through Kal Pyrthin Bay. If they get past the Pyrthin navy, they will lay siege to the city and send their ships up the river to attack Kylep."

"And capture us in a vice," the King added.

"How many men do you mean to leave behind to hold Kal Pyrthin?" another of the advisors asked.

"I mean to leave none behind but the city watch."

The advisors looked at the King incredulously, but Casstian did not balk.

"This is not the time for conservative tactics. We'll need every able-bodied person we can muster if we hope to stand against Sargoth. The fate of our city lies in the hands of our navy, and Prince Parmenios. He knows the tactics of the Valarion navy better than any and is familiar with the waters at the southern edge of the bay. I am putting him in charge of our naval force."

Parmo nodded as all their eyes turned upon him. His thoughts, as they did often, returned to Makarria. After freeing Casstian, he had asked the King to let him lead the search for the airship, but Casstian was convinced Taera and Makarria had been abducted by the Emperor. "The only way to get them back is to take Col Sargoth," he had said and so Parmo stayed. *I don't know where Makarria is,* he told himself for the hundredth time. *This is all I can do to aid her: help defeat Guderian.* He steeled his resolve again and spoke to the men gathered around Casstian.

"I will do all in my power to keep your city safe. At worst, we will keep the Valarion fleet floundering at the edge of the bay for months, but I mean to do more than that. Pyrthinia and Valaróz have always been allies, even during the Dreamwielder War, when all the other kingdoms were at war with one another. I mean to make them allies again. Just as you are all loyal Pyrthinians and have fought to free your king, so too are the Valarions loyal and proud of their kingdom. They have no love for the usurper Don Bricio, but they have had no one to unite and lead them. Until now. I will declare my rightful claim to the throne of Valaróz, and if Don Bricio has the courage to face me, I will cut him down."

"Courage is not the way of Don Bricio," Casstian remarked. "Always he has resorted to secrecy and treachery. He will not face you but rather renounce your claim as false and scheme to murder you by some nefarious means. He will lie, bribe, blackmail, and kill to make people do his bidding. You risk much if you declare yourself."

"We all risk much, and as you said yourself, this is not the time for conservative tactics."

"So be it," Casstian conceded.

"Your Majesty?" a wiry man spoke from the outer edge of the circle of advisors. Few of the others had hardly even noticed he was there until he spoke. "If I may…"

"Of course, speak your mind, Leone," Casstian told him.

"If the prince means to declare himself, then we could use it more to our benefit," Leone said. "There is little hope for surprise regardless. The houndkeeper escaped upon your rescue, Your Majesty, and Guderian no doubt has other spies in the city. He will know before long that we are mobilizing for war so why try to hide it? Let us all declare ourselves. We are not alone in our hatred of Guderian. Others may join us. I can spread the rumor through the city that Prince Parmenios Pallma has returned to reclaim his throne. The news will spread like wildfire. I will send messengers to Pyrvino, Tyrna, Makady, and Kylep. I have loyal men and women who will go from there to spread the word into the other realms. Let the people of Valaróz know their prince has returned. Let the people of Sargoth know that Pyrthinia has declared war and means to free all the Five Kingdoms from the tyranny of Guderian. We might just find that we have many allies out there, both big and small. At the worst, Guderian and his lapdog Don Bricio will have their hands full keeping their subjects scared into submission."

Casstian pursed his lips thoughtfully for a long moment before responding. "Do it," he said, finally. "As you say, Leone, we have little hope of secrecy anyhow. And if nothing else, it will make your task somewhat more feasible, Parmenios. The people of Valaróz will be more inclined to believe your claim if they have already heard rumor of you."

Parmo smiled. "I like it."

"Done then," Leone said, slipping back into the shadows of the assembled group.

"Very well," Casstian said. "Leone and Parmenios, you have your tasks before you. The rest of us will make way to Kylep with our ground forces. We will strike Lepig first, and if all goes well, march on Weordam. If we move fast, we can bottle Guderian's troops up on the high road through Forest Weorcan."

"What of Golier and Norgland?" one of the advisors asked.

Another of the advisors answered. "King Lorimer of Golier will be first to come to Sargoth's aid after Valaróz. It is too late in the year for Lorimer to send troops through the mountain passes though. All he can do is send troops by ship to bolster the forces massed at Col Sargoth. As for Norgland and King Hanns, we needn't worry about them yet. If we are able to march on Col Sargoth, they may pose a problem, but that is all. Hanns's loyalty to Guderian is questionable. He won't risk sending their ships around the northern cape at this time of the year. The same is true of the western Valarion fleet and Golier's navy. They are of no concern until spring at the earliest, and even then they would have to voyage for many months to reach Kal Pyrthin Bay."

"For good or ill, this war will be over by then, I think," Casstian said. "I don't mean to throw Pyrthinia into an extended war. We are risking everything and making a sprint for Col Sargoth."

All the advisors were silent for a long moment as the gravity of the King's words sunk in.

"And what of Wulfram?" Tharon asked at last. "Do we have no

plan to contest him?"

No one was fain to hope they could defeat Wulfram, and none had the answer.

"What plan is there for one of his likes?" Casstian asked.

"Perhaps there are more sorcerers in hiding?" one of the advisors asked. "We used to provide safe harbor to them. They might help."

Casstian shook his head. "Even if there are any sorcerers still alive in the realm and supposing we could find them, they wouldn't help—not after what Wulfram did to those girls in our very courtyard. We're on our own, I'm afraid."

"Let us be preemptive at least," Tharon said. "We can be vigilant. We can place archers with the advanced scouts, solely for the purpose of espying him. If we can see him coming when he is in raven form before he reaches our main force, perhaps we can catch him unawares and shoot him down."

"Yes, you are right," Casstian agreed. "Do it. Put together small teams and we will split them up. We'll send some forward with the scouts, but let's take your plan further. Wulfram poses the most danger if he comes upon us when we're gathered in mass. He can kill hundreds with one fell swoop. We'll move our troops in segments so that we never have our forces massed in one place except during battle. He will be less prone to attack then, for fear of killing his own troops. We'll place teams of archers in each regiment, with the sole purpose of defending against Wulfram if he should attack. Is there more we can do than that?"

No one had anything to add.

"Very well then," Casstian said. "You all know what to do. Let's get to work."

Though it was nearing midnight, Natarios Rhodas was admitted immediately to Emperor Guderian's private study high in the easternmost of the five towers of Lightbringer's Keep. Natarios was bedraggled and muddy and near exhaustion, but he knew his news could not wait. He had made it to Col Sargoth from Kal Pyrthin in an astounding fourteen days, taking a new horse as often as he could manage in the towns and cities he passed through and riding at least four of the poor animals to death. He was not overly fond of riding in the saddle, but his fear that King Casstian would send men after him to keep him from reaching the Emperor was enough motivation to keep him pushing on each day long after he would have stopped otherwise.

The Emperor's quarters occupied the uppermost five levels of the eastern tower, and the study was on the lowest of the five. It was a large, semi-circular room, not nearly as warm and inviting as King Casstian's study in Natarios's estimation. A cast iron heating stove stood at the center of the room and around it were an assortment of rigid, high-backed wooden chairs. At the far end of the room was a balcony, though the doors and curtains were shut at this hour. To Natarios's immediate left, next to the door through which he had just entered, was a strange scaffold-like structure rising up from the floor and through a square opening in the ceiling. A strange grating noise began emanating from the opening as Natarios stood there, and suddenly there was a deafening release of steam spurting down toward him.

Natarios leapt back with a yelp as the steam billowed around him. The smell of heavy oil nearly gagged him, and the grating noise grew louder. A platform dropped slowly through the opening, and when the steam finally cleared Natarios stood facing the Emperor. Guderian wore a sleeveless leather cuirass—exposing his heavily muscled shoulders and arms—and tight fitting leather trousers with a bulging steel codpiece. *If those are his nightclothes, I shudder to think what he wears by day*, Natarios thought.

"Natarios Rhodas," the Emperor said, stepping from the platform of his lift. "Why are you here and not in Kal Pyrthin as you should be?"

"I'm afraid that Casstian has been freed, Your Excellency," Natarios said with an apologetic bow of his head. "I do not know much, as I was barely able to escape with my life, but his commanders, it seems, acted of their own accord. They snuck into the keep in the night, tried to kill me, freed the King, and seized our tower. Otherwise, I would have sent a raven, of course."

Guderian's expression did not change, but Natarios could see the muscles bulging in his jaw. "You best sit and tell me everything," he said.

Natarios waited for the Emperor to sit first, then took a seat beside the heating stove across from him. He told the Emperor everything, from waking in the night and going down to the larder, to his escape from the keep, to his discovery that his men and the scent-hound in the tower had been killed, to his hasty flight from Kal Pyrthin. When he was done, the Emperor merely stared past him for a long time.

"Your pet has done as well as could be expected, I suppose," the Emperor said finally.

Natarios frowned, confused by the Emperor's words. "I don't understand—" he started to say, but a hand suddenly grabbed his shoulder from behind, and he jumped to his feet with a startled yelp only to see Wulfram standing there behind his chair. *Shite!* he swore inwardly. *How did he get in here without me hearing or seeing him?*

"Sit down and be silent," Wulfram said.

Still unnerved, Natarios took a seat well away from the sorcerer.

"He is a coward but a useful one," Wulfram said of Natarios to the Emperor.

"You heard all he said?" Guderian asked.

"Yes. The death of our scent-hound in Kal Pyrthin is most unfortunate. It makes our task very difficult now. I will go there and put an end to Casstian once and for all, if it is your desire."

"Not yet, I think. Where have you been? What have you found out about the prince?"

Wulfram stepped away from the stove into the deeper shadows of the room. "As the Prince's captain revealed to you, there is a passageway beneath a loose flagstone in the prince's room," he said. "I found his liaison dead in the tunnel beneath the room and beyond that discovered a network of caves and tunnels beneath the keep that lead to the city sewers beyond. The prince could have escaped through any number of drains and pipes leading to the streets."

"That is of little help."

"I think it was not the first time he used the passageway though. And I found the tracks of at least one other person. They led through the sewers to a cellar beneath a warehouse. There was a meeting of some sort there and a fight. The walls were scorched, and one wall was completely collapsed. It was the work of a sorcerer."

"That would account for the activity our houndkeeper detected before the prince's escape," the Emperor said. "It was in the northeastern borough, yes?"

"Indeed. And what's more, it was less than a hundred yards from The Thirsty Whale."

"Where the prince's brother was killed," the Emperor mused. "Perhaps the rumors are true then. One of the sorcerer's guilds has reformed. Do you suppose then that the prince joined up with them?"

"That is my belief, yes. Perhaps he told them of his sister, hoping that they would help protect the two of them."

"They think she is the one."

"Likely," Wulfram agreed.

"Well, let them continue thinking it. She's gone and of little concern."

"There's more," Wulfram added. "It may be nothing, but I have heard rumors of the airship again."

The mention of the airship put Natarios's hair on end. *Roanna,* he recalled. *Does Wulfram know?* He shrank back further into his chair. It occurred to him briefly that he could tell them of his meeting with Roanna, but he quickly dismissed the thought. *They would flay me alive if they knew.*

"The timing does not coincide," Wulfram went on, "but there were sightings of a strange flying object rising from Forrest Weorcan beyond the high road leading south. It is possible this sorcerer or other members of the guild went after the princess."

"Let them have her. She's of no concern to me—little more than a half-witted seer."

"Do not be so sure, Your Excellency," Wulfram warned. "She is not the one, but her fate may be linked to the other. We still know too little to take the princess lightly. She may very well lead us to the one we seek."

"Very well then," the Emperor said. "Continue your search. If the guild is back, there must be members still here in the city. Find them, and if you can't get information from them, bring them to me and I will do it myself. I want to know what they're after. I want to know where the prince went."

"And what of Casstian?"

"I had hoped to make an ally in young Caile and have him take his father's place, but this will perhaps suit us better. Casstian has declared open war with his actions. We will make an example of him just as we did with the Pallma house in Valaróz many years ago. My machines are ready. I will send them south along with the strength of our army to crush Pyrthinia. We'll set Don Bricio upon Casstian's rear to take and hold Kal Pyrthin Bay against retreat, then crush Casstian backward one step at a time. He will see the destruction of his greatest cities before he dies. It is time the world sees what the Empire has become—what we are capable of. And when Casstian is dead and his rebellion with him—when Kal Pyrthin is nothing more than rubble—none will ever dare to defy us again."

"And our misplaced houndkeeper?" Wulfram asked, indicating Natarios.

"Take him to the High Houndkeeper to put him to work. There are ravens to send and much to do before we march."

26
The Secret Discovered

Makarria lowered herself from her handstand and plopped down onto her bed, wishing Siegbjorn would return already. It had been four days since she had separated the linked rings, and that meant four days of solitude in the chamber while Taera continued her training with Roanna. The first day after separating the rings Makarria had been exhausted and slept much of the day, but by the second day she was recuperated and bored already. The subsequent days seemingly stretched on for an eternity. Makarria would try to sleep as late as she could each morning, but inevitably she would wake when Roanna came to fetch Taera and be unable to go back to sleep again. So she would get up, run laps around the room, move the beds around to create obstacles to leap over, do handstands, somersaults, cartwheels, push-ups, try to run up the wall and touch the stone ceiling—anything she could think of to pass the time. She would do that for what seemed like hours, then sit and still have to wait for the guard to deliver her midmorning meal. She would stretch the meal out as long as she could, but then the bulk of the day was upon her, and she would have another eight or more hours to occupy.

After four days, Makarria was absolutely done with it. *There has to be something better I can do to pass the time.* She looked the room over, but it was the same barren chamber with two beds and a lantern by the door. Her dirty plate, spoon, and cup were the only foreign items in the room, but she saw little use in them. *If I had a knife instead of a spoon, then that would be something,* Makarria thought. She got up from her bed and knelt down on the ground where she picked up the wooden spoon and idly rubbed one edge of it on the ground to try and sharpen it. She had sharpened sticks often enough on rocks when she was younger, grinding the tips to a point that was sharp enough to stab soft-shelled crabs in the shallows and tide pools near her home. The floor here in the cave was polished smooth though, and did little in the way of rasping away the edge of the spoon. Makarria plopped back onto her butt with a sigh. *I could always change it another way.* It was almost as if a voice outside her own suggested the idea to her. She had been thinking much of her ability since disconnecting the rings. It was the first time she had changed anything on purpose, and with that knowledge, the possibilities of what she could do had kept her up late each night, but she had pushed the thoughts aside, always telling herself there would be time for it later, when she and Taera were free and safely away from Roanna and Kadar.

Makarria stood up with an exasperated huff and took the spoon with her back to her bed, unable to push the thought of transforming it into a knife aside, even though she knew it was dangerous. *Taera and Roanna won't be back for hours,* she told herself. *No one will ever know.* Still, she hesitated for a long time. Only the thought of being in the tiny chamber all alone with nothing to do but somersaults and cartwheels convinced her to chance it.

Her mind made up, Makarria clutched the wooden spoon in both hands and closed her eyes. She cleared her mind and relaxed her breathing, as she had done before. When her mind was clear and her heartbeat steady, she envisioned the spoon in her hands and imagined its shape changing to that of a dagger. The image formed in her mind easily, but as before, she felt herself grow cold and weary. She could clearly form the image of the dagger, but it was as if the dagger was out of focus, and the closer she came to solidifying it, the more resistance she faced. She stubbornly refocused on the image in her head. There was a brief moment where she felt the resistance almost push her to a stop—like a rope stretching to its limit and holding for a split second before breaking—and then suddenly all resistance was gone and the dagger was there in her mind.

Makarria opened her eyes with a gasp and looked at the wooden utensil in her hands. It was the dagger as she had imagined it: long and slender with a sharp tipped point and an edge along either side of the blade.

"I did it!" she said out loud, unable to contain her excitement. She ran one finger across both edges of the blade and was surprised to find how sharp it really was. Being wood, it would nick easily and lose its edge of course, but it was sharp enough to gut a fish. Or to stab someone. Makarria brandished the dagger and spun, as if striking out at an imaginary assailant. Halfway through her spin a hand snatched her wrist and yanked her to an abrupt halt.

Makarria gasped. The door was open. Lost in her trance, she hadn't even heard Kadar step inside the chamber.

"Show me what you have done," Kadar said, prying the wooden knife from Makarria's fingers.

Makarria's strength wilted beneath his grip, and she fell to her knees. Waves of pain shot down her arm into her shoulder and chest. "Nothing," she gasped. "I didn't do anything."

Kadar let go of her and held the dagger up to stare at it in wonder. Makarria shrank back from him, unable to tear her gaze away from his black teeth.

"It is as I thought," Kadar said. "You are a clever little girl to keep this secret from me."

Before Makarria could catch her breath or respond, he yanked her up by the scruff of her tunic and shoved her forward. She struggled to free herself, but it only made it worse as he tightened his grip and caught up strands of her hair in his fist. He pushed her out the door past the guard standing there placidly, and then to the right into the main cavern past the other side chambers. When he reached the chamber where Taera met with Roanna each day, he kicked the door in and threw Makarria bodily to the floor inside.

Roanna jumped to her feet in surprise, and Taera rushed to Makarria's side protectively.

"What are you doing?" Roanna demanded.

Kadar thrust the wooden dagger in front of her face. "See what the little one has been doing. Turning spoons into knives behind our backs. It has been her the whole time."

Roanna stared at the dagger for a long time. When she spoke it was little more than a whisper. "Impossible."

"Do not tell me what is and is not possible," Kadar yelled. He turned to Makarria. "Who are you, girl? What is your name? Who are your parents?" He threw the dagger to the ground and it splintered in half.

"Leave her alone," Taera said, sliding forward on her knees to protect Makarria from him. "She's no one, just a farm girl."

"Liar!" Kadar hissed, and he grabbed Taera up by her hair and smacked her across the face. "Liar. How long have you known and kept it secret from us?" He smacked her again and blood trickled from her mouth. "Who is she? Where did you find her?" He raised his hand to strike her again, but Roanna grabbed his arm.

"Enough," she yelled, but Kadar shoved her away.

"Do not tell me my business, woman. Be gone and take the little one if you must protect someone. She is the one we want."

Roanna cowered back as Kadar turned his attention to Taera again.

"This one is mine now. She will suffer, and she will answer all my questions before she dies. Leave me."

Roanna hesitated.

"Leave me, I said!"

Roanna curled her lips and grabbed Makarria by one arm. She yanked her out of the chamber and slammed the door closed behind them. From within the chamber Taera cried out again. Makarria tried to rush back in, but Roanna held her back.

"No!" Makarria screamed. "Leave her alone."

Roanna slapped her. "Be silent, fool!"

Makarria fell to the ground stunned. Her hands shook, and she felt near vomiting. Taera's screams continued, punctuated intermittently by Kadar's yelling. Makarria closed her eyes, thinking she could dream something to help Taera, but her thoughts were scattered, and she could not concentrate. She crawled to her feet, half expecting Roanna to hit her again, but when she looked up she saw that Roanna was staring at the chamber door, her eyebrows furrowed and her jaw clenched tightly.

Without warning, Roanna barged forward through the door. Fire sprung from her palms, and Kadar flew back from where he knelt hunched over Taera. His robes flared up brightly as his body slid down the wall.

"Go!" Roanna yelled, yanking Taera up from the ground.

Kadar groaned as he flailed about in his burning robes. Roanna hurled fire at him again, but Kadar somehow pushed the flames aside with a sweep of his shoulders and stood, disrobed and free from his burning garments. His eyes flashed with anger, and his black teeth grit across one another audibly.

"Go!" Roanna yelled again, and she flung herself forward at him.

Makarria lunged into the chamber and grabbed Taera by the hand. As they sprinted out, the room lit up behind them with a flash. Makarria turned to the right for a moment, but then remembered Siegbjorn and the airship were gone, so she turned back the other way, dragging Taera along behind her deeper into the cavern. Screams and explosions echoed behind them, and Makarria quickened her pace only to come to a sudden halt as the guard at their chamber door stepped forward to impede their progress.

"Please, help us," Makarria pleaded. "They're fighting each other."

The man looked from Makarria to the sobbing Taera to the flashes of light behind them. "You're a friend of Siegbjorn, so you're a friend of mine," he said with a nervous nod. "Come, this way."

Caile stood at the back wall of the large chamber, well behind Talitha, who was the center of attention amongst the *Snjaer Firan*. The two of them had searched for days at the base of the mountain for the entrance to Trumball's cave. They found the remnants of the main entrance easily enough, but it had been collapsed years before and was little more than a rubble-filled crater in the mountainside. Talitha told him there was another entrance, a narrow tunnel higher upon the mountain that joined the main passage a mile or more in, but the terrain had changed much since Talitha had last been there, and the *Snjaer Firan* took great care to keep it hidden. When they found it at last, Caile's relief was short lived. The secret passage was little more than a gopher's tunnel in his estimation. The opening was three feet in diameter at best and utterly dark beyond.

They had unsaddled and set their horses free before continuing on, then climbed in, Talitha leading the way. How far they crawled on their hands and knees in the dark Caile could not guess. It seemed miles, though rationally he knew it must have been much less than that. On several occasions they reached narrow sections of the tunnel where they could barely lift their heads or move and Caile felt as if the mountain was crushing the breath out of him. Talitha seemed to sense his fear though, and each time he felt on the verge of panic, she would speak out to him and encourage him onward.

When they had at last reached the main cavern, Caile was much relieved to be able to stand and walk on his feet again, and even the two days more of walking deeper into the mountain was tolerable beneath the blue light emanating through the glacier above them. They were challenged by a guard on the second day, but when Talitha told the guard her name, they were ushered immediately into the massive cavern harboring the city of Issborg. Caile had gotten little more than a few minutes to marvel at the strange underground city before the both of them were rushed to where they stood now, in what appeared to Caile to be the town hall. It was long and narrow, with an arched ceiling, and carved literally into the face of the cavern wall.

Dozens of fur-clad, hairy men, and only slightly less hairy women crowded around Talitha. It was clear enough to Caile that they knew her and seemed to regard her highly, but they all spoke in a language he had never heard before, and he could discern little more than that. It seemed they were intent on bringing a parade of people to greet her, but she was insistently waving them away and asking questions of the most prominent men and women around her. Eventually, they settled into some sort of hushed conversation around her, and after several minutes of speaking, Talitha waved Caile over to finally join her.

"Your sister is here," she told him. "In the caves at the far end of the cavern."

Caile felt a surge of triumph and at hearing the news. "Let's get her then."

"It's not as simple as that. There are sorcerers holding her. Two of them. One is the woman from Col Sargoth, it seems, but the other hails from the Old World. It is as I feared."

"Are we safe here?" Caile asked her. "Can these people be trusted? Will they turn us over?"

"They can be trusted," she assured him. "They will do whatever I ask of them, though I will not throw them into harm's way if I can help it."

"You're one of them, aren't you?"

Talitha smiled. "Yes, but it's more than that. I am Trumball's daughter, Caile. I am their chieftain."

Caile stared at her, surprised, yet at the same time not. "Why didn't you just tell me before?"

"Because I have been away for decades now and I was not sure they would recognize me or honor my claim to lordship. I did not want to give either of us false hope."

"But you said they will do whatever you ask of them now, right? So, let's go get my sister."

Talitha sighed. "These sorcerers are very powerful. The two of them alone have managed to enslave my people. We cannot rush headlong to face them, or we will all end up dead. Even if we succeeded in killing our enemies, they might kill your sister first to spite us."

Caile opened his mouth to protest but did not know what to say. The thought of being so close to his sister and doing nothing to rescue her filled him with impotent fury. Equally as infuriating was knowing that Roanna was within his reach. She had used him for his knowledge of his sister, and she had betrayed him. She had tried to kill him. Caile wanted nothing more than to return the favor.

"We will stay here hidden for the time being," Talitha said. "Some of my people work in the outer caves as these sorcerers' servants. We will question them and learn the routine of our enemies so that we may sneak up on them unawares."

It made sense. He knew Lorentz would advise him to be patient, too, but Caile could not shake the feeling in his core that now was the time to strike. He felt as if danger was nearer than Talitha realized, that if they didn't act soon, it would be too late. "I just feel... I feel that—"

Before he could put his thoughts and words together, there was a commotion at the entrance to the hall. A group of newcomers pushed their way through the doors, although, they were blocked from Caile's and Talitha's view behind the gathering of people inside. Caile felt a tinge of warning run down his neck. He pushed aside those around him to meet the newcomers, and as the crowd parted he came face to face with his sister, her face battered and bleeding.

"Taera!"

"Caile?"

Taera could hardly believe it was really him until he grabbed her in his arms. "You're alright now," he told her. "Everything is going to be alright."

Talitha looked over Taera, and at Makarria standing beside her, for a long moment, then spoke sharply to the man who had escorted the two of them in. "Where are the sorcerers?" she asked in the tongue of the *Snjaer Firan.*

"They are fighting one other. I was frightened, so I brought the prisoners here."

Talitha pursed her lips and turned back to Taera.

"They found out about her," Taera kept saying to Caile. "They found out about her."

"Found out about who?" Caile asked.

"Makarria. He'll take her away now."

Makarria looked away from her hysterical friend to the crowd of people around them. She was able to surmise who Caile was—Taera had spoken of him often enough—but how he had gotten here she had no idea, and of the rest of the people she knew nothing. *If only Siegbjorn were here.*

"Please help us," she said. "Kadar is going to kill Roanna, then he's going to come for us. He's going to kill Taera, then he's going to take me away."

"He will do nothing of the sort," Talitha replied. "If they are fighting each other, now is the time to strike. We can't let them reach the city."

Caile pushed Taera up from where she sobbed and bled on his shoulder and unsheathed his sword. "Yes. I want their blood."

"No," Talitha told him. "This is my task and that of the *Snjaer Firan*. You must protect the girls. That is your task. Take them back the way we came—through the tunnel. With any luck our horses will have not wandered far. You are their protector now. I will follow you if I survive. If not, take good care of them both. They are the key to everything."

Caile swore. "I'm not running away."

"Caile. You must."

"I'm not leaving."

"Hide at least," she begged of him. "Go into the southern passage beyond the city and wait. If I do not return soon, if the fighting reaches the city, then you must take the girls and flee. Otherwise, all is lost."

Caile grit his teeth and sheathed his sword. "Fine," he agreed, knowing Talitha was right but not liking it. He wanted nothing more than his revenge but protecting his sister was more important. If he lost her now, he would never be able to live with himself.

"Go then, quickly," Talitha urged him, then turned to her own people. "Gather the twelve mightiest warriors amongst us and send them after me into the northern passage," she said in their tongue. "The rest of you: hide!"

27
Trumball's Heir

Makarria sat huddled up against the cavern wall with Taera's head in her lap, awaiting Caile's return. He had left the two of them in the cavern at the south end of Issborg to go fetch water from the lake, and Taera had immediately fallen into a fitful sleep. Her face was swollen and the blood on her face had dried into a black crust around her nose and mouth. Makarria, for her own part, found herself nauseous and overcome with an empty feeling inside her like a great sorrow. Part of it was a sense lethargy from having transformed the wooden spoon into a dagger, she knew, but the sense of loss she could not explain except from having been so scared by what happened with Roanna and Kadar. Her cheek stung where Roanna had slapped her, and poor Taera had faired much worse. The sight of her face made Makarria want to cry. Makarria closed her eyes, fighting away tears and wishing everything could just go back to the way it was before, when she was back with her parents on their farm. She could barely picture her parents' faces anymore. For that matter, she could barely picture her grandfather's. The thought of him left behind on *Pyrthin's Flame* pained her. She desperately hoped he had somehow escaped the burning ship.

"Is everything alright?" Caile asked, startling her.

"Fine, yes," Makarria said, rubbing the tears from her eyes.

Caile knelt down and handed her a waterskin to drink from, then turned his attention to Taera. He had dampened a cloth in the lake and he used it now to wipe the blood from her face. She moaned but did not wake.

206

"Kadar was beating her," Makarria said. "He would have killed her, but Roanna set him on fire."

"Roanna saved her?"

Makarria nodded. "She's mean but not as mean as Kadar. He's got black teeth."

Caile frowned at the thought but said nothing. He rinsed the blood from his cloth with water from the skin and continued to clean up Taera the best he could. When he was done, he sat down beside Makarria and sighed.

"How is it that you came to be captured with my sister?" he asked.

"I was stranded at sea, and your sister rescued me," Makarria said, and she told him how she had been rescued along with Parmo by *Pyrthin's Flame*, only to be taken away with Taera by Roanna on the airship a few days later. It felt good to talk to someone and speak her grandfather's name. She said nothing about the prophecy or Taera's visions however.

"Roanna has a flying ship?" Caile asked. "Are you sure you didn't just dream it up?"

Makarria laughed at the irony in his question. "Technically, Siegbjorn is the captain of the airship."

Caile thought her laugh odd but wrote it off to fatigue and delirium. *She's little more than a kid,* he realized now that he got a chance to look at her up close. Her arms were skinny but well-muscled, and the way she had walked into the town hall holding up his sister, he mistook her to be much older than she was. She had seemed very much an adult the way she carried herself. She was very pretty but younger than Caile by several years at least, by his estimation.

Makarria blushed under his prolonged gaze.

"Sorry," Caile said, realizing he was staring. "I just thought that... I mean—"

Taera gasped and woke with a start, cutting Caile short. "No!" she cried out. She pushed herself upright, panic on her face.

Caile grabbed her hands. "Taera. It's me, Caile. Everything is alright. You were just having a nightmare."

Taera took a deep breath and grimaced at the throbbing pain in her face. "Not a nightmare," she said. "A vision. Two visions at the same time. In one, Kadar stands over our bodies, and Issborg is destroyed. Ice falls from above and crushes the houses, crushes everyone, and Kadar is laughing. In the other, Makarria is standing there, and the city is safe. Kadar is swept away into darkness. I see both visions on top of each other. I don't understand. They can't both be true."

"It's a choice," Makarria said.

Taera's eyes refocused as she heard Makarria's words. "Yes, I think you're right, but what do I do? What choice must I make?"

"It's not your choice," Makarria said. "It's mine." She couldn't explain it, but when Taera had described the visions, Makarria could see them in her mind too. Two contradicting visions. The choice was simple enough. If Makarria did nothing, Kadar would kill them all and destroy Issborg. Makarria didn't know how she could stop Kadar, but she knew she couldn't stand by and do nothing. The people of Issborg had helped her and Taera. They were Siegbjorn's kin and friends. She would not let Kadar kill them. *Kadar is swept away into darkness...* Makarria repeated Taera's words in her mind. She could see Taera's vision. An impenetrable curved wall surrounded Kadar, and the light receded around him. Panic overcame him, and he scratched at the walls. Makarria knew the feeling. It was the same sense of dread she felt being trapped in her stone chamber day after day. That was it, she realized. She knew what she had to do.

"I have to go help the *Snjaer Firan*," Makarria said, standing.

"No, you can't," Taera said. "Kadar will do horrible things to you."

"It's alright. I know what to do."

"Hold on, what do you mean you know what to do?" Caile started to say, but Makarria ignored him and sprinted off back toward the city before the words were halfway out of his mouth. "Get back here!" Caile yelled, but Makarria paid him no heed.

Taera watched her leave. Her heart ached, but she too knew

Makarria was right. The visions represented a choice, and that choice was Makarri's to make. "Go with her," she told Caile. "Do whatever you can to keep her safe. She's the one."

"What do you mean, the one?" Caile asked, exasperated that he never seemed to know what was going on.

"The one prophesied to kill the Emperor."

"What? I thought that was you."

"No, Caile. It's her. Go!"

Caile snatched up his weapons with a curse and ran off in the direction of Issborg. At the edge of the city, he caught sight of Makarria nearly halfway to the other side—the only movement in the entire city. The *Snjaer Firan* were hidden away in their homes and had closed the shutters over every window. Only the blue daylight protruding through the glacier illuminated the city. *Damn it all, she's fast,* Caile swore inwardly as he chased after Makarria. When he finally caught up to her at the far end of city he grabbed her shoulder and dragged her to a halt, heavily winded.

"Stop. Wait!"

Makarria pushed his hand aside and trotted on. "Please don't try to stop me."

"I'm not here to stop you. I'm here to help. Now just slow down for moment and tell me what it is you think you're going to do that two sorceresses can't."

"What two sorceresses?" Makarria asked, glancing back at him.

"You said Roanna tried to kill Kadar. And now Talitha is going after him."

"Talitha is a sorceress, too?"

"Of course. She's the one who saved me when Roanna tried to kill me in Col Sargoth."

"I didn't know that," Makarria said. "But it doesn't make a difference. It wasn't Roanna and it wasn't Talitha in your sister's vision. It was me."

"Fine, but you still haven't told me what it is you mean to do."

They were getting close to the chambers now and Makarria slowed to a brisk walk. "I need to get Kadar into one of the chambers."

"Alright, that's a start. What chambers?"

"A few hundred yards down the corridor on the right, there's a bunch of caves with doors."

"Does it matter which one we get him into?"

"No."

"Alright," he said again. "And what do we do after that?"

"Then I do my work. Quiet now. We're getting close."

Caile bristled at being shushed. "Slow down then," he whispered. "We don't want to rush headlong into something if Talitha and Kadar are fighting. Or Roanna."

As if on cue, a heavy concussion echoed through the cavern.

"I've heard that sound before," Caile whispered. "That's sorcerers fighting." He left his sword sheathed and instead strung his bow and notched an arrow, remembering what Talitha had told him about trying to kill sorcerers. *Surprise them. Be unpredictable.*

The sound of concussions and bellowing flames grew louder and more frequent as they continued on, and before long they could hear voices, although, they could not make out the words. Talitha's indecipherable shouts were little more than guttural moans, while Kadar's heavily accented words were taunting in their tone. They heard nothing from Roanna. Suddenly, dark figures appeared before them, and Caile almost let loose his arrow but luckily held it back at the last moment, realizing it was the *Snjaer Firan* warriors who had accompanied Talitha. There were only four of them, and they all huddled close to the wall at their right.

"We're here to help," Makarria whispered when one of them turned back to see her and Caile approaching. It was the man who had been guarding her room. "Where's Kadar?"

"Up there," the man said with effort, and Makarria and Caile saw that he was badly burned on one side of his face. "Talitha is trapped on the far side, below the glacier."

"What about Roanna?" Caile asked.

The warrior spoke to the other men in their tongue, and they all shook their head. "We saw no sign of her," the man said. "She must be dead."

"Where's the rest of your men?" Caile asked. "I thought there were twelve of you?"

"There were."

Caile pursed his lips and pushed his way forward past the four men to peer farther down the corridor. A torrent of flames spat forward in the distance, and for a brief moment Caile could make out Talitha's form huddled behind a stalagmite twenty yards ahead and Kadar a little farther beyond her. Then the flames were gone and he saw only shadows again. Caile stepped back safely out of sight. "He's got her cornered, and he's too far away for me to get a clean look at him," he whispered to Makarria. "How is it you think we're going to get him into one of those caves?"

"I'll get him into the open," Makarria said. "When I yell, start shooting."

"I don't see how—" Caile started to say, but before he could get the rest of the sentence out Makarria strode forward into the middle of the corridor.

"Kadar!" Makarria yelled. "Kadar! It's me, Makarria. Stop, please."

"Makarria, no, get back," Talitha's voice rang out.

Makarria ignored her and walked on, fear in her belly. *He won't risk killing you—you're too important to him*, she told herself, but now that she was exposed, she wasn't so certain.

Kadar peered out from his hiding spot and began laughing an oily, rodent-like laugh. "It is alright, Makarria. Yes, come to me. I would not hurt you."

"Leave the woman alone," Makarria said. "And then you can have me." She stopped parallel to the first of the caves on the right. She saw in front of her the smoldering bodies of the other *Snjaer Firan* warriors but quickly averted her eyes and kept her attention solely on Kadar.

"But I can kill her and still take you," Kadar said.

"Not if I'm in the way, you can't," Makarria retorted, and she stepped forward to place herself firmly in the path between the two sorcerers. "Go," she said, looking back toward Talitha.

"Are you mad?" Talitha hissed. "You'll be killed."

"Just go," Makarria told her. "Trust me."

In the distance, Kadar laughed again. "Go on. Let the little girl save you for now."

"Go," Makarria said again.

Talitha paused for a moment longer, then sprang from behind the stalagmite and scurried back into the cavern behind Makarria toward the others.

"My end of the bargain is met now," Kadar said. "Now it is your turn. Come to me."

"I'm right here. Come get me."

Kadar stepped forward from his hiding spot, and when he spoke there was menace in his voice. "What is it you hope to accomplish, girl? Do you mean to stab me with a wooden knife? Your dream powers are weak and unhoned still. I could burn you to ash or bring that ice crashing down upon your head before you even close your eyes, let alone dream."

"Not if you want me to kill the Emperor, you can't."

Kadar smiled and his black teeth glimmered as he slowly stepped forward. "You are a clever girl. Too clever for your own good."

He was almost upon her now. She waited one breath longer, then turned and sprinted away. "Now!" she screamed.

Caile stepped out into the corridor and loosed his arrow. It whizzed by Makarria's ear, and Kadar leapt to the side, just narrowly dodging the projectile. He raised his hands to strike back, but Makarria had changed her course to run right for Caile, blocking Kadar's line of sight. Caile fired another arrow over the top of Makarria, and this time Kadar had no choice but to jump for cover in the nearest of the chambers.

"He's in!" Caile yelled, notching another arrow.

Makarria skidded to a halt and plopped down on her butt, facing back toward the chamber. "Keep him in there," she said breathlessly and closed her eyes.

"I only have four arrows left—move fast," Caile yelled, but

Makarria was already halfway in her trance, and Talitha and her men had jumped to his aid besides.

"What is she doing?" Talitha grunted out as she hurled fire at the doorway.

"I don't know," Caile said as he fired another arrow. "Just keep him trapped in that cave."

Beside Talitha, one of the *Snjaer Firan* warriors hurled his war hammer at the doorway when Kadar tried to peek his head out. Kadar flung a tight ball of blue flames at the man and ducked back into the cave as the war hammer slammed into the wooden door. The fireball flew true and knocked the *Snjaer Firan* warrior back onto the ground, where he died with a truncated scream.

Makarria was aware of none of the fighting around her. Her breathing was calm, her thoughts focused. In her mind she envisioned the door to the chamber and closed it.

The door closed with a bang that echoed through the cavern.

Makarria now pictured the living rock around the door frame. She imagined it blending with frame and door. She imagined the rock bleeding into the wood. She imagined the entire door turning to stone, becoming one seamless wall of rock. The same coldness and resistance she felt before washed over her but stronger than before. It was as if she herself was running headlong into a stone wall. But she pushed through it and solidified the image in her mind. Over and over again she pictured the door turning to stone. She clawed her mind through the resistance, she envisioned the door becoming stone. She projected it outward and made it so.

When she opened her eyes, all was silent.

"Did it work? Is the door stone?"

"Yes," Talitha said, stunned.

"Will he be able to get out?" Makarria asked.

"If it were wood, perhaps, or steel even, but you've made it solid stone. He is trapped. He will die, either of starvation or lack of air, whichever comes first."

Makarria pushed aside the knowledge that she had just killed a human being and let out a breath of vast relief. *We're safe now,* she consoled herself, and slowly all the nervous energy left her body. She felt herself slipping away into unconsciousness but could do nothing to stop it. Caile saw at the last moment as her body began to collapse and jumped forward with a startled yelp to catch her before she hit the hard ground.

When Makarria awoke, she was lying in a proper bed. She was startled for a moment, not recognizing where she was, but she soon remembered what had happened and realized she must be in one of the stone houses of Issborg. She was in a small square room with a window along one wall through which she could see the glacier above the city. In a chair near the foot of the bed sat Talitha.

"I'm glad to see you're awake," she said. "You've slept a long time."

"Is he dead?" Makarria asked, rubbing the sleep from her eyes. "Kadar, I mean."

Talitha nodded. "If not yet, he will be soon. The air in that chamber can't last more than a day or two."

"What about Roanna? I didn't see her anywhere."

"Dead. Kadar must have killed her before I arrived." Talitha grabbed a tray of food from a table near the door and placed it on Makarria's lap. "Here: eat, drink. You need to regain your strength."

Makarria sat up and looked over the food in wonder. Her meals back in the caves had been nothing more than bread, dried meat, and water twice a day. The plate before her now consisted of bread, fresh meat, cheese, and an assortment of berries she had never seen before. She dug into the food like a starved animal. When she finally finished and washed it down with a cupful of honey wine, she laid back content and tired again.

Talitha was not intent on letting her sleep yet though. "What you did yesterday, Makarria, was terribly brave but also terribly foolish," she said.

Makarria knew the truth of it, but she didn't see how she could have done anything differently, and besides, she felt this woman should be saying thank you rather than lecturing her. *I did save her life after all.*

"You are too important to be risking your life needlessly," Talitha went on when Makarria said nothing.

"There was plenty of need for it," Makarria retorted. "Taera had a vision, and I saw it too. Not only would you have been dead, but the whole city would have been dead too."

"I know. Taera told me what she saw. And don't think I'm ungrateful. It's just that I fear for you. You used yourself as a human shield. You can't go on taking your life so lightly."

"I don't take it lightly," Makarria told her. "It's just, Kadar and Roanna were using Taera and me for so long—because they knew what we could do and they were greedy and wanted to control us— it somehow seemed right to use that same greed against him."

Talitha smiled. "You are more astute than you might know. When people learn you are a dreamwielder, they will go to all ends to control you, to manipulate you, and to tempt you with promises and riches in order to make you do their bidding. And if they know of the prophecy regarding the Emperor, they will have even more reason to manipulate you. Some will try to win you to their side for their own selfish purposes, others—like the Emperor himself—will want you dead. But there are others, like myself and perhaps even Kadar, who understand the fragility and flexibility of prophecy."

"What do you mean?"

Talitha closed her eyes. "What seers see is merely an image of a possible future. Probable, yes, but not definite. Seers absorb the thoughts and feelings of those around them, sometimes of those far away, and in some way their brain translates these into potential events yet to come. They are by no means certain though. A thief might be inclined or predisposed to steal my coin purse as I walk by, but if I foresee this happening and eye him warily, or if a marshal walks within eyesight by happenstance, or if any other random act occurs, that thief might be persuaded to change his course and the prophecy becomes false. Alternatively, a seer might foresee something and try so hard to avert it that he or she actually sets in motion the very sequence of events that make the vision come true—the self-fulfilling prophecy.

"So you may ask yourself, Makarria, are you the one spoken of who is foretold to kill the Emperor? I would answer yes, but I would answer also that this does not mean you *will* kill him. Yes, the Emperor will try to kill you to preserve his own being, and yes, most of those who hate the Emperor will keep you safe in order to kill him for their own means but not all of them. Prophecies leave much to chance. People are unpredictable, and even those who want something from you might sooner kill you than not get their way. Kadar easily could have done so. Do you understand?"

"Yes."

"I don't mean to chastise you," Talitha said, looking kindly upon Makarria. "I just want you to be more careful, that is all."

"What I want," Makarria replied, "is to know what it is *you* want from me?"

"A fair question. Do you know who I am?"

"I know your name is Talitha. I know you're a sorceress, and you saved Caile. The *Snjaer Firan* follow your orders for some reason, too."

"Yes, it is because I am their chieftain. I am Trumball's daughter. Like him, I am a follower of Tel Mathir. I have spent my life learning the ways in which all things, both living and dead, are linked to her. Everything in our world is connected, Makarria. It is a world of complex cycles, all interconnected. Understanding how Tel Mathir operates gives me a greater understanding of the power you and I wield. It does not necessarily make me more powerful—indeed, Kadar, who knew nothing of Tel Mathir and little of what he was capable of, nearly slew me—but it does give me greater purpose and makes me better able to teach others.

"I will not lie, Makarria. I too want Guderian gone. He murdered my father, but it is much more than that. Guderian means to rid the world of all magic. He does not realize that magic, too, is one of the many cycles of Tel Mathir. If he succeeds in his goal, he will change the earth irreparably. The link between humans and nature will be gone. He cannot be allowed to succeed. If you choose to face him, I will assist you in whatever way I can. But I will never force you to do anything against your will, for that too would be contrary to the will of Tel Mathir. And the fact of the matter is, Guderian is not invincible. Another could kill him. He could simply catch a cold and die. There are an infinite amount of possibilities. Yours is merely the most probable."

Makarria's head swam with everything Talitha had told her. She was less certain now than she had been before. "Tell me this at least," she asked. "Both Taera and Kadar and now you have said that I am the one from the prophecy. But the prophecy says it's supposed to be a prince or princess, and I'm just a farm girl. I understand what you say, that the final result of a prophecy can be wrong, but how can it be so wrong about such a simple part? I'm not a princess at all."

Talitha smiled. "To answer that question, I think it's best you hear the news your friend Siegbjorn brings."

"Siegbjorn? He's back?"

"Indeed, he returned while you slept, and he has much you must hear."

28
Grave Decisions

Makarria and Talitha joined Siegbjorn in the town hall, who sat waiting at a large table along with Taera and Caile. The enormous room was otherwise empty and seemed overly large for their meeting. Makarria found herself running an awkwardly long distance to reach Siegbjorn and throw her arms around his chest.

Siegbjorn guffawed and ruffled her hair. "A good deal of trouble you've gotten yourself into, I hear. Can I not leave you for a moment?"

"I'm glad you're back," was all she said and sat down beside him.

Talitha sat, too, and regarded them all silently for a moment. Taera's face was bruised and swollen, but she sat erect and proud. Caile slouched forward with his arms on the table, again annoyed that he had no idea why they were meeting or what was going on.

Talitha sighed, then turned to Siegbjorn. "Tell them what you've learned."

"Yes," Siegbjorn said and cleared his throat before continuing. "At the bidding of Roanna, I traveled south to Weordan to gather news of what events have befallen the empire. She has spies there—part of her sorcerer's guild, although they are not sorcerers themselves—and they gather what news they can from the Five Kingdoms. Usually they would have little to say but much nonsense, but it seems much of import has happened of late. Wulfram himself was sent to Kal Pyrthin to dethrone King Casstian when the Emperor heard of your escape, Prince. Your father's imprisonment was short, however. He was set free several days later, and Pyrthinia has declared war upon Sargoth. Already as I was leaving, their forces were assembling at Kylep."

"Father?" Caile asked. "I didn't think he had it in him."

"It seems he does," Siegbjorn said with a shrug. "The Emperor is not one to sit idly by, however. The dark army of his is mobilizing in Col Sargoth, and it is common belief that the Valarion navy will set sail for Kal Pyrthin the moment Guderian's army begins to march."

"Those are not good tidings," Caile said. "Our navy is no match for theirs."

"Perhaps not, but there is more," Siegbjorn went on. "The wildest rumor I was to hear is that the heir to the Valarion throne has returned and allied himself with Pyrthinia. His name is Prince Parmenios Pallma, they say. To hear of him, he is young and quick with a sword, and it was he himself who freed King Casstian."

"Impossible," Caile remarked. "Parmenios was killed with the rest of the Pallma house. Don Bricio himself told me he saw him drown in the harbor of Sol Valaróz. And besides, he was young thirty years ago. Even if he were alive now, he'd be an old man."

"Perhaps not," Talitha said. "Siegbjorn, what do they say is Parmenios's nickname?"

"Parmo. And there is something more. It seems he was there on *Pyrthin's Flame*, Makarria, and somehow survived."

Talitha looked to Makarria. "Do you understand now? Why don't you tell us your grandfather's name. Tell us also where he is from and what you've done to him."

Makarria could not answer at first, she was so surprised. She was happier beyond description to hear that her grampy was alive but still could hardly believe her ears. *Why didn't he tell me?*

"My grandfather's name is Parmo," she said at last. "He was born in Sol Valaróz but lived with me and my parents near Spearpoint Rock. He was old and sick and about to die, and I was so sad I accidentally dreamt him a young man again. That's when we ran away and got rescued by *Pyrthin's Flame*. He explained a lot of things to me, but he never told me he was a prince."

"It was out of necessity he never told you," Talitha said. "If word reached Guderian that the true heir of Valaróz still lived, Guderian would stop at nothing to find and kill him. And whether your grandfather knew of the prophecy or not, he would know that your life was in danger being both a sorceress and of royal blood. You were safer if you didn't know who you were."

Makarria said nothing. She loved her grandfather, but at the same time she was mad at him, and Talitha trying to defend him only made it worse. In the long run, Parmo's secret had done Makarria little good. He was off fighting a war and here she was, freed from capture at last but facing danger nonetheless and her identity known.

"What do we do now?" Caile asked, breaking the silence. "Are we going to sit idly around while Pyrthinia goes to war against Sargoth?"

"That is for you to decide," Talitha replied. "I will tell you something more before you all choose your course of action. We are all aware of Wulfram, of course, and the danger he presents, but he is no longer the Emperor's most dangerous weapon."

"He has more sorcerers?" Taera asked.

"No, something worse. He has created machines of war. In the factories of Col Sargoth, he has been building steam-powered wagons meant to destroy everything in their path. They stand fifteen feet tall, eight feet wide, they are fully armored and armed with battering rams, scythe-like blades at the sides to cut down enemy troops and horses, and turrets along the top for archers. They are of the likes which the world has never seen. Only the half-human, half-machine horrors of the Dreamwielder War surpassed them in destructive power. King Casstian is marching into a death trap."

"How can you be sure?" Caile asked. "I was in Col Sargoth and saw nothing of the sort. Steam-powered wagons, for sure, but nothing like what you describe."

"I was not in Col Sargoth only to look after you, Caile," Talitha said. "I've been spying upon Col Sargoth for many years. The Emperor's factories are in the ground, deep beneath his smelting factories, and he only allows slaves to work on them so as to keep their existence secret. He has hundreds of these machines, and they will cut through the Pyrthinian troops like a scythe through wheat."

"Then we have to warn Father," Caile said.

"To what end?" Taera asked. "Father has committed Pyrthinia to war. They cannot retreat now. The Emperor will not let this act go unpunished even if we were to surrender."

"She is right," Talitha said.

"We still have to warn Father," Caile insisted. "I don't know what he has planned, but we have to tell him what he's up against before he faces these machines in the open. He'll have to change his tactics, draw the fighting into wooded areas, something."

"It's possible," Talitha conceded. "It is also possible the Emperor will send his machines on regardless—let your father's troops nip at their heels while they destroy every Pyrthinian city in their path."

"He'll turn our people into homeless vagabonds," Taera said, and they could all see that she had slipped away into a trance. "I see Kal Pyrthin in ruins, our ships burning in the bay. I see our people wandering aimlessly, hurt and hopeless."

Taera opened her eyes only to stare away at the table below her. They were all silent for a long moment, lost in their own thoughts. Makarria remembered the sight and smell of the slain *Snjaer Firan* she had come across in the cavern while confronting Kadar. *And that was only eight men dead,* she remembered. *How many will die in this war? Not just warriors but innocent people in the towns and cities? Hundreds? Thousands?* The numbers were incomprehensible to her, but the faces of those dead she had seen were enough. *What if that were Grampy dead? Or my parents? Or Siegbjorn? Taera and Caile?*

Makarria turned to Talitha. "Can I stop all of this if I face the Emperor?"

Talitha regarded her silently for a long moment. "It is impossible to say."

Taera dropped her hands away from her face. "Makarria, no. Don't even think about it. You're too young. You can't hope to defeat the Emperor. Not yet."

"If there's any chance of her succeeding, then she has to," Caile objected. "If the Emperor dies then all this stops. Think of the destruction and death we will avert."

"She's just a girl, Caile," Taera said, an edge in her voice. "She can't go alone."

"Of course not. Talitha can go with her. They can take every last *Snjaer Firan* with them, too. What does it matter? If she's ordained to kill the Emperor, how can she lose?"

"It doesn't work that way, Caile," Talitha said. "Nothing is for certain, especially prophecy."

Caile dropped his hands down on the table in frustration but said nothing. All of them were silent for a long moment.

"Should I do it?" Makarria finally asked of Talitha.

Talitha sighed deeply. "I cannot decide for you, Makarria. My heart and hope was that I might be able to teach you the ways of Tel Mathir. With knowledge and maturity, your powers would grow and you would be better equipped to face the Emperor if you chose to do so. But this war changes everything. My only advice to you is to disregard the prophecy, all of you. Forget you ever heard it. Caile, if you believe you can aid your father in warning him, then you must go. Makarria, if you believe you can defeat the Emperor and stop this war, then go. Know, however, he has killed sorcerers mightier than you. Though not a sorcerer himself, he has the ability to stint magic right when you are on the cusp of using it. Wulfram may very well be at his side, too. Together, they have defeated all who face them. If you think you can somehow do what others have not, then go. Otherwise, stay here with me. You will be safe for the time being."

"Whatever the rest of you are doing, I'm not staying," Caile said.

Makarria nodded. "I will go too, though I don't know the way to Col Sargoth."

"You can't, Makarria," Taera pleaded.

"I have to."

"If that is your decision," Talitha said, "then I will guide you and help you as I may. What is it you think you can do to stop Guderian?"

"I don't know," Makarria admitted. "I have to meet him first, then I'll know. Hopefully."

Talitha closed her eyes and nodded but said nothing.

"Then what of me?" Taera asked.

"I want you to stay here," Caile said. "If Father and I die, you alone carry the Delios bloodline."

"Your choice is yours," Talitha said. "Stay, join Makarria and I, go with your brother, or do something altogether different if you think it best."

"I will go with Caile," Taera decided. "My place is with the Pyrthinian people. Perhaps my visions can help us win this war."

"Very well then," Talitha said. "Everyone is decided."

Siegbjorn cleared his throat. "If these are the choices you would make, time is of utmost importance. Let me take you on the airship. There will be danger with armies on the march, but we can sail by night and travel quickly. Perhaps I can get you to the Emperor before the fighting even begins, Makarria."

"You can take us as far as Arnsfeld," Talitha said. "From there it is best she and I travel by foot, I think, so as to arrive unnoticed in Col Sargoth. From Arnsfeld, you can take Caile and Taera south to wherever they wish to go."

"It is done," Siegbjorn agreed. "Let us leave tomorrow. Already the snows have started, and we cannot tarry if we hope to make it over the mountain passes."

29
Converging Paths

Natarios Rhodas's chest heaved and his thighs burned as he tromped up the stairs to the Emperor's private quarters. He had been summoned from the houndkeeper's tower, and that meant walking down some four hundred stairs to the main keep and then back up again into the Emperor's tower. *Now I know why he created his steam lift,* Natarios thought, idly wondering if the Emperor would allow him to use the lift next time. When he finally reached the top of the stairs and the doorway to the Emperor's study, two guards opened the doors and stood to the side to allow him entry.

Wulfram and the Emperor were waiting for him. The Emperor motioned for Natarios to sit beside the heating stove, and Natarios did so wordlessly.

"I have a task for you to perform, Houndkeeper," the Emperor said. "You are to go to Pizer with all due haste and be my eyes and ears. You are to keep a lookout for a girl."

"Of course, Your Excellency," Natarios agreed. "Who might this girl be? How will I know her?"

"She is young. No more than thirteen or fourteen years old. She will be coming from the northeast, beyond Ulmstadt, perhaps by airship, but more likely she will be on foot so as not to attract attention. She may have one or more sorcerers from the guild with her. She may also be accompanied by the Pyrthinian prince, Caile, or his sister, Taera. You should be able to recognize them, no doubt. You will take with you gold to pay for information. Bribe innkeepers, farmers, whoever you deem useful to pass on what they may see to you. She must not get by you unnoticed."

"Yes, of course."

"You will take with you three ravens," the Emperor continued. "Send me word the moment they arrive in Pizer. Then follow after them in secrecy if you can and send the other ravens if you are able to learn anything more from your spying."

"There is a chance," Wulfram added, "that she may not come at all or come by another route."

"No," the Emperor said. "You have gathered the pieces well, my wolf. It is a complex puzzle, but a puzzle that is becoming clearer. The guild has found this girl and has hidden her away from us beneath the Barrier Mountains, but she will come to me. Who comes with her I cannot say, but she will come. I have a sense for these matters. It is in my blood."

"As you say," Wulfram conceded. "Still, I wish you would allow me to stay here with you. You may need my assistance."

"No, your job is to lead my army against Pyrthinia. I will stay here and await the girl. I fear not the prophecy of my childhood. I have done much to change the face of the earth we walk upon. This is not the same world which that seer saw. And besides, you have brought me a great gift, a token of insurance that the girl will surrender herself to me. We cannot fail. Go now, both of you. It is time to bring forth the Sargothian Empire to its true glory and strength."

It was still dark, some hours before dawn, and the wind was cold on the deck of the airship. Caile bundled his cloak tighter around his shoulders and gazed over the bow at the lights far below them.

"There lies Kylep," Siegbjorn said.

Caile could still hardly believe how quickly the trip had gone. They had left the cavern of ice at first light three days before and traversed the mountain passes in the safety of the daylight, then continued on throughout the night and left Makarria and Talitha several miles east of Arnsfeld with a few short goodbyes and well wishes. It had been hard for Taera to let Makarria go, but she was strong and smiled for Makarria as they flew away. When dawn approached, Siegbjorn set the airship down to anchor in the highlands to the south and east of the city. They stayed anchored throughout the day, then when the cover of night came again they took to the skies and continued southward, only to stop again when the sun rose. Now on their third night, Siegbjorn, Caile, and Taera approached the city of Kylep. It was a journey that would have taken three weeks by land, even if they had horses and pushed their mounts hard. *The world is changing,* Caile mused, thinking of the airship, the steam wagons he had seen in Col Sargoth, and the war machines Talitha had spoken of. *And not at all for the better.*

He left Siegbjorn at the helm and went into the cabin to join Taera. "We're almost there," he told her. "You're sure you want to do this?"

"Yes, I'm sure," she said, looking up at him.

She had shed her dress back in Issborg and adorned herself in the attire of the *Snjaer Firan* women: fur cloak over a skirted leather tunic, fur leggings, and soft leather boots. At her belt, she wore a long skinning knife. She looked more a savage warrior woman than a princess. She could sense Caile's reticence at leaving her behind.

"I'm tired of being afraid, Caile," she told him. "I'm tired of feeling powerless. I want to fight back. At the very least, I can warn Father as well as you can. You go on to Kal Pyrthin and carry out your plan."

Caile frowned. His idea had seemed better to him the night before when the prospect of leaving his sister behind wasn't at hand. *Still, she's right,* he told himself. His idea was simple enough. Makarria's grandfather, Prince Parmenios, had made his claim for the throne of Valaróz, but it was an empty claim as long as Don Bricio controlled the Valarion navy. Caile meant to remedy that. He knew the ways of the usurper.

"Let's get you out there, then," he said to Taera, grabbing her hand and leading her outside to join Siegbjorn.

Siegbjorn hardly noticed them walk onto the main deck, as his attention was focused on landing the airship without being noticed. He skirted the ship well around the eastern edge of the city and across the River Kylep as they slowly descended, and then at last set down at the edge of the high road to the south of Kylep. Caile helped Siegbjorn with the gangplank then walked Taera down.

"Identify yourself to the first Pyrthinian soldier you come across," he told her. "Command them to take you to Father straight away."

"I know what I'm doing, Caile."

Caile frowned. "I know, it's just…"

"I can take care of myself," she said and kissed him on the forehead. "You do the same."

She turned and ran off down the road then, and Caile walked back up into the airship. Siegbjorn wasted no time in pulling up the gang plank and getting them back into the air and away from the city.

"These are Pyrthin lands still," Caile said, hoping to keep an eye on his sister a bit longer. "We needn't be so secretive anymore."

"The Emperor has eyes even in Pyrthinia," Siegbjorn replied. "If you wish for your mission to be kept secret, then we must hurry for cover."

Caile said nothing, and they turned east, following the river. When the first hint of the sun peeked over the horizon, Siegbjorn set them down again to anchor in the treetops along the northern shore and wait the day out. The two of them retired to the cabin, and though Caile knew he should sleep, he found himself restless. The danger of the task before him weighed heavily on his mind. Don Bricio was a dangerous man, both devious and manipulative. Caile found himself reliving countless memories of his time in Sol Valaróz and trying to remember every nuance of Don Bricio's ways—how he turned conversations his way with sophistries and leaps of logic, how he kept his men loyal to him by turning them on one another and punishing treachery with death, how he forced women into his bed and threw them aside when he grew bored of them, but mostly how he taught Caile to fight in hand-to-hand combat. During his time in Sol Valaróz, Caile had daily private lessons with the master-at-arms, but on several occasions—usually when Don Bricio was drunk—Don Bricio took it upon himself to teach Caile a few of his personal tricks: sleight of hand maneuvers to distract the opponent, feigned injuries, and a whole slew of tactics most warriors would find dishonorable. Caile knew many of those tricks now, but he knew Don Bricio had not shown him everything.

Caile eventually did fall asleep, and Siegbjorn let him sleep through sunset and on into the night to pilot the ship by himself. When Caile awoke and joined him late that night they said little to one another. They had to anchor again the following morning, still almost a hundred miles east of Kal Pyrthin, and again Caile was left to his own thoughts. When night finally fell, they set off and passed over Kal Pyrthin a few hours later to head out across Kal Pyrthin Bay. Caile stood at the rail and watched his home city recede behind them. He couldn't help but wonder if he would ever see it again.

It was still several hours before sunrise, but Parmo could not sleep. *It figures,* he thought. *Now that I'm finally away from the war councils and have some time to rest, I can't sleep.* He got up out of his bunk and exited his quarters up onto the main deck of *Pyrthin's Valor.* It was quiet on deck but for the steady breeze flapping the sails and the prow of the ship cutting through the water. The few sailors on deck at this hour tended to their duties and left Parmo to his own thoughts. He'd had much time to ruminate those thoughts since setting sail from Kal Pyrthin two days prior, and yet he still didn't know what to make of it all. He had acted foolishly taking Makarria from her parents, he knew. He had been intoxicated with the vigor of youth when Makarria remade him and had acted the part. His rashness had likely cost Makarria her life by his reckoning, but there was no going back now. If Makarria was alive, she was on her own, and Parmo had declared himself the heir to the Valarion throne. King Casstian and all of Pyrthinia were counting on him, not to mention his own countrymen. *It's time you act like a prince for once, borrowed time or not.*

He walked to the bow of the ship and gazed to the east. Come midday they would pass by Spearpoint Rock and his farm. That was, assuming they didn't run into the Valarion fleet first. If time allowed it, he would go visit Prisca and Galen, tell them what he'd done, and warn them of the impending war. He owed them that at least, he decided, as much as it would hurt.

A shadow crossed over Parmo, almost imperceptible in the pre-dawn darkness, but he sensed it nonetheless. He looked up and saw high above him the silhouette of the airship passing overhead. A surge of hope and anger washed over Parmo. The airship was heading in the same direction they were, likely to join up with the Valarion fleet he guessed. It was too much to hope that Makarria was aboard the airship, Parmo knew, but still, having found the ship after all this time validated his decision to lead the Pyrthin fleet and strengthened his resolve. *Makarria may not be on that ship, but whoever is onboard knows where she is, and Tel Mathir help me, I'll have it from their dying lips.*

30
The Long Belated Claim

"We have an hour at most before the sun rises," Siegbjorn said. "If we don't spot them soon, we'll have to take cover on shore."

Caile nodded. They had passed Spearpoint Rock an hour before and turned south, skirting the Pyrthinian shoreline, but still had seen no sign of the Valarion fleet. Caile suspected the fleet was not far off but could not be certain. Don Bricio was sometimes unpredictable. If he suspected much resistance from the Pyrthin navy, he might have waited to set sail, or he might have led the fleet farther to the north, far from sight of the coast, to turn around and enter the bay at its northern end. Caile kept his eyes peeled regardless. Don Bricio was also an arrogant man, and with any luck he would sail in the most direct route toward Kal Pyrthin.

The minutes passed, and still they saw nothing. The eastern horizon brightened, and Siegbjorn looked toward shore for a suitable place to hide.

"Not yet," Caile urged him. "A few more minutes." The thought of waiting another day to finally face Don Bricio was more than Caile could bear. *Where are you, you bastard?* he muttered beneath his breath.

They traveled onward and just when Siegbjorn was about to insist on landing, Caile spotted dark shapes on the horizon.

"There!"

Siegbjorn followed his gaze. "Indeed, there they are. But it is nearly light now. We would not be able to approach unnoticed."

"Yes we will. Drop down low and turn dead east. We will wait and use the rising sun to come at them in their blind spot."

"Of course," Siegbjorn agreed, disappointed he had not thought of it himself. He dropped the ship low, no more than twenty feet over the rolling waves, and turned eastward toward the sun. A mile out, he stopped the propeller and brought them to a halt. "Now we wait."

Caile nodded and wordlessly prepared himself. He took off his boots and shirt, rolled up his trouser legs, and removed his sword and scabbard from his belt.

"What plan do you have?" Siegbjorn asked.

"Stay low as we approach," Caile said. "I will jump into the water on their starboard side and climb aboard as you sail past. Once you're past them, stay low so they see you. The sight of the airship will distract the crew so I can get aboard unnoticed."

"Those ships will be under full sail and moving fast," Siegbjorn pointed out. "How do you mean to get aboard from the water?"

"I'll need a short length of rope, something to hook around the anchor, and this won't do me much good," Caile said, throwing his sword into the cabin. "Have you got something smaller I could have? Something easier to swim with?"

Siegbjorn took the skinning knife from his belt and gave it to him, then unwrapped one of the anchoring ropes from the rail of the airship.

"I just need a loop, five or six feet long," Caile said. "The anchor hangs no more than a few feet from the water line on the portside of Don Bricio's ship."

Siegbjorn looked at him skeptically, but tied the rope in a loop nonetheless, then tied a wide knot at the free end of the rope. "You are in for a sore surprise, you will find, if you think you will be able to pull yourself aboard a fully rigged ship."

"Trust me," Caile told him. "Let's go."

The fleet was parallel to them now to the west. Siegbjorn reengaged the propeller and they turned toward the Valarion ships. With the sun at their back, they were completely invisible to the Valarions. Caile tucked the knife into his belt and looped the rope over his head and one shoulder, then went to stand at the bow of the airship in front of Siegbjorn.

"You'll want to board the flagship, yes?" Siegbjorn said over the wind.

"No, the one at the rear. Don Bricio never sails in the flagship. He commands the fleet from the rear."

"He commands the fleet from that tiny caravel?" Siegbjorn asked incredulously, spotting the ship at the rear.

"That's the one. She's maneuverable and fast—easier for Don Bricio to escape if things go wrong. Cut us right across her prow, then make a good show to keep them all distracted. Maybe yell some curses at them in your tongue just to really get their attention."

Siegbjorn couldn't help but laugh in appreciation of Caile's brazen confidence. "As you say, Prince."

They were approaching now at a fast clip. Caile climbed up onto the railing at the bow and stood at a crouch. He could see the water speed by below and realized they were going faster than even the fastest horse could run. *This is going to hurt,* he told himself. *And it's going to be damned cold.*

The brunt of the fleet had already passed before them, and they were on a near collision course with Don Bricio's caravel at the rear. Caile waited until the last possible moment, then dived forward off of the airship. The impact was violent, but he cut into the water as best as he could hope. Still, his head was ringing when he surfaced, and he had to gasp for breath. He spun in the water to catch his bearings and saw that the caravel was bearing down right on him. He kicked and backpedaled with all his might, and then suddenly the surge of water at the prow of the ship hit him and pushed him clear. He scrambled to get the rope from around his neck and took the loop in one hand, the knotted free end in his other. Meanwhile, the ship was zipping by before him. He spied the anchor hanging from a porthole racing toward him. *You've only got one shot at this,* he told himself, then kicked with his feet to push his upper body up out of the water and heaved the rope.

His aim was true. The loop in the rope caught on the forward rung of the anchor, and before he knew it he was yanked forward with so much force his arms nearly came out of their sockets. It took so much concentration to hang on, he couldn't even cry out in pain. His legs and torso slammed in and out of the water as the ship crested each wave, and it took every bit of his will power to hold on to the rope. With great effort, he pulled himself up out of the water to grab hold of the anchor. The rusty metal scraped the skin from his fingers and palms, but the pain only steeled his resolve. He climbed hand over hand up the chain, then pulled one foot up into the porthole and heaved himself up onto the main deck. He looked around and saw thankfully that the men on deck were all at the portside of the ship, yelling and pointing at Siegbjorn's airship.

Caile pulled himself up as quietly as he could manage, then darted to his left down the stairs leading beneath the sterncastle to the captain's quarters. *This is it*, he told himself. *Don't be fooled by his smile*. He pulled the knife from his belt and took a deep breath, then threw the door open.

Don Bricio stood hunched over, facing away from him as he yanked his britches up. "What is all the damned yelling about?" he asked, thinking Caile was his first mate.

"Why don't you look and see," Caile said, closing the door behind him.

Don Bricio turned and stared in shock at Caile, his tight, rotund belly hanging over his trousers. "*You*. How did you get on board?" His hand reached instinctively for the sword at his hip, but his sword sat in its scabbard along with his belt on the bed. Caile had literally caught him napping.

"You taught me well the ways of stealth and treachery," Caile replied with a smile.

"Yes, yes, you always were a quick learner," Don Bricio said and smiled. He brushed his thin, gray-black hair slickly back over his head. "I taught you a little too much perhaps, but this is still good I think. Yes? It's not too late, you know. Join me and you will be rewarded handsomely. The throne of Pyrthinia is still yours if you league yourself with the Emperor. You can become my equal.

Again, Valaróz and Pyrthinia will be strong allies."

"Under the yoke of Guderian? I don't think so."

Don Bricio held his hands palms-up and waggled his fingers, as if beckoning a child to come sit on his lap. "Come, come. Put your weapon down. Let us not be hasty with one another. I was like a father to you, yes? Let us embrace, then we will go to the galley and discuss matters over a few cups of fire nectar. It will be like old times."

Don Bricio stepped forward, ostensibly to hug Caile, but also closer to the sword on the bed.

"Don't take another step," Caile warned him, crouching forward with the knife held at the ready.

Don Bricio's smile disappeared.

"There's nothing to discuss," Caile told him. "You have nothing to offer me because you are no longer King of Valaróz. Prince Parmenios Pallma has returned."

"Nonsense!" Don Bricio spat. "You speak of rumors from that treacherous liar Casstian. The Pallma line is dead. Quit being a damn fool and drop your weapon. You try my patience, boy."

"I'm not a boy anymore."

"No, you're a dead boy now," Don Bricio said, and he lunged as if he were reaching for his sword. Caile leapt onto the bed, lashing his knife outward, but Don Bricio pulled back with surprising quickness and darted around the bed for the door as Caile tumbled across the bed. Caile let his momentum carry him to the far side of the bed and hurled the knife at Don Bricio as he spun to his feet. Don Bricio grunted and stumbled into the door as the knife struck him in the back of his right shoulder.

"Whore's whelp," Don Bricio swore, leaning heavily into the door. He reached back over his shoulder with pained deliberation and wrapped his fingers around the handle of the knife. "I'll kill you and your entire family, just like I did with the Pallma line," he said and yanked the knife free. He let the door support his weight and turned to face Caile.

"I think not," Caile said, and he ran Don Bricio through the neck with his own sword.

. . .

Parmo looked upon the familiar sight of Spearpoint Rock from where he stood at the forecastle of *Pyrthin's Valor*. There was no time for side trips or reminiscing though. Their scouting ship had spotted a fleet coming from the south. *I hope you're ready for this*, he told himself as he turned to Rufous, now captain of *Pyrthin's Valor*. "Signal the fleet to hold here," he yelled, "then raise the yellow flag for a parley. We'll face the Valarion fleet alone."

Rufous carried out his orders, and within a few minutes *Pyrthin's Valor* sailed southward alone. The Valarion fleet soon came into sight, and Parmo looked to the top of the mainmast to make sure his yellow flag was flying. It was a symbol honored by Valarion sailors of old, but Parmo was not certain the Valarion fleet would honor it now. He could only hope they would. His plan was simple. If the Valarions agreed to parley, he would state his claim for the Valarion throne and challenge Don Bricio to single combat. If Don Bricio refused, he would attempt to win the hearts of the Valarions over and mutiny against Don Bricio. Snippets of phrases and ideas swirled through his head, but he had no set speech in mind. *Speak to your own heart, and you'll speak to theirs*, he knew. If that failed, it was war. Rufous would signal the rest of the Pyrthin fleet at the first sign of trouble, and they'd all sleep at the bottom of the ocean, Pyrthinians and Valarions alike.

The first ships of the Valarion fleet drew near now and Parmo saw with some relief that they were lowering sail. In fact, the entire fleet lowered sail and formed a perimeter around *Pyrthin's Valor*. Rufous ordered his men to drop their own sail, and soon two hundred ships were drifting off the eastern shore of Pyrthinia, all of them, but one, Valarion ships.

A lone caravel sailed forward to halt alongside *Pyrthin's Valor*. Parmo put his hand to the hilt of his sword and yelled across the span of water between the two ships.

"I am Parmenios Pallma, rightful heir to the throne of Valaróz! I demand to speak with the usurper, Don Bricio."

A sailor stepped up onto the sterncastle of the caravel and shouted back. "I am Socorro, Admiral of this fleet. If you have something to say, say it to me."

Parmo glanced at the ships surrounding *Pyrthin's Valor*. On the deck of each and every one, Valarion sailors crowded forward to hear what he had to say.

Rufous saw it too. "Word of your return has gone before us," he spoke quietly. "They are yours to win over."

Parmo breathed in deeply, then spoke, projecting his voice out over the water. "I have come to retake the throne of Valaróz! Thirty-four years ago, my family was slain by the Emperor and the usurper, Don Bricio. King Provencio was shot in the back with a crossbow, like a common thief. Queen Lauda and Princess Maysa were burned alive on the steps of the palace in Sol Valaróz. Maysa was only four. Four years old! These were your countrymen, your just and faithful rulers, descendants of Vala herself. In their place, the Emperor placed a foreigner from the Old World, a weasel who rules by force and cares not for the welfare of Valaróz. How many of your friends—of your kin?—have died or felt the sting of the whip at Don Bricio's hand? How many have disappeared never to be seen again because they were an outspoken Valarion and unafraid to stand up for truth?

"I remember a time when Valaróz was proudest of the Five Kingdoms, the never-wavering force that kept the Old World at bay. The kingdom of the sun, home of the finest wine, the best catches of the sea, and the most beautiful women. I remember a time when all Valarions were free to live and prosper without fear of pain or death for speaking their mind or disparaging Sargoth. I remember a time when Valaróz and Pyrthinia were allies, when we fought together for justice and peace. But now, Valaróz is nothing more than an extension of Sargoth. Our once proud kingdom has sunk lower than Golier, even!

"But we can regain our glory, my countrymen. Join me. Let me lead you, and together we will once again ally ourselves with Pyrthinia. Together we will defeat Sargoth. Together we will remake

Valaróz into the kingdom it deserves to be!"

A great murmuring rose up from the Valarion sailors, punctuated with intermittent shouts, but Parmo could not make out their words, whether they were for or against him.

"Silence!" Socorro yelled. When all was quiet again but for the lapping of the seas against the ships, he addressed Parmo. "How can we know your are truly of the Pallma line?"

Parmo withdrew his sword and held it up for all to see. "Because I bear the sword of my ancestors. Bring forth Don Bricio and he himself will recognize my face. He was there when I was thrown into the bay of Sol Valaróz thirty-four years ago. Let him speak for himself, and if he still lays claim to our kingdom's throne, I will cut his heart from his chest."

All was silent for a long moment. Parmo held his breath. He didn't know what else he could say to sway them.

"I'm very sorry," Socorro said finally, "but Don Bricio cannot vouch for you."

A young man stepped forward onto the forecastle of the caravel to join Socorro, and he flung something toward *Pyrthin's Valor*. One of the Pyrthinian sailors caught it out of the air and held it up. It was a burlap sack. The sailor looked inside and pulled out the severed head of Don Bricio.

"Don Bricio no longer lays claim to the throne of Valaróz," the young man said from the other ship.

Rufous ran forward to stand alongside Parmo. "Is that you, Prince Caile?"

"So it is, Captain," Caile yelled back with a smile.

"How is this possible?" Parmo asked, stunned.

"Perhaps you should come aboard," Socorro said, "and we can explain… Your Highness."

On board Don Bricio's caravel, Caile explained to Parmo and Rufous how he had snuck aboard and killed Don Bricio, then confronted Socorro.

"When he showed me that head, I didn't know whether to kiss him or kill him," Socorro laughed. "But he somehow knew you were with the Pyrthin fleet, King Parmenios. We'd all heard rumors you were back but didn't dare to hope it was true. I'm glad it is."

"As am I," Parmo agreed. "But how is that you knew I'd be here, Caile?"

Caile shrugged. "It was not hard to guess. I'd heard the rumors you were back, too, but I happened to know they were true because I've met your granddaughter. And if you're anything like she is, I knew you'd be with the Pyrthin fleet."

"Makarria?" Parmo could hardly believe what he was hearing. "She's alive?"

"Alive and well last I saw her."

"Makarria?"

"Yes, Makarria," Caile said with a smile.

Parmo gave out a hoot of elation, then picked Caile up in a bear hug and swung him around in a circle before kissing him on the forehead. "Where is she? You're sure she's fine?"

"She's in Norgland with a sorceress—the daughter of Trumball himself—so I imagine she's safer than the rest of us," Caile said, and he proceeded to tell Parmo how he'd been rescued by Talitha and traveled with her to Issborg to free Taera and Makarria from Kadar and Roanna. He told Parmo everything except where Makarria was headed. That information Talitha had made them all promise to keep secret. *You're not to tell anyone, not your father, not Parmenios, not anyone*, she had said. *Even those we trust can unintentionally let secrets slip, and if the Emperor learns Makarria is coming, she is lost.* And so Caile kept his promise and made it sounds as if Makarria was still in Issborg.

When Parmo was content that he had heard everything and that Makarria was safe, they set about discussing what to do. After much deliberation, they decided to split up. Caile would go with Rufous and the Pyrthin fleet back to Kal Pyrthin, then upriver to reinforce Kylep, while Parmo would return with Socorro and the Valarion fleet to Sol Valaróz and make official his claim to the throne. Parmo's initial instincts were to go with Caile to Kylep and help Casstian fight the Emperor, but he knew Socorro and Rufous were right: he'd better serve the war against the Emperor by unifying Valaróz under his rule and striking out both by land and sea.

Less than an hour later, their plans were made, Caile was gone with Rufous on board *Pyrthin's Valor*, and Parmo stood at the sterncastle of Don Bricio's caravel which he promptly renamed *Makarria*.

"Are we ready to set course for Sol Valaróz, Captain and King?" Socorro asked him.

"Send the rest of the fleet on ahead of us," Parmo said. "We'll catch up with them shortly. There's something we must do first."

"What would that be, Captain?"

"Set course for Spearpoint Rock. We're going to fetch the rest of the royal family."

31
The March to Col Sargoth

King Casstian looked at the fray before him and commanded his reserve troops forward. The Sargothian cavalrymen from the Lepig garrison had cut deeply into the ranks of the initial Pyrthinian force, but Casstian's small army vastly outnumbered the Sargothians, even if his army was hastily assembled. Upon Taera's arrival in Kylep and after hearing her news, Casstian had made haste toward Lepig with his advanced troops to take the city. If the rumor of Guderian's war machines was true, Casstian knew his only hope was to bottleneck the machines in the confines of the high road where it passed through Forrest Weorcan and that meant securing Lepig and Weordan first. All was going as planned so far.

The reserve troops surged forward onto the plains surrounding Lepig and swept over the Sargothian cavalrymen. A few small pockets of resistance persisted, but the fighting was all but over. Satisfied, Casstian turned his horse about to face his High Constables. Taera was there with them, sitting on her horse still clad in the savage furs of the northmen. He had tried convincing her to stay back in Kylep, but she insisted on coming, and he didn't have the heart to keep her confined there by force.

"It is done," Casstian told his constables. "Let's form the men back up into ranks before we march into the city. I want everything orderly and clean. No looting, no drinking, nothing. First order of business is to secure the garrison and round up any other Sargothian soldiers. Once that's done, post the bulletins and send out criers to announce a curfew and our purpose. We are here to free these people, not enslave them. Put down any disobedience quickly and quietly. Otherwise, the people may go about their normal business. Send out our field marshals to recruit whoever is willing into the general infantry. Is there anything I'm forgetting?"

"What of me and my men?" Leone asked.

"Your work here is done," Casstian said. "Sneak your men past Weordan into the forest. Do what you can to block the high road. Fall trees across it, dig holes, do whatever seems most feasible to stall those wagons from reaching us. Our main troops are ten days out still, even under a forced march."

Leone was listening, but his attention was focused beyond Casstian. "Your Majesty," he said suddenly. "Behind you."

Casstian turned to see four Sargothian cavalrymen rushing up the hill toward them. They had somehow fought through the Pyrthinian forces and broken free.

"Form around me," Casstian yelled, drawing his sword. "Taera, stay here."

The constables drew their weapons and formed up around Casstian. When he saw they were all ready, he called the charge and they spurred their horses forward. They were six against four and at the last moment one of the Sargothian's reigned in short and veered away. Casstian thought little of it, thinking the man merely a coward, and the three remaining cavalrymen were pummeled from their horses in the initial onslaught. The fourth cavalryman, however, did not flee; he merely skirted Casstian and his men and charged straight for Taera.

Taera realized what was happening immediately and pulled her skinning knife from her belt. A twinge of fear ran down her spine, but instead of letting it paralyze her she took a deep breath and let the fear fuel her anger. *Damned coward,* she cursed the soldier charging toward her. *Go after the one girl on the field, will you?* Taera squeezed her legs and gave a little chirp to urge her horse forward, then kicked him in the flanks to meet the charge full-on. She let loose a yell from deep within her gut.

Casstian turned to see what was happening at the last moment and screamed, but Taera did not hear him. The cavalryman's flail swept out toward Taera's head, but she ducked beneath it and swiped at the man with her knife. The collision nearly broke her arm the force was so great, and she was knocked clean from her saddle to land on the ground with a thump. She pushed herself up with a groan, ready to fight even though there was no air in her lungs and she had lost her knife. The cavalryman had been unhorsed as well, she saw, and he was still down, her knife stuck into his belly. He flopped and convulsed on the ground like a fish, trying unsuccessfully to grasp the bloody handle of the knife and pull it free.

Taera stepped on his chest with one booted foot to hold him down and yanked the blade out of him. The man groaned in pain and looked up at her with wide eyes, but she felt no pity for him. With a savage yell, she brought the knife down into his throat, and his startled cry ended in a wet gasp.

"Taera!" Casstian yelled as he reigned his mount to a halt. "Are you alright?"

"Better than I've been in a long time," Taera remarked, flinging the blood from her blade.

Casstian was off his horse by now and looking her over to make sure she wasn't wounded. "What were you thinking?" he demanded. "You're just as much of a damned fool as Caile is."

"That's because we both take after you," Taera pointed out. "Now quit your fussing over me. We have a city to secure."

Casstian couldn't help but laugh, he was so surprised by her demeanor. "As you say, Your Majesty."

Makarria came to a stop at the top of the hill and sat down on a rock alongside the road to wait for Talitha to catch up. The morning sky was dull and gray with clouds, but after being trapped in the cavern of ice for so long, it seemed almost bright and cheery. It was liberating to be in the open air, to be surrounded by trees and grass again. The only thing missing was the ocean. Still, the land around them was beautiful, and Makarria felt guilty for not enjoying it more. Knowing where the road before them led took the joy out of everything for her.

They had been walking more than a week now since Siegbjorn dropped them off outside Arnsfeld. Their days consisted of breaking camp at first light and walking as far as they could before the sun set again, sometimes covering as many as thirty miles or more. When the mornings were fresh and they were not yet weary, they talked. On their first day, Talitha had made Makarria describe every instance she could remember where she had dreamed or used her power. Makarria's stories were frequently interrupted by questions from Talitha, and on more than one occasion, Talitha had demanded that Makarria elaborate and provide specific details. She was particularly interested in how Makarria had transformed Parmo into a young man—she asked much about the dead fish—and also how Makarria had managed to trap Kadar inside the cave. The subsequent days had been filled with discussions about the cycles of Tel Mathir and practicing various small exercises. Makarria's part in the discussions was limited mostly to asking questions, but she was content to listen to what Talitha had to say about how plants grew, reproduced, and died, how water evaporated from the ocean only to fall from the sky again in the form of rain and snow to cycle through the ground to feed the rivers and lakes, and how animals created a great hierarchy of prey and predators. Makarria had no idea how any of it was meant to help her face the Emperor, but she dutifully listened and learned from Talitha. If nothing else, it was a welcome distraction from what faced the both of them in Col Sargoth. As for the exercises, they were limited to achieving a meditative state where Makarria was half asleep yet half awake and still able to walk and function at a rudimentary level. Talitha absolutely forbid Makarria from trying to use her power in any way, for fear the Emperor and his scent-hounds might detect it.

"You're a fast walker," Talitha said when she reached Makarria at the top of the hill.

Makarria shrugged. "In the morning, I suppose. Probably it's only because you're the one carrying the pack."

"Let's remedy that then, shall we," Talitha said and hoisted her shoulder sack into Makarria's arms. "That'll slow you down for a while so we can talk."

"What are we talking about today?"

"Do you remember how you described to me the feeling of resistance you experienced when you were trying to trap Kadar?" Talitha asked, leading the way down the opposite side of the hill.

"Yes, it was like climbing a steep mountain," Makarria replied, recalling the sensation. "A mountain I could barely get to the top of."

"Indeed. The apex of that mountain, the wall you must break through—however it is you perceive it—that is the border between your dream state and reality. If you do not push through that boundary, your vision becomes nothing. There were probably many times when you were growing up where you dreamt things, and they started to become real only to disappear the moment you awoke. This, partly, was because you did not yet have the strength or ability to push through that border, but mostly because you were not purposely trying to dream things."

"My grandfather said I used to have lots of dreams that would show themselves then disappear," Makarria said. "Every once in a while the dreams would stay. The dress stayed and then my grandfather himself, of course."

Talitha nodded. "Yes, those were the times you pushed through the boundary and solidified your dreams. The danger comes when you commit yourself to dreaming something too big, when you create a hill too tall to climb over. If you try make that dream reality and do not have the strength to make it happen, you will die. You see, Makarria, you cannot make something from nothing. When you utilize your ability, you are drawing upon the life force within you and the energy around you to literally change the fabric of matter. In the case of the wooden knife, you rearranged the particles of wood from a spoon shape to a knife shape. In the case of the door, you did something much more difficult: you changed wood to stone. But if you do not have the strength in you and the energy around you to draw upon, you will fail and you will die."

"That's why I was so cold and so tired after changing the

spoon," Makarria said, remembering the sensation.

"And why you fainted after trapping Kadar. What you did in that cave with so little heat or energy around you was very dangerous. It is fortunate you are a strong young lady."

Makarria couldn't help but take the statement as a compliment and smile. "So that means if I get stronger I can create anything I want?"

Talitha shook her head ruefully. "No. There are always limits. Much of it depends on your imagination and your spatial cognition—you cannot create what you cannot visualize. It also depends much upon your understanding of Tel Mathir though."

"But how did I make my grampy young again when I didn't know anything about Tel Mathir? You said that was the most difficult thing you've ever heard a dreamwielder do before."

"It is," Talitha conceded. "I can't fully explain it myself, but in simple terms, you needn't be taught the ways of Tel Mathir to understand Tel Mathir. Some people simply have a connection with the natural world and have an innate sense of how it works. Do you remember what I told you about the limitations of prophecy when we were in Issborg?"

"Yes."

"Good. Well, the limitations of being a powerful seer and being a powerful dreamwielder are much the same. Do you see that tree there?"

Makarria looked at the large birch Talitha was pointing toward. "Yes."

"And that one?" Talitha asked, this time pointing at a cedar tree.

"Of course."

"They are quite different, aren't they? And yet you know that they are both trees. How?"

Makarria grimaced. "I don't know. Because they both look like trees."

"Your answer is a dodge, but nonetheless correct," Talitha said, smiling. "The essence of Tel Mathir is that she creates templates—perfect images—of all things in existence. We see trees around us,

GARRETT CALCATERRA

and each of these trees is a copy of the image of the perfect tree. Each squirrel is a copy of the perfect squirrel image. Each rock is a copy of the perfect rock image. Those of us with the power to wield magic have a connection with Tel Mathir and access to these images whether we are cognizant of it or not. Seers see an image of the future because they see in their mind the end result of a perfect equation with many variables. They see people of specific persuasions in unique circumstances and are able to see the outcome if everyone acts according to their innate persuasion. One variable is a greedy husband, another variable is a jealous wife, and the outcome would be easily predicted if the variables stayed true to their perfect images—if the husband remained greedy and the wife remained jealous—but as people, we rarely stay true to our perfect forms, and hence the unreliability of prophecy. The randomness of people can never fully be accounted for."

"I don't think I understand," Makarria said, shifting the pack on her back.

"I have a hard time understanding it and putting it into words myself," Talitha admitted. "Let me put it this way. Most dreamwielders are limited to combining things they can see with their eyes. The horrors of the Dreamwielder War were creations of this sort: dogs melded with sorcerers, sorcerers melded with coal furnaces to become fire-wielding machines of destruction, warriors melded with steel weapons to create inhuman assassins, and so forth. But a truly powerful dreamwielder understands the perfect forms and images of Tel Mathir. She can see past the boulder and envision the perfect form of a tree and literally break the matter apart to reform rock into tree. In the case of your grandfather, you saw him in his perfect form—a young man in his prime—and were able to make him so, despite knowing nothing of how the body ages or works. This is a rare ability, Makarria. In my years traveling the Old World, I saw this only on two occasions, and neither were as significant or profound as what you did."

Makarria walked on in silence for a long time as she pondered Talitha's words. The road stretched out before them, a brown ribbon through sparsely wooded rolling hills. "I understand, I think," Makarria said at last, "but how does this help me against the Emperor? He's immune to magic, right?"

"I don't know how it helps you, Makarria. All I can say is that you should follow your instincts. You have an unusual knack for visualizing the true nature of things. Do what seems right to you, but just be aware of your surroundings. Don't push yourself beyond your limitations."

"But what if you were me?" Makarria pressed. "How would you try to kill the Emperor?"

Talitha shook her head. "I honestly don't know. To me the only thing that makes sense is to try to attack him from afar. If he can't see you, if he can't detect your presence, he would have no way of stopping you. But at the same time, if you can't seem him, I don't see how you could kill him either."

Again, Makarria nodded and contemplated Talitha's words. They walked the rest of the morning in silence. At noon they halted briefly to take a quick meal of dried meat and cheese, then continued on. As was the case every afternoon, the walk turned into a mind-numbing blur where Makarria merely focused on putting one foot in front of the other. Each curve in the road, each hill and valley was gone from Makarria's mind the moment it was behind her. She didn't notice Forrest Weorcan come into view far to the south, and she didn't notice the little town in the distance late that afternoon as they crested yet another hill. Talitha had to point it out to her.

"I think it best if we pass straight through town and make camp when it gets dark," Talitha said. "We're getting close now. It's not wise to chance exposing ourselves by letting something slip in a random conversation at an inn."

Makarria just nodded. As nice as sleeping in a bed sounded, she had bigger concerns on her mind. They were getting close, Talitha had said. They were getting close to Col Sargoth and the Emperor.

. . .

Natarios Rhodas sat at a bench in the common room of The Mountain Jewel, the most luxuriant inn the small town of Pizer had to offer. Ostensibly, he had chosen the inn because it stood along the main thoroughfare through the center of town and gave him an ideal vantage point, but in reality he had chosen it because it was the only inn that had proper down mattresses. And also because of the mulled cider. *I love mulled cider,* he thought fancifully and tipped his flagon back to take a hearty swig of the sweet substance. His four days in Pizer had been a welcome relief to his time in Col Sargoth. With the gold the Emperor had given him, it had been an easy matter to bribe the other innkeepers in town and also the farmers on the outskirts of town to stay watchful and bring him news of any travelers. He'd accomplished all that on his first day, and since then had just sat tight in The Mountain Jewel and enjoyed himself.

"Another cider," he yelled at the innkeeper.

The innkeeper grunted and waved in Natarios's direction noncommittally. Natarios grumbled at the man's insolence but said nothing. He knew the cider would come eventually if the innkeeper wanted his coin. Natarios laughed inwardly at the path on which fate had set him. From Kal Pyrthin to Col Sargoth to Pizer. He had lost his riches Roanna paid him but now found himself with more gold than he could spend in this small town. He smiled, more than a little satisfied with himself. His self-satisfaction was cut short, however, when a stout woman suddenly burst through the doors into the common room from outside. She saw Natarios sitting there and rushed to his side.

"You said you were looking for a girl coming from the east, yes?"

"That's right," Natarios replied, setting his flagon aside.

"Well, I've seen her. She just walked into town with an older woman. Now give me my gold."

"Hold tight a moment. Where is she? Where did they stop for the night?"

"They did not stop, idiot. They kept on walking right through town to the west. You best hurry if you want to catch them. But give me my gold first, I tell you."

32
The Tide Turns

From his ship *Makarria* in the Sol Sea, Parmo looked upon Sol Valaróz, the city he once thought he would never see again. It was nearly as he remembered it, stretching up and away from the harbor in a series of tiers to the Royal Palace, its white marble buildings glimmering in the setting sunlight. Parmo did not feel as triumphant as he felt he should though. Here he was, returning as the Prince of Valaróz, on the cusp of leading an entire kingdom of subjects to war with Sargoth, and yet all he could think about was two specific people: Prisca and Galen. It had been a week and a half since he'd taken charge of the eastern Valarion fleet and gone to Prisca and Galen's farm near Spearpoint Rock, hoping to take his daughter and son-in-law away with him.

He had found the farm abandoned.

While there had been no signs of fighting or attack, he nonetheless knew something horrible had happened there. He told himself that Prisca and Galen had in all likelihood gone to Pyrvino looking for him and Makarria, but he did not believe it, and the haunting fear and guilt ate away at him. His only solace was the thought that Makarria was safe in Issborg. *You're the crown prince of Valaróz now,* he reminded himself as his ship approached the piers. *You need to think beyond your own personal concerns.*

Word of his arrival had already reached the city and by the time his ship was docked, a massive crowd of people swarmed over the docks. The cacophony was deafening, and it took Parmo a few seconds to realize they were chanting his family name.

Pallma! Pallma! Pallma!

"We will escort you to the palace the best we can," Socorro said as the crew secured the ship and lowered the gang plank. "There are a lot of cursed people out there though. If you get separated, just push your way through."

"I know the way," Parmo assured him and led the way down the gangplank and up the pier to face the crowds.

Before they reached the crowds, however, a regiment of soldiers pushed their way forward to bar the way. Parmo felt the prickling sensation of danger. So far the transition of power from Don Bricio to himself had gone smoother than he ever would have imagined, but sailors had always been loyal to the Pallma line of kings and queens. Dealing with the city soldiers and aristocrats could prove to be an entirely different matter, he knew. Parmo put his hand to his sword hilt, ready for trouble.

It proved to be unnecessary, for the captain of the soldiers bowed as soon as his men were in ranks and at attention. "Welcome, my prince," the captain said. "My name is Antonio Haviero. I am Captain of the Royal Guard. Your coach awaits you and the palace has been prepared for your arrival. The houndkeeper and the rest of Don Bricio's men have been taken to the dungeon, except those who resisted—them we have flayed and fed to the desert cats. Also, the Assembly of Chancellors is gathering in the palace as we speak. They await your arrival to begin your hearing. If you can validate your claim to the throne, they mean to anoint you this very day."

Parmo could hardly believe the words he was hearing. He'd expected resistance of some sort, but it seemed the people of Valaróz were more than ready for him.

"Thank you, Captain Haviero," Parmo said with a smile. "I am much relieved and pleased by the warm welcome. Socorro, the rest of the men can stay on the ship now that we have an escort, but you best come with me. The chancellors will want to hear what you have to say."

"Aye," Socorro agreed, and with a few curt commands he dismissed the rest of crew to return to *Makarria*.

"Captain Haviero," Parmo said, "Please lead the way."

Captain Haviero gave a harsh whistle, and his men immediately sprung into action to clear a path through the crowd from the docks to the harborside streets where an armored coach awaited. The crowd seemed unperturbed by the soldiers pushing them aside, and they continued to chant: *Pallma! Pallma!*

Parmo felt himself become flush with excitement. It had been decades since he'd heard that name. A woman in the nearby crowd pushed her way onto the shoulders of the soldiers blocking her way and threw a bouquet of flowers at Parmo. "May Vala bless your soul," she shouted over the din. "We love you!"

Parmo bent down to pick up the flowers and blew the woman a kiss in thanks.

Pallma! Pallma! the crowd chanted.

They reached the coach and Captain Haviero offered his arm to help Parmo up. "Your ride, Your Majesty."

Parmo stood there for a moment, basking in the adoration of the crowd. "No, I think we'll walk, Captain."

"You're sure?" Captain Haviero asked with a nervous glance at the people flooding the streets around them. "We are but a small regiment. We cannot keep the crowd at bay if they decide to mob you."

"It'll be fine," Parmo assured him. "The people of this city have been waiting a long time for their king to return. They deserve to see my face."

King Casstian yelled out at his troops to reform behind him as he yanked his horse to a halt in the outskirts of Forrest Weorcan. They had come upon Guderian's war machines on the road just south of Weordan two days before, and nothing they could do slowed the iron-shelled wagons. The machines cut down the Pyrthinian troops just as Taera warned him they would. Casstian had ordered Taera and the rest of his constables and field marshals to sound the retreat back to Lepig, and then led his own small contingent of troops onward into the forest to harry the Sargothian infantry marching behind the war machines. Three times now the small Pyrthinian brigade had successfully darted from the trees to charge through the Sargothian lines and quickly retreat back into the safety of the forest. It was nearly dusk and Casstian desperately hoped they were nearing the Sargothian supply train. He knew the Emperor's war machines needed fuel; if they could succeed in destroying the supply wagons, they would effectively stop the war machines in their tracks.

"Draw your weapons," Casstian yelled to his men grouped around him. "Archers, stay back at the perimeter of the woods. If we come upon the supply train, set your arrows aflame and take out the fuel wagons. They'll be carrying coal or naphtha or something of the sort and should be easy to spot."

Casstian drew his own sword and steeled himself. "For Pyrthinia!" he yelled.

"Pyrthinia!" his troops screamed back in reply, and he spurred his horse forward to lead the charge.

The forest thinned in front of them as they rushed forward through the trees and the supply wagons suddenly came into view on the road. Casstian felt a surge of triumph and spurred his horse on faster. He could clearly make out the supply wagons on the road, guarded only by a meager force. *They're just sitting there, waiting for the taking.* He could hardly believe it, but gave it not a second thought.

"For Pyrthinia!" he yelled again, and the forest opened up before him.

Captain Haviero's soldiers cleared a path through the crowd and marched forward, away from the docks toward the center of the city. Around them, the city folk still chanted the name Pallma. Parmo followed in the wake of the soldiers as if in a waking dream, and he had to remind himself not to get caught up in the reception. *These people have lived for thirty years under the rule of Guderian and Don*

Bricio, he reminded himself. *Of course they welcome you.* He forced his mind to the tasks before him. The people would want to celebrate his return and draw out the coronation ceremonies, he knew, but he had no intention of sitting idly by while Pyrthinia fought against the Emperor. *I will insist on a quick coronation,* he decided. *Then it's off to Sevol to set forth the western fleet for the Gothol Sea. If we leave soon, perhaps we can take Lon Golier and Col Sargoth by surprise before Casstian is even fully engaged. And whatever infantry we have, we'll send to Makady to reinforce the Pyrthin troops.*

His escorts pushed now through the lower boroughs of Sol Valaróz and up the long slope leading from tier to tier toward the Royal Palace. The buildings surrounding them were as he remembered from his childhood: irregularly shaped with white and yellow stucco walls, a wide array of balustered balconies and windows, and orange terra cotta tiled roofs. The smell of braised, spicy meat cooking in hundreds of homes and taverns tinged the air, intermingling with the briny harbor odor. More and more Valarions were crowding around in the streets now, eager to see their prince, but Captain Haviero and his men kept the path toward the palace clear. Parmo looked up to see men, women, and children waving at him from the second and third story balconies of the buildings along the streets.

Pallma! Pallma! Pallma!

He could not help but smile and wave back.

Startled shouts rose up from the Sargothian soldiers along the road and Casstian let out a cry of triumph, but then from nowhere, a dark shape appeared to his right and his horse locked its legs in fear, nearly throwing Casstian from the saddle. Before he realized what was happening or fully regained his balance, he was bodily knocked from his saddle to land sprawled out on the ground. The fall knocked the wind out of him, but he pushed himself up to stagger clear of his panicked horse and survey his surroundings.

His men were nowhere to be seen. Terrified screams echoed from the shadows of the forest behind him.

Without a second thought he abandoned the Sargothian supply line and dashed back into the trees. Around him, men and horses cried out in fear and pain. He saw them only as silhouettes flitting between the trees. One of his men ran toward him, only to collapse, his throat torn out and gushing blood. The hair at the nape of Casstian's neck stood up on end and he gripped his sword and shield tighter.

Suddenly, the wolf appeared from the shadows. Horses and men alike fled, leaving Casstian alone. The black wolf was impossibly large, its eyes and snout somehow human looking. Casstian crouched low and held his sword at the ready.

Pallma! Pallma! Pallma!

It still seemed unreal to Parmo to hear his name being shouted by thousands of people, but he waved and smiled nonetheless. When one of the soldiers beside him suddenly yelled out a warning, Parmo hardly noticed it over the cacophony of shouting and whistling around him, and even when he felt a sharp pain in his chest and was knocked backward onto the ground, he did not fully understand what was happening. "Where am I?" he whispered to Socorro, who was kneeling over him, but Socorro did not look Parmo in the face. His attention was on the feathered shaft protruding from Parmo's chest. Socorro tried to pull the shaft free, and the sudden searing pain nearly blinded Parmo. "*Merda!*" he swore. "Leave it," he tried saying, but warm blood oozed into his lungs and he fell into a fit of coughing.

Around Parmo, the crowd was screaming and yelling in a frenzied panic. Captain Haviero and five of his men surrounded Parmo in a tight circle, and the rest of the troops Captain Haviero sent rushing into the building from where the assassin had fired his shot. They returned mere minutes later dragging the killer—a loyal follower of Don Bricio: an aged warrior from the Old World—and while Captain Haviero promptly disemboweled the assassin, none of it could keep the life blood of Parmenios Pallma from spilling onto the white cobble stones of Sol Valaróz.

I love you, Prisca, and my dear Makarria, Parmo spoke inwardly, hoping somehow his words would reach them. *I'm sorry, dear Valaróz.* And then all faded to black.

"Come on, you filthy animal!" King Casstian yelled, and the wolf swiped a paw at him, renting his shield into a dented mess and breaking his left arm. Casstian staggered back with a gasp, only with great effort willing himself to stay conscious and on his feet.

The wolf growled, a low chortling rumble, as it circled Casstian. *It's toying with me,* Casstian realized, and with sudden fury he lunged forward with a sweeping overhand sword strike. The wolf merely sidestepped his blow though, and sprung back at him. Casstian tried but failed to raise his shield, and the wolf's claws dug into his shoulders, driving him back into the ground with impossible strength. The wind was knocked from Casstian's lungs and his ribs cracked beneath the force. He reached for the dagger at his belt in a desperate last attempt, but the wolf was again too fast. It snarled and snapped its fangs together like a whip, crushing Casstian's skull beneath them with ease.

Taera awoke in her saddle with a scream.

Caile gasped, startled as much as she by her sudden outburst. He had been lost in his own thoughts and hadn't even realized she was in a trance. Just hours before he had been making haste toward Weordan and come upon Taera and the High Constables retreating with the mass of the Pyrthin army. After having sailed six days up the River Kylep just to get to Kylep and find his father had marched on without him, Caile had wanted nothing more than to continue on to Weordan to help, but Taera had entreated him to return with her to Tyrna and prepare the city for attack. Caile had reluctantly agreed.

"Are you alright," Caile asked Taera. "Another vision?"

"I've seen everything," she said, her breaths coming in short gasps.

"Tell me," Caile said, his hair standing on end. He could sense in her voice that something was very wrong.

"I've seen everything," Taera said again, numb from her visions. "Wulfram has come, and Father is dead. Sol Valaróz weeps. And Makarria: she's walking into a trap."

33
Into Darkness

The winter rains had finally come, soaking the lands east of the Gothol Sea with a cold, relentless drizzle. Makarria and Talitha stood shivering and drenched for a long time upon the hill looking down at Col Sargoth from the eastern high road. The soot-stained buildings and smelting factories belching smoke into the air radiated outward from the towers of Lightbringer's Keep like a feculent sore, and while only a handful of farmers passed by Makarria and Talitha on the eastern high road, the high road leading to the south was another matter: a solid mass of wagons and troops extended outward as far as they could see, trailing into Forrest Weorcan and Pyrthinia beyond. In the bay beyond the city, ships flying the blue and yellow banners of Golier made way for the harbor bearing even more troops.

"I know what I have to do," Makarria said, casting her eye upon Lightbringer's Keep.

"You're sure?" Talitha asked her.

"Yes."

"What is your plan? What can I do to help?"

"Just get us into the city," Makarria said, "somewhere where I have a good view of those black towers."

"You're going to tear them down?"

Makarria nodded. "I'll turn the foundation to sand and bring the whole keep tumbling down on the Emperor. It's the only way. You said yourself, it's best to attack from afar."

"So I did," Talitha conceded. "It could very well work, but we best wait for the cover of darkness to sneak into the city. There will be guards on the high road at the gates, and they might be looking for us."

"We don't have time to wait," Makarria said, determined to go now that she had made her decision. "I'm scared to think what all those soldiers will be doing to our friends if we wait."

"Don't be foolish," Talitha told her. "Another few hours will make little difference. We did not come this far only to be taken captive the moment we step into the city. Besides, the chances that we'll catch Guderian in his tower are better at night. Come, we'll take shelter in that copse of trees until it's dark."

Makarria nodded sullenly and followed Talitha off the road to wait beneath the trees. The trees were barren of leaves and did little to shelter them from the rain, but they at least shielded the wind somewhat and kept Makarria and Talitha from standing in plain sight. Talitha divided what little food she had left in her pack between the two of them and they ate silently, each lost in her own thoughts.

The sunset was indiscernible behind the rain clouds, and the western horizon merely faded from gray to black as time passed. When Talitha deemed it was dark enough, she motioned for Makarria to follow her. "The city is not walled, so we will have little trouble entering unnoticed," Talitha said, veering off the high road into the mud. "I need you to stay close beside me though. We'll be entering in the northeastern borough. There are many unsavory people there. If anyone speaks to you, just ignore them and let me do the talking. Stay focused on what you need to do with Lightbringer's Keep."

"I will," Makarria promised.

"And one thing more, Makarria," Talitha said, grabbing Makarria by the shoulder and bringing her to a halt. "If things go awry, I promise you I will do all that I can to help. If Wulfram finds us, I will give him the fight of his life and try to lead him away from you. If Guderian finds us… I cannot hope to hurt Guderian, but if nothing else, perhaps I can distract him and give you time to do what you must. If it comes to that, you must act quickly though."

"I understand," Makarria answered, and the two of them continued slogging wordlessly down the hill. It was still a mile or more to the outskirts of the city, and they were slowed by the mud and rain, but time held no meaning for Makarria—she was not aware of her feet carrying her one step at a time closer to the city or even of the rain pelting her in the face. Her eyes were locked on Lightbringer's Keep, still visible above the city, a black shadow even in the night. *There's no other choice,* she told herself again, trying not to think about the hundreds of innocent people who would be killed when she brought those towers toppling down: the porters, the cooks, the maids, the stable hands, and then of course, all the horses and whatever other animals were kept in the keep. The very thought almost brought Makarria to tears. She pushed them away and steeled herself. She had gone over every possible tactic she could think of in her mind, and there was no other way. She had to attack the Emperor from a distance, just like Talitha had said. Otherwise, he would simply stop her magic. And that meant innocent people would have to die. To protect the lives of others.

The ground leveled out before them, and they began passing the outermost buildings of the northeastern borough. The buildings were little more than dilapidated huts and sheds made of building scraps that rattled in the wind. Most were dark and lifeless, but a few had pitiful fires at their doorsteps where groups of people sat huddled together. If any of them noticed Talitha and Makarria passing by, they said nothing. The buildings gradually grew larger and more permanent-looking, and before long they were walking on a tar-paved road. Between the buildings, Makarria could still see Lightbringer's Keep though, and her attention was focused entirely on its dark visage. She followed Talitha wordlessly, not even noticing the steam powered rickshaws, the gas lanterns lighting their way, or the increasing number of city people crowding the streets. When Talitha finally brought them to a halt, they stood at the intersection of two large streets that was absolutely bustling with people making for the center of the city.

"Something's not right," Talitha muttered. "There are never

this many people in the streets of Col Sargoth."

Makarria tore her eyes away from Lightbringer's Keep and took in her surroundings. She'd not been in enough cities to know what was normal or not. "Maybe it's because of the war. Could the Emperor be forcing people into his army?"

"He doesn't need them," Talitha said, shaking her head. She waved at an old woman passing by. "Excuse me, what's all the excitement about tonight?"

"Haven't you heard?" the old woman replied. "There's a public execution in the city square. The Emperor is killing the King and Queen of Valaróz."

"That's impossible," Talitha said, shaking her head. "We were told the Pallma line was killed off years ago."

"So we were. So we were. I guess we were told wrong."

"Wait," Makarria said. "My grandfather—"

"Hush now," Talitha interrupted, covering Makarria's mouth and waving the old woman away. "Thank you, Ma'am."

Makarria pushed Talitha's hand aside, annoyed she was being treated like a child. "Don't do that. What if it's my grandfather the Emperor has?"

"I don't see how that's possible. The last we heard, he was in Kal Pyrthin, preparing to sail for Valaróz. In all likelihood this is all just a ruse."

Makarria didn't believe it. The moment she had heard the old woman utter the word Valaróz, she knew something was wrong. She couldn't shake the feeling that her grandfather was in trouble. "I have to find out if it's him."

"Don't be rash," Talitha said, but Makarria was hearing none of it. She dashed off into the crowd of people and began making her way toward the center of the city. "Wait!" Talitha yelled, hurrying after her, but it was hopeless. Makarria was swallowed up by the crowd, and being shorter than most of the city people, she was impossible to spot. Still, Talitha forged her way forward, frantically looking for her.

A good distance ahead, Makarria wormed her way through

the slow-moving crowd. When the street finally opened up into the city square, the crowd dispersed somewhat, and Makarria saw before her thousands of people mobbed around a huge platform in the middle of the square. She sprinted forward, and as she got closer she could see that two people were being held captive on the platform in pillories. By the time she got close enough to make out their faces, she was in the midst of the crowd and could see nothing. She shoved her way forward, frantically looking for a break in the mass of people. She spotted to her right a statue in the near distance and changed course toward it. Once there, she scrambled up onto the base platform of the statue and pivoted around to finally look upon the prisoners on the platform.

It was not her grandfather she saw.

She didn't know how or why her parents could be there, but it was them in the pillories, their hands and heads protruding from the cruel wooden framework, both of them badly beaten and shivering in the cold rain. Galen's face was hardly recognizable it was so bruised and swollen, and Prisca's nose was bleeding, her clothes tattered and sodden with blood. The crowd was jeering them with curses and insults, and those close enough threw rotten food and garbage at them or spat on their faces. As Makarria watched stunned, a man pulled himself onto the platform and grabbed one of Prisca's hands where it protruded from the large wood beam. He guffawed at the crowd, then yanked her fingers back with a savage twist, mangling her fingers into a broken mess. Prisca screamed out in pain, and at the base of the statue Makarria screamed. Both screams were lost in the yells of the crowd. Makarria tried to jump clear of the statue, but hundreds more people had crowded in around her, trapping her where she was. The man on the platform sauntered to where Galen was held, backhanded him across the face, and Makarria could take no more.

She closed her eyes and envisioned the pillories. She imagined them turning to sawdust and a great whirlwind blowing the dust into the crowd to chase everyone off. She felt the resistance in her core as she pushed the dream toward becoming reality. In her periphery, she heard her name and faltered for a moment. *Makarria, no. It's a trap.* Still in a trance, Makarria opened her eyes and saw Talitha there, trying to pull her away. Beyond Talitha, Makarria could still see her parents in the stockades, being kicked and spat upon. Again, she envisioned the pillories turning to sawdust…

A sudden gut-wrenching pain ripped the image from Makarria's mind. She opened her mouth to breathe but could not. The wind had been knocked out of her, and rough hands were pulling her from the statue. Someone smacked her across the face, and she was dragged to the ground to lie on her hands and knees. When air finally returned to her lungs and the tears cleared from eyes, she saw that she was surrounded by soldiers. Six of them surrounded Talitha, the tips of their pikes held inches from her throat.

The crowd, which moments before had been filling the city square with shouting, had gone completely silent.

In the silence, Makarria heard heavy footsteps approaching. She pulled herself to her feet and blinked the tears back from her eyes, as a giant of a man strode forward bearing a sword that was taller than Makarria. The very sight of him made Makarria's skin prickle with fear. *It's him,* she realized.

"Welcome to my fair city, Dreamwielder," Emperor Guderian said, coming to a halt before Makarria. "You've arrived right on time and saved your parents further public humiliation. They'll be happy, I'm sure, to return to the safety of the dungeon." The Emperor smiled thinly and winked at her. "I trust that you will be a polite guest during your time here. You and your sorceress friend, both. If either of you try any sort of magic again, you will be killed on the spot and I'll have your parents disemboweled then stoned to death to suffer for your crimes. Are we understood?"

Makarria could only stare at him in stunned silence.

34
The Dawn of a New Age

Caile rubbed the weariness from his eyes and looked over the Pyrthinian troops digging ground fortifications in the fields at the western edge of Lepig. "Can you do it or not?" he asked the guild master of the carpenters who walked at his side.

"I cannot get a tank that size fifty feet up in the air," the stout, mustachioed man replied, shaking his head. "Thirty feet is the best I can do, and even then I can't promise the tower I build will hold the weight once that tank is filled."

Caile pictured the contraption he had conceived the night before. He wasn't certain that thirty feet would provide the pressure he was after, but it would have to do. "Do it," he told the carpenter. "You have two days, and it better hold. I have every barrel of naphtha from here to Makady on its way. That tank holds near five thousand gallons and I want it full."

"Two days?" the carpenter balked.

"Work day and night," Caile told him. "Get whatever men you need, and promise them whatever pay you must. If we succeed, I'll gladly pay it. If we fail, well, it won't matter much anyway—"

The color drained from the carpenter's face, and his mouth clamped shut. All he could do was nod that he would do it. Caile sent him on his way and turned back to the city to see to the coppersmiths who were making the long, tapered pipe and nozzle he would need. He had taken his idea from the miners in the mountains north of Sol Valaróz who used creeks and streams to create water cannons to strip down the sides of hills and unearth silver. Caile's contraption wasn't meant to hose down the hillside though. It was meant to douse the Emperor's war machines in naphtha once they got stuck in the trenches the Pyrthinian soldiers were digging at the edge of the city. *I just hope that the same principles apply to naphtha as well as water, and that thirty feet is high enough,* Caile fretted.

"Your Highness," a soldier called out to him, disrupting his thoughts.

Caile stopped in the middle of the road to see that it was one of the men assigned to protect Taera. "Yes, soldier, what is it?"

"Your sister has sent me to tell you that she has left."

"What do you mean left? Left where?"

"She did not say, Your Highness. She said to tell you that she had a vision and that she would be back with help if she could. She took off on her horse to the south."

"Damn it all, man," Caile swore. "You're supposed to be with her at all times. Go get her and bring her back!"

The soldier coughed uncomfortably. "She said that you would say that, Your Highness. She said to remind you that she is the heir to the throne, not you, and that she's in charge."

Caile glared at the man but said nothing. By Pyrthin tradition and law, she was right. Still, Caile was angry she had gone off without at least consulting him first. *Damn that girl,* he swore to himself. *She better hurry, whatever she's doing. We have three days at best before we're under siege.*

Emperor Thedric Guderian sat hunched forward in his throne, wearing his black leather jack and trousers with plate armor at the forearms and shins. Held before him in both hands was his massive claymore, its point resting on the floor between his feet. At his side stood King Lorimer of Golier, a wiry, gaunt looking man with stringy blond hair. And filling the throne room were an assortment of dignitaries, Sargothian aristocrats, and thirty soldiers from the Imperial Guard who stood at the ready around the perimeter of the room with long pole-axes in hand and short swords at their waists.

The main doors opened, and Makarria was escorted in through the main doors alongside Talitha. Makarria tried to take it all in, but she was still in shock from what had happened the night before. She and Talitha had spent the night alone in a solitary jail cell beneath Lightbringer's Keep, watched over by twenty soldiers and warned not speak to each other. They slept only fitfully on the stone floor, and when morning had arrived, they were given nothing to eat or drink. They were merely escorted out of their cell and led in a long, slow procession through the keep to the throne room where they now stood. They were travel-stained and weary, exhausted and terrified, and worst of all, they had no idea what the Emperor was going to do them.

For all the potential danger they posed to him, neither of them had been bound or shackled, Makarria realized, and that gave her some semblance of hope. *He's not afraid of us. Maybe he's not as evil as everyone says. Perhaps he's willing to listen to me.* She did not know what she meant to do if the Emperor didn't listen to her—for that was her only plan now, to try and reason with him.

"Bow before the Emperor!" a herald yelled when Makarria and Talitha reached the dais before the throne.

Around them, everyone in the chamber bowed. Makarria and Talitha followed suit, prompted by the spears at their backs. Emperor Guderian's dark eyes followed Makarria's every movement.

When everyone finally stood again, Guderian spoke. "Welcome, Makarria; daughter of Galen and Prisca Spero; grandchild of Parmenios Pallma, last prince of Valaróz; dreamwielder. The good people of Sargoth would like to know if you have come here today to kill me?" The corners of his lips curled up into a sneer as he asked this last question and Makarria could see well that he was putting on a show for the people there in the throne room.

"I only came here to ask that you end the war, please," Makarria replied shakily. "Let the people of Pyrthinia live in peace. Do that and free my parents, and we will go far away. I promise. I don't want to hurt anyone. I don't even know you—I don't want to kill you."

GARRETT CALCATERRA

The Emperor snorted and looked from Makarria to his subjects filling the throne room. "You see," he announced to them, "this is what remains of magic in our new world: a little girl begging to spare the lives of traitors." Snickers filled the room, and Guderian stood up from his throne as he spoke on. "The mightiest seer of the Old World foretold that a dreamwielder would slay me. Well here she is, my people, and she says, *please, I don't want to hurt anyone.*"

Again, laughs of derision filled the room. Guderian stepped from the dais, claymore in hand, and stopped to stand towering over Talitha. "And you, woman, you are Roanna, the mighty sorceress who meant to renew the sorcerers' guilds."

Talitha kept her eyes downcast, but shook her head. "No, you are mistaken. Roanna is dead—slain in the caverns of Issborg. Along with her, Kadar, sorcerer of the Old World who longed for your throne, has been sent into oblivion. For that you have Makarria to thank."

If Guderian was surprised by Talitha's revelations, he showed no sign. He grabbed her by the jaw and yanked her head up to face him. "Who are you then, woman? Your face looks familiar to me."

"My name is Talitha. I am a turnip farmer. Perhaps you have seen me in the marketplace."

A few of the audience members snickered, and Guderian's eyebrows quivered in anger. He released his grip from Talitha's jaw, then struck her with the back of his hand. The force of the blow knocked Talitha to her knees, and Makarria stepped back involuntarily.

"Talitha who?" Guderian demanded. "You have the look of northmen in you. What is your full name?"

Talitha shot a glance toward Makarria then wiped the blood from her mouth. "My name is Talitha, that is all. I am daughter of Trumball, chieftain of the *Snjaer Firan*. And I've sworn to protect this girl. I've sworn to protect all who would live a life free of your tyranny." The words still hanging on her lips, she suddenly lunged toward the Emperor, fire sprouting from her fingers.

The crowd gasped and shrunk back, but the flames made it no

266

more than an inch from Talitha's fingers before petering out like a spent candle flame and Talitha collapsed to her hands and knees with a groan, as if she had been kicked in the stomach. Makarria realized too late what Talitha had intended to do. *I was supposed to act when she distracted him!* She tried to close her eyes and think of something to dream, but the Emperor's sudden shout wrecked her concentration.

"Trumball's heir indeed!" he bellowed, and he kicked Talitha in the side, sending her sprawling across the floor. "Think you can use sorcery against me? Fool woman!" And he kicked her again.

Blind fury welled up inside Makarria, and she leapt forward with a savage scream. She had never hit anyone before, but she wanted to hurt the Emperor now, more than she had ever wanted anything before. She swung her arm in a wide arc, fist clenched.

Guderian merely turned and watched as her fist struck him harmlessly on the hip.

Makarria cried out and staggered back, her fingers throbbing. She closed her eyes and pictured the Emperor in her mind. *Make him dead,* she told herself. *Make him dead!* She pictured his face and how she wanted it to be crushed...

Suddenly Makarria's eyes were open, and she was staring at the Emperor crouching before her. "Let's not be having any dreams, little one," he whispered. "I warned you once already, and I'm not ready to kill you yet. You haven't suffered nearly enough."

Makarria felt all the anger and strength drain from her.

Guderian winked then stood and turned to the crowd again. "This is the fruition of what magic has brought to the world, my people. To your left is the daughter of Trumball, the mightiest sorcerer since Sargoth Lightbringer himself. Talitha, she says her name is, and she is a turnip farmer. To your right is the last of the Pallma line, a dreamwielder, and she says she would very much like not to hurt anyone, even if they be traitors, thank you very much, and yet she strikes out at me like an insolent whore." The crowd broke into mirthful laughter at his words, but he stamped the tip of his claymore into the stone floor to silence them.

"This is why I say magic is dead," he said in a dreadful tone.

"This is the dawn of a new age, my people. The age of intellect and human achievement. No longer are we dependent on those who are born with magic. No longer are we slaves to the whims of nature. The world is ours. As we speak, the combined forces of Sargoth and Golier march on Pyrthinia. Already, King Casstian has been slain. Soon, his heirs will be dead with him, and the last safe harbor for sorcerers will be destroyed. Parmenios Pallma, defender of the old ways will be killed and his claim to Valaróz along with it. We will not be slaves to the sorcerers' guilds of old. We will not be subjected to the horrors of the Dreamwielder War again! This is our world—the world of men!"

The crowd broke out into applause, but Guderian waved their claps away and turned to Makarria and Talitha.

"Daughter of Trumball, you are now my slave," he declared, addressing Talitha. He dragged her up to her knees, tore the cloak from her shoulders with one hand, then grasped the collar of her tunic. As she knelt there, cradling her bleeding face in her hands, he slid the length of his claymore up the back of her tunic and slit it open. He then grabbed her by the hair and yanked her up, naked but for her britches. "Bring chains to bind her hands and feet and a scold's bridle to curb her tongue," Guderian yelled. "Trumball's daughter shall be my pet from this time thenceforth. Let her faun and prostrate herself beside my throne, naked for all to see, as a reminder of the pitiful past we have left behind. And if she ever raises her hand against me, or attempts to use the sorcery in her blood again, I will strike her head from her shoulders. This is magic for you, my people."

He pushed Talitha away, and two soldiers rushed forward to grab her and bind her hands behind her back.

"And you, Dreamwielder," Guderian went on, "for now, you will live as a monument of man's dominion over magic, a monument of my power over prophecy. You may spend your last days with your parents, as you wish, but know that the day Pyrthinia is defeated, all of you will die." Guderian turned to the audience now. "This is my gift to you, my people. On the day Pyrthinia is defeated, this dreamwielder and her kin—the last of the Pallma line—will be executed, and with her I will put to rest Wulfram, last of the sorcerers of old. So will pass the age of our ancestors. So will dawn the age of the Sargothian Empire. On that day, let the Old World and the entirety of civilization across the earth quake, for we will not be stopped."

Rise of the Young

Taera reigned her horse in as she reached the center of the small town of Tritea. It was little more than a village really, but Taera recognized it from her vision. She dismounted and led her horse to the only inn in town, a nameless boarding house made of wood— squat and sturdy. Inside, only a few elderly townspeople sat eating in the common room. The innkeeper sat too, wiping clean his wooden mugs and goblets. The lot of them looked up and gawked at Taera in her outlandish furs.

"I'm here to see the refugees," Taera said to the innkeeper.

"I... I don't know what you speak of," the man stammered.

Taera didn't have the patience for games. She strode through the common room and pushed her way through the door past the innkeeper into the private dining room she knew would be there. It was just as she had pictured it in her vision. The people sitting there eating though, were not as she had hoped they would be. They were a pitiful lot, all seven of them. Like frightened children, they looked up at her from where they sat hunched over a long bench eating from bowls like a pack of feral animals. They were a mixture of males and females, young and old, but they were all emaciated and wild looking, filthy beyond description. Some of them were dressed more scantily than Taera herself, others wore clothes that were worn to shreds.

The innkeeper barged in behind Taera and clutched at her sleeve apologetically. "I meant no harm. They're homeless vagabonds. All I did was feed them. I swear. They were hungry."

"Don't apologize," Taera told him. "You did what was right." She turned her attention to the seven sitting at the bench. "All of you have come here because you have heard that Pyrthinia is at war with Sargoth. You have lived many years in hiding, I know. You have been afraid. You have been hunted. Well no more. I am Taera, Queen of Pyrthinia, and I say that you are outlaws no longer. I am like you, a sorcerer, and I ask for your help now. If you would have a Pyrthinia where you can walk freely and do as you will, I beg you, join me. Help me defeat the Emperor."

Makarria relaxed her arms and let the shackles binding her wrists above her head support her weight. Across the circular chamber from her, on metal racks the same as hers, her parents were shackled against the wall. Her father hung in a trance, his face a mutilated pulp and his left shoulder grossly displaced. Her mother was conscious, but only with great effort, and she breathed in long deliberate breaths.

The sight of it all made Makarria begin crying again. She wanted nothing more than to use her power to make the chains and wounds go away—to make her parents free and happy again—but she knew she couldn't dare use her powers. When she had been escorted up the tower stairs two days before, the guards had warned her to not use her magic. "The scent-hound's tower is no more than a hundred feet away," the captain of the guards had said. "Be still and your remaining days will be painless. Try to use your ill magic and the houndkeeper will sound the alarm, and the Emperor himself will come to kill your parents first, then you." Makarria had said nothing in reply. She felt helpless then, as she did now. The realization that her friends were likely suffering as badly as her parents only made matters worse. *Poor Talitha,* she thought, the memory of Talitha naked and battered flashing through her mind. Of Siegbjorn, Taera, and Caile, Makarria knew little, but she knew they were at war— she had seen the soldiers marching from Col Sargoth and she knew what those soldiers meant to do. And then there was Parmo. A sense of dread and emptiness filled Makarria when she thought of him. She couldn't help but feel that something horrible had happened.

"Makarria?"

Startled, Makarria looked up to see her mother awake, head held up weakly.

"You're crying."

"I'm sorry," Makarria said, sniffling back her tears and sobs.

"Don't apologize. It's perfectly alright to cry, darling."

"No, I'm sorry for all this. I'm sorry I couldn't save you and Father, that I couldn't save anyone."

"Oh, Makarria," Prisca lamented. "It's not your fault. I'm the one who should be sorry. And your fool grandfather. Why did he ever take you away from me, where I could keep you safe? I hope he's still alive somewhere so I can get my hands on him." She said this with a wan smile, but the effort drained what little strength she had and her head slumped forward again as she barely held onto consciousness.

Despair filled Makarria again at the mention of her grandfather, but she smiled for her mother and tried to convince herself that Parmo was fine. "Grampy's wonderful," Makarria said, and she proceeded to tell her mother everything. She told her how she had made Parmo young again, how they had fled on the skiff—and how sorry they both were for leaving without saying goodbye—and then about the storm at sea and how they were rescued by Taera, their kidnapping by Roanna and their time in caverns of Issborg, and lastly, the news of Parmo's return and the rebellion against Sargoth.

The news seemed to breathe strength back into Prisca. "I hope he gets to see Sol Valaróz at least once more," she said when Makarria had finished her story. "He's always dreamt of going back and he deserves that, if nothing else."

Makarria smiled and said nothing.

"It's true," Prisca said after sighing deeply. "You are a princess. I see now it was pointless to try and hide things from you, but I did what I thought was best. You are a princess of Valaróz, Makarria.

Neither you or I have ever seen it, but we belong to the land of the sun, the kingdom Vala founded when she crossed the Spine." A single tear, atrophied by dehydration, ran down Prisca's cheek. "If it's true, Makarria—if you are the one ordained to defeat the Emperor—then do what you must. I know he has threatened to kill me and your father if you defy him, but please, don't worry about us. I would gladly die to know you have killed him and made the world safe. There are others in this tower who have been tortured; I have seen them and spoken with them in the darkness of night. All of them would gladly die to know you have prevailed. This is your time, Makarria, not my time, not your grampy's, not anyone else's. Do what you must. Don't let all our suffering end in vain."

Makarria slumped forward and stared at the cold gray floor below her. "I would, Mother—I would kill the Emperor—but I can't. I tried. He knows how to stop magic. I tried to hurt him, and he just made the magic go away." She began crying again.

"Shush, darling," her mother told her. "Men of his ilk always try to destroy the magic in the world, but I promise you, no one can make all the magic surrounding us go away. The Emperor is an ignorant child if he thinks he can overcome magic, or that he can live without it. It's part of us, all of us, Makarria. Don't you ever forget it."

Prisca went silent then and fell into unconsciousness.

Makarria looked at her mother and father hanging there at the opposite wall. They were little more than husks of the people she remembered when leaving her farm. A cold determination filled her insides. *I have to kill the Emperor,* she realized. *But how?* Her mother's words ran through her head again: *He needs magic to live, and he's a child if he thinks he doesn't. A child...*

Makarria closed her eyes and pictured Emperor Guderian in her mind. She did not picture him as a grown man clad in armor and sword, however; in her mind she saw him as he once was, many years before and still a child.

• • •

Caile rushed from his pavilion into the rain as the warning horns sounded around the city of Lepig. He looked first to the massive tower harboring the tank of naphtha to make sure it was safe and breathed a sigh of relief when he saw it still standing there. His deepest fear over the last two days was that Wulfram would come flying from above and set it aflame. The tower stood as he last saw it though, thirty feet tall with the steel-banded, five-thousand gallon tank of naphtha at the top. The tank was covered in every spare skin and fur his soldiers could rustle up in town and soaked in water to ward off any burning arrows the Sargothian troops might shoot at it. Caile knew all would be lost if the tank was set aflame before its highly flammable contents were sprayed onto Guderian's war machines.

"Keep your eyes on the sky!" Caile yelled up at the archers stationed on the tank tower. "Keep Wulfram the raven at bay, and I will keep you safe."

The danger was not coming from the sky though. Caile looked to the west and saw an endless line of Sargothian war wagons approaching along the high road from Weordam. "Take your positions!" he yelled to his troops, but the Pyrthinian troops were already where they were supposed to be. The half dozen archers on the tower looked to the sky; two soldiers manned the spout nozzle; the remaining archers hid behind their ground fortifications, ready to light their naphtha-tipped arrows aflame upon command; the cavalry waited at the ready behind the nearest buildings, ready to ride outward and flank the war wagons once the machines were mired in the trenches and pits barring the road into the city; and the ground troops were ready to charge and kill whatever Sargothians came past the machines.

Satisfied that all was ready, Caile wiped the rain from his brow, buckled his shield to his left arm, and drew his sword. An intoxicating sense of power and invincibility rushed over him, and he felt compelled to run forward and meet the war wagons headlong, but he knew better than that. His father, Lorentz, and even Don Bricio had taught him well. The adrenaline-fueled sense of invincibility was a mirage, he knew, and he dutifully fell back to his command post at the outskirts of the city and waited.

The Sargothian wagons approached faster than seemed possible, emerging from the rain-shrouded horizon like nightmarish iron-clad monsters. Even having seen the steam-powered rickshaws and wagons in Col Sargoth, Caile still instinctively expected to see the enemy lines approaching at the speed of a cavalry charge, at most, but these wagons were charging forward over the rain sodden road faster than any horse, faster than anything he had ever seen. Smoke billowed up from their stacks, and the sound of the three hundred plus wagons filled the air like a violent thunderstorm. Steam pistons thrummed like an earthquake, drowning out the deluge of rain hitting the ground.

"Wait for my word!" Caile yelled out.

The wagons barreled forward, armored in steel, scythes stretched out before them like plows.

The rain fell in torrents.

The first wagon reached the outskirts of Lepig and augured nose first into the ground; the front wheels buried themselves in the ditch the Pyrthinians had dug, and the wagon upended itself to land upside down in the mud before the city. The second wagon followed suit. The third wagon slowed and merely slid into the ditch, and the wagons behind it skidded to a halt.

"Release the naphtha!" Caile screamed over the cheers of his troops.

The men at the tower released the control valve, and five-thousand gallons of flammable fuel began rushing down the copper pipes to stream forward and shower the stalled wagons. The stream of naphtha shot with the same force Caile had imagined, just as powerful as the water cannons of Sol Valaróz. The viscous liquid splashed over the steel shells of Guderian's war wagons.

"Archers," Caile yelled. "Draw, aim… Fire!"

Two hundred burning arrows arched into the sky. Nearly all of them struck the doused wagons, but the flames did not take. The burning arrows clanked off the steel hulls of the wagons harmlessly, and while a few of the burning spears set the naphtha alight, the downpouring rain promptly put the flames out.

Caile stared at the enemy machines, his hopes snuffed out along with the flames of the arrows. He watched as the Sargothian troops rushed forward to begin digging the war wagons from the ditches. Sargothian foot soldiers surged forward and Sargothian archers took aim at Caile's men on the tower.

"Cavalry, charge!" Caile yelled. "Archers, aim and fire!"

The Pyrthinian horsemen charged past Caile, and a hail of burning arrows rained down on the Sargothian troops and wagons again, but the burning arrows did little more than sputter and fizzle out as they struck the armored shells of the war wagons. The heavy downpour of rain extinguished everything as the Pyrthinian troops engaged the Sargothian force.

Makarria had seen many strange things in her dreams the past few months—everything from girlish fantasies to visions of the future to immaculate forms of rock and human life itself—but she had never seen before what she now envisioned. *The past*, she realized. *Guderian's past....*

She had seen glimpses of Taera's visions of the future, but this was vastly different; it wasn't a potential future but rather the very real past. In her mind she saw Emperor Thedric Guderian as a boy... and the Dark Queen...

Thedric jumped from the boughs of a tree in the garden and ran toward his mother. She flung wide the folds of her black cape and knelt down to take him in her arms...

The Pyrthinian cavalry rushed forward, but as intent as they were to steer clear of the war wagons, the wagons were faster. The steel-shelled machines barreled outward from the road into the fields to bar the cavalry's progress and Caile could only watch as his soldiers were mowed down like stalks of grain beneath the scythe. The screams of horses and men filled the air.

"Fire, fire!" he yelled at the archers, but still their burning arrows fizzled out on the hulls of the war wagons.

Makarria beheld the throne room of Lightbringer's Keep, but in her mind's eye she saw Thedric Guderian as a lad of three. Beckoning the small boy was his mother, the Dark Queen...

'Hurry, Thedric. I have news for thee.'

Thedric ran forward and grasped his mother by the waistcoat. Outside, balls of fire rained down on Lightbringer's Keep and men screamed in agony...

Caile blocked the sword stroke of his nearest assailant and swung his own sword into the Sargothian soldier's thigh. The man went down with a grunt, and Caile yanked his sword free only to thrust it back down into his adversary's throat. The man died immediately, and Caile looked up barely in time to see a Sargothian cavalryman baring down upon him. Caile sidestepped the warrior's flail and slashed with his sword to take out the hind legs of his enemy's horse. The horse collapsed with a scream, and the cavalryman flew over the saddle to break his neck in the mud.

"For Pyrthinia!" Caile shouted in triumph, but suddenly a dark shape moved toward him on all fours.

The deep toll of a bell thrummed throughout Lightbringer's Keep and Emperor Guderian rose to his feet from a chair in his study. He was sincerely surprised and glared at Talitha who sat naked and chained to the floor beside him, as if the warning toll was somehow her fault. He had not expected Makarria to act out against him, but the alarm from the houndkeeper's tower was quite clear: magic was afoot.

Caile raised his shield barely in time to block the deadly talons of the black wolf. Even so, he was knocked to the ground.

He pushed himself back to his feet with his sword raised. "Fire, fire, fire!" he yelled, and a volley of arrows streamed downward, but the wolf was gone already and the arrows embedded themselves into the muddy ground.

It's Wulfram, Caile realized, and spun around to look for help. There were a few archers in the tower still, but the men at the base were all slain. Without thinking, Caile ran to take up the nozzle spout. He yanked back on the nozzle valve and sent a torrent of volatile liquid forward onto the stalled war wagons.

"For Pyrthinia!" he yelled, but then the black wolf was there in front of him again.

Makarria envisioned Lightbringer's Keep, but she envisioned it fifty years before she had seen it in real life. In her mind, Thedric Guderian was but a lad, and the Dark Queen sat on the throne before him. Makarria erased the floor beneath her and everything but the walls and manacles holding her and her parents. She made the torture chamber a blank slate and the half- formed images of the past came to life…

'Come to me, my boy,' the queen said. 'War is upon us, and you must flee. Take care of yourself and someday you will be welcomed here again. You will return as the king you are meant to be.'

At her bidding, a sorcerer grabbed up young Guderian and carried him away, but the crown prince of Sargoth looked back and saw behind him the might of Col Sargoth, what could be. He was taken away on a ship across the

Gothol Sea, but still he kept his sight on Col Sargoth. South he went, to the Old World, and with him his dreams. But still, he remembered the glory of Lightbringer's Keep....

Wulfram knocked Caile away from the spray nozzle of the naphtha tower, but Caile maintained his footing in the muddy turf and slashed back. Wulfram snarled and sidestepped the stroke, then lunged forward again. Caile took the brunt of the attack upon his shield and spun away, managing to strike a blow across Wulfram's snout with the butt of his sword.

Before Wulfram could attack again, Caile sprinted away through the rain to the nearest of the war wagons. He jumped up onto the main deck, slick with naphtha and water, and cut down the soldier sticking his head from the foremost turret. The Sargothian archer collapsed back into the hollow of the wagon, and Caile turned again to face Wulfram, now below him. The wolf leapt up, knocking him back against the turret, and Caile's sword fell from his grip. Caile pushed Wulfram away with all the might he had in him and spun away to fall to the ground.

"Fire!" he yelled to his archers, but he was too far way for them to hear him now, and Wulfram leapt down from the wagon to face him, eye to eye.

Thedric Guderian barged his way through the doors into the lowest chamber of his torture tower and froze, disorientation sweeping over him. He was not in the torture chamber he remembered. Rather, he stood in the throne room, which he had just left moments before. But it wasn't the throne room as it was now… his mother and Wulfram were there. Impossibly.

What would you have me do? Wulfram asked, his voice young and strong.

The Dark Queen contemplated his question silently for a long moment. *Send my son away to the Old World,* she said finally. *Then destroy Lon Golier. I want the city burned to the ground. If nothing else, I will have my revenge on Golier.*

Wulfram bowed and swept away.

The Dark Queen turned then to Guderian. *Come to me, my boy,* she said. *War is upon us, and you must flee. Take care of yourself and someday you will be welcomed again. You will return as the king you are meant to be.*

"No," Guderian said, squeezing his eyes shut and shaking his head as if it would somehow make the visage of his mother disappear. "This isn't real," he said, turning to Makarria where she hung against the wall. "I'm not a boy. Make it stop."

Makarria half-opened her eyes, still in a dream trance. The image of the throne room she held steady, half-formed but not yet solidified into reality. She saw the Emperor standing there in duplicate: a child in her mind's eye but a grown man in real life.

"It's your life," she muttered. "You make it stop."

Flames suddenly spurted past Caile and Wulfram leapt back with a yelp as his black fur took flame. Caile had no idea where the fire came from, but he didn't care. He scrambled up from the mud and darted around the wagon to grab up his sword. When he looked up, he saw before him Taera, surrounded by seven mad-looking vagrants. A pack of coyotes rushed past one of the men and fell upon Wulfram, who had already extinguished the flames in his fur. Rain and wind swirled over the top of one of the other women and she flung it forward to send three Sargothian cavalrymen flying back into the mess of war wagons.

Sorcerers! Caile realized and rushed away from the wagons to join his sister. "Fire, fire," he yelled. "Set the wagons on fire!"

One of the women at Taera's side raised her hands and fire belched out from above her to bathe the wagons in flames. The naphtha hissed and took flame even in the downpour of rain.

"Again!" Caile shouted in triumph.

Another firewielder joined the first, and the two of them struck together. The whole line of wagons near the tank tower went up in flames.

Wulfram was still there though, in wolf form, and he tossed aside the coyotes harrying him.

Now's your chance! Caile realized, and he ran yet again to the tower of naphtha.

"Make it stop!" Emperor Guderian yelled.

Makarria looked at him through her blurry eyes but kept the vision of the throne room and the Dark Queen firmly in her mind—half dream, half reality. It took all of her strength to hold the vision at the brink of the hilltop. "You make it stop," she whispered. "You have the ability to stop magic."

Come to me, my son, the Dark Queen said, beckoning him.

Guderian screamed in fury and clenched his eyes closed.

Caile opened the valve and aimed for Wulfram. The torrent of naphtha washed over the giant black wolf and knocked away the remaining two coyotes.

"Fire!" Caile yelled.

The firewielders lashed out at Wulfram, but he was too quick. He leapt away from the flames and bolted. Even as he ran, his body began to change into that of a raven. Caile cursed and grabbed up a bow and arrow from one of his fallen men as he sprinted after Wulfram. The dark sorcerer was already flapping his wings, and he took to the air. Caile skidded to a halt at the first burning wagon he came to and lit the tip of his arrow. He notched it quickly into the bow string and pulled back with all his might.

Wulfram arched up and away from him through the rain.

Caile took aim and let the arrow loose. The flame at the tip sputtered as it cut through the rain, but it stayed alight and flew true. It struck Wulfram in the breast, and instantly his naphtha-soaked feathers burst into flames.

Wulfram's half-human, half-raven cry carried over the battlefield. His mighty wings flapped twice more, then he began to plummet from the sky. His burning body shifted and changed as he fell, at one moment a man, the next a wolf, the next a raven. Down and down he fell, then stopped with a thud as he struck the muddy ground. The impact snuffed out the flames, but Wulfram's body was already burned and broken beyond repair. He took one last breath then died.

Emperor Guderian shook his head and looked away from his mother, who he knew was not real. She had been dead and gone for fifty years.

"You will die for this," he told Makarria and moved toward her. He raised his sword and even as he did so he reached inward to feel Makarria's magic and stint it.

Makarria felt the image in her mind suddenly yank free from her grasp. She screamed out in pain and felt her mind tumult back down the mountain of resistance.

Around them, everything flitted away: the throne room, the Dark Queen, but also the floor beneath Guderian's feet. Makarria had turned the floor to nothing before she had created the image of the throne room, and now when Guderian stripped Makarria's half-realized vision away, the half-dream floor was stripped away with it.

Guderian bellowed as he plummeted downward between the spiraling staircase at the perimeter of the tower wall. His claymore slipped from his grip and he dropped sixty feet to the ground below. Body and sword hit the ground simultaneously. The sword shattered. Guderian died with one last blood-filled gasp in a broken heap.

When the echo of Guderian's yell finally died, Makarria forced her eyes open. She saw her parents across the room, hanging from their wrists the same as she. Darkness tugged at her mind, and she felt herself drooping into unconsciousness, but she fought it off. She reformed the floor in her mind and made it so. She dissolved away the shackles binding her and her parents and made them gone. Her parents slid limply to the ground, and when she saw that they were finally free, she too collapsed to the floor and fell into unconsciousness.

In Emperor Guderian's study, Talitha broke her chains and stood. She yanked the barbed scold's bridal from her head, then strode out the doors, erect and uncaring of her nudity. The guards at the door tried to stop her, but she struck out at them with her power, and they were hurled back to shatter against the far wall like dried twigs.

She walked down the steps from the Emperor's tower and killed all who tried to stop her. She made her way through the keep, then to the base of the torture tower where she found Guderian's broken body. She nodded with satisfaction and strode up the stairs, sixty feet up to the bottom-most torture chamber, and there she found Makarria, deathly cold and breathing in shallow gasps. Talitha sat down and put Makarria's head into her lap, then closed her eyes. Very slowly, she pushed life energy and warmth back into Makarria's body.

"You've done it, Makarria," Talitha whispered softly. "You've done it."

36
Epilogue

Makarria looked out from the balcony to watch the sun rising over the white city. *Sol Valaróz*. She'd heard much of the city from her grandfather over the years, but even his stories did not do it justice. In contrast to Col Sargoth, which was enormous but rigid and menacing, Sol Valaróz was a beautiful, sprawling mess of ancient buildings covering the mesa, each and every one of them different from the others. *I suppose I'll have plenty of time to explore it now,* Makarria mused, but she was cheered little by the thought. All she could think about was her grandfather.

"It's nearly time," Prisca said from inside their room in the Royal Palace. "Here, I have something for you"

Makarria went to her stiffly, still unused to walking in a gown and heeled shoes.

"It's your grandfather's ring," Prisca said, taking Makarria's hand and slipping the ring onto the thumb of her left hand. "He left it for me to find when the two of you left. It's yours now."

Tears filled Makarria's eyes at the thought of the day she fled with her grandfather on the skiff, seemingly a lifetime ago.

"Don't be sad for him," Prisca told her. "His time had come. He knew that long before you ever made him young again."

"He's one with Tel Mathir now," Makarria replied. "That's what he told me would happen."

Prisca smiled and kissed Makarria on the forehead. "Come now, it's time to go. You have a kingdom to rule."

Makarria sniffled back the tears in her eyes and nodded. "Alright."

Outside in the corridor, Caile stood waiting for her. "Are you ready for this?"

"I guess so."

Caile grinned and ushered her forward. "It'll get easier and don't worry, I'll be there right beside the throne with your mother and father. Once the coronation is over, take your seat on the throne and wait. Today's business will be simple enough, just a bunch of aristocrats, ambassadors, and guild masters coming to swear their fealty to you. Just thank them, and I'll fill in any necessary formalities you might miss."

Makarria nodded wordlessly and followed after him toward the throne room. It was as if she was walking in a dream. The last two weeks had been such a whirlwind she could hardly keep track of it all. With the death of Guderian, the Sargothian advisors had surrendered, along with King Lorimer of Golier. Talitha called for a council of all the highest Sargothian officials and together they began the long process of choosing a new ruler. The Sargothian Empire was officially dissolved. By then, Siegbjorn had arrived in Col Sargoth, along with Caile. Caile brought news of Wulfram's death and the surrender of Sargoth's generals. Taera, he explained, had gone back to Kal Pyrthin to be anointed queen now that the war was over. At hearing this, Talitha urged Makarria to go to Sol Valaróz with all due haste. "You are needed there," is all she would say. Caile offered to accompany her, seeing as how he knew as much about Valaróz as anyone, and so they set sail with Siegbjorn on the airship: Makarria, Prisca, Galen, Caile, and Lorentz, who had been freed from the torture tower along with all the other prisoners.

When they had arrived in Sol Valaróz, they learned of Parmo's assassination. Makarria was devastated. She cried and cried and could not be consoled for days, but Prisca finally put an end to it. "There's no time for crying like a little girl anymore," she had said. "You're to be queen now, and a queen must be strong."

"A queen?" Makarria asked incredulously. "Me?"

"I've renounced my claim," Prisca told her. "I am a farmer and a mother—that's what I've been my whole life. You are young and already stronger than I've ever been or ever will be. Valaróz is your responsibility now. Prince Caile has promised to stay here as your advisor, and your father and I will be here... to be your parents and to help you."

The weight of it all had pushed all other thoughts aside. And now, here Makarria was in the throne room of Sol Valaróz, standing before hundreds of Valarions, all of them staring at her adoringly. The crown Vala herself once wore sat on a cushion beside the throne, waiting for Makarria to place it on her head.

Nothing will ever be the same again, she realized. *I'm a queen now. More than that—I'm a dreamwielder. Grandfather would be proud.*

Continue Makarria's journey in Book Two of the Dreamwielder Chronicles,

SOULDRIFTER

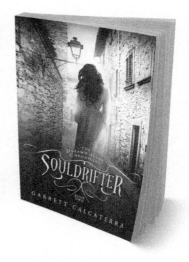

In the shadow of Emperor Guderian's fallen empire, young Queen Makarria finds her throne—and her life—in grave danger. The Old World Republic has come, demanding that Queen Makarria bring order to the struggling Five Kingdoms by forming a new empire, one she would rule as the Old World's puppet. When Makarria refuses them, the Old World threatens war and unleashes a nefarious spy to sow discord in her court. Before she knows it, Makarria's budding romance with Prince Caile has been exploited by the spy, and Makarria finds herself embroiled in a complex game of power and lies in which she can trust no one.

Betrayed and lost, Makarria is forced to shed all pride and discover the true nature of her power as a dreamwielder in order to recreate herself and face the sprawling threat that is the Old World Empire.

CPSIA information can be obtained at www.ICGtesting.com
Printed in the USA
BVOW08s0029261015

423450BV00016B/71/P